THE SCORPION GRASSES

Shivram K

Invincible Publishers

First published in India in 2019

ISBN: 978-93-89600-16-2

Registered Address: 201A, SAS Tower, Sector 38,

Gurgaon-122003

Printed at Thomson Press (India) LTD

I dedicate this book to two great storytellers- and of course, they taught me storytelling quite earliest when I didn't know what storytelling is!

My

Grandmother

&

Grandfather

Acknowledgement

If it would not be customary paying gratitude in the book for people who help knowingly or unknowingly while writing this book, still I will be thankful for some of the people who really assisted me making me a writer.

I'm greatly obliged of my family- my grandparents, who taught me storytelling, my father – who never bother me being lost in imagination and my superb brothers- Vikas Sharma and Vishal Sharma- supported me every while who have made my life immeasurably so easy and better providing a confined solitude that I can think more and write more. I really feel gratitude toward my pretty wife, not calling me at the time of editing of this book and provided me with a comfort zone to ruminate my story.

I'm profoundly grateful towards Dr Prarthana Vardhana and Mr Anil Pandey who set writing spark in me which is fueled by Prof. Dipti Ranjan Patnayak, Dr PS Mishra, Dr Indrajit Mishra, Dr Sangeeta Jain, Dr Bandana, Dr Mala Srivastava, Dr Aliya Rifat, Mr P C Pandey and Dr Leonard Ekka.

I am profoundly indebted and feel gratitude toward Dr Ashish Mishra, Dr Nitish Thakur, Amit Mishra and Prashant Upadhyay for supporting and motivating me even in my hard time and making me believe as a complete writer.

I thank some of my friends, confidantes and fellows Nishant Bhardwaj, Arun Kumar, Vimal Kumar, Khurshid Ansari, Mrs.Anjali Piyush Mishra, Mrs.Nidhi Gupta, and Ms.Nidhi Tripathi.

I thank Mr.Sameer Ahsan, Mrs Nidhi Sharma and Mr Praveen Kumar for reading and giving their critique that really helped me to straighten this book.

I thank my commissioned editor Ms.Pooja Mishra, Ms.Tamanna and entire Invincible publishing team.

Finally, I thank Almighty to choose me to be a writer.

Thank you all for picking up this book, turning its pages and inspiring me to write another story.

Prologue

She walked out of the room, possessed a stunning looking beauty. I gazed her and gazed her and gazed her.

I woke up out of dream when she winced and grinned indulgently assuming my open mouth. I shook my head and smiled back.

“I don't want to spoil your dressing.”

She giggled, pulled my hand and said, “Don't be crazy now. It’s getting late.”

She paused for a moment before opening the gate, stood still in front of me, constant lingering her glance at my either shoulders, mending collar, buttoning shirt, setting tie and having a bland smile at her lips.

I conjectured, she desired to say something, so I looked straight into her eyes, assuring her tacitly.

“Our living together has given people a reason to gossip. After a long time, you will be in the department before fellows, teachers and acquaintances. It may be a little weird situation for you, but you have to be patient,” said she, convincingly.

“I can’t imagine how embarrassing it has become for you. The comments and mocking you have to face these days. You carried all. You bore it.” I held both her arms delicately, leaned my head onto her shoulders..

“When you are with me, I’m unabashed. And gossiping amongst people will die a natural death.”

And we hugged.

After the accident, it was my first day in the department. Urvashi had submitted my medical certificate to Head of Department though.

As my name announced for poetry recital, the gathering hailed me with a thunderous round of applause.

I strolled and rose to the dais. I prepared myself to read my emotional expressions as the poetry outloud before the crowd. The clapping stopped; a deep quietness pondered everywhere in the echoing auditorium hall.

After a brief greeting and introduction, I began, my verse-

Meeting with a Stranger

You

Nobody I knew

When we met very first

Sat at a bench under the verdurous tree

Of a random park

Where tramps ramble

-laymen, old age and pairs

We shared our sour blend sweet past

We talked, laughed and shared

A gender sensation when

You touched, relieved me

Being untouched.

Her metamorphosis beauty in broad bordered Bengali sari, glittering earrings, wistful bangles style, and her charismatic smile had transformed her into Venus. Sharpness, child-like traits, and frankness of her utterance vanished from her demeanour. She was now a grave, humble, and peculiarly quiet girl. She began to study late night, inspired me, too, to do the same. Though she was on the stage amidst crowd, yet her concentration was only on me. Her dance at the fresher's party exhibited two different personalities of Urvashi. The moment her eyes met mine, she smiled; I was standing quite away watching her like a spectator.

She escaped friends and reached to me. It got few while summing up the whole program.

“Sorry,” said she, reaching to me.

“Mention not. Loved your dance,” said I, smiling.

“Let’s go. I feel hungry.”

“Where?” I followed her. She was rushing down through the stairs.

“VT,” she answered. She questioned, stepping down the stairs, “Don’t you feel hungry?”

“Yes, I do,” I said.

“Why didn’t you tell me? “

She rode us to VT. Her hairs brushed my face with the wind brisk hurriedly passing back.

The best thing I liked about her was her incredible intuition the way she knew my unquote inmost.

Tyro

Day- One

The sweet, soothing evening beauty, the refreshing breeze and the sights of boat's plying at Triveni Sangam, Allahabad, fails to purge the pang and agony of Prabha's mind.

She declines her friends' invitation to go with them on the ferry. Needless to say, her spending evening here was their plan to relieve her grieving. They get into the boat together, leaving her behind. The boat drifts away passing underneath Naini Bridge and keeps going afar into the water till it resembles a tiny speck, just like all the others.

Twilight breaks and the sun's crimson rays have painted the clouds, drawing nets of a reddish hue over the smooth flowing streams. People stroll with ease, a few enjoy watching the sailing boats, and few partially-naked young lads are too keen about the idea of fishing with their long nets.

Prabha rambles on the bank of the river, listless and thoughtful. Often she looks at the birds, flying just above the currents, as though playing a game. She watches the boatmen as they pass with people on the ferries: mostly families with kids enjoying the holidays.

The beads of sand disperse as she rambles by the bank. She is heartbroken and deserted by the way Avinash has decided to walk apart and snaps a promising relation of three years.

Wandering near the bank, she pauses in her strides to watch the surges of the river. Her eyes fall over a wrapped- up bundle of paper lying a little ahead. Inquisitive, she walks to the bundle and picks it up. It's a leather covered diary, wholly drenched, dripping. She turns it around to look for any marks left by the owner but finds none. Curiosity now piqued, she holds the diary in her palm tenderly lest its dilapidated pages get spoiled and ink get messed-up. It has thread-bound around to keep it shut. Prabha places it on a newspaper that she picks up from the bench next to her in the faint evening sunlight to let it dry before it could satiate her curiosity.

She walks a couple of steps, looking in the west direction but her friends can't be seen anywhere. They have sailed afar.

To avert her isolation and bitterness of life, she has recently bought some books and developed a habit of perusal. She has been reading a novel on love and friendship by a debutant author. She goes on leafing the pages of the book for next some twenty minutes but still, nobody is visible nearby her. She stands up and makes a shade by her palm above her eyes, gazes again far across the river, ruminates precisely the fleet of the boat, but it is too challenging to recognize which one are they sailing in.

She wanders to and fro, then sits down, and opens the book and engages herself in reading anyhow. Then suddenly she gets distracted by the relentless haunting thoughts and slams the book again and puts it aside.

Suddenly the attention of unknown diary swamps her mind; she picks it up and holds it delicately. Although the water is drained out, not dripping anymore almost but still there is moisture between the pages.

It is undoubtedly somebody's diary that somehow fell into the river and came floating by the currents, she speculates.

She unfolds its cover, tries to turn it and finds it tough to reach to its scribbled pages.

Prabha realizes somebody is patting over her shoulder slightly; she is shocked a bit and immediately turns around.

"Hey! What's up?" Nazarin asks. She is smiling, staring at her surprised face. "Why are you looking at me so strangely?"

"Nothing," says Prabha. Gently she closes the diary and places it on her lap.

"What's nothing?" says Nazarin, kneeling down on her haunches. She notices already, she is reading something from that wet lumps of paper. "What an irony! You're doing something and saying nothing...Hmmm, it's ok if you don't want to tell." Pretending displeased she sits beside her.

"It's nothing just someone's a lost diary," says Prabha, emphatically, to pace down her curiosity.

"It's already wet," says Nazarin, staring at the diary strangely that laid in Prabha's lap.

"Yeah, I found it floating in the water. I haven't turned its pages much. It's fragile enough and risky to turn its dilapidated pages."

"So, what is there inside?" asks Nazarin.

"I can't tell you now until I go through. I read mere few paragraphs, it's someone's life's story," says Prabha.

She pauses, ruminates something in self and begins uttering beholding straight across the river, steadily. "I think, our life is like this diary too. We don't know what secrets are there in its pages, what will happen next? Which detour life will turn? Who will come, who will leave you in the middle of the life's journey? What will happen? It's all just a mystery, a myth." She turns to Nazarin and adds, "Don't you think we are following a maze of shadows?"

"It's the beauty of life. When the future already gets predicted, life will turn monotonous and will lose its thrill. And Prabha, it's enough, stop behaving as if somebody died." This time, Nazarin asserts firmly. "Please! Come out of your vain dreaming. Stop befooling yourself speculating about the person who doesn't care about you, who was never yours. Stop haunting about the worthless past and fantasying about the future, which nowhere exists. Live the moment where you are. Insha-Allah, God will heal every wound and mend the broken path of life with the the passage of time."

"I am hungry!" Prabha says, cutting her in the middle of her quote.

"What?" Nazarin startles to her changed mood.

They laugh together and move toward a chaat and panipuri vendor.

The sun almost conceals in the west, but still, its light lingers in the sky. It seems as if the nursery kids have poured down a bucket of color over the canvas, sprawling all around moving the brush vaguely and have yet created a masterpiece. Gradually the birds' chirping decreases, they begin returning to their shelter to feed their kids. The idle clouds are creeping listlessly, and vanishing at the horizon. Boatmen, begin to anchor the boat at the shore. The light of the day is diminishing, darkness is falling. The appearance of people rambling there is mere shady- a silhouette image, you can't recognize them clearly. Darkness is prevailing over the sphere.

Prabha and Nazarin both keep waiting for their friends for a good deal of time. Prabha squats down on the floor and rests her chin on her knee, wrapping her hands around her legs. She keeps looking inquisitively at their path. Now she is impatient while waiting for hours.

Again Prabha stands up, strolls a few steps, and commence to speak impatiently, "Where have they gone? Now, it's enough. I can't wait for them any longer. I'm getting late." She frowns.

"I don't know where they are now." Looking in the same direction as her Nazarin says. "Leaving me on the bank, they sailed to another side. Let's wait for ten more minutes, if still, they won't come, we will leave."

"Let's go to that side. ."

Nazarin stands up, brushing the dust from her back. They walk by the bank of Yamuna, glancing far across the river, there is hardly any boat sailing now. The level of anxiety and annoyance rises simultaneously on her face.

Suddenly, they hear a vague muttering at the remote.

She apprehended something untoward happened and briskly walked towards the crowd. Nazarin followed her. When they reached there, they saw a strange man lying on the ground, unconscious. He was wounded; blood was oozing out from his head, hands and wore small cuts over all his limbs.

"What happened? … Who is this guy?" asks Prabha, controlling her gasping.

"We don't know. Just a stranger," says Manoj, turning to Prabha.

"He is bleeding!" repeats Prabha. Her voice is more exclamatory than a quest.

“He jumped off from the bridge,” says Sammy.

“Ya Allah! Why?” exclaims Nazarin, gasping, putting her palm over her mouth to control her shock.

“This is the common day to day story of this place,” reports the boatman. Everybody starts looking at him, questioningly. . He adds further, “Occasionally, broken heart lovers jump off the bridge to commit suicide…”

“It’s not the time to listen to such stories. Arrange to take him to the hospital. He is bleeding extremely.” says Prabha worrying.

Bending down, she asks Nazarin to bring dry soil. Nazarin quickly turns around, ransacks the sandy ground and brings a fistful of soil. She gives it to Prabha. Prabha rubs it over his wounds where the blood has been oozing out from.

“Don’t you think it can infect?” says Rohit, in a rather mild voice.

“No. It will help to stop the bleeding instantly,” says Prabha, still rubbing soil at the scars.

“If police investigate, then?” says Manoj, being worried.

“Forget it,” says Prabha, moving to him. “What if you were lying here, then?”

“What will you do if there will be a police case or if he turns out to be a criminal?” asks Rohit.

“What nonsense you are talking about! Who knows this stranger? Who knows why he has jumped from the bridge? Who knows he is not our friend except us present here?” Prabha harangues rather aggressively. She pauses, looks over them for their response. “It is you and me.” Prabha bandages his bleeding head with a handkerchief. “We can’t leave him here dying. Let’s take him to hospital.”

“Uncle!” says Manoj to the boatman, handing him some rupees. “Take this as your boating charge and these fifty rupees extra.”

“And we request you not to reveal this to anyone.” Prabha’s another friend comes in front and pleads him.

Meanwhile, Manoj rushes to fetch the car, and carefully they place the wounded man on the back seat and drive him to the hospital.

Avowed, Prabha decides to look after 'The Strange Man' until he reaches to his kin. She gets him admitted at the hospital. Due to the layer of dry soil rubbed over the wounded areas, for the time being it had restrained the bleeding. Doctor, too, has consented, the man is lucky because of their providential decision to bring him to the hospital in time. Neither it might have been life-threatening because of overt bleeding.

Prabha tells her friend, who has an exam the next morning that she will stay back at the hospital for the night. They didn't tend to leave her alone in the hospital. While Prabha and Nazarin are free now everyone else has bidden their goodbyes and gone to their hostel wishing her a good night.

Prabha sends Nazarin to bring her some cash from the ATM, some clothes and something to eat. The treatment has already started. Her avid interest in the diary and selfless service for a stranger has brought an arduous complicit. She has a deep epiphany with her inside and outside world now.

In fact, besides sitting in the corner of the room, shedding tears it's better to borrow someone's tears, and you will experience, it dismisses your distraught anxiety and sprouts a vista of compassion; fuels in you a sense of fortitude.

She does all the formality of filing the form and paying the initial amount of fees from her pocket. She tries to kill time sitting on benches, places at reception which are crowded with the idyllic attendants, occupying chairs along with their indigenous bags, bottles, and packets of food.

Some of them tire staying there in the surroundings of medicine and the typical hospital smell and lie-down between benches on the floor. Some of them sprawl on the benches covering space sufficient for two men their eyes set at the muted television. Some stay motionless looking closely at the hospital's gate waiting when they would receive any good news about their near one.

She can't endure the sweating stink any longer, sitting there, and begin roaming in the corridor, makes jaunt outside in the lawn.

She sits down on the lawn, awaiting for Nazarin. To consume her leisure cum stressful time, she takes out something to read from her satchel that she can pass her tedious hours with.

She wears her spectacles; fixes her quaint eyes into the dotted pages of the Lost Diary.

Chapter 1

Twenty-four years ago, I was incarnated on the planet in a pastoral setting of a small Indian village near the bank of the Ganges River.

The land where I was born is also known as the carpet city of India, situated in the midst of Allahabad and Banaras. Putting the name of my village in URL, it might navigate you to the interior region, quite far away from clamour of the town, where you could not find any transportation to reach. Hardly any if you are lucky enough. It can take half an hour of constant driving of your personal vehicle dangling over chasm spotted road, giving you surges of jolts that might draw the water inside of your stomach to your mouth until you reach to the periphery of my village. Yes, reaching at the doorway of my village, you need not to use the Google map to navigate my resident. You can ask anyone reading my name- not Siddhartha, but my domestic name- Saddhu- the person would lead you straight and leave you at my threshold.

You might be thinking why I'm telling all these.

The irony is that, I had never visited any city till my graduation, even after crossing my twentieth birthday. I was not fortunate enough to walk through the buzzing streets due to over scare of my Grandma. If you wished to explore a town you had to travel ten to fifteen kilometers to find transportation for big cities.

My life was like a planet which revolved around my home, my school and my village until I joined the university.

Though I was born of my parents, yet I was nurtured by my Grandma, whom I called 'Maae', that means mother in folks' language.

God is the greatest conspirator in my life who has plotted against me to snatch everything from me, whereas He had given two such a sovereign souls to survive in this lonely world– my Grandma and Meera who accomplished my life.

Meera was my world that I knew after my Grandma in those days of tenderness.

My father passed away in sickness, my mother couldn't come out of the nostalgia of his commemoration, and she died in the sickness of his thoughts. Grandpa could not bear this adversary and got a cordial attack one late night in sleep and fallowed them.

And afterwards, Grandma held herself strong within, fought with every circumstance to bring me up, and educated me.

My Grandpa was a renowned, respected and worldly scholar without receiving any degree from any college or university.

Folks used to come to him for his advice on crops, harvesting, husbandry, social issues, and more. He was a good landlord with no conceit, people of the opinion.

Similarly to once upon a time— story like other carpet businessmen, my father had a prolific weaving business he earned well, but he had to face the deterioration of carpet market too, like others. Export ratio got down; helplessly he had to stop carpet trade like so many other people related to this industry and started farming with Grandpa.

After their demise, responsibility came over my Grandma. She gave lands to the sharecroppers. She paid my fees and ran household through the farming.

Grandpa had left a great legacy behind him, which was enough to survive our life.

I recalled the moment when I heard snipped of my fancy turned into reality, counseling letter came from the university which I ever dreamed of.

Though it was a rainy season in India, yet the sun was still scorching, brooding in the widespread sky. Seldom had it rained- an irregular monsoon. The farmer had to depend massively on methodical irrigation- canal, tube well, village pond and diesel engine.

I was engaged in preparing the Babawala Khet, farm which was situated across the canal on the west side of *taal* to crop paddy. *Taal* covered around three square kilometers, which was surrounded by approximate ten villages at its periphery. The area was quite appropriate for paddy and wheat harvesting due to its clay soil and water availability.

And this area was prosperous from the irrigation point of view. There was a canal which partitioned the village colonies and cropland three ponds adjacent to each other, sometimes made by the ancestor of yore. There was just a dilapidated bridge for crossing the canal. In cropping day, the whole field divided into queues, lines, and block and dappled with hundreds of folks working their chore.

And most particularly bucolic ladies in kaleidoscopic sari, adorned its pastoral beauty.

I had been dripping drowned in muddy water, My clothes colored into the spongy grey mud. The folk lady on daily wages had been sowing the seed bending down, murmuring folk songs, and oft engaged in occasional garrulous dialogues. Their topics varied but themes mostly remained familiar primarily, candidates of the village election, cursing away the landlords for paltry wages. Or sometimes they appreciated another landlord for taking their proper caring for lunch and generosity.

Most of the land, Grandma had given to sharecroppers against my will, except a few of them. She told me to focus on books instead of farming.

She used to tell me one should do only the chore what he is made for.

A large piece of land had been given to Chhottani—a lineage sharecropper, who had a rather big family consisting of his wife, three daughters and two sons. He was an honest man which he had received from his ancestors. He was a landlord without having land. He worked hard, and his wife was the equal partner in his every struggle and toil.

They always gave respect and looked after us.

Chhottani easily arranged waged laymen for harvesting because of his repute in pariah colony. My Grandma told me many stories of loyalty of his father and forefathers. Even Chhottani himself was a brave and braw man, who honestly used to execute his chore. And my Grandma never suspected his loyalty that you can guess. She had never gone in the field to see, or divide ripens crops. After Grandpa's death, she appointed him supervisor of our estate. He did all- threshing of grain, packing in bags, and storing at home in the granary.

It was a bright, breezy day; clouds were drifting to the eastern sky like scatter cotton pieces, a frequent thick overcast gave a relief to the farmer community. Wading through the water and mud, I was picking out grass, dry leaves and stalk and collecting in the corner of the field. As it could have an adverse effect on the crops' growth, once when it would sprout out of the soil and formed into the tiny plant.

"Siddhartha brother, take some rest," said Manju, eldest daughter of Chhottani. She was quite sincere and frank, who had continued her study after passing twelfth. She used to help her parents in her spare hours. Chhottani canceled her marriage when I counseled him against the evil of child marriage.

"Betawa, (son) She is right. You would be tired now," said her mother.

Really, I fatigued wading in muddy water, felt an ache in calf and thigh of my legs. I washed my hands and perched at a suitable dry place and beheld them laboring.

The trees had been rattling and the branches were swinging. It relaxed my body and mind, both.

"Bhai, brother," Manju stopped sowing seed plant. Straightening her back, she said. "Meera Didi is calling you."

I turned back and saw her standing at the barricading wall of the canal. She was calling me. Due to the strong winds, her voice wafted, didn't reach me audibly. She was calling cupping palm one side of her mouth. She was showing some paper in her hand, rafting in the air. I thought better to go there and asked instead yelling in vain standing at my place.

"Have you gone dumb. My throat becomes panic calling you" said she, mocking me.

She was so breezy, entirely besotted for me and with Grandma.

"Hey *Bhagawan*! (God)" she said, drily, being surprised. Putting her one hand on her forehead when she glanced me from head to toe, tittered. "Were you bathing in mud?"

"No," I said, looking at myself. "What is in your hand?" Finally, I asked, suggesting the envelope that was in her hand.

"Guess." She said, wearing a sparkling smile. I was baffled and unable to anticipate . Seeing me puzzled, she handed me the envelope to open it myself, sprightly.

Next moment I was filled with overjoyed, which oscillated inside me. I could not express my happiness. She sensed my innate emotions overwhelm into my eyes and glowing complexion. Was the delight adventurous?

An advent sojourn was imminent, awaiting my tramps. A fact, I tell you, first time, I was to travel via train. Before this, it was just a picture in my mind.

I went to college and met Shashank, a friend. Within two days, I had to assemble all the essential documents. I encountered one of our veteran teachers, Dr P C Dwivedi, a young man in fifties who was at the verge of retirement, usually found taking lectures, roaming in campus, or working in the office. I adored him, and he admired me often in the class for my somber and gentle behavior. He was happy hearing the news that I was called for counseling from BHU.

He wrote a note on a piece of paper. And that note had done all my works so soon, than I had imagined. Issuing migration certificate was left, for which I had to go to the affiliated university that was not possible on that day.

Up to now, it was a brooding afternoon. Humidity was at its height; seldom drifting cloud shadowed from the sunlight had relaxed us. Wiping the sweat from the forehead, I complained about the heat of the day. Shashank gave a sarcastic smile and said, "When people feel the heat, besides planting trees, they plant AC in their room and contribute to the growth of global warming…a self-funeral rite of man by man."

As I was coming out of principal's office, leading towards the cycle stand, I encountered Mohan, a peon in the college.

Often I spent time with him whenever I went to take my cycle. And he used to share views about the world. I found it more vogue and vigorous than the crammed lectures I received in the classes.

I imparted him the news.

He smiled and raised both hands in blessing and said, “It is a good news son. Leave this place. Here, students are only pampered by a local politician, behave rowdiness, beat teachers and tease girls.” He told us, last day when a teacher stopped a boy while teasing a girl in the class, who was the nephew of a local political leader, came with a group of scoundrel boys, and had beaten professor bitterly. “They are few, but they are enough to spoil the whole water. Good students like you will suffer here. We are just an employee. We have no option…God bless you son.” Took a heavy breath of grief for the incorrigible problem of the college and endured it. Again he raised his hands in blessing, commenced to speak once more, “But you have proved me wrong.”

“How *Kaka*?” asked Shashank.

“*Betawa*, (son). I have been working there for more than twelve years.” Widening his eyes, he said, added farther. Years could be seen through the drawn lines over his forehead while speaking, “I was thinking, here, I could find only rogue and rascal. But forgot, the lotus can be found in mud only.”

“Leave all these things Kaka,” Shashank said, changing the subject of the topic, . “His migration certificate is still remaining…. Is there any *jugar* to avail his migration… without going to university?” He said in a rather low voice.

He nodded. “It will be possible...” After speculating for a second, he said, “It will cost two hundred rupees. A man usually goes to the university for such works and he charges money for it.”

Immediately, Shashank handed two hundred rupees in his hand.

We went to our favourite confessionary shop - *Dagga Samose Wallah*. Man in the black coat having a terse tie usually flattered in his shops, and discussed some judiciary dictions- as prosecution, bell, evidence et cetera and et cetera. And in the end, they stood up. And the gloomy man appeared in shaggy cloth of *dhoti kurta* used to paid the cost of sweets and *samosa* stuffed by those white collars *li-ar.*

Dagga's shop was entirely in front of the district civil court.

The waiter, a young boy in his teenage, served us samosa then after l*aung-lata* at our table our usual recipes. After devouring bites of samosa, I took water. Shashank was totally concentrated on his every bite.

"I'm thinking where I will stay there?" I was concerned.

"Where had you been last time?" he asked after chewing the hot bite that was already in his mouth.

"Last time…Entrance day?" I pondered just for a moment and continued. "I had to spin whole night lying over a plank of a vendor near Ganges' ghat. The whole night I had to encounter mosquitoes and local dogs. Meanwhile, a constable arrived there, suspected me as the thief."

"Thief?" he laughed. "Perhaps he couldn't see your face clearly."

"Yeah, that's true. I pleaded him I showed him my entrance and admit card. Then he turned generous. He took me to the near police station, and allowed me to sleep there on a plank."

"You love to write, that's why God gives you new experiences." He giggled. He stopped to see my grave.

He perceived my mood, balanced himself and said, "Why don't you contact Manish, your last year, friend?"

I recalled Manish one of my friend who went university last year. I was disappointed next moment for I had no contact number. He flashed his cell phone, scrolled over the screen, ransacked his number out of his digital contact list. He read, and I wrote in my notebook.

"How will you contact him after reaching there?"

"I will call him from the PCO."

“I knew your answer would be something similar to this…Take this.” He handed me a black and white Nokia cell phone. You can return it when you buy a new one.” Though he knew I couldn’t afford one in near days.

He dialed Manish, informed him about my arriving there.

Further, he suggested me to catch an Intercity Train the next day at 4:30 p.m. from Junghai Junction.

Chapter 2

The parting day had arrived.

Though we knew I had to return within a couple of days, yet our underlying sub-conscious admitted covertly the extended bon-voyage of my life. Bitter but it was the truth, I was to shun my home, my loved ones and native land for study sake.

Seldom was I compelled to speculate what the things were that forced me to force me to be away from the people. Their happiness was related with me and mine with Grandma, Meera, my lands, mango orchard and my natives which were to resign. And we had to accept it.

I never understood why I left my Grandma, who had spanned her whole life in upbringing me. The sun rose in the east and set in the west in her life and followed the day mere for me. For her, things started from me and ended to me

Sometimes I realized guilty of my selfishness. I yearned to prove her sacrifices turning into prolific soaring height and achievements.

I believed she was an angelic form, incarnated into the world to adorn my life and make it beautiful.

I recalled her shedding eyes when she had admitted me in the village primary school because I used to be away from her the whole day. That time I was too young to read her fainted face, shedding tear's spots beneath her eyes. Now I was a grown-up child. And this time, indeed, I was not going to the village school. It was a university, miles away from my home.

Overtly she showed delight on hearing of my counselling letter, but I discerned her strife with very own self, not to break down before me.

She was calm, moving over her stumbling feet, arranging my scattered things, occasionally reminded to pack up my essential stuffs. She instructed Meera to wrap *paratha-sabji* in a used newspaper paper. She was scared of me getting late. Due to their intermittently emphatic plead, I hurriedly swallowed some bites like ghosts, devoured it within a fraction of seconds.

"Dear son," she said to me. "Before you leave, go and bow your head on the shrine of Chaura Mata and feed bread and juggler to the cow."

I had been watching people praying before the Chaura Mata, a shrine of village deity. It was located amidst the village. There were various vaguely shaped stones around the idol, over a high dais around the trunk of an old neem tree in the middle of the village.

The sun was brooding, showering heat; hardly people had been seen ambling outdoor.

I hastened my step back to my home. I had put on my tailored new cloth. I feed juggler and bread to cow and touched her feet. I did this as a ritual or in faith, I can't tell. But I had seen a great belief of Grandma, so I received her believes voluntarily.

\For, I loved her, and I never found her doing anything irrelevant. She also used to say, "God is not present in the stones. He is inside us. Sitting in front of idols in praying posture, we just enlighten the spiritual spark inside us. And it always helps us."

Obviously, we all have received a way of believing from our far or near people or late ancestors. It doesn't matter whether knowingly or unknowingly.

I asked permission to take leave. She muttered words of blessings which resounded into my ears when I bent down to touch her feet.

Gulabo aunty arrived there. Hanging my bag on my shoulders, I bowed to touch her feet too. She read a chain of blessing, "May Goddess Mother keep you flourish by day and night." She turned to Meera, instructed her. "Meera daughter, accompany him till the road."

I prolonged, kept handkerchief covering my head until I reached the road.

Walking a hundred meters straight from my house, the brick path met a canal, which led to the main road. We halted under a lush shady banyan tree; we waited for the arrival of the bus, gazing over far stretched melting charcoal road. Due to furious sunlight, there was serenity prostrated either side of the road in the colonies of the village. Villagers had been napping on cots under the tree fanning; some were playing card wiping sweat from their perspired body.

"Perhaps, we are late." Meera anticipated, gazing over the road under fiery sunlight.

"I' m thinking, too," said I.

I strolled a few steps further on the road to see the vehicles.

"Sadhu, don't go in the sun. Come back! NoryYou will fall sick."

I thought, too, to remain stayed beneath the tree, than becoming sandwich between burning sky and melting charcoal vainly.

"Sadhu!" said Meera, in lowing tone. "Ask Mangal Chacha. He may tell you."

Mangal Chacha had a small general shop, selling tea and paan masala as well. He was just a sort of news channel for villagers. In the early morning and at evening, a thong of villagers flocked together there, conversed over ample of topics and had fun banters. That proved to be jovial and amiable hours for him, and folks gathered there.

When I reached to his shop, I found, he was dozing gasping his mouth. There was no one there, and he had been inside the shop and outside there were dogs. I called his name three times intermittently. Finally, I had to speak at a high pitch. For seconds my voice echoed between the walls of his shop. He woke up, collected himself being shocked, rubbed his eyes, and looked at me winking. He yawned widening his mouth.

I asked him about the bus.

"12 o'clock bus …" he paused, collecting his memory moving tips of the finger into his dense beard. He glanced at his watch and said, “No. it hasn’t passed yet. Stay and wait… it’s about to come.....The time is approaching.”

Another yawn he took. This time, one could count his betel painted teeth meanwhile.

“*Pranam Chacha*,” I joined palm, asked his blessing and moved away from there.

“Are you going somewhere?” He asked.

“Yes, *Chacha,*” I said. “Banaras.”

I returned to Meera. She frowned at him on asking about my destination.

It is believed ill-ominous in my village to ask a man about his destination if he is ready to go out somewhere.

After ten minutes, the bus appeared out of the meandering of the road around two hundred meters away from our standing place. I lifted the bag, waited for its approaching near to me.

I got into. I waved a hand to Meera to go back home. She watched me until the bus geared and beganrolling down. She covered her head by her apron and retreated back to home as the bus rolled afar.

After a jig-jag jolting velocity of bus travelling, I alighted at Junghai Junction. Paid fare, I walked crossing buzzing lane and followed a straight road from where I could read the name of the station written in the giant font. I asked for the ticket counter from a vendor softly. I moved in the direction told by the man, waited my turn at the window and took my ticket.

I walked with sluggish steps scanning around. People were spotted in twos- threes group here and there, some occupied benches, some standing in group chuckling over their comical comments. I glanced across the platform to have spare space that I could perch.

I kept strolling. As I told you, it was my first journey with Indian Railways that was why I was a little hesitated. I was plotting within self how I would enter into the train. I heed my prudent ears listening announcement sagaciously. Often I asked about the train's arrival time and platform from people standing near to me. Coolies were kind and generous. I think the railways' enquiry department should be thankful to them.

I accosted a bench. Next moment, it crammed with people. I asked one of the reticent men to move a bit, who gave me an intense glare. I thought better to stand up and leave that place. Seeing them next, I figured they were strangers to each other as I was to them.

I moved on another bench. Beside me, an elderly man was reading newspaper resting his spectacles over his nose. The silence of surround was broken with his occasional flapping of newspaper. I, from the corner of my eyes, rested my glance at the back page of the newspaper, tried to read the headlines and had just an aborted attempt to see the picture printed in the newspaper.

I thought I should ask for the newspaper. Next moment my inner philosopher restrained me and thought about what I would feel like if the man declined. I decided to control my reader spirit.

Having been tired of sitting, I stood up after a few minutes, stationed on the verge of the platform, peeped over track waiting for the train like an inquisitive child. Again I returned to my place. I asked the man about the train's arrival time that couldn't seem to say anything.

He raised his eyebrows, looked coldly and said, "Enquiry counter is that side."

I embarrassed at his behaviour. I remained silent for the next five minutes. I opened my crammed backpack and took out my counselling letter. I held it in my hand, turned it time and again pompously its main cover, printed Banaras Hindu University that that man could see it. And I succeed in this plan. Gradually the man initiated a discussion with me. He asked the trick of how his son could do well to crack university exam. I detailed him. He paid his ears to me like a slave. I could see now at his face an ineffaceable reverence for me.

If you want, people to respect you. You must be consummated about how to demonstrate yourself. All the skills are just another way of befooling.

I felt ecstasies while surmounting my skill at the man who showed me his ego a few minutes ago. I killed my idle time oozing my gregarious sermons.

Meanwhile, the announcement occurred. Massing together, the passengers started aggregating at the verge of the platform waiting for the final stop of the train.

I didn't know why I had a strange sensation, knotting around inside my stomach as the train getting slow to stop. I felt a prescient effervescent. I clutched my bag; I was ready to have my egress. People leaned forward when it reached at the platform, I glanced too. It seemed like the only engine was gliding down coming closer to our place. My heart throbbing raised as the train approached nearer. For a moment I did my best to segregate myself closing my ear, eyes when the train passed by just before me, slowing down puffing thick smock behind.

The train finally stopped, people alighted. I used all my force to pierce the crowd, thrashed into the compartment. I was hailed by an abysmal centenary smell. And a wretched-looking orderly couple had been sitting between both latrines boxes. I locked my nose to stop the obnoxious stink and walked inside, looking for a vacant berth.

I halted at a berth where two young boys were sitting already. When I was about to sit, they asked me to look for somewhere else. I strictly asked the reason why I would. They didn't rebel further, and I enjoyed my freedom. I stipulated reasons for their urge to me to be away from there. For there was a beautiful girl at the opposite bench, they cracked jokes, relished jolly comment and if ever she smiled a bit over their glib, slippery talkative, they filled with pride and happiness and triumphant. That was why they weren't ready to allow any other to intrude in their realm. They had developed an acrid, I envisaged, sentiment against me.

But they got down after some three or four stations. One of them, who looked little handsome and jolly, waved hand from the window to her. She remained listless. And train horned. It began rolling down. The atmosphere got relaxed after their departure. I shifted my seat over the window seat. Though now she was before me, honestly, I hadn't changed it to stare her. Everyone loved to sit in the window seat. Suddenly she took out something from her ears, it was ear-lid. Now I understood why oft she smiled. After the boys departed, now she might feel free. She glanced around occasionally.

She was a desi belle- a full-blown, dashing youth. Oft her sportive locks were falling over her healthy mysterious eyes and, very next, her fingers flipped those locks behind her ears, was adorable. She had been constantly looking across the window, beholding plants, field, houses, and cattle disappearing running behind, in the vice-versa direction, equal to the speed of the train. The wind stroked her silky hairs. She spoke less or, if I say, she didn't talk, as I hadn't listened her any mouth-spoken words yet. In her humble dressing- a kurty over jeans and a scarf- she appeared beautiful at first sight in her unpretentious attire. Perhaps, she was nescient and starkly unconscious of her surroundings.

The sight of her offering biscuit and snack to the poorly looking old couple who were sitting beside centenary demonstrated her poignant beauty blend with generosity.

She fetched them to make them sit beside her.

I ransacked my bag, took out the novel, Candida, and started rowing through its pages. Whenever I got chances, I pleased to gaze her escaping through the pages throwing my glance upside of the book.

Though I didn't believe in love at first sight, yet I could not resist the insistent of my innards man to have a glimpse of her now. It was the first time; I was beseeched and cherished by any womanly charm.

Obviously, it wasn't loved. For me, love was the theme of romantic books, plotted in Shakespearean dramas, a title of the book by Eric Segal and typical Bollywood story.

But to gaze her for me that moment was like gazing beautiful mountain landscapes, newly bloomed flowers and tossing myriad blossoms at the break of the day, chirruping birds, fluttering leaves of trees with the slightest gust, or watching a smiling child. In fact, she was at the moment was just 'a thing of beauty joy forever.' And nothing else.

I was reading the novel. Suddenly I heard a lucid, soft voice. To confirm it, I looked at her.

"Is it Candida?" asked she, softly smiling.

"Yeah," I replied positively.

"How many pages have you done?" asked she.

"Not so much. Still, I'm going through," said I.

Her chain of questioning was stopped. I didn't want to lose this opportunity to turn a monotonous jolting journey into chatting with a beautiful girl.

"You?" I looked questioning.

"In my last vacation, I finished it."

"Just an amateur?"

"Hmm…You can say it was amateur reading." She said, pondering for a second "….actually, this book was in my B.A. Honour Syllabus and that time I hadn't much time to devour it within a few days. I had to read other books too. So I decided to cram in my free time."

One thing, I anticipated that she was a literature student too.

"And you?" She said, a mild smile floated over her lips.

"Actually... one of my teachers, a Muslim daughter, mentioned her experience while delivering the lecture that once her father had stopped her to read this book when she was quite young. Since then, I thought to read this book."

"Oooow I see," she said rather excited.

"What is there inside the story? Can you summarize it?"

"Beauty of reading a book- don't try to know its story before you finish it. Flow with the line."

"Time is one factor. It does consume lots of time." I gave a reluctant expression.

"Reading a book, I don't think you need to fix time. Of course, you can utilize your spare hours in reading fiction-while travelling, at breakfast, before sleeping you can spend few amounts of time, which will help you to digest haunting thoughts of the day."

I giggled as she uttered, '…to digest the haunting thoughts of the day.'

"Ticket please." A man in a black dress was next to me, asking tickets from the old couple who were sitting beside the girl. Ticket Collector likes creature I had heard many times but saw first time vividly.

I pleaded with the ticket collector, not to ask tickets from the poor old couple, they appeared wretched. He turned to me and asked mine. I was rummaging ticket in my wallet. Meanwhile, she handed him two tickets. He saw it once, checked. He instructed the old couple to change the compartment at next station and moved further.

"I had a ticket," I said her showing mine to her.

She smiled, looked at me. "Don't mind." A constant smile lingered next for minutes at her face. "Are you travelling first time in the train?"

I nodded, yes. She was looking at me, startled. "I was joking." She said.

"But I'm not," I said solemnly and asked further with my curiosity. "Why did you show the ticket on my behalf while I had already?"

"Because it's an AC coach. And you have a general ticket. He might have caught you and impose some heavy penalty or could take some legal action against you. ."

"O….My …God!" I imagined those unwanted situation fo a second, what if he caught me without having a ticket?

I thanked her.

“One of my friends was about to come with me, but in the end, she declined due to some important work. Anyhow, we couldn’t conceal her ticket,” said she..

“How did you know? I had a general ticket?” I was looking at her astounded.

“When you were adjusting your ticket in the purse, I saw it. But honestly,” she held the skin of her throat. “I didn’t guess you were a novice train traveller.”

Indeed, never I was enthralled so much as I was feeling now watching her beauty stealthily, sometimes conversing common talks. But I ventured not to give my attention neither I wished for any magical happening.

I managed to balance my flamboyance innate, overwhelmed emotions. Her mild and pleasant cheered face, lively humour and frank gesture, filled the surrounding mirthful and my heart too.

Day- One (Evening)

Prabha's absorption in dairy snaps with the shush arrival of Nazarin. It seems as if Prabha was in some dream sequence.

Nazarin has carried a stuffed bag with packed food, fruits, juice, clothes and blanket. The clock has struck nine-thirty of night.

The gloomy silence of the hospital often splinters with the tramps of doctors, nurses and attendants. The visitor throngs at enquiry counter muttering something in dark tone querying about their near ones admitted in the hospital. The mute television fluctuates. The security guard defies people to assemble at the reception area, in the hallways or on the stairs.

Nazarin: Take something in. You might be starving.

Prabha: Yup, I am. But I want to change my clothes first and want to freshen up.

Nazarin: Better if you chose to eat something.

Prabha (Probes, pointing out to the bag): What's in it?

Nazarin: Cheese and puree, salad, apples and juice.

Prabha: Hold it. I'm coming.

She strolls to the reception.

"Excuse me," she said to the receptionist, a beautiful girl in sari .

"Yes, madam, how can I help you," the young girl says. She pauses a while, stares at Prabha vigorously. "If I'm not wrong, you are Prabha Mam?"

Prabha smiles vaguely and says, "How do you know me?"

She stresses over her memory, trying to recall the girl's pretty face.

"Guess?" says the receptionist, smiling.

"Okay. Let me guess." After a few seconds, she commences saying, "You are Shreya. Right?"

"How are you here?" asks she.

"One of acquainted is admitted here. Treatment is going on." She adds. "I need to change my clothes, can I have…" Prabha falters in her following words to complete the rest of the sentence.

The receptionist takes them to a comfortable and well-furnished room.

"You can stay here."

"Won't be any problem if we stay here?"

"Nope. It's only for lady staffs."

"Thank you," Prabha said.

"Welcome, Mam." She is about to shut the door. Suddenly she halts and turns to Prabha. "Anyway. What's the name of the patient? If there will be an update about the patience, I will let you know."

"Siddhartha."

She leaves.

"Siddhartha? …Without knowing him, how do you know his name?" Nazarin gets puzzled.

"From this lost diary," says Prabha, nonchalantly looking at the diary.

"Ah…How can you say, this diary belongs to him?"

"I don't say it belongs to him. Randomly I mentioned this name. I didn't find any name when she asked."

"We don't know who is he. Maybe a criminal, terrorist, or rapist?" yells Nazarin, worrying.

"Why are you so scared?" asks Prabha.

"Because we are girls."

"Ah! See. A rapist and a lover— both are a man. Then why do you think a man can be demagogue only?" Prabha counsels and continues. "And of course, a terrorist or criminal will not jump from Naini Bridge, you know that. You know how that place has become popular for committing suicide for brainless lovers."

They finishes dinner quite early . Nazarin sails into the bed and falls asleep. Prabha can't resist the alluring thought of reading the pages of the diary before her eyelids compel her finally.

The utter stillness of the night often has been interrupted with the frequent ambulance alarm and mourning of relatives of patients in the hospital. But the flipping of the pages plays an antidote for the disturbances coming from outside.

Chapter 3

Banaras is a city of beauty, simplicity and truth. If you ask in one word, you will find a universal answer- *Har Har Mahadev*.

Indeed, the simpler it appears, the more it holds depth within. Indeed, its simplicity is what called mysticism of Banaras and to discern it. Equally, you will need to possess a simple soul. It's the land of knowledge where all the veil of illusion and ignorance disappear. This is an immortal city. This is the land when one can attain their destination. It's only place where people pray to find death, where one can find the truth of life, turns indifference to mundane truth, merely roaming through the buzzing streets, wandering aimlesslynd ruminating in the corner of temples. It's the land where one hails with resounding slogan *Har Har Mahadev*, forgetting all. It is the land where you can hear a foreigner reciting '*Shanti Shanti No Kranti*'. It's the land where best social, economic, political analytical debate you can hear just sipping tea in soil cup at the tea stall, by any scholastic spokesmen. Here, magistrate of the city is perennial Lord Baba Kaal Bhairav.

It's the city where poets are named *Saar Banarasi, Chakachak Banarasi, Bedhab Banarasi, Danda Banarasi* and dot dot dot. It's the city where the depth of friendship is fathomed at the pitch of "*Bhosari Ke*", a sort of city anthem which your ear can have a chance to listen to it at any crossing, corner or nooks. Such an incident happened to me.

The exhibition of *pichh- pachh* artist's masterpiece, you can witness at the wall of the city. It is the city of amenity where oft you can see commoner, standing at traffic; help people to navigate out of the crowd. Here, if the ball goes directly into the Ganges means out in cricket.

Here, people are not Bengali, Gujarati or Marathi, whereas they fusion with its aura and become Banarasi Bengali, Banarasi Marathi Banarasi Gujarati and the chain of suffixes go on.

Apparently, people find here cattle, dong, traffic, and the thugs, but they are not real Kashi. As much I understood this city through my whole experience- to know it live in Kashi, feel Kashi, study Kashi, roam in Kashi and find the truth and mysticism of life hidden in its breathing.

Quit exotic. I, standing just across the road in front of exeunt point of Cant Station Varanasi, was reading faces. But honestly, it was the first time I couldn't identify any single one. Behind me, there was a small temple under a tree, red-painted wall, few saffron dressed men wore dense silver beard had been reciting hymns, beating an antique drum and rest clapped with the rhythm of beats.

Inside, at the centre of the temple, there was Lord Shiva idol. Outside, over the dais around a tree's stem, several Gods and Goddesses' dilapidated picture and statue laid down there in exile.

I bowed, prayed for my admission and betterment of the future.

Fear of your fortune can make you more religious, isn't it?

I always remained a man of impatience, particularly in waiting for somebody. I uplifted my head, trying to recognize Manish among fleetingly rushing faces. Now, the white bulb of shops began glittering, high stood flood light thrown its focus all around and to see the city first time at nightfall showered in brightness, my tyro soul blazed up even, and I gazed eagerly. Auto men were yelling several names- *Lanka bichchu- Lanka- Bichchu, Maidagin, DLW, Godaulia*.

I was familiar with these names from Radio Mirchi, but I didn't know where and which part it did exist. Later I came to know, 'Bichchu' was a mispronunciation of B.H.U.

It was a completely new world I had seen the first time.

"Hello, Mr.," somebody called me. When I darted, the girl, whom I met in the train, thrashed out her head from the auto. "I think you are new in the city?" She had put on a beautiful smile, comically."If you are looking auto for Lanka, it can take you there." Seeing my indecisiveness, she said, comically. "I can guide without charging you any penny."

Obviously, I was an innocent young man, but not fool that I would skip such chance to sojourn with a beautiful girl who herself was offering from the front. I better thought to drop a message to meet at Lanka. And I plunge into the auto without any presage.

I had been eagerly gazing the shops, malls and people in fancy attire. I was feeling as I was on a different planet and travelling with an alien girl. Everything was new, springing inside a fountain of strange pleasure which I could not understand.

Our auto dawdled along with other hundreds of creeping vehicles. The driver took a heavy breath of tense, slowed down the pace of the auto. The road was blocked ahead. And after some time, everyone struck still. I looked around, found every vehicle- auto, bike, and bus and rickshaw man- turned as stagnant lake water in midnight and madly blowing the horn, like crazy hounds illogically.

I couldn't take much time to understand what people prognosticated about the city's road. I heard ever a popular phrase about the busy road of the city. And it was also my first time to experience the creeping speed of the stormy car. Before this, I had heard about Banaras' traffic jaam news at Radio.

It was also the first time I experienced one of the oddities of the city when a rikshaman tried to overtake, and unfortunately, his rear wheel touched a bike. The man on bike raising his head, adjusting paan chewing in the mouth, burst out indignantly over wretched man, abusing "*Bhosari Ke*." And rickshaw grinned triumphantly and next turned in defending state, said, "*Babu... bhaiya* ...excuse me."

That time, I received it as a derogatory term, but couldn't imagine I, too, would be accustomed to this cult and would chant-like blessing word.

"What happen *bhaiya?*" asked the girl.

"There is a digging work going on the road. Telephone Corporation, City Municipal Corporation and sometimes local people dig out the road. It has become a routine of the city," he complained.

"Don't know when this Banaras will get rid of this incorrigible sickness?" said she, grudgingly.

Listening to it auto man chuckled a bit and returned, "This is Banaras Mam, and people of the city turned accustomed to such unpredictable inconvenience. While they don't know it is the loss of time, money and energy for public and government both."

"Actually, the problem lies here in the people. They have accepted facing it like day work," said she, rather sternly.

She popped her head out partially, craned slightly, scrutinized traffic and returned to her seat. She said after passing a couple of minutes, "*Bhaiya,*" appeared worrying. "Is there any other route that you know?"

She waited for his response. He remained quiet, pondered and finally took a long sigh and turned auto into a street. He was rowing through the streets like any Hollywood action hero. And the streets had a quite unpredictable meandering. Sometimes, auto had to stop passing through narrow, chaotic gullies due to lingering masses, cattle, relentlessly in front of it. The driver blew the horn, geared it and again moved it on.

However, he emanated us out of the tangle and left us at our destination- Lanka, BHU.

I came out of the auto and found standing under an arch gate. I fumbled inside my pocket to take out the fare. Before I came out in action to pay money to the auto man, she handed him twenty rupees and nodded for not to pay.

I requested her to only pay for herself. She declined and said next if they met, I would pay the fare. She left, and I watched her going away, mounting on a rickshaw that drove her across the arch gate of the university. I sensed she was a student at the university.

I remained standing there in dummy bird scare pose looking for Manish.

The gateway of the university was gigantic glittered with yellow light, busied with the tramps. I startled when I turned my head left to the right side and caught Manish next to me.

He greeted me in a poised Indian way, joining hand wearing a cheerful smile. "*Namaskar Maharaj.*"

He asked me to follow him and I, like a child, obeyed his commands. We drank juice, and then he took me adjoining tea stall, offered me first *kulhad.* "This is *Pappu'*s tea stall," took a sip, "remember this place. You have to spin here complete two years."

"Why?" I asked, taking my sips.

"Students of this university have a special epiphany with this tea stall; some goes a step ahead and tries puffing with the sip." He said. We threw our used *kulhad* into the cane. Then he led to a restaurant and ordered a meal. He collected the packet and moved out of the restaurant sluggishly. While crossing road, he bowed before a giant statue, situated in the middle of the *chauraha.* I also followed him, I had no idea why I was doing that by then, but I did. Amidst hue and cry of vehicles, he steadily crossed the road, sometimes threatening coming van nearer to us.

He hired a rickshaw. We mounted and occupied its back seat. The rickshaw man drove us, paddling, as it ran dangling, a nocturnal panorama opened before me which amazed my eyes. And could amaze anyone at first sight- the vista of glittering lamppost, series of hostel in queue and its sparkling rooms, panorama of the trees in rows either side of roads and whole premise washed in light.

As rickshaw stirred on through the serene road, my eyes widen seeing the beauty of the campus and its aesthetic. I felt I was sojourning through the dreams that some time ago I had seen.

Manish imparted me about the places, points and detours which fell in the way.

He told me about PMC- *Piya Milan chauraha.* I was astounded when he told me the history of the university, how a single man had founded it accumulating capital by begging. It was unbelievable to accept that such a grand university was set by a Brahmin man begging throughout the country.

As a campus, it is marvelous and unforgettable which reflects Indian culture, art, science, carrying the world's modernity as well.

The caravan of wavering rickshaw journey got over; it halted before Raja Ram Mohan Rai hostel.

After washing, getting fresh, it struck 10 p.m. Soon we made our dinner.

"Check your document once and arrange it now," he said taking brush and pest from the drawer. He thrust it into his mouth, and rushing it around his teeth, he walked towards the bathroom. Returned with a dripping face and held the towel, wiped droplets. I was already prostrated on the bed, feeling drowsy being tired of the tedious day. Hardly had he switched off the light, left on zero watt bulb, just then somebody bumped over the gate. Manish glanced at the gate, then to me and hinted me by putting his finger at his lips not to speak.

Suddenly, a chorus proclaimed together his name at a high pitch. He didn't speak. I surprised to listen to the slogan just next, whereas Manish was smiling.

"*Manish Bhaiya ki,*" One of them led and read the slogan.

"*Jai,*" A group of voice followed.

"*Manish Bhaiyaa ki,*" This time louder.

"*Jaiii,*" others.

"*Manish Bhaiyaaa,*"- louder.

"*Jaaaiiiiiii,*"

The last slogan startled me more and broke the Utopian image, which I had a few minutes before, about the university. This time all voices came together at the highest pitch.

"*Maaannishhhawwaaa Bhhoooshaaariii Keeee.*"

Chapter 4

Manish opened the windows; morning lucid beams intruded and flickered into the room and blazed up the whole interior texture of the room in yellow light.

Deliberately my eyes squeezed, I tried to restrain it falling over my face shading palm and rubbed my partially slumber eyes. I tried to glance through the hazy morning eyes but couldn't.

I walked and peeped through the windows, gazed the morning sun.

It was my first morning in Banaras. I remember still, I had never seen such exquisite 'morrow' ever in my life. It appeared cool, crisp and bewitching as I had heard.

The sun appeared bounty. Its crimson soft beams kindled in the entire sphere.

Now I sat in the wooden chair, calmly watching chirruping birds, hopping from one to another bough and frequently disappeared in the bushes in the backyard.

I looked down, bending my head, resting at the bars of the window. It was crammed with canes, plastic bags, dry rotten leaves and twigs. It seemed as it had gone ages when somebody downtrodden over there.

By now, Manish had done his morning routine, got into the room back, pushed the door opened gliding its plank into vice versa direction slowly.

He sat on the next bed, reading beads of the rosary, muttering some Sanskrit shlokas vaguely. I was impressed by his way of beginning the day, I fancied to start my day, too, once I got admission.

He looked at me from the corner of his eyes, rolled his eyes waving hands to go to the bathroom without derailing his chanting.

It was not tough to find the bathroom that day. I just followed half-naked boys' marching, brushing teeth, hanging the towel over shoulder.

I bathed under the shower for the first time in my life that morning. The experience under the bathroom shower was quite similar to the experience cropping paddy in the field under the rain.

When I returned, Manish was not in the room. I wiped out wetness dragging *gamachha,* across the torso. Henceforth, I put on my cloth.

The gate opened. I caught Manish in formal decorum- white shirt, black pant, simple footwear and wore his oil combed traditional hairstyle.

"Are you ready?"

"Yes"

"Come" he held his bag, hung by the right shoulder and asked me to follow him. "Have breakfast. Lunch will be after 11:30 o'clock."

We devoured *paratha*- sauce. Manish suggested me to scrutinize all the important documents once more.

We strolled out of the hostel. He gave a key and kept another one with self.

It was 10 A.M. now. The sun was light sharp soaring at our back, but walking under the vista turned scorching July into blissful. As I headed toward the department, where counselling was to go, I was getting a strange excitement and my heart throbbing increased.

We walked on the road shadowed by the row of verdurous trees either side. The sunlight drizzled through the foliage, dappled the pavement, soft breezing, occasional hooting cars and bikes, students' strolling hanging bags, series of hostels in queue and arch faculty building- it all was just coherence or planned in the mind of its founder? It was a question haunting in my mind. Whatsoever but I relished its aesthetic.

Quite then, I saw an arch peak of a temple. Still, I was in a dilemma if it was a faculty or temple. Startling I asked Manish.

"It's VT." After a while, he elaborated, "New Vishwanath Temple. It was the dream of the founder of this university that there should be a Lord Shiva's temple in premises."

I bowed my head slightly.

Tacitly, I vowed if I got an admission I would visit that temple at least twice in a month.

Walking now we reached in front of social science faculty. He wished me 'best of luck' and parted. Now I led lone toward English department. The closer I was getting, I found commotion outside of premise and whirling inside me.

As I crossed the threshold, I was amidst the flood of strange faces, chaos and chattering. Its gallery was utterly filled with tramps, resounding of candidates' chattering. I bewildered initially. Asking I reached to the classroom where counselling was going one, scarcely I intruded through the crowd, approached to one of the professors sitting at the right corner of the dais who was collecting and checking the documents and detailing essential instructions patiently.

I asked about the cut of the list.

'250,' he told. I was disappointed. He asked my score. I said '249'.

Hearing me, he gave me a form to fill it up and submit it within ten minutes, promptly.

Gladly, I rushed to the adjoining room. I filled the choice form. I organized my documents and returned in the same stuffed, murmuring room.

After submitting my form, I engaged a chair of the hall. There were two boys; oft conversed something in Banarasi slang whisperingly.

"Kamalawa...Ka bey ... Are you watching?" said the short-heighted.

"Hmm…It appears we are Bohemian before these sophisticated rascal, aren't we?" long- heighted.

"…I'm scared… Likely, we are going to lose Hostel life this year?"

"Mahadev knows."

They remained quiet. Now, a bald-headed man stood up on the daise, announced that after half an hour, the final list would be declared.

"But Rehanawaa," said long-heighted, who had worn a thick glass spectacle. "Haven't you noticed, it seems as if all the Bollywood beauties come down on the floor for the catwalk?"

"Really," supported another. "Let's see if sitting with them on the bench is in our destiny or not?"

I controlled and pacified my impatience man and waited for the final list.

"What is your score, Bhaya?" I turned. One of them was asking me.

"249," I said.

He patted my shoulder and assured me of my admission. The same bald man stood up again, read the list of those who were finally selected for admission.

"Your?" I asked homelily.

"Too low than you," he said, smiling and added. "Just I70."

He announced the name from general category first. I was listening inquisitively for the announcement of my name.

At last, I found me fortunate enough. I heard what my ears awaited to listen. I was called. The professor, a middle-aged woman, looked me and finally commenced to say, "Your name is on the waiting list." My breathing stopped for a while. "You will have to wait. In case if anybody declines, then you will have a chance? Till then, please have a seat and wait."

I returned to my seat. And the list of Gen, OBC, and then SC & ST announced. The first time, I realized India has got redeemed from casteism but created another option of social war- classism.

I heard a thong of students speaking infrequent Hindi, sometimes in a strange language which I had never heard of before. I was just guessing it whether it was Uriya, Bengali, Tamil Telugu but whatever, I was sure it was not Panjabi.

The professor started announcing the final shortlist. I was mumbling, praying to Lord Shiva as with ach name from the list articulated.

As the crowd began disappearing from the room, shifted to the next room, I felt a pang in the heart. I looked those selected candidates as a heavenly creature, moving out taking confirmation letter as they were prized to brood in the heaven permanently. The more students had been shifting, the deeper I found pessimism inside me. I had an *abysmal* pang when both boys sitting near me got selected, in spite of having a lot less mask than me.

I was asking my fault of sitting there alone just harking names from the list. I gazed them walking out. Now there were only a few counted candidates left-back and I was one of them.

But thank God. I was delighted when my name was called. First I waited and watched if there was somebody else of the same name in the hall. Again my name was called. This time, it was more prominent. I could not believe the sound. I stood up; pace toward the dais "Son" a middle-aged woman said "You are lucky. A top rank girl preferred girl's college."

I thanked God taciturnly. I was told to move the next room for document submission. A bald-headed man, a professor, stopped her, 'Ma'am. Just wait. She might come for the campus. She is a good student. I know her." He mumbled. For a while, my heart stopped beating. The girl arrived there for some official interrogation.

"Hello, daughter," the professor said. He proceeded. "All are renowned professors in the campus. Still, I don't understand why do you want to go to an affiliated college?"

"Sorry sir," she apologized with a soft smile.

"See," he indicated to me. He kept continuing, "People are dying to have an admission in campus, and you have a chance, you are denying."

Believe me, for the moment, I thought to return to my last college.

To be poor is affordable, but to look poor can be harmful for your personality. Because in the pompous world, 'what you are?' is the matter of less bothering, than how you look apparently. My pastoral silence and sober trait had created a misconception about my covert world.

She glanced at me.

"Sir, my parents want me to admit me in a woman's college. Sorry," she returned him cordially.

"You need not be scared...," as he started to speak, she cut him off and said 'Thank you sir' and moved away. He kept looking her going away blankly.

And this way, I got a confirmation letter.

It was 3 o'clock up-to-now.

The whole room clamoured with mumbling, chatting and ambling of teachers, students and parents. Affiliated teachers, having the list in hand, were wooing good rank students. All were engaged in stapling form, sticking photographs and submitting the photocopy of essential documents.

Manish, rowing through the crowd, arrived. I had already completed all my formality, but still, I had to wait next for half an hour. I could see famish stress on his face after receiving tedious lectures. Since morning we had only breakfast. I suggested him better to move to the hostel and had rest.

It was a glorious evening, amazing, very special to me. I had changed my dream into reality now. The sun was rushing down to its destination after the day-long walk. Now, it appeared in an utterly mollifying round like a red coloured disc, cool and soothing.

I retreated to Raja Ram Mohan Ray hostel, quietly gazing thing around delightedly that now I was a part of it.

I set out my feet dreaming my upcoming days. It was difficult for me to evaluate the state of pleasure and pangs I was carrying simultaneously, deep inside.

It was tough for me to survive, for we had no permanent earning resource, so monthly expenditure haunted me oft -'How?'

Now I could not pull back my feet, which I knew well.

Now, I approached at the threshold of the hostel, the sun was hidden behind buildings. A group of students assembled in front, gossiping day affairs, and class matters. Of course, it was not related to their study. As I passed by them, their jargons buzzed in my ears.

The corridor, rooms, yard of hostel glittered with white CFL light. After a long curving walk, climbing stairs, tramping I reached in front of room no. 212. It was unlocked already. I pushed the gate gently inside, peeped. A half-naked strange boy was doing yoga. I conjectured; he might be Manish's room-mate, whom Manish used to talk about, often.

I walked into the room straight, kept the bag on the table. I unbuttoned and stripped down my sweaty- sticky cloth and wrapped towel. He spoke to me in a homely as he already knew me for a long time...He wished me for my admission. I paid my gratitude.

Negligently in towel and innerwear, I went to the bathroom and ensued back into the room with the dripping face.

Wiping moister from the skin by *gamchha*, I was looking intrinsic through the window, dreaming.

He conversed on various points. Sometime evading him my eyes took jaunts of the room, struck to his bookshelf. I read titles which were mostly economics entitles, covered with dust layers;

it failed to raise my curiosity to read it. Some magazine were scattered on their beds. I did my senior secondary in math, but all the interest in mathematics was dead almost after studying literature.

Slowly the gate glided wide rattling. Manish plodded into the room.

"Where were you?" I probed.

"I went Lanka," he put some stationery on the table and fell sluggishly on the bed. "You could call me," he said.

"I called you, but the network was busy there," I pretended.

"Anyway. Have you submitted your fees?"

"Hmm," I nodded.

"Why did you need to stay late?" he asked.

"I was on the waiting list. They wanted to be sure. That's why."

"I thought you were trying to know your FFC," he put on lower.

"FFC?" I puzzled.

"Future Female Colleague," he wore a mischievous smile

"No. No." I said, shying.

"I just thought. But mostly beautiful girl migrates in the English Department," he said pretending to be serious.

His room-mate was gazing him, smiling.

"*Bhosari Ke*… you are looking as if you will eat me up," said Manish tossing sarcasm over his smiling demeanor. "Take away your lusty eyes."

"You are my darling. I love you. I won't molest you," he said. They laughed. I was silent, just watching them astonishing. Manish got fresh. I engaged in the reading newspaper.

"How do you know each other? Is he from your village?" room-mate interrogated to Manish.

"Noooo," Manish gave a longer no. "He is Siddhartha. I told you about him. He is my previous college fellow."

I kept observing Manish's gesticulation, the way of talking, and demeanor. I caught he was not the previous local college student. Everything was changed except his dressing and saving every single penny to spend on the unnecessary thing. He was frank than the previous shy local boy.

A swarthy young boy of fifteen opened the gate, remained stood on the threshold, wore half pant and an antique shirt, sleeper, and held a bulky sack in the right hand. His sticky skin shimmered in the light. He took out four storey lunch box, put down as usually bereft saying anything.

" *Chhotu,*" said the room-mate. "You have to bring one diet more."

"I have already done," said the young lad, looking to Manish. "*Bhaiya,* already told."

"Ok," roommate nodded. He left.

"Spread paper."

Manish untangled the bolt of the lunch box, took every box separately. His roommate bent down, picked a few old newspapers, and spread it on the bed. Yellow stains on its pages demonstrated, they used to spread it.

Manish had put two thali, and people were three. "I will manage in the box," said the roommate.

We began our dinner.

"In English Department, the majority student is Bengali," said roommate, thrusting his bite. We were silently chewing our swallow, giving him an occasional glance. "You can find only three things in Bengal." He counted on his fingers. "Culture, art, and beauty. And English literature they received as a gift for being the first victim of colonial power." He took a slice of bread wrapped in palak- paneer.

"How a Bihari can expatriate about Bengali so fairly," Manish snapped jokes. Roommate, too, smiled and replied jovially,

"Beta, I'm three in one." I looked questioning. He sensed it and said, "By birth Bengali, paternal Bihari and doing degree in Banaras. So, I know more than you." We remained calm and focused on our meal. The roommate came out with another visionary assertion, "You will have a precious chance to drive among Bengali beauty…They are amazing…Especially their eyes…Have you met anyone today?"

I tried to hide my blush, nodded 'no.' I smiled abnegating his question, but at the moment, a panorama of beautiful faces seen in counselling flushed in my mind.

"Are you non-veg?"

"No," I replied immediately. "I'm also Brahmin."

Manish laughed.

"I mean, do you have sex?"

Suddenly, my breathing for the moment choked, I took several sips of water. He still was looking at me for the answer.

"No," I reverted, swallowing bite of mouth down through throat.

"Smoking."

"No."

"Drinking."

"No."

"You must have taken your girlfriend on the bike, mustn't it?"

"Neither I know the driving, nor I have a girlfriend," said I rather confidently. Whatever question he had hurled over me was exotic. Beyond study, nothing got success to knock the door of my mind. It was just malpractice to me as I used to think. I glanced at him. He was smiling.

" Shut your mouth rascal…take your dinner silently," said Manish to him, bluntly. "We are honest, Brahmin, son, unlike you."

"Sorry, friend," said roommate. "...but I don't find this convincing." He turned to Manish. "Either he is lying or befooling us. If a young boy, particularly English student is saying. He doesn't like pretty girls, neither smokes nor consumes alcohol and doesn't have an intercourse experience. Then there must be a question over him. If it happens, either he is telling the absolute truth, or the man needs to consult a doctor...Bro," he mumbled, emphatically.

"But now something seriously I suggest," he couldn't stop, delineated. "Don't ever be room partner of any Bengali if you are vegetarian and don't like lingering smoke in the nose."

"Why?" Manish asked my question, mocked.

Roommate smiled.

He prepared himself to utter headed toward me, "Bengali smoke cigarette outdoor and burn the pile of *biri abysmal* indoor. And also, they are quite frank about sex, cigarette, non-veg and modern perceptive." He halted for a while, prolonged his speech, this time accentuated, "The second point...Never rely on the charms of Bengali beauty and their oceanic deep, inquisitive eyes ... 'A thing of beauty' has so many chance to be contaminated and to be fooled."

"Nice research!" Manish bragged.

"And brother. I'm giving you the essence of my one year experience- float through the current of vogue. Avoid taking deep interest...neither will you drown... keep safe yourself...Keep remembering your purpose of coming her...," he said solemnly.

Chapter 5

After slicking, I packed my indispensable essential belongings and treasured the counted sums between the pages of the book; I reached at Manish's hostel next week.

Giant, arch mason, wide stretched well-equipped ground, long smooth roads along with pleasant vista and rambling students had truly, filled my heart and mind with rupture.

I reckoned as I stepped on, 'Is it a reverie? …Am I walking in a dream or reality? A dream -that I had seen yore of time.

Absolutely we are just an image of somebody's dream. We are just character just performing accordingly. We all are captivated by the enormous mind of some human being- just an x-rox copy of somebody's imagination.

I was already late to join the class. There was a commotion in the corridor, and it seemed busier but unlike clamorous and vociferous admission day. Of course, I was damn nervous, but I tried hard to hide my inside face plastering a soft smile over my face. Staring on the ground, I walked through the hallways. Nobody cared who I was. The students appeared less friendly. Professor quietly made their way through the crowd. It was stuffed with unfamiliar and strange faces.

I stopped seemingly a young girl and asked humbly where the first semester postgraduate- English Literature class was being taken.

"Fresher?" she looked at me scrutinizing.

"Yes," I nodded.

"Go straight to room number 25." She directed me, pointing her finger.

Thanking her, I walked, collecting confidence, speculating how I would get into the classroom.

My heart was throbbing like the diesel engine. I had a notebook in hand and a pen in my pocket. Up-to-now, I carried homemade bag, stitched. I could not afford extravagant, stylish satchel. But I could not carry that old-style home-made bag now anymore.

I halted before I pushed the door. Hundreds of thoughts were flying hurriedly in the arena of my psyche. I stood struck in front of the door, collecting to intrude inside. I rambled a couple steps back and forth to make easy myself. I faltered to knock the door. I could hear a frail voice of teacher lecturing inside coming through the chink of the door.

Backside to me, their shoes clattering synchronized with the beating of my heart. The lady I met passed by. She stopped her stepping, seeing me and approached me, "What happens?" She glanced the number plate pinned on the door. "Yes, this is the classroom." She prolonged and pushed open the door partly and peeped into.

"Excuse me, sir! Sorry to disturb you." She made space for me. "He is a new student." She turned to me and asked my name.

"Siddhartha," I said meekly.

The professor hailed me with a comely smile. And she went on her way.

When I pushed the door gently, it glided with a fragile rattle. I entered. I caught myself in already engaged classroom stuffed with a throng of some know and some strange faces. Everyone's eyes struck at me, gazing, as I was standing in a strange land. I made me brave, prayed Mahadev.

I marched through the space between the benches beholding faces. I walked as if bombs set in the ground. I felt like it was the toughest journey I was travelling to find the vacant seat in that already crammed classroom. I found an unoccupied seat at the end of the row, the quest got over.

A girl patted on the chair next to her. I sat down.

She was smiling. Amazing. She was the same girl I met on the train. 'Wow! What coherence!'

She had a constant smile over her face.

"Hi," she said whisperingly. I shrugged, 'hey.' I turned attentive to the lecture.

It was just an introduction class. Professor asked about students' aspirations, lectured a bit on literature and language.

In the recession, before another teacher arrived, students introduced one another, interrogated about their last college, gossiped among themselves. Being found myself in a flood of strange faces, I shied and hesitated to speak.

After ten minutes gap, the gate opened again, another teacher entered the classroom. It was the same lady whom I met very first in the corridor and assumed her a student.

The whole class stood up in greeting. She gave a broad mesmerizing smile.

She was beautiful and young enough possessed an indeed transcended youthfulness. One couldn't assume age.

A beautiful woman is not one who posses beautiful curve only.

She scanned the classroom and said, "Good morning here to Siddhartha."

All eyes turned to me for once.

"I think, I have seen you somewhere…?," she asked the girl next to me, speculating.

"MMV," said the girl, blushed. "You went there for the guest lecture."

The teacher asked her name.

"Urvashi." She mentioned.

"Yeah…That's right…So, you have changed only the building…Right?"

She nodded, smiled softly.

"Where are you staying now?"

"Triveni hostel."

"Help you, friends who are new for this place," the professor suggested.

"Hmm," the girl nodded.

Throughout, I was reading her expression; I figured out, she was meek before the professor.

"It means you have done your graduation from here?" I demanded.

"Fortunately, by mistake," said she smiling errantly.

"I don't think anyone can qualify an exam of such a grand university by mistake?"

"But a fortunate one can."

"I don't agree."

"Maybe. Even this time too, I used *andazification* in the entrance exam, chanting Jai Mata di A B C."

We have been conversing scribbling on the last page of the notebook.

We remained quiet, attentive at the lecture.

"You are from Allahabad University?" She wrote.

"No,"

"Then?"

"KNPG College."

"Where is it?"

" *Gyanpur*- a local town- in between Allahabad and Banaras." I detailed. "It's around 70 kilometers away from Varanasi if you move toward Allahabad."

"I know… I Know." She said abruptly. After a brief pause, she commenced, "I think, you are befooling me."

"Why need I to fool you." I jot down on the page. Now we were silently conversing bereft making notice to anyone.

"If it's true, it shows, you are laborious and intellectual....Coming here from a small town...graduating from a local college...It's a big thing."

I restrained my inner philosopher, who was to come out about my originality that I was not a small-town boy while an idyllic boy.

"Are you from Allahabad?" I questioned.

She shrugged. "You can say."

The professor discerned our secret conversation. She turned a bit exasperated as our listless distracted her. I was not willing to be famous on the very first day of university. When teacher popped up her head to lecture the class, she turned her lingering eyes toward us, we masqueraded having engrossed in her words.

"You are a genius, that's why you are here." She penned down. I found it if it was a sarcasm. "We can be good friends." She offered her hand to me, escaping teacher's eye, underneath the bench.

It was getting over for me. I couldn't digest it now.

"Sorry. I haven't come here to make friends."

"Wow. Attitude! Take your time." she pumped a gasp.

We kept our nose straight towards the teacher.

"Where can I buy books?" I couldn't help asking her.

"Again, I'm offering you proposal of friendship." She offered a proposal for making friendships.

I gave her a cold response. I could not violate Grandma's promise.

"You will repent when you know that Urvashi hadn't offered her friendship to any boys in the entire university." She said bragging.

To see her beauty, I knew, boys would die to accept such an offer. But for me, the situation was different. My purpose constrained me to prompt to move across my study, for what I was there.

"It means you will not tell me about the bookshop." I tried to make up what I was to mass-up. "It's ok."

"You are strange."

"Then?"

"Nothing." She got agitated a bit. She pretended better to focus on the class than to talk a boring guy. I drew a smiley in her notebook.

"I'm a quite tyro in this city," I looked at her, being vulnerable. "You must help your friend, you promised to Mam a few minutes before."

She glanced at my visage, pitied, "University publication. You can catch an auto from Lanka. There you can find all sorts of books. In common friendship, you can have only information."

"If it would be handshake-friendship, then?" I demanded.

"I, myself, Urvashi, will take you to the shop."

"Thank you so his much for this kind job," I said.

We remained taciturn the next few minutes until lecture got over.

"And canteen?"

"Are you hungry?" she asked me.

"Hmm…Haven't you taken breakfast?" Pang of starvation was reflecting clearly over my face, which anybody could read.

Up to now, the clock crossed 12 o'clock. My mind began losing its grip on consciousness.

"Oh…Where are you staying?

"With the friend in Raja Rao Hostel."

After the next fifteen minutes, teacher left the class. She assembled her notes, books and put it into her bag and asked me to follow her. I collected mine, walked in her footsteps sheepishly in search of the remedy of my hungry exhausted stomach.

"Are there any more lectures to go?" I asked her, strolling over her trodden path, navigating through the students loitering in the corridor.

"How can I tell it?" she scoffed, partly turning her head toward me. I sensed the reason for her quick temper.

"Perhaps?" I doubted, "What do you mean?" following her steps. "You mean, there may be some professor come for lecture?" I concerned.

"Yes, but it is the first day. The teacher will come and preach about career, syllabus planning, and a bit about subject. Serious classes will run after passage of couple weeks," she said. She checked her hurried stepping. "Listen. If you long to go canteen, then pursue me. Don't show that I compel you to bunk the class…Ok," she was firm in her tone.

I pursued her steps. Absolutely I was hungry. I can't assure you whether I was infatuated of trailing her beauty or my appetite. It was happening the first time in my life. Throughout her way, she was garrulous describing everything zesty that came in our walking way- even tea and samosa shop under a tarpaulin shade in front of the main building, adjoining faculties, departments, leading roads and its destination.

In my college days many times, I attended the class without having food in the stomach, bore every pang but never bunk or skip lecture, which I was to violate that day.

I was baffle whom I was following- my starve stomach or my heart?

Overtly, I personated to my conscience, I was following my stomach whereas, in truth, my ears felt amused in her chirruping and frank tone.

We were strolling parallel when she asked me to maintain a distance from her, and she paced down her tramps. I kept walking. First I caught it embarrassing situation for me, but soon I understood when a girl came straight to her, they screeched, yelled, hung around the necks, and looked as they met after yore days.

I stopped at a nook and waited for her a few meters away from her.

You know, if a girl meets another girl from her previous school or college in any corner of the world, if unfortunately, she is her best friend, and then it's terribly awaited moment. Just keep gazing creeping needles of your watch.

I was steady looking toward them; likely, she caught my sight standing alone and returned in her conscious self. And it happened. Seeing me standing alone beside the road as the dummy, she fluctuated toward me while talking her friend.

I didn't know what discourse happened between them, her friend also turned to me simultaneously. They shared smiled and parted in the opposite direction.

"What I was worried about, the same thing happened," said she, gasping.

I darted at her, being puzzled. I couldn't sense what she meant. She continued having a mystic smile on her lips, "She thought you are my boyfriend."

"Oh." for a moment, I faltered, hearing word, 'Boyfriend' which pragmatically I didn't experience before that.

"She was my graduation college fellow." She was looking in the direction of her nose. Just then, deliberately, she asked me, "Where would you like to go?"

"For what?"

"Stupid," she spoke in high intonation. "I'm asking about lunch."

'Stupid,' what an amiable affectionate word! It imparts how near is someone who you speak to you. I felt the word sweet and sour at the same time. Sour, for no one ever dared to say this way to me. And 'sweet' because none ever any exotic girl called me so affectionately.

"How would I know?" I said, emphatically. "I know only, I'm just hungry."

"Would you like to go to VT or Matri?"

"I haven't seen both yet."

"Matri is a university cafeteria, and VT is Vishwanath Temple where there are several good restaurants."

"Means you are really new in this campus?"

"Was I saying something else?" I said in a sarcastic tone raising my eyebrows.

She simpered slightly and detoured from the T-point of the road. She led me in the direction where several vehicles were rushing down.

If you ever are roaming in this university in July and August, you will be fortunate to experience life- a kaleidoscopic picture-fresh flower, fruits, foliage, and new faces.

After five minute walks, we were in front of an arch temple, a classic epitome of architecture. I uplifted my head, just beholding its gargantuan standing vault.

"Hello Mr.," she called, raising her pitch a bit high to pull me out of my reverie, clutched my arms and dragged me aside from the road.

"Let's have something in our stomach. Later I will take you there," she stated. My right arm was still in her clutch, the feeling was peculiar, striking, and unremarkable. "By then, keep patience."

He had worn that day *Anarkali* style churidar kameez with a sheer *dupatta,* her pesky arms covered with a diaphanous sleeve. Still, it was enough revealing due to the transparency of muslin clothes. She was around 5 feet 4 inches high, absolutely a lush ambience, a sculpted womanly figure, cheerful complexion as if her lips were the most beguiling place for the smile. And above all her dimple could detain attention of anyone, of course.

Oft light wind stroke her locks blew it away, sometimes it teased her eyes, and she ironed out, dragging it behind her ears.

Words were so spontaneous; deliberately, it had been uttering out of her mouth that helped me to emit weigh from my chest that I bunked class first time, roaming with a girl whom I met just few days before.

Walking with her, listening to her musing tone, beholding her gaits was like opium taking- oblivion of all tenses of the world. I knew I was wasting my precious time, though.

"What do you like to eat?" asked she.

"Anything you want." I took a pause. "You know about here better than me." I played a trick. "And I know I'm not specific about food."

That was true adequately. I was not a foodie adventure. I loved and enjoyed even Grandma's handmade dapple bread lubricant with ghee and salt.

While walking amid the swamp of students in front of the shops, I observed puffing tea breathing through the craned chimney of teapot and delicious samosa, lingering discussions, gossiping of gathering young minds on some common talks, some concerned for jobs, some bearded researchers busied in new ideas and the progress of their thesis, but one thing was common in almost, they wore spectacles. Graduation and post-graduation students appeared a bit relaxed engaged in dandy talks, new syllabus, and new girls in the department. Some political minds were appreciating a mass movement, 'India Against,' occurred at Jantar Mantar, New Delhi.

"*Samosa* and hot tea is favourite for all." She darted at me, "You will be habitual, too, soon."

We entered a shop, occupied chairs, face to face either side of the table. She ordered *chhola-bhatura*. Scrupulously, I was also haunting about my pocket, whether the more money I had in my poecket, was it adequate for the bill.

Samosa and tea were before us on the table. She began swallowing.

"Hello! What are you shying for?" she said, in the middle of her eating.

"I'm not shy. It's my natural speed of devouring," I said, chewing down food in my mouth.

I was moderately taking my food, chewing easily, and then devour but she seemed as if she had to go somewhere. Hardly had we done our share, she ordered two glass of *lussi.*

"You know what?" she said, wiping food particles stained over lips, assembly herself. "Thank you. I was extremely hungry, honestly." I could not hold me steadfast without pouring out my inward. "If you would not initiate, probably I killed my hunger in the classroom."

Now, it was time to pay. I fumbled my hand in the pocket to take out money. She proffered a hundred notes on the counter.

"Perhaps you don't like to meet me anymore?"

"Why?" I was a bit astonished.

"Then, save your money. Next time you can pay," she said.

I shrugged.

Just then, my black & white phone beeped in the deeper side of the thigh pocket, and its vibration raised a surge of sensation in the whole body. It was Manish who was asking where I was. The problem was he came to my department to visit me. And I didn't want to be exposed and degraded my image at first day, bunking the class.

She urged me to go inside the temple premise, but I denied. I asked to go back department. While returning to the department I told her reason for my haste. She giggled. "OMG! Aren't you alien?" She incessantly kept chuckling, bubbled comic comments. When I glared her being teased, she retrained her guffaw, and after an interval again she burst into the cackle.

I halted, turned back, and glared her furiously. "Had I laughed at you when you told me to make distance seeing your friend coming near you?"

Her giggling evaporated from her face. I prolonged.

"Hey, I'm sorry," she followed me begging pardon, repeatedly.

I brisk on, envisaged Manish would be waiting for me there.

I didn't reply to her. She stopped and meandered for her hostel.

Now it was around 5 o'clock. Henceforth, the campus was gradually enveloped under evening, mythical serenity. Not finding him there, I plodded his hostel.

Chapter 6

Banaras's roads are always struck in horn, clamour and rush; but there is no haste, no rashness. You can experience a classic example of harmony on its road. You can discern all three tenses within one city- the city of Lord Shiva- the most ancient and only living city of the world. If you are a cultural, spiritual, and intellectual adventurer, explorer of mystic life and divine in the material world, peace in the era of chaos, Banaras can be the appropriate answer to your every question. You can find the most significant philosophy even while roaming through the streets.

India is a country of festivals and celebrations, but coming Banaras is not less than any gala. You can encounter rarest species of human race ambling there, comes from the corner of the world.

Banaras is a mini-world in itself and home city of Master of Universe- Lord *Baba Vishwanath.*

Manish, Thakur, and I struck at Godiliya- focal point of Banaras city. We had our own reasons for forbearance standing amidst the crowd. Manish needed a lamp for study, Nitesh had to buy multipurpose *gamchcha* and, you know, I required a backpack for carrying books and stationery. And we reached *Dalmandi* Market, solution point of our requirement, a multi-shop market of the cheap prize.

After purchasing we had planned to visit Lord Baba Vishwanath temple. Though they were regular comers, for me it was the first time.

We were stuck in a *jaam,* irritating traffic. Manish gave an exasperating glance to Nitish. He was being fed up cemented at one place amid the hue and horn in the middle of the road for twenty minutes. Nitish winked in returned.

Staying there, I realized, any road of the world can take you where you want to go. The things you need, envisaging your destination, and quite crystal clear.

“*Bhosari Ke”* Manish bellowed. “It was your idea to follow this route.” They indulged in entertaining Banarasi slangs.

After the next ten minutes, we were fed up. It seemed like the motion of earth stopped its revolving and horn of vehicles, continued piercing our ears. Now staying there anymore was intolerable.

Suddenly mob began scattering apart running hither-thither.

“*Guru*…run…run fast,” Manish screamed, jolting back, bubbling a thunder of chuckles. I saw aside. OMG! It was a black muscular Banarasi bull, coming swaying through the traffic. All around, people were scattering, collapsing in confusion, but the bull kept on walking over his course. Someone in the crowd was shouting, "Don't run. Be easy. It's his routing walk. He won't hurt any. Don't make chaos." But in confusion, no one gave him any heed. The crowd sprawled wherever they found space.

We three intruded into a nearby lane, trailed its curvy and narrow cave- labyrinthine buzzing alleys.

And after a constant walking next for ten minutes, we reached at *Dasashwamedh Chauraha,* around hundred meters straight eastward to *Godiliya Chowk.*

We prolonged some fifty meters from there, and again they turned from a corner into a street. I followed their tramps. I was a little canny, caught me slavish in abyss predicament where I was rambling about and what the road I was walking on. Thakur gave a solemn glance to Manish. He sensed.

“We should visit the temple first,” Nitish suggested. “It would be easy to get into the premise as it would be least crowded now. Afterwards, we can go to *Dalmandi* and from there; we will go straight to watch Ganges Arti. What do you think?”

They swirled from next detour and, as usual, I pursuit their footsteps, strolling through the congested street crammed with shops of flowers and garlands, cosmetic and Banarasi sari either. Some young lad harangued in front of the shops trying to woo the devotees marching toward the temple.

Placing sleepers in a corner, we stood in an ethnic queue of multi-lingual speaking people-Tamil, Telugu, Bengali and many more. But they were similarly obscure to my ears.

But, after creeping next one hour we were fortunate enough to enter into the main temple. No sooner, we stepped inside the main temple, had a glance of Shivaa's shrine, a security person, standing next door, pulled us clutching the arms and flung out.

From there, we navigated through the crowd straight to watch auspicious Ganga Arti.

"Why is there a rush everywhere today?" I asked them curiously.

"It's the usual scene of the roads on Monday," Manish said, gravely.

I could sense fatigue over their face.

Wandering through roundabout narrow streets, I was feeling dizzy. And the strange sight we saw, a man was pissing over the wall when a throng was passing by there. He attained rapture emitting his loaded liquid, clutching his member, uplifting his head upward toward the sky and closing his eyes in vigorous pleasure.

Walls seemed as if some painters as sprayed dotted lines and tried to make some abstract painting. It appeared the wall had been facing such chronicle assault.

And no sooner we had overcome the predicament, I felt like my feet wrapped into some greasy stuff. The moment when I looked down at my feet, it swaddled into brown dong.

I yelled, squeezed my nose, whining.

"Hey, *Mahadev!*" Manish laughed,, seeing me in bafflement. My feet enwrapped with cow dung.

"*Bhosari ke*," Thakur said, dragging. "One side, someone is in trouble, and you are giggling."

We statue there as the dummy, surveillance across the street to have water but alas! There was nothing. A man halted near me, uplifted his mouth, settled paan chewing inside, prepared himself to speak, " How does this happen? Wait." He fetched a mug of water from a neighboring house. I cleaned my feet and thanked him.

Banaras is the only city where the existence of everyone finds equal consideration and importance- either is it commoner, the foreigner, old, young, ox, dog or anyone.

We hurried toward Dalmandi.

"Make sooner...Ok. Ganga Arti schedule is at hand," Manish said. Rambling shops to shops, checking, choosing, at the end they selected a cheap one. They showed me for final approval first before they went for bargaining. They purchased things whatever they wanted to.

"What is your budget guru?' Manish asked, scrutinizing bag turning it left-right, back-front, dragged its zip and checked its sustainability.

"Let me know whether you want to use bag or sticker. No need to spend on the brand." Nitesh satirized commenting at Manish. "Choose only which is reliable and durable in the cheap prize."

"Three to five hundred," I declared my pocket's sustainability.

Manish asked prize of the bag from the shopkeeper calling him aside.

I didn't know what they murmured among themselves together, said, at last, they would pay three hundred. And then twenty-minute business dealing went on between shopkeeper and them. And finally, shopkeeper got ready after negotiation at three hundred thirty rupees.

"Seven hundred rupees bag, in three hundred thirty rupees…wow…amazing…How?" It was surprising to me as I was always a bad bargainer at shopping. For me, it was surprising because I never succeed in the bargaining of the prize.

"Local shopkeepers' hike twice of the actual price," said Thakur. "And the customer gets busy in bargaining. They show kindness over costumers reducing some meager of their set prizes, and trap the customer."

I held the bag in my hand, visualizing in inward eyes how I would be carrying it hanging at my back, dreaming.

I missed their tracks. When I resumed my consciousness, I recalled and looked around, back and forth far ahead of the moving crowd craning. But nowhere had they appeared. I didn't understand what to do now. Sometimes I walked ahead; sometimes I tramped back, hoping I would find them. Being worried, I searched them in the swamp of unknown faces. I stood aside at Godaulia Chauraha and thought if they would pass from there, I would catch them easily. There were thousands of people jostling before me, but I realized acute loneliness, standing amidst the crowd.

I learned a secret about this heart; it doesn't want many people, whereas it longs somebody who can share its abstract presence, who always stand with it and avert its isolation.

I fell into an extreme dilemma whether I would wait and search them at Dasashwamedh Ghat or should return to the Hostel.

I remained calm, wore serenity over face, locking my inward disquiet and chaos. I set eyes over the floating crowd and tried to recognize them among the passerby but it was in vain.

Sometimes I looked right, sometimes left, sometimes I considered searching for them somewhere else but I stopped after speculating they might come there as soon as I left the place, I would miss chance. So, I thought better to stay there without displacing a bit from there.

Quite behind me, a throng, all were Banarasi, set a mini-parliament at the betel shop, "None single politician is crystal clean. They all are the scoundrel looting our share," said one of them licking white greasy lime from finger and hurled some small pieces of betel into the mouth, uplifted his mouth. "They have made this country miserable since colonial power returned to their nations."

"Bhaiya, they are the actual problem. And I will say, they are an ulcer," another interrupted.

"Do you know why all parliamentarians have gone against Anna's Lokpal Bill?" the betel shop owner said wrapping the betel leaf. “They knew if the Bill comes, all currupts will get fucked up.” And others burst into a giggle.

“Because they are corrupt,” another one added, who standing quite behind me.

“ Bhaiya, look,” the shopkeeper said, spitting red chewed betel as spraying at the rear wall. “Everyone is corrupt…” pointing his finger. “You …you …you…and I’m also. We all are corrupt. Whenever we go to any government office, we carry some surplus money that anyhow we need not stand in the long tedious lines and wait for the hour. We feed money to clerks and do our work. Before to cry, we must think about whether we are ready for the change. Do we want the change?” He said, added emphasizing. "A real change? Are we ready for it?" He paused and continued. “And those who assembled at Jantar Mantar, you will see, many will set their shop after the dispersal of the movement.”

“Right bhaiya!” They echoed together in chorus. “Mahadev!”

I felt as somebody patted at my shoulder. I turned. I caught; Urvashi was standing beside me along with some girls likely her friends, whom I hadn’t seen with her on campus.

“What are you doing here?” asked she.

“Nothing,” said I, jaunted my glance across the mob that was drifting toward ghat to watch Ganga Arti. “I’m searching my friend. We came together but I missed their track in the crowd.” I failed to feign the façade of perplexity and wariness from my face.

“Why don’t you call them?” she suggested which I had applied already. Manish’ number was switch off and I hadn’t Nitish’s cell number.

“Let’s go for Ganga Arti. You might find them there” She introduced the other two girls who were walking behind us. I greeted them. There was an enormous crowd as flooding in the same direction, we were flowing on.

With creeping crowd but we marched on.

Due to hustle, her friends also separated from us. The nearer we crept approaching Dasashwamedh Ghat, drizzling of light brightened. She took out her cell phone, dialed her friend's number whose head mere appeared at around ten meters distance and told them to meet at Godaulia Chauraha after Arti.

Next while, they vanished from our eyes, dissolved into the strange faces.

"Is there everything okay?" I asked. I scared whether they were feeling uncomfortable because of my presence among them.

She simpered. "They have come here to meet their boyfriends."

Boyfriend- I heard this word very first if I don't count when I read it in book or magazine or social media.

"And you?" I asked, stepping downstairs of the Ghat. "Their boyfriends wanted to meet me but I didn't like this idea." Walking down of arch stairs of the Ghat, she stumbled once but immediately I clutched her arms as I was stepping slight behind her.

She went straight right and then paddled ascending the stairs reversed and sat at a height from where we could behold Arti, crystal. I faltered a bit before sitting with her, but soon I got confidence when asked me to sit down beside her.

I started my miles away journey with that moment.

Tourist, pilgrims and devotees had taken their place comely, without making any clamour. Some VIPs were sitting at the roof nearby building.

"Banaras is also known with another name as Varanasi, Kashi. Kashi is a sacred place for pilgrimages according to Hindu mythology, the oldest city of the world at the bank of holy Ganga where it flows in the opposite direction," said she.

A group of young priest in the yellow dress, traditional dhoti-kurta, which was tight-bound with a long towel at the waist, made preparation for *arti,* making a collection of five elevated planks, held a big and heavy multi-tiered oil brass lamp having snake hood at the edge of the river, an idol of goddess Ganga, flowers, incense sticks, and a conch shell in each priest's hand.

A group of the boat crammed with the spectators was stagnant in front of *Ganges'* Arti performing place in the river. Every eye was gazing toward the dais and waiting for the commencement of the auspicious event. Some of them were recording videos, some busied in taking snapshots, and some fine art students were using their brushes portraying scenes. It began. The young priest was performing the ritual of Ganges *Arti* accomplished by chanting the mantras, ringing bells, and blowing conch at an interval.

That fine evening, I experienced an aura of spirituality and divinity lingering around at the Ghats. The crowd I was sitting with, it was enormous than the crowd crawled on the road, but there was no commotion, no hue and no cry.

People assembled there, they were of a different colour, caste, community but over their face, one could read serenity of oneness; a pleasure had taken place- which was similar.

I was next to her; hardly dared I to glance at her face. Sometimes when she darted another side, I gazed her. I could see only one side of her face and swinging ornament by ear. That evening, she was in her new incarnation. She had put on tight jeans and a t-shirt.

Most of the male's first glance falls at the curved fabrics, but I can't tell you about me at meeting with the woman. What I had seen when I glimpsed her very first time that evening. - Was it her sportive hairs over her shoulder? -Her deep eyes? -Her whole sculpted fabrics? -Her sweet smile? -Her gait? -Or she as the whole? - I can't tell you.

It seemed as she woke up of a dream from her hypnotic state of watching Arti. She called a tea-vendor who was rambling down, selling tea to spectators. He had a kettle fitted above a grate. I felt some raindrops on my face. I looked upward toward the sky, there was cloud drifting in the wide firmament. The density of drizzling raised, but people remained cemented at their place, they were still enjoying the eloquent Arti performance.

"Today, I will taste your flavour of Banarasi tea," she said, winking.

Seeing her smiling face, I wished to entitle her 'Smiling Princess,' but constrained my all willful.

She bellowed in the high pitch to the tea vendor. He plodded toward us, mounting the arch stairs from the narrow space between the people. She looked at me and smiled. "I love this tea."

The man arrived. "Bhaiya! Give two glass of tea," She ordered.

He poured down puffing liquid, chopped a lemon apart and squeezed its juices into *kulhad*, desi cup. It was brown lemon tea.

I sipped. Indeed I hadn't ever relished such a desi flavour.

Her smile got broader, her silver teeth flashed between her luscious lips. Her lips gleamed rather than usual. She had applied some gel. Her midnight like raven black silky hairs was tumbling over her shoulders whenever she stirred her head tilting to see things happening around.

She clad in the western dress still she had a comely impression, maintained her modesty and elegance. Her crescent sporty cheerful eyes were the centre of her beauty which reflected innocence, faith and simplicity.

"Waah," I said, trying to draw her attention.

The second time, she paid money. The man pulled out a long crumbled plastic bag pulling out of the secret pocket of his baggy pant, kept ten rupees into it and moved for other customers. 'Lemon tea…lemon tea' yelling, he disappeared.

She shook her eyes brow, taking sips, "How is it?" I displayed thumbs up.

She illuminated transcending my confused evening into a special event with her enlighten presence, elevated soul and beautiful smile.

The Ghats were glimmering under the lights, lamps and, of course, moon poised the beauty of the river and its sandy shore. The milieu of Gange's Arti and its aura had erected the grandeur of that evening. My eyes often jaunted to Arti, often to gatherings at Ghat and often to Urvashi whenever I ensured she was looking at another side.

"How many times have you come here?" I asked.

"Me?" turning to me, she put a rhetoric question. She glanced far delving into pondering. "Hmm. Many times. I can't count."

"Approximate?" I had no subject to prolong our talk.

"I couldn't count, but yes, throughout my graduation, I visited this place with my friends." She darted where Arti was going on and turned it back to me. "I don't know, but I loved this place." now her face was again in front of me. "Not only Arti but everything like its Ghats, ferrying in Gange river, measuring Ghats through my tramps. " Once you have accepted this city, you will love it. Because it accepts everyone." Her face brightened.

"How?" I questioned.

"Banaras doesn't ask people anything in return except one thing…do you what?"

"What?" I repeated her words.

"Open your heart" she stretched her arms. "Be Banarasi, be Bindas"

"Means?" I wished to listen to her more and more.

"Banaras is not only famous for religion, spirituality, education or tourism, but it is also famous for its lifestyle. It's called Banarasi masti." She became attentive at the blowing of the conch, she joined hands in praying poster and closed her eyes. "You have two years to feel and imbibe Banaras."

"To feel or know?" I tried to rectify her verbal mistake, but she defended.

"To imbibe Banaras, you need not only have a healthy mind, but also you must carry a beating soul too, for Banaras is itself a living organism- a breathing city. Never apply your mind to understand it, you won't succeed. Apply your heart; Banaras will unfold every mystic tales about her before you. And I can detail you everything without imposing any cost," said she. She smiling from the right corner of her lips.

She had a fantastic, charismatic charm over her complexion, which I couldn't help without staring her in the lights.

I saw a good number of people offering .diya, a small lamp in a cup made of leave and flower "It is lamp offering to Maa-Ganga." she explained.

I engrossed in beholding lamp offering, melodious prayer, drumming sound, chanting mantras, fire and strong incense. The huge crowd gathered there, they had travelled miles from across the nation and abroad to witness this auspicious ceremony. My eyes stuck seeing a boat laden with devotees ferrying in the river, taking snapshots.

" Come," she pulled me to stand up.

"Where ?" I asked.

She halted at the verge of the flowing river. A ferryman was calling seeking clients to take them on water jaunt via boat.

"What is the prize for two people?" she probed to the boatman.

"Hundreds," said he.

She agreed without bargaining, she asked me to enter into the boat and take place. I dithered, for me; hundreds of rupees were not a small amount. She voiced me to wake me up out of my indecisive mind. She bought two small lamps for the offering.

Boatman loaded a good number of passenger until it filled to its required seats. Another man, his help, freed ankles, began stirring it to let it move out of the fleet. The generator had been puffing out, leaving its ominous dark smoke behind. As it reached in the middle of the stream, she asked me to lit the lamp and flew it in the currents.

The boat sailed southward ripping water apart, foams flew away from its mast, circumnavigating leaving behind series of Ghats one by one as I was watching a telescope.

Stairs of Chetsingh Ghat enveloped with students who were singing some choirs. As it passed by Harishchandra Ghat, everyone present in the boat, wore a graveness at face, beholding the truth of life- cremation of the corpse- where a pile of wood was set afire, and funeral smoke lingered in the sky, alongside few grieved kin awaiting blowing off of the pyre that they could collect remains. Adjoining buildings' colour turned dark due to perpetual burning soaring funeral smoke.

A bitter truth- a stalk truth.

The series of Ghats ended reaching in front of Asi, crammed with tourist, youth and some phenomena Banarasi folk.

“This is Assi Ghat,” said Urvashi. “Ages ago, it was ruminating place of saint Tulasidas, Kabir and Saint Raidas. Now it is the most favourite place for a foreigner, students, poets, writers, musician, scholar and explorer?”

“Do you come here?” asked I another monotonous question to break the silence between us. Her face flashed up, brightened. The boat swirled around to return to Dasashwameth ghat.

“Yeah,” she shrugged her shoulders. “Often if my mood goes ok.”

“If your mood goes okay, may I come with me… next time?” I paused, and again I repeated, ‘If…’ reminding her it was not compulsion

“Yeah,” said she. “If things remain fine in my life… but I can’t promise. I will let you know whenever I will be free.”

“I will need a guide,” I said, in a humorous tone.

She laughed, tilting her head backwards, facing up.

While I fumbled and took out some folded strips of Indin currency to pay the fair, she again stopped me.

“Let me invest some more money,” I said.

“I will give you a chance. Don’t worry,” She propelled passing fair to the boatman. "We have two years to study in the same class."

And our evening gala snapped here with her dazzling smile. I kept looking at her going away.

"Ka ho Maharaj!" being astonished, I turned immediately. It was Manish and Nitish. "If you have done the meeting, can we move now?"

And here start their mocking, laughs, comments until I slept and went for a dreamy nocturnal.

Chapter 7

First one month had gone in acquainting campus life of the University was buzzing with the fresher parties, tramps of newly admitted students and fellows and acquainting city milieu existing outside of the fence. Old students were busy in organizing the fresher party – a juncture of the meeting point of two generations.

Banaras, indeed, doesn't take much time assimilating newness in its profuse colour. Within the month, I sojourned every major road, streets and places, mapped it paddling cycle when I had spare hours after class, mostly on the weekend.

One fine day, Pandey sir halted at threshold, when he was to leave after taking the lecture. He peeped inside from narrowly opened door and said addressing us, "Your seniors may come to have an introduction session with you. They are good guys, quite helping nature. So, mingle with them and know them and set a fraternal atmosphere." And he ended his words wearing a smile.

After ten minutes, an assemblage of students, who oft appeared haunting in campus, entered into our classroom and scattered around. We were sitting on chair whereas they stood in around dais before us and some of them skipped at the rear side of the classroom.

"They are really senior," Pummy Ghosh whispered to me. She was one of my class fellows, coming from Bengal. "See…How muscular, tall mature they are!"

"Are you looking for a suitable boy?" Rehan whispered coming closer to her ears, restraining his chuckle.

She turned her head slightly, looked from the corner of her eyes, and frowned, "No way."

"Then, why do you bother, Pummy? -Just give-take intro and move on," he voiced.

A fair girl in front of the dais commenced addressing, with an adulating smile having a titillating dimple on her cheek.

"I'm Anamika. And today we are here to congrats you and wish you all the best for the brewing session."

Then, she led her class fellows. One by one, they asserted their name only. Soon, they finished their list.

Now, it was our turn. One by one, students mounted over dais, delivered a brief introduction-consisting of the name, hobbies, dream plan and so many things. Few stammered as they reached dais began uttering fluently, some babbled as any beast was trailing them behind. For me, it was an experience, fusion mixed with excitement and hallucination. It happened with me; hesitation lingered inside me, knotting something in the stomach until I reached the stage.

I remember, the first day of my last college when professor was asking students to speak something about self. Standing at the dais that day, I realized, how less one knows about oneself.

Now I was called. I reached dais, stood comely, and stayed looking for their response. They asked me the usual question, 'Tell about your…favourite things.'

As I articulated beginning slowly ascended the fluency of my speech. Hearing my hometown, one of them intervened, interrogated several things related to my native.

Later on, he told, he was too a domicile of my native town.

Knowing that I liked reading and writing poetry, they urged to recite some piece of my poetry.

I sauntered to my seat, opened my bag, took out my diary and read poetry that I had written last night.

The moment I was inscribing words into rhythmic sounds, I realized, there was none except tranquility around in that stuffed human classroom. As I ended recitation, whole room clattered with clapping. Now I could read my written lines implying in the expression over their face.

It was a bounty sunny later half of the afternoon. I was glad, ambling through the corridor, kneading thoughts in my mind primarily the glory I met a few minutes before.

I was speculating how, the way, I would tell those entire things to Meera. She would be glad, I thought.

The corridor harangued with a loud voice. Somebody was calling an exotic phrase, 'Mr Poet.' It dawdled pace of my walk.

'Mr Poet,' I found it fascinating.

"Wow," said Urvashi, coming nearer to me. "You never told, you also write poetry."

"You never asked about it," said I.

"You mostly remained dummy," said she caricaturing. Coming closer to me, she said almost in whispering, "Actually, you are a bit shy."

I smiled in revert.

We dragged our feet toward the main gate of the faculty. The watch struck at 4 o'clock by then.

The tramps echoing had vanished- no rush, no commotion, mere falling cool evening. Occasionally, professors one by one locked their cabin left for their residents. Oft, the building, was reverberated with the fluttering wings of the long domiciled pigeon, fainted chattering of clerks and peons.

The sun was rushing down in the western sky, hiding behind trees. We moved through thick foliage shade. The dribble sunbeams sprinkled out of the bushes, fell over our eyes seemed as the sun peeped through the chink between boughs and bushes.

Her hazel eyes, glowing fair face, unvarnished modest form and her sheer words were enough to hold my undivided attention and threw me into complete forgetfulness.

"Would you like to come for tea?"

"Where?" I asked.

"Matri Cafeteria,"

'Matri' was a canteen in campus situated beside Social Science Faculty. I tried to restrain my implicit hastiness from accepting her offer. Comely I nodded in her suggestion.

She put her cell phone into her satchel, unlike girls who gazed into the screen.

"How many people do know about another self?" I queried.

"What?" she was a bit baffled.

The waiter brought our tea. We clutched our glass of tea which was quite warm. After having her first sip, she said, "What haven't I disclosed from people?" She ordered *samosa.*

"That you are not what you show. You are what you disguise within the self" said I, taking a bite of samosa with the sip of tea.

"I don't understand," said she, pretending to be innocent. She stopped her eating, mere to listen more, looking equivocatingly.

"Inside classroom you have a different personality, and outside different," said I.

She chuckled for a while. Finally, she controlled herself, struck her eyes at sealing and preparing herself to answer me.

"Very few are privileged who knows my second self," she said, looking into my eyes, stagnant, with a soft beam at her lips.

I connoted her words well. Although I didn't sense, why I didn't tend to understand her words any further of that. Grandma's suggestion used to resound in my ears and reminding my obligation. But however, every time, my heart succeeded to woo me, seek some excuses to evade Grandma's alarming words. Her amiable traits enticed me. I liked to watch her cheery eyes.

"What are you going to wear on Monday," asked she.

"Monday?" I puzzled what was on Monday.

"Fresher party, idiot!" said she emphatically.

"Anything …neat-clean," said I abruptly.

She grinned mysteriously. I asked the reason, but she ignored it.

My Nokia 1100 black & white phone beeped. Manish called me in the Social Science department. We took apart, I left her at hostel road, and I retreated to meet Manish. I stood at the gate, watched around searchingly. I waited for him. Nitish Jha appeared walking toward me. “Ka Ho,” reaching to me, he questioned. “How are you here? …Waiting for Manish?”

He instructed me to go HOD office. I walked as cautiously as I was moving as a child to a new school, reading nameplate suffixed with ‘Dr’, ‘Professor’, and ‘Asst. Professor’.

I halted my loitering steps at the door, reading the plat at the door of the chamber, ‘Head of Department’. I peered from a distance; I saw Manish was standing aside, resting his hands backside. I shuffled back and forth outside in the corridor.

A sharp moustache man, with round baggy belly, came to me, interrogated reason why I was loitering there and returned to his place knowing the reason. Manish came out of the department trailing the wobbling walks of the professor to his car and waited for him until he drove away.

We barely carried few meters away from there, it began drizzling and dappled the charcoal road, and a rhythmic sound began musing in the surrounding, resounding sounds of drizzling.

It's cooling breeze soothed, an ineffable beauty, rich, mellifluous echoes descended and enveloped the whole campus. Manish mocked if any couple passed by us driving bike- girl clutching boy across his belly dripping under the rain.

The sight brought fictitious imagery of my farming field, floated before me. I delighted to ponder the pale paddy plant would restore to its rejuvenation, would be painted in vigorous foliage.

The falling drops are life for farmers and the pleasure that he receives, no words can define.

After a while the rain got slow, we decided to move.

At Birla Chauraha, a man was peeping into wounded hoof of an ox. He was bandaging that wretched animal.

“What happen, sir?” asked Manish.

He turned his head clockwise, looked at us and again busied in his job.

“Nothing,” said the man, without intervening of his errand. “Some inhuman rascal hurt to this poor animal.”

“Can we do anything, sir?”Manish asked again

“No. It’s done already,” said the man, standing up. He tackled up his first aid box, put into his car and drove.

“Who was he?” I asked, looking at his car running away and suddenly disappeared from the next turn.

“A senior IIT professor,” said Manish. “He treats unwanted wounded animals.”

On Monday, nobody left any stone unturned to present themselves appealing.

I had put on my regular dress- a formal white shirt and black paint. Last evening I had spent ten rupees to iron it.

I cherished seeing myself being part of the fresher party. It occurred in my imagination as if I was watching any movie. And then my name announced on stage for poetry recitation. I stood up, walked with throbbing heart and mounted stairs of the stage.

Now I stood at the lectern. I put the diary on the plank, turned its pages, in which I had scribbled something. I began reciting. The whole auditorium hall was prone with utter silence.

It was the first time I loved my own voice. It was the first time I realized my ambience. It was first time a crowd was listening me without any interrupt. It was first time my poetry got my voice. It might be rhyme words for the audience; but it was my absolute innate, scripted into words since I left my home.

The hall reverberated with the thunder of claps and remained continued until I got down.

The needle of the watch was telling the course of the sun. It was the evening. The sun was getting down hastily.

The performer's a stunned audience with their dance, music and mimicry. High volume sound I could not bear, so I escaped the engaged eyes and got out of the hall while they casted their eyes at the stage; their feet motioned with the beat, head tilted. Backside on the chairs, a horde hooted at every appealing step of dance performance.

I found a cool shelter near a pool of water beside the trees. Some ducks were swimming in a pond, were playing the game of hiding and seek in bushes.

I sat beside the pond, gazed them navigating.

"*Arey wah*," somebody said. I turned around. It was Urvashi. "Far from madding crowd." She made a burlesque comment. I gave her my usual response, a partial smile.

"Searching some poetry here, hmm?" She probed humorously.

"No." I stood up, strolled to her. "Why would I search poetry if poetry comes searching for me?" I said with a soft smile.

A blush manifested over her face. She had worn Anarkali style suit, coiled her dupatta in her right hand, adorning accoutrements such as glittering accessories in ears, neck and wistful bangle.

"That's great if I become the reason to inspire a poet's mind," said she, in a gleeful way.

I pacified surges rising inside my heart. But I failed to stop oozing out it in my eyes.

"You like such solitude place?" she beseeched, with a vigil glance at the pond, trees and sportive wakeful birds.

"Yeah," I said. "I think serenity can converse more honestly than human."

" Then, I will show you a place, you will love it," she promised.

CHAPTER 8

It was on Saturday. I had planned to go home after the dispersal in the evening. Manish also consented to go home.

Unfortunately, I got late leaving the department. Hurriedly reached the hostel. Due to bad weather and my delayed, Manish cancelled his plan. I hopped from beds to closets, tackled up my clothes, books and other essentials stuffs.

"Guru, stay today. We will go tomorrow together," said Manish, lolled in the chair.

"I don't want to spoil my tomorrow in running and travelling. I want to spend it with Grandma," said I.

The sky was turning grey, a dark giant cloud creeping to envelop the whole city, slowly its laden fluffy dark cloud overcast.

I shook the hand, embraced and asked adieu from him.

I had mere a ten rupees note in my pocket. Eventually, I had no money but eventually deterred to go home. I ran to catch the train at Bhulanpur station, passed the university fence through the shortcut- a narrow passage.

Bhulanpur is actually a suburb halt of Banaras city

Grandma's face was lingering in my eyes and going back to home seemed as Adam's restoration to Eden garden.

I trailed the road. I halted my steps sometimes and asked wages from passing vehicles. I displeased and deserted of their ignoring of my plea. I prolonged my tramps once again to cover remaining distance. My thighs tighten, and the calf was panic. But I didn't stop for any while. Asking route from people, I entered in DLW campus. Roads were smooth, wide and clean. The architectural design of houses appeared similar all around. It was greenery all around wherever I glanced.

I detoured from a corner. I was now plodding over the way went parallel to the railway track.

I pulled my doggedly trudge. A man on cycled told me to make haste. I heard the train horn behind me. I ran as fast as I can do with the jumping satchel my back, reached station controlling my gasp.

It was a one-sided platform having the only couple of small teen shad. There was an assemblage in front of a small cabin. They were thrusting their hands and pulling out receiving their tickets through a chink; I had ten rupees only, so I walked away from the crowd to save it and looked for space to sit under the open sky.

Soon, before the train's arrival, the platform was swamped with passengers.

There were few people, busied in rubbing tobacco; few were puffing *biri,* a second Indian version of the cigarette, and few in group swallowing the remaining meal of the day.

I strolled scrutinizing the platform. I found space and sat down on the edge of a bench where already three people were sitting. Folk sitting beside me had shabby cloth, wrapped multipurpose *gamachha* around their neck. Their skin was glittering with sweat. It was intolerable to my nose to bear it. And when they smiled, their black-spotted flushed out between their lips, as they were painted it for some dramatic scene. Cheek was glued with the jaw.

Seeing such a miniature station and such an enormous crowd, I was already amazed. I couldn't resist my inquisitiveness and asked them, "What's the reason for this rush?"

One of them, who were sitting at the next end, stirred and leaned forward to contact eyes with me, "It is the everyday business."

We settled in our previous posture. And again they got engaged in gossip. I agitated for getting late. Sometimes I stood up gazed on track for imaging arrival of the fourth coming train but no sign we had.

"*Bhaiya*...Today, the passenger train is too late." the man said.

"Why?" I concerned, added further. "Is it the everyday business?"

"It came late already from Allahabad," said he. After a brief pause, he asked, "You are here the first time?"

I nodded in affirmation. He seemed wiser out of them. He was somewhat organized and tidy than other shaggy companions.

"That's why," said he and continued. "You come here to work?"

"No," said I, proudly. "I'm a student. I study at BHU."

"Achchha!" said he, reverently and asked a usual question. "Are you a doctor?"

I smiled softly remembering my Grandma's word who considered I would be going to have an admission in medical science. In the nearby district, common folk knows about BHU for its Hospital and medical faculty.

I nodded in 'no'.

"I'm doing M.A. English," said I.

" *Chutiyanandan*!" That man sitting on verge said drily. "BHU is not only a place for *doctory*. There are many subjects that are being taught there. Right *bhaiya*?" he looked toward me for assurance.

I shook my head in yes.

Their traits changed toward me.

"We are a worker who every day comes to Banaras for the day job every day," he said, pointing to folk stood there conversing, cutting jokes on fellows, rubbing tobacco. "Among them, somebody is the mason, and somebody is laymen. They belong to the rural area at the periphery of the city. We, every morning, come here by train, boarding cycle and search contractual jobs. And we returned with evening passenger train." He leaned forward a bit, looked in a similar direction and continued speaking in Banarasi dialect. “Don’t know why *sashuri* gets so much time.”

The man, who was in the middle, said. “In the morning we come with a shining face having hope and return with an exhausted body- a hanging face.”

“After getting fucked off, everyone loses shine of one’s face,” they laughed together.

Now my voyeurism got the wing and longed to know more about them. I started taking an interest in them and their mannerism.

“Do you manage to find a job every day?” asked I.

“Sometimes we returned with evening train without having a job,” said he. I inquired about their job. “We spent time in the field if we don’t have any job.”

I looked in the train’s direction relentlessly.

“It’s late from its usual time,” he said. “You may catch Lichhvi Express.”

I hadn’t ticket; the new man in the city inside me scared of being caught without a ticket. I dared not to take a chance.

Sudden, there was a commotion in the crowd I saw. “Signal is fallen.”

The green light blew up.

Every one began murmuring muffling. They started assembling themselves, grabbed the handles of their cycles. I too stood up in the queue waiting like inquisitive children.

The train flashed out at the meandering, trailing its long stretch compartment, curving from the turn, blowing the screaming horn.

I scrutinized compartments. I scanned if there was any TC roaming there. I stood still gazing the train glided cluttering on the track before us.

"Maheshawa. Get into in this boggy," the man yelled. They had tied their *gamachha* around their head. I too tried my best to pierce the crowd and secured a seat. As the gate turned open, a flood of human swept into the coaches.

I occupied a window seat.

One can't compare the happiness of a person who gets success acquiring a window seat in the train, most notably in general compartment.

It's nothing like anything- a heavenly bliss. As the train passed through provincial stations, passengers alighted in the throng. The stopping train was now sojourning across the pastoral settings which were showered in the moonlight. The train moved leisurely jolting, blowing horn kept on cluttering over the iron track. The compartment was almost vacant except few one sitting here and there.

In front of me, a middle-aged man was ruminating looking through window, unfolded bundle. He opened it. It was bread and roasted potatoes. He tore the piece of bread, mixed with vegetable and put into his mouth. He chewed. After a couple of stations passed, he was the only reason to realize life on the earth. His face was swarthy, had worn shaggy cloth alike other laymen as like I encountered at the Bhulanpur station.

After crossing few couples of stations, I was alone in the compartment. To avert my loneliness, I began reading of stations name, banners, hoarding and gazed passing the small town, village, and mango garden quite crystal clear in the mercury white moonlight. I mused songs softly that I knew nobody was there to be disturbed by my novice voice. And this way, I span those tedious minutes before, I got at my station.

It was 8:30 p.m. I got down at my station. It was quite late to have any transportation for my village. So I thought to walk to reach the main road. The white moon followed me whatever route I took for.

If ever I stopped, looked back to see any possible vehicle, the moon also paused awaiting me.

I reached to the Jeep Stand where we used to catch auto for the village, but there was no vehicle available.

I thought better to walk rather waiting for any luck or chance staying there in isolated place. People who were connected with me, they knew it well that I scared walking alone in the night. I, chanted shloka, recited Hanuman Chalisa briskly. And I ran using my all stamina, breathlessly if the road led across any dense garden or haunting place.

I asked for the lift from vehicles seldom passed from there nugatory. But none stopped seeing me walking on the lonely road as a stranger.

I asked for the lift from a tractor. Thank God! He belonged to my neighbouring village. He left me at the outskirt of my village, from where my home was just at a few walking distances.

Milky moon still trailed me, didn't leave me alone for a second throughout the journey.

I reached in front of my house. Cots were vertically made a stand under neem trees. But a cot was laid there flat still, and dogs had made it their bed, squatted, coiled and buried his face into their coiled belly.

I veered into the tattered thatch- a dilapidated cow shade. I went inside the hut, calling the name of my cow, '*Kamali*'. I touched her face searching in dark hut. She stood up, fluttering her ears and twitched her tail. I brushed my palm over her back.

I caressed her forehead, promised her to see in the morning, and I moved out.

Hardly had I reached the threshold, I heard most lucid, sonorous, as all the saccharine of the world fusion in that one word "Bhaiya!" I heard the rattling of cots. "Wait..., I'm coming," said Grandma from inside of the house.

I never understood the craftsmanship of God- what engineering, He has done while creating the soul of a mother.

Mother's love is natural. But the love of a grandmother is more peculiar, possesses profundity and grandness.

"I have been waiting for you" I heard her tramps, strolling nearer to the door. She strived to utter words, "I knew, you would come today. I felt it." The door opened with a metallic jingle.

"Bhaiya," she held my arms, her voice filled with cheer. She dragged her palm across the shoulder, neck and finally cupped my face, gesticulated my face. We could not see one another in darkness clearly. I had only her silhouette of her torso. I could figure out her ecstasies in her words.

I clutched her by shoulders assisting her to her bed. She urged me to sit her beside. She overhauled her hands at my back, belly, and face.

She concerned about my health.

"Meerawa was asking about you since evening whether you came or not? …Just hardly twenty minutes before she went from here" said, Grandma

She asked me to take a meal from the kitchen and eat. But the exhaustive journey drained off me. I was tedious and drowsy. I devoured without having hand-wash. And soon, I fell over asleep.

"Wake up," Meera tugged away from my blanket, uncovered me.

The sun rose glorious rising over the trees, cold wind lured me to remain still in winging in loose woven khat. Partly I woke up; partly I was in the dream. It was a long time, I had rested. The morning commotion of village fell in my ears dimly. I could hear every utterance, but still, I could not connote in slumber.

Some dilapidated coughing I felt approaching near me. Grandma was sweeping the floor, creeping. I opened my eyes, sat straight, and waited for my complete consciousness to grasp.

I walked out of the house, halted at the threshold and beheld the morning. I felt morning coolness and its idyllic serenity as it had concealed perpetual within.

I couldn't understand it until I left my village.

Holding water mug, I marched toward at outskirt of the village, in search of bushes to release the morning burden.

Dews hanging over paddy simmered in morning beams appeared as the myriad of pearl fallen down from the sky during the night and entwined with foliage. Trees were calm; seldom had `its leaves motioned with brisk.

The birds were chirruping, hopping over branches and fluttering their wings.

I saw *Chhottani* along with his family plugging out the weed, tugged unwanted grass.

After doing morning ease, I reached to the paddy field. Seeing me arriving, *Chhottani* stopped his work.

“When did you come, *babu*?” asked *Chhottani.*

“Last night,” said I.

He walked off the bog.

“Your health is down, babu,” said his wife, scrutinizing me from toe to head.

“For how many days have you come?” said Chhottani, questioning glance.

“Today afternoon,” said I, dryly. Both looked at me amazedly. Further, Chhottani discussed harvesting and his action plan for the coming session.

I thought to take a jaunt of other cropping fields, so I went next to vegetable farms. I cherished to see the rich greenery of the plants.

They were not only crop but our hopes and means of survival.

Grandma was waiting me sitting at the door. Meera was cooking something inside.

“Where did you stop, meanwhile?” said Grandma.

“he would be busy in gossip?” Meera hit sarcasm.

"Shut your mouth," I poked fun at her height that I used for teasing her since childhood. He was not short heighted though

Chapter 9

I booked a rickshaw.

The rickshaw riding dangling in jam-packed traffic can be a bit tedious in Banaras, but quite suitable to look at the city jointly.

The rikshaman informed, there was a student's strike at the Lanka gate. Therefore, the vehicles declined to go on that route.

Rickshaw man said, faltering, "Babu Ji. What is the use of their education pursuing in such grand university?" He was slightly sarcastic in his tone. He kept on mustering his sinews; meanwhile, he conversed to me, "You are also studying in university?"

"Yes," said I.

"Bhaiya!.... You are….. lucky," he said. The whole sentence came into installment while paddling. "I have witnessed, there are many young scoundrels who are always seen in political issues." He exhaled heavy breathing. "Never fall in the group of these scoundrels and never be part of any unnecessary strike. To attain some recognition, they snatch our bread."

He paused instantly.

"How?" I asked.

He reverted, "The day they struck passage, that day, me like a poor rickshaw wallah had to return home without a penny." He faltered but summoned his courage. "And these *chutiya* accused rickshaw man that we spend our earning on wine. They call us drunkard." He paused his words and pacified. "I have seen their night escapade. I have dropped many at hostel in an unconscious state."

"How can you say this?" I objected. It was my hypocrisy, pretending that I could not bear words against students.

He chuckled. "I have been smudging my buttock pulling rickshaw for fifteen years in this city."

I got fresh, changed my dresses, combed hairs and reached faculty. It was deployed with students chattering professor's lecture. Handshaking culture with peer again started. I still received applause from students. The hangover of my poetry still hovered in the department. Junior students did Namaste.

Some girls reached to me praising for my poetry.

"How do you write poetry?" a girl asked.

"Do you have friends?" asked I.

"Yes," she said.

"I don't have," said I and moved.

I met Urvashi after the lecture.

"You lie?" she asserted, staring.

"Never," I said.

"Who am I?" she puzzled me.

But I answered her straight. "Of course, Urvashi."

"Not a friend?" stared me steadily.

I sensed. I tried to evade her point. I began ambling toward the classroom.

"Hello, Mr Poet." She called stopping me. She had a perpetual smile. "Would you like to visit Asi ghat?"

I, turning back, smiled and said. "Soon I let you know."

The clock struck above 10 p.m. The commotions of hostel's corridor turned into a strange serenity. Sometimes stillness broke up with fluttering slippers, or sometimes with a loud slogan, 'Bhosari Ke' or two friends late-night gossip.

I was studying, leafing pages. Manish had gone somewhere outside. There was very less possibility of his returning that night.

Somebody knocked on the door. I stopped my study, concentrated at the door, waiting for the response.

“Open the door,” asked a boy. It was not a familiar voice.

“Who is there?” I asked walking toward the door. I peeped through the half-opened gate.

“It’s me,” said a trim bearded boy. He was Manish’s class fellow.

“What are you doing?” he inquired.

“Nothing,” I mumbled.

“You must join us. You might be feeling bored,” another one suggested.

Their words were so compelling and amiable that I couldn’t deny them.

I followed them. I stopped as they halted in front of room number 225. They knocked once, twice, and at the third time, they bumped at the door.

A boy opened the door, popped out his head and hailed us into the room. As I got in, he slammed the door immediately behind us. Both boys were standing behind me. Light of the room was off. A laptop was open. And I could anticipate the density of the room through the shining heads, scintillating by laptop’s flash. They patted me gently to move on; I didn’t guess who the boy was.

There was some motion picture displaying over the screen. Everybody busied in the gazing film. I focused. Initially, I couldn’t assume the picture, but the room echoed with an amorous sighing sound, ah…uhm. They made me sit. When I paid attention I saw, some naked images were playing the amorous game. It was porn. My eyes widen. I was to stand up, but the boys sitting behind me pulled my shoulder and held tightly. I could not escape.

“They will not let you go, better sit and watch,” said a boy sitting next to me. Probably, he was also fresher.

“You will experience something new tonight,” said another boy. He was Thakur I confirmed him with his thick spectacle.

It was the first time that I never felt as restless in my genital, a sensation in my every inch of the body as it occurred that hour. While watching those skin flickered adult film wondered my senses, zip of my pant swelled upward. My breathing was tougher a bit than usual.

The nude amorous images kept lingering in my mind throughout the night.

Everyone left for their bed in their respective room. Gradually all the glittering of the hostel's light was gone off, except big ones.

I found me fragile to restrain the lingering thoughts of those lingering seductive images played on the laptop screen.

The first time, I felt an utter sort of restless. Often my hand slipped inside the trouser, cradle member and I experienced with every touch a tickling effect as my finger crawled crouching over glens. I caught a freak emotional and physical change which stimulated me for further crouching. The more I fondle, the more my Adam went stiffer.

I took out my head out of the blanket, tried to check whether the room partner was still awakening or snorting his nose. I calculated with his echoing nasal bubbling sound that he was soundly sleeping.

The romantic fantasy had overtaken my brain to the firework. It was not the first time I had such a great urge of sexuality. It happened but never succeeded to conquer my brain. Some of the night, I had realized, I pissed out something sticky liquid dreaming in the sleeping night.

But tonight, it turned the volume at acme which I felt tough to endure any longer.

Silently, with pressing toe, I got out of my bed walked toward the bathroom on the voyage of exploration of self-pleasure.

I decided to walk barefoot, thinking not to give any clue of my waking up to this late night.

It was a placid night, everywhere, unlike day, serenity prone all around- corridors, rooms, roofs and the big yard was showered under mercury light. Yes, lots insects were fluttering around the bulbs, and with their presence, I had no harm.

I stood in front of a giant mirror of the bathroom, gazed my portrait as reflection. So, without delaying any second, I strapped down my trouser, gazed my primitive feature reflected in the mirror as truth as white.

I hadn't control over my impulses that hour. Being nescient of the onanism procedure, still, my clutch accesses as successfully as a regular user does. I felt as if I was flying mounted over the wing of absolute pleasure which can't be scripted into words although.

I remember I hadn't remembered anything that hour as I enhanced rotating couch. I forgot everything, dissolve in ecstasy, headed upward toward the roof having closed eyes.

Suddenly I felt a strong urge of a stream of something bolting out from the vein of my phallus protagonist, felt as to piss out as it was while dreaming.

Certainly, it was incredible, epical in pleasure. Of course, it was my first organism after crossing my age of twenty.

With the floating of days, I developed many reasons for happiness in the 'city of light'. Ghats, grooving Ganges River, central library, VT temples and of course campus life; like these, one fine evening, Urvashi took me such a cool spot to hang out- LC and DGC Adda -which were en route of IIT faculties. It became our favourite spot for munching samosa and sipping tea.

Kamal and Rehan too became part of my amusement. Kamal was rather taciturn, and Rehan was garrulous. Both mostly found around the girls, making them laugh, cutting jokes full-time entertainer and sometimes rushed to Lanka to photocopy of notes if any girls asked them.

There could be seen a good tuning between Urvashi and Rehan. They addressed me name, 'persona' 'doctor' 'poet'.

We – I mean Urvashi and I- always averted conversation in department, averted eyes of gathering to catch us together. We had signed a silent bond between us without writing anything paper that we would keep our friendship secret from else.

I helped her in poetry, and she provided me with important notes, for she had an impressive link with senior girls.

She performed as a guide for me to show Banaras free of cost and became a reason to ruminate in most of the hours. There was no such spare hour, apart from study, when I hadn't been nostalgic of her. I didn't feel conscious when I sick of her memory.

One right evening, she asked me to follow her steps, and I did like all time I used to do. I conjectured her intention; she would be going to VT. But no. She surpassed the VT, headed toward IIT. Now, we walked en route IIT faculties, and her steps paused at a hut-shaped-shed which gave shelter to dozens of people, munching samosa and sipping tea. There were autos and bikes honking, leading to the main gate or hostels.

The stall swamped with bikes, cycles, and gossips. She brought tea and samosa.

"This is a famous spot of BHUites – DGC" sipping tea she said. My eyes stuck to a couple and her eyes at my curiosity. Students rambled in half pant t-shirt, sleeper in feet and the blazing cigarette in right hand in between the fingers and puffing glass of tea in the left hand.

"How do you feel here?" asked she, putting her glass on a stool.

"Nice," said I. "Far from madding crowd."

"It is famous for couple's haunt," she said, smiling. There was a blush on her face which she tried her best to hide between her sips and swallow of samosa.

"Evening seemed so pretty here," I gazed in the western sky drifting grey cloud. "with a pretty girl."

I didn't spare any chance to waste.

She clearly blushed and reverted, "Wow! Thank you... Thank you," she said dryly. I busied in gazing the drooping evening.

“Sometimes, I don’t understand your poetry. And when I do I enjoy” said she.

“I will try to make you understand,” said I, added, “You have to glide with words wherever I do take you. And sometimes you feel familiar with the sense of poetry.”

“I think people, write poetry when they fall in love or deserted in love. What is the case in your own context?” she browsed.

“Not always. Poetry comes to seer mind. When you start understanding life and time, then universe passes your poetry. Life and time, both, is the biggest teacher in human life. And in my case,” I paused my rolling eyes away in speculation. “Life has given love and desertion both. So I write.” I added. “I think everyone has the poet inside. Every human has emotion which overflows. Everyone has a heart which speaks a language. Few are skill who able to pen it down into words. They are called a poet, writer. A gazer might be a good poet if he can describe his experience of the day into fine rhyming.”

“And you have a language to speak. Right?” said she, smiling into my eyes.

“I…I don’t know … I feel something and try to put it into words,” said I, after a bit faltering.

“Can you portrait your emotion about me in words?” asked she, comely, still looking into my eyes.

I felt a sudden scintillating vibration ran throughout in my vein and rushed toward my heart. My heart always talked about her to me, taciturnly.

“I will try to portrait my innate saying,” said I, although at same moment content already scripted in my mind.

“Try to listen to it, and you should.”

Honestly, I could not sustain my dart into her eyes constant. She brushed her locks from her eyes and hung it on the backside of her ears.

Throughout the night I strife with words, my recollection and understating of her character with the pen to scribble over the paper. My emotion was dense, so I was searching for such diction which could paint my inner portrait.

So writing the first draft was not any difficult task, but by going the second draft, cutting down whole pages sometimes, I found, writing second is like molestation of words which an author has spent hours to script it previously.

I considered it a chance to talk about her and me. I wrote, rewrote and read, again I repeated the same process. I tell you, I was not writing poetry, but I was writing herself the much I had perceived.

I didn't know I fell asleep. But I woke up with the fluttering sleepers and tramps sound passing by my gate.

I hastened, got ready for class as fast as like wind. I was late today. I didn't know when I fell asleep exactly. My attendance was only in the register, not in class these days. Urvashi had occupied my psyche absolutely.

Till 4 o'clock, I reached at LC. I had been waiting. According to her plan, I should leave first, and she would come later escaping from the eyes of fellows.

She had covered her face by a scarf. Only her eyes were open. Yes, I didn't recognize her when she reached to me and patted over my shoulder.

"Come," said she to me. And she prolonged further.

"Where?" asked me. I was baffled where she was going to this time.

"Today I will show you a secret place which I haven't share with anyone yet." Her eyes stopped for a while at me. "It's my favourite place on campus."

"So, why me?" asked I, walking beside her. She darted at me, said softly, "It's something special to someone special."

After few minutes, she detoured through the most solitary vista. It was a lonely road. We crossed a gate. Now we were standing before a huge area of plantation. I bowed in front of a small temple which was near the gate. We sat on the cemented dais under the shed of the trees in the premise of the temple.

"It is nursery farm of Agriculture Science faculty," said she, suggesting toward the field.

There were several students doing something bending down and next hour they noted down something in their notebook after study of the plants. Few students were wandering still hanging bag.

"You told right about the place," I said to her looking across the farm.

She took me to the farm and stopped at a small pool of water. There was a bench. We sat there. The evening was quite clear, the sun was drooping down behind far stood fence of the university. Few phantom images of human being appeared rambling moving back to their destination. Few local female folks, who were trying to wrap up the grass that they had accrued, one by one, they, also, began returning to their kitchen work.

"You know well, this place?" I asked rhetorically.

"I have spent three years of my life in this campus."

We discussed many things, eating Kurkure and snacks that she had put in her bag. It was pleasing to see exotic species plants, blossom and organized queues. We were in the widespread arena which was coloured in blue, green, red, acute kaleidoscopic panorama was in front of us. Behind us, there was the narrow cemented passage, sometimes honed with the passage of bike.

The sky turned grey, dark overcoming scenario.

"You had promised to compose poetry for me. Where is that?" she whined like any child.

"I have?" said I.

I ransacked my bag and opened my diary. She delayed her glance at me, eagerly waiting for my words like an inquisitive child. Now we were alone in that field except few birds chirruping in bushes, few were returning to their newborn babies. The sun was set already, mere its lingering light in sky ablaze. The night was slowly gliding down.

"What would I get as royalty in return?" said I, kidding her. I flipped the pages.

"What you wish?" asked she.

"You decide."

"Ok. So start now. That I will decide."

As I finished the poetry, she travelled the gap between our faces. She touched my lips with her. It steered my all senses mesmerized my whole anatomy. I felt a strange experience. It was newness.

Anyway, after that scintillating touch, we met frequently in the department, and that place became our favourite visiting in evening. We entitled it Sunset Adda. We used to chat, joke, and smile. Gazing evening sight with her was a coruscating moment. But we never talked anything about that touch.

Chapter 10

Her company had healed and helped me to avert the feeling of the grief of native place. My suffering of nostalgia, yearning and isolation dwindled.

I found me; I became fond of Urvashi's company, her way of smile, her ways of wording, and her traits. I didn't miss any chance to spend my minutes with her. I could afford her as a guide without paying any cost. Ghats, Sarnath, DLW, and labyrinth Banarasi gullies, I made a list. Oft I went out tramped through its roads, narrow lane, but mostly on Sunday. But whenever I wished to visit Manikarnika ghat, she precluded the thought every time. But I was quite eager to see life's most prominent philosophy lively- cremation of somebody's near and dearer before their eyes.

But to behold her was itself a lively dream. So I decided not to stress. However, I convinced her jaunt in Marnikarnika Street before Diwali, for we planned to be a focus afterwards. Semester exam was coming closer.

I planned our meeting point at an intersection of Triveni- a girl's hostel in the campus.

We caught an auto-rickshaw from Lanka for Gaudolia. The driver, haphazardly, set his haunch however and made sit three people along his side. Comparatively, Banaras' road remains relaxed on Sunday than else days. No hustle-bustle, no hue and cry. No creeping traffic. Foreigners, wearing a hood, Capri and light T-shirt, click snapshots, rambling being lost gazing around, sometimes pause at any corner astound, they gazed Banarasi people but Banarasi less bother of their exotic presence, for they become used to of haunting White people.

"Come," she signed me to follow her. She jaunted to a restaurant. "I'll take you on food adventure today" She ordered typical Banarasi food, *Chhola- kachori*. And hardly, I had finished my bites, she ordered jalebi. A man, in shaggy oily spotted cloth, brought the plate of jalebi.

"Banaras also is a tremendous place for delectable food recipe," she mumbled stopping her chewing. "And particularly it's morning jalebi and *Chhola-kachori*."

With every bite, my mouth filled with sweet syrup. I faltered before her. It was not the first time happening with me. It occurred to me all the time if ever I ventured before anyone. But I liked Banarasi jalebi. Though I had tasted it several times in Gyanpur market in the lunch break, at my neighbouring village shop, it was different.

Banaras's traditional food cuisine is like Banarasi way of life- soulful.

When I returned to my chair after cleaning my hand from the wash tub, there was *kulhad* filled with cardamom flavour, topped with a generous layer of cream. It was terrible. There was no space in my stomach. She suggested me to have a jaunt around.

"I can't go this Banarasi beverage" I pleaded her to cancel the order. But she was headstrong.

"Now sit down," said she, emphatically. She looked me intentionally. Her chide was loving. "The place that you are eager to see, after seeing that I don't think, you will dare to take bite till evening. So better, drink it."

It was the magic of her bewitching anatomy, I forgot the world. She was like opium taking whose company threw me in forgetfulness, cut me off from the world- a complete oblivion state. Her deep, health eyes numbed me.

Her entire attires embellished her beauty of simplicity. She had put on pink salwar, kameez. The length of suit hanging like bell reached all the way down to the ankles. And churidar salwar was tightly fitting buttoned cuff at the ankle. The excess length fell into folds and appeared like a set of bangles resting on an ankle. Her dupatta hung either side of her right shoulder and blew sometime with the stock of wind. We entered into typical serpentine streets of Banaras-Marnikarnika gully.

The coloring of the wall, perhaps, was done years ago, might be before independent of the nation, rather appeared dark due to soaring smoke from the furnace of adjoining sweet shops. We needed to be careful while walking. We partly looked ahead, somewhat down our stepping escaping cow dong. The lump of dong was not less than an explosive bomb. It could devastate the interest of the day, so I was cautious of my tramps and her too.

She held my hand, trailed behind me. She grabbed an arm and shrunken behind whenever any funeral procession passed by us reciting truth in the melancholy tone; '*Ram naam satya* hai' 'Lord's name is the only truth.' Her holding my arms, watching from the backside of my shoulder was an amusing moment to me.

"Banaras itself is a myth and mythology is mixed in the breathing of the city," said she stepping parallel.

"Myth?" said I, blended with the exclamation.

"Maybe there is no space for 'maybe' about Banaras' credential," said she. This time, she was a bit firm in her voice.

"How can you say it is a myth?"

"From ancient time, Banaras remains the epicentre of knowledge of Hinduism for the saintly soul. Even god wishes to visit this city."

"Were they told you?" said I, teasing her. Later after uttering, I realized my blunder.

"No. Absolutely not," said she. "It is the city of myth and Mahadev for those who faiths, not for those who expect just live stunt."

"Ok. Ok," said I pacifying her. "Why are you getting angry?" I noticed her frown.

We stood aside, made space for rikshaman to pass on.

"If anyone becomes able to understand the mystery of this city, that person can feel Lord Mahadev presence and he won't require anything, but it happens according to the wish of Mahadev."

We swerved from the point. There was an ethnic group of foreign tourist marching in the direction where we were leading to.

"Do you know about the myth of *Marnikarnika*?"

"No," I said. Up to now, I started getting interested in the gospel. "Do you know?"

"Yeah"

"How do you know this much?" asked I.

"Of course," said she, emphatic. "I have spent my three years of graduation and love of Mahadev. Shiv Shambhu"

"Oooow. So, what is the myth of *Marnikarnika?*"

Meanwhile, pyre processing passed by us, and every time she shrunken behind me, grabbed my arms.

"There are several stories behind it," said she, continued. "Marnikashina- If you go through its etymological study of Sanskrit, it means earring. Feeling disgraceful, Mother Sati flamed herself alive in the fire of yagya organized by Her father, Dakshya-one of sons of Lord Brahma.

Just then rickshaw cluttered bell. We stood aside, but she continued sporadically.

"Why had she sacrificed?" I asked curiously. "For her father tried to humiliate Lord Shiva by not inviting him in *yagya* conducted by Daksh himself."

"Oh," said I. I grieved. "So, Lord Shiva got anguished in animosity. Lord Shiva took her body from Himalaya. Lord Vishnu, seeing the wrath and deep unending sorrow of Lord Shiva, cut the body of Sati into fifty-one pieces through his divine chakra. They are also called Ekanya Shaktipeeth. Wherever it dropped, Lord Shiva, later on, established Mata's Shaktipeeth. Here at Marnikarnika, it is believed Mata's earring had fallen."

"Ok. That's why it's *Marnikarnika,"* I tried to be sure.

"Yeah, this shrine is one of the important place of worship for Shaktism of Hinduism.

"There are some more stories also behind this name. It is also the myth, Lord Vishnu, after austerity prayer, trying to please Shiva, to woo him not to destroy the city, Kashi when he was destroying the world. Lord Shiva was convinced and appeared before Lord Vishnu with Mata Parvati to grant him his wish."

Now we could see the smoke of funeral hovering in the sky, soaring and uplifting in the sky.

At the opening face of the street by river crammed with people and my ears were engaged to her lecture and eyes were curious to see the scenario of the ghat.

We strolled quite closely, for the funeral procession had been passing by now.

"Lord Vishnu dug a kund, well for the both of Lord Shiva and Mata Parvati. When Mother Parvati was bathing, a jewel of her earring fell in the well, that's why; it is called '*Marnikarnika'*. And third myth" she was to start when I interrupted. "Is something more beyond it?" I interrupted

"Yeah," said she, started further. "When Lord Shiva was dancing in wrath after Sati's self-immolation. His earring fell into kund, the well. This is also one of the reasons to entitle it *Marnikarnika*." After the pause, she looked at my face rather in eyes. "It is believed."

She denied moving anymore further saying; the woman was not allowed to enter the cremation premises. She stayed before the periphery of cremation place- Manikarnika Ghat.

I stopped quite before the place where people were sitting with the dead body of their relatives waiting for their turn of cremation. There was hush serenity over the face of mass who, I think, didn't like to come before their actual death.

Nisadraj who function cremation procedure, bargaining the rate, busied in piling the wood, making a bed for final sleep. Arranging fire, instructing them to follow the custom, he called the kinship of dead man to set ablaze the wood log. No spark of sadness or a blink of pang, I could see over their face. No emotion, no sentiment. The overcast world's truest truth was before my eyes.

After the accomplishing one, they arrange immediately, and some small boy fumbled something in the ashes.

At a time, I saw several pyres burning, and the sky turned dark cloudy with funeral smoke lingering. A quite youth was made laid down over wood pile and next thing fifteen minutes after his healthy youth physique turned into ashes. Seeing, it blew my heart. I felt helpless to stand there any longer.

My phone beeped in the right pocket of my jeans. Urvashi was calling. Before to receive the call, I beheld her around but didn't appear in remote places of my stay. She called me near the water tank, four Ghats ahead of Manikarnika. I caught her waiting for me there, acutely. She took me next side of the river rowing across the Ganges by boat. I couldn't speak anything since I return from there. We sat on the sandy floor, gazing a panorama of Ghats across the river as if any child had set boxes, toys in order to play.

It was late October. The sunlight was pale from turning rather cooler. A family had been playing with kids, couples were riding horse gleefully, and boys playing flying a kite and yelled '*baaaw kaatey'*. She tried to talk to me but I, as if, lost my mind still at Manikarnika Ghat. Still, funeral fires had been blazing up in my mind. I was gloomily dealing with sudden questions, memories and consequences of the past. She, sometimes, stuck at me, stared, tried to read my expression I wanted to ask but didn't utter anything. She was feeling a bit aligned being my aloofness in pondering vacuity.

"I lost my mother at my birth. My father couldn't endure this tragedy, lost his mind. He became mentally paralyzed. One day, till late evening, he did not return, and then he returned never. My grandpa and villagers searched him all around and in the neighbouring village but he was not found anywhere. Within year grandpa caught cordial attack. And left a loner world behind us and since then Grandma brought me up."

I kept my face straight looking across the river to a series of Ghats. It was not only truth, whereas I was trying to hide oozing out tears from my eyes. To control that uninhibited liquid was not in my grip.

“Where is the Grandma now?” asked she, mildly.

“AT home in the village,” I said, added. “She is breathing because of me.

I looked her, tears gushed down wetting my cheek.

“How would she look after herself at home?” asked she.

I was not able to escape. It seemed like any lump stuck in my throat, seeing my helpless to speak, she begged ‘sorry’.

“Meera looks after her in my absence,” Meera was her next question but she didn’t think it better to ask that moment. I was in the condition to speak her anything as somebody had glued my lips.

Day- Second

The bell of the room is rung along with some gentle knock on the door at an interval, intermittently.

Nazarin shakes Prabha to wake her up. She moanes in drowsiness. Prabha is still in partially dream, she woke up late night turning the pages of the diary.

Both are partially awake and partially numbed.

Finally, Nazarin squeezes her eyes, rubs it with the back of her palm to see the vaguely seeming texture, and anyhow opens the door over staggering feet. Seeing receptionist at the front, she collects her consciousness. "Is everything okay?"

Hearing it, Prabha gets alert.

"Shreya is calling you here."

"Call her in," says Prabha, controlling yawn covering mouth with her palm, sprawling still in the bed.

"Good morning Mam," the receptionist wishes her with an affirmative smile.

"Hello, Shreya. Good morning." She mumbled.

" Actually, my shift is over mam. It's my leaving time," she tells.

"Oh." Prabha says. "We will leave this room soon after getting fresh.".

"No. No. I didn't mean anything like that," says she, apologetically. "Actually, manager sir wants to meet you."

"To me?"

"Yup. I told him about you, so he wishes a professional meeting with you," says she, smiling softly. "Get ready. I'll come after some time." She is to move out, Urvashi probe about the patient.

“Till now there is no issue. If the doctor gives any input of patient, I have mentioned my colleague, they will inform you.”

Prabha gets ready, take Nazarin and shuffles through the tramps exhilarating to see the Strange Man. She staggers at the meandering of wards.

They enters the ward, strolls through its middle space to which either side there are beds for traumatic patients. Nazarin shatteres seeing their pathetic state. Prabha grabbes her hand to encourage her.

His dashing and elegant look has perplexed them.

He is enwrapped with bandage from head to toe. Doctor set a neck-belt to straighten it.There is a plaster wrapped in the right leg.

He is calm and quiet, looking blankly. She exhibits no emotion or expression over face.

“Hello Mr. See who is here to see you?” calls the ward boy. He turns toward Prabha, “He hasn’t spoken a single word since he comes in consciousness. We tried to talk to him but he is silent. Doctor of the opinion, the accident might have left an impact on his mind. I’ll say, if you leave him alone, it will be better for him.”

Seeing him mute, Prabha is filled with an extreme anxiety.

“Where is the doctor, who is doing treatment of our patient?” Prabha demands.

“He is not available. He comes every day at 12 p.m. you may wait for him,” the ward-boy informs him.

“When will we take him to our home?” inquires Prabha.

Nazarin frowns and whispers, “Have you gone mad?”

Prabha winks at her to be remained pacify.

“That only doctor can tell. But seeing his wound, he might need to stay in the hospital until his wounds get healed. Here in hospital, he would be under doctor’s vigilance,” he says.

"Mam is also a doctor herself" Shreya asserts.

"Okay," he pauses his words further on.

She glances at Nazarin's tense and frown face.

"Can we be alone for few minutes with our patient?" beseeches Prabha.

"Of course," he asserts. He moves, the receptionist follows him.

"Have you gone mad Prabha?" Nazarin's whispering has changed into protest.

Prabha feels uncomfortable with her high pitched voice, echoing.

"Can you imagine what you are saying?" says Nazarin, emphatic. This time, she is rather low in her tone.

"What's wrong with that?"

"Where would you keep him?" asks she.

"In our house."

"This girl is really gone mad." She mocks. "Why are trying to be Mother Teresa?"

"Why are you showing so much concern and interest in rescuing a strange man?" says Nazarin, emphatically.

"It's not just about a strange man. It's about myself- mustering my inside humanity. As you know well, I don't leave anything incomplete until I make it." She pauses for just caesura sake and continued.

"How can we live in the same house with a strange man?"

"Darling" Prabha addresses jovially. "A rapist and a lover, both are a man and born from woman."

Prabha disregards Nazarin's unnecessary concern wearing her perennial soft smile.

Nazarin can decipher Prabha's anthological impulse which intrudes in her intrinsic despair of life which she is trying to surpass.

On another hand, Prabha decides to construe with the situation together and holds the responsibility of the strange man until he finds someone his near one.

She heads toward chamber of the manager. Gently she pushes the transparent door manager's office and mused, "May I come in sir?" and with his slight nodding, permission is granted.

"I heard, you have pursued your study in medical science." He keeps straying his eyes for a moment at her face for her assurance.

"Yes, sir."

"What's your specialization?" He questions. Although he has made already a research over her that Prabha senses it well.

"I did in the surgeon…?

After having formal queries, he comes on point and offers her a part-time job to consider only having twice visited in a week and she will be paid a good amount as her fee.

He also exempts some percentage of medical fees and shifts the patient from general ward to a private well-equipped-room.

Chapter 11

Diwali holiday was over. We returnedto our hostel. Since I shifted in Birla hostel, the experience never went better; rather it was bitter to me. Especially with my room partner and his two friends who had occupied the adjoining room.

They ridiculed on my going Temples on barefoot and worshipping God and deities. Sometimes being scared, I escaped to pray, chant shloka and make red round spot on the forehead in the hostel room in presence of them. I mentioned Manish my problem, urging him to change my residing room of the hostel.

I never came to know what their problem was, whereas I used to see them putting the poster of some saints, favourite great personality on the wall. I never reverted them whenever they went Ravidas Temple. Oft I went with them too.

Another trait, I couldn't tolerate- their sound making eating while moving tongue. My room partner unable to tolerate hunger any longer whether he had to bunk the class. He rushed hostel as the class dispersed. He used to be very first to reach in the mess as if it was like any race. Obviously, none could rival him if it would be competition. I never dared to take my meal with him. I averted it if I found him around. The sound of their tongue resounded like dog's eating made me irritated.A devotee of Carl Marx. Great critique of elite class, particularly Brahmin and unfortunately he knew my clan.

Kamal used to call them 'chutiya gang' and Rehan entitled them 'chindi chor'.

Rehan and Kamal advised me to alter my room and shift into with them if they were only my problem but I found my psyche fed up with hostel life and its ways. The exam was at hand I had not much money that I could afford a separate room outside of campus. I thought better to bear the situation.

The exam was to start from fourth of December and on 17th it ended. It was chilled bone shaken cold. The day I attempted the first exam I was excited. And I was at the culmination of pride, I proved my dream being part of such grand institute when I received question paper in my hand and wrote my roll number.

I didn't mention you that my title, surname puzzled among caste, community seeker. I felt an internal dilemma among teachers, friends and hostlers. Few considered me elite class Brahmin, seeing my white reddish complexion and my usual going temple; few thought me lower caste by surname 'Gautam'. And those who were unaware of my name and surname, seeing me, at first sight, misunderstood me, recognized as a north-eastern or Nepalese, Garhwali, by complexion; few studied me by my natural French beard as a Muslim lad.

Once after a long conversation with Japanese, I came to know at the end, he had been assuming me any European. Later I laughed constantly for few minutes. And when I told him my nativity, he chuckled too.

To avoid it all and hostel's garrulous atmosphere, mostly I studied in the central library, sometimes at VT with Urvashi.

Months passed.

It was the last lecture of the first semester. Urvashi sat beside me. Today HOD Mam was taking the class. She recently returned from the USA after attending the seminar. Meanwhile, her research scholar had been taking lectures in her behalf.

The greatest tragedy of Indian institutes, somewhere I believe, professors who receive the handsome amount in their bank account, spend time in their chambers, in copy paste seminars, making trips, feeling proud to deliver the lecture in foreign universities. And those, contract tutors, who keep continuing the pace of institution, complete the syllabus; they receive scale not better than day wages.

Anyway, after many days, Urvashi was sitting on the same bench with me. She pushed a notebook before me, written 'Hi' on its last page, made the smiley.

'Hello,' wrote I, made a big smiley.

'Looking happy?' asked she.

"Yeah," I wrote.

We both voluntarily escaped being together in the class. Our communication with each other was limited, academic discourse only whenever we were in the department. We rarely sat together in the class, since we came together.

"Why?" asked she. "What is the secret behind this?"

"Department's most beautiful big eyes belle is sitting with me. I am fortunate and feel an honour blended pleasure." I scribbled down and pushed it to her.

"This seat is the most favourite seat for this most beautiful big eyes wallih girl. Perhaps she may feel more honour than you if she gets chance to accompany you."

"You are most welcome. You may sit wherever you wish to" I wrote further. "Can I know what the reason behind your happiness is?"

"Sure," she darted to me for a while and again ran her pen "I'm happy because I'm sitting with the most sensitive and sincere boy of the department... And do you know what another special thing about you is?"

My hunger to listen to me rose to the level; I longed to listen to it sooner.

It is natural to me to be delighted being a human being. And it was my first live appreciation, so it became more natural to swell with elation. But I didn't reflect my internal image over my complexion.

"Sure. I want."

"You are the rare species of the boy who don't flatter behind the girl, who don't believe rushing after fake world. You are genuine version. One thing more, here every girl keeps jealousy to me...You know why?" she asked and wrote answer herself. "Everyone wants to chat you but you don't allow anyone to come closure, whereas every boy haunts behind some girl, but you ….no way. It's you who don't flirt me. B'coz I had booked you before coming in this world…lovvve yooouu soooo much."

It was her way of expressing her love. It was first and foremost time when out of us has asserted our innate world into words.

Bubbles sprung out throughout my body.

“Actually I look the way I’m. It’s the beauty of you who see, frame me this way…but anyway thank you so much being a fellow walker.”

We shared glance watching into each other’s eyes. She bent her head and began jotting down in the notebook.

“This is...This is the things that draw me closure to you and make me sometimes crazy about you…your cuteness… simplicity… innocence and less networking.”

“Wow. You are crazy about me!! OOOO,” I exclaimed. Obviously, I felt the delight to listen that most beautiful girl of faculty had a crush on me.

“I know you are stupid too.” She made a smiley.

“A girl never haunts behind any boy. She can’t walk any step if she doesn’t see any heroism. You must read George Bernard Shaw and his ‘life force’ philosophy. Poet like character gets dumped by his heroine. You can see in his book Man and Superman and Candida too…” I was just trying to listen more from her.

“Then you must read Carlyle’s philosophy of heroism...a man of the letter is also a hero. And I don’t bother about other’s philosophy. I listen to my own heart.”

“What does your heart say?” I wrote abruptly. My fathomless pleasure buried in my heart still. I never learned how to explicit my emotion in a fair way, particularly before the girl. I was waiting for her reply.

“My heart informs me you are my hero ...That’s why… I love you… Rest I don’t know anything beyond it. I always follow my heart.”

I was looking into her eyes stealthily escaping from the professor. I dared not to show her what my soul was saying. I wanted to say her...I love her too… fathomless as water in ocean…measureless as unbound sky… I wished she must read the wordless beating of my heart. I wanted to say her, I watched her when she didn't notice me, escaping from her eyes. I wanted to say her, I failed to understand my relentless the day she couldn't come university anyhow and I failed to have a glance at her face. I didn't sleep throughout the night when I couldn't hear her voice once in a day. Whenever I walked with her even through thoroughfare, I seized most beautiful and charming hours of my life. I realized I was opium eater when I found myself with her. I didn't bother about paths where I went whenever I trailed her tramp. I just followed her and wanted to follow throughout my life.

"It's ok. You need not bother. I won't disturb you and your study. We'll be rather a good friend." She looked into my eyes when she didn't find any responses. I couldn't help my eyes glittering with the instance delight I received. I saw a latent sparkle in hers too.

I really wanted to embrace her tightly and planted kisses if I forgot I was in the class.

"Thank you," said I, returned a smile.

On 17 December exam got over. It was chilled winter. We had planned to visit Sunset Adda at last day of the exam before we left for our home.

We took a packet of Kurkure, her favourite and tea in disposal glass, walked to our serene place. We talked about spontaneous topics. We never found us blank, without topics or words if we were ever together for few recent days. We stopped chatting only when our hearts communicated. Time hurried past whenever we found one another amity together.

"When are you leaving for home?" asked she, taking a sip.

"Tomorrow morning," said I, crunching kurkure's salty jig jag light pieces.

We finished our tea and Kurkure. We started strolling on the narrow road made between farms. Frost prevailed all around. You could not see people walking in the distance of ten meters clearly. The fog had covered the leaves of plants and grass with her greyish cloak, appeared silver layer over them. Birds didn't bother to sing and vanished to any strange land. But it was an inexplicable fascinating day to me.

I had covered my ears with a black round head tight cap and hood of my sweatshirt over it. She had put on jeans, a leather jacket and muffler wrapped around her neck.

I was helpless to imagine. Had God framed the ears of girls with some armour metal? Didn't they feel cold? Or just a pomp? Or they didn't want anyhow mishap of their hairstyle? Whatsoever I didn't know but scared about her, she might be caught cold.

"You?" said I.

"Tomorrow," Replied she and asked me further. "And returning?"

"As soon as winter vacation will get over," said I.

"I knew. You are not going to miss your class anyhow. But I'll come back after Makarshakranti, 15th of January. Classes will also begin regularly after 15th of Jan. Before that, it will be just casual classes." said she.

We stood up from the bench. But honestly, I was reluctant while moving. I yearned to spend time with her. To think, I could have a chance to see her after winter break, I despaired. I paced down of my tramps. I wanted to stop. Perhaps she understood, she walked rhythmically with my steps. We stopped walking at manoeuvre, standstill quite opposite to each other, sharing dialogue, glances, smiles and foggy puffs.

"I'll miss you," said I, hesitating. However, I collected courage to utter this to her.

The more I was frequent to split down words over pages, equally, I faltered to utter out words from my mouth.

"OOO really?" said she, amazedly.

"Yeah… so much," I said rather confidently. I got encouraged with her positive response.

Now, we were almost stopped face to face. We moved a bit against each other. She placed her both palm against my chest. I slowly dragged my arms around her waist grasped her, pulled her closure, looking into her eyes and her in mine. She lifted her face enhancing her height lifting herself over her paw. I leaned my head toward her. And she rubbed her nose over mine, chuckled. We hugged. She was in my arms, a mesmerizing experience beyond any dream, I felt.

"I'll miss you too ...soooo much," said she.

Suddenly, she tilted her head back, still locked holding our arms clutching to each other waist.

"I'll miss you I understand because I love…," she winced, wearing a soft smile. "But I suspect on you… why do you miss me?" she knew all, just trying to listen in my voice.

Love what exists in the heart, if portrait into words, it soothes immensely.

"Yeah," I giggled at her as she was looking at me, naughtily. "I'm not a fool who spent time with a girl."

She became calm; her smile suddenly vanished from her face, asked ahead. "So?"

"You are not only stupid in love," said I, tightened my grip.

She blushed with a smile. Still staring, beholding our true images through the reflections into each other's eyes.

Our warm embracing circulated a heat in our vein. Cold elapsed, snow inside melted. Our relation was transcending from a class fellow to a fellow traveller. This transformation was not sudden. Nature had decided it already; frost helped to avert my shy from mass and had provisioned me a sense of privacy. Serenade of our heart went on musing. I could overhear her. I believed, she listened my nocturnal too.

Time detained in the surrounding. Space between us dissolved. We drew to each other. Our eyes were closed and lips instinctively were moving toward each other. Suddenly, I felt a sparkling touch, a current ran through my veins, my pulse raised high, heart throbbing. Our eyes were closed, forgot where we were dwelling? What were we doing? We forgot ourselves who we were exactly? It was the true epitome of transcendentalism.

My eyes were closed. Even I didn't get conscious to look around. I felt some soft gliding, slipping and sailing over my lips. My lips and tongues reacted parallel spontaneously. I didn't know where it had learned to move this way. It was an aesthetic flow from our lips through the lake of conscience and we discovered the most wonderful experience of our life. I felt unknown waves of ecstasies ran as currents in my whole body, sensitized me. Invisible obstruction of shyness, thawed. After a minute of our mesmerized sojourn, we opened our eyes. I looked her face which was glowing and her bright eyes were sparkled with delight.

After a while travelling through heavenly experience, we struck apart, smiling into each other's eyes. We felt more closed one. I still felt the touch of her lips over mine. Now, I was rather confident and cupped her face in my palm, stared into her blushing eyes. As I again moved my lips towards her, she closed her eyelids, lost.

We were once again started our voyage of love sailing through mine to her coral lips which drainage to our soul.

Finally, I stuck my lips from her, still cupped her face in my hand. We devoured quietness. I glanced at her face. It was glowing. I didn't sense why she appeared bewitching. Skin of her face turned reddish, still blushing. She dropped her eyes now, shying. And she buried her face in my chest, embraced me.

Chapter 12

Entire winter vacation spent in netting dreams of true lover's knot, myriad brooks of affection sprouted and glided through the valley of my tender heart. My psyche was crammed with the thoughts; a new promising year was awaiting the commencement of the new era of my life.

I engaged most of my time speculating how I would encounter Urvashi or the way she would hail me after reopening of the department, how I would be the utterance of my first word, or spelling time with her at Sunset Adda, together.

She had promised to take me for a jaunt at Sarnath after her returning from home. I fancied the gait we would walk; spent time together in the antique land of Lord Buddhism.

Sometimes my fancy was tossed and enraptured when I thought she used to go Allahabad via Junghai Junction, and the breezing might have touched her, then perhaps to me while blowing to eastward. For Junghai was not that much far from my home.

I occasionally jaunted there for books, nursery seed and miscellaneous works. Might be she was on the train when I was passing by the station. It might be we had passed coming from two opposite direction and being unconscious; we couldn't care and acquainted with each other's faces being stranger in that fortunate hours. Whatsoever but I was sojourning the most beautiful emotional journey, sighing in the remembrance of her that worked like burning grate in my heart, it kept me warm and fresh and lost.

This December was turning diabolic. Newspaper usually published this year's cold had broken several years' record. Grandma had already collected a heap of firewood that she had been doing it before every wintry season. Before winter reached door she used to collect woods log, dry leaves and rice husk. While assembling I had noticed she rejoiced it and devotedly did this considering an essential errand. And almost whole wintry days had gone with a constant cheerful fire burning inside the door to make the house warm. Somebody or else of my neighbor or villager you could find d sitting by fire accompanied Grandma discussing some local issues- cattle and their newborn baby's health, status of crops, local politics, the heart shook icing wind's blowing, prevalent of frost, invisibility of sun - sometimes tilted their head aside rubbing their eyes to avert smoke's stroke.

As the day began getting darker and needle clock sloping down, Grandma busied in making fire ablaze. I took an axe, split wood logs apart and fetched it to the fireplace. Grandma never allowed me to work or feel a single spark of pang; it was another thing I never followed her urge not to work, but rest. She picked up small pieces of wood after I returned collecting chopped long pieces of wood.

Oft I went to the vegetable farm to look the growth of plants- its foliage. It had really helped me, for extent, resolved my monetary problem.

It was cauliflower, tomatoes and chilies season. Productivity and selling both were a great mass. We earned adequate amount of money that we could save after day to day expenditure. I helped Chotani in the field, dealing with the folk customer doing the calculation. He was an honest man. There were several popular stories of honesty related to his ancestors. Whenever there were any marriages in my family, his father used to take responsibility to execute it successfully. They looked after house and woman laden with jewellery, holding lathi, a strong stick, guarding throughout the night until people returned after wedding ceremony next morning.

Every morning, after brushing teeth with neem twig, Grandma fed me stomach struck, forcefully with an unfathomed latent love and caring.

I couldn't disturb Chhottani, therefore I, myself, took responsibility to do the entire chore, for Makrshanrati was at hand.

Sankranti, particularly in rural territory of India, is celebrated delightedly. Women prepare several sweet recipes made of pure desi, indigenous material.

Meera assisted Grandma in her household. Early morning she fetched her all pots at hand-pump and took our too when we used to remain in bed, she cleaned it rubbing it with ashes and husk. After accomplishing her chores, she used to come to our house, make tea and serve me when I used to be in bed even.

I worked hard and settled things. I carried paddy to neighboring market to thresher the rice and stock it in the house that Grandma needed not to trouble seeking the help of somebody else. Albeit Chhottani was always stood for any job but he had also a family and he had an obligation toward them. So I did my deeds by own.

The winter vacation was over. We were again in class for a new semester with a new syllabus. The result was to release very soon. Everyone was excited to see the outcome of their first six months and stood before notice board every morning before going to their respective classes. Especially Bengali students, they became so chirpy. They raised their eye-brows being concerned as if somebody had set the bomb under their feet. They were friends, hostel mate but covertly reveller as they were fallen into a secret tug of war against each other that one could see the expression over their faces on the day when the result was to move out.

They busied so much in cramming notes till the late night before the exam being commenced. Urvashi told sometimes she was unable to sleep underwent her night ineffably in the hostel before the exam.

Urvashi didn't come yet. I didn't feel interested in class anymore, waiting for her even I knew she would come after 15th of January, she had told me already. I, usually, span poetry in her memory. I recited and kept listened by self-sitting at Sunset Adda. I ambled at Ghats, beheld Siberian birds and wandering tourists.

Time flew as if it has thousands of arch wings when you are moving with your chosen person. It behaves vice-versa when you are alone moving with some loved one's memory.

I was enduring it.

Memories are sweet which send you into the world of fiction with real character.

Next day when I reached department, my class swamped around the notice board and poking their head-tossing up, dragging their eyes up-down, down- up.

They were not only counting their own marks but also their friends also- who was the topper and who was the loser. I apprehended it as I crossed the threshold and entered the corridor.

I made my way through the throng of students, peeping into the list and searched my name from the bottom, for the first alphabet of my name began with 'S'. Seeing the number before my name I rushed out of the department with gloomy face instead of going for taking the lecture.

First time I experienced, scorecard could fuck the smoothness of your mind, disturb you. Within minute thing turned relentless in my sphere of life.

My dream, I felt as it was shattering into pieces. Grandma's face and her struggle to save money that I could study, Meera's hope and her pray to God every morning for my life and its betterment lingered before me. I grieved. I sat alone in MP Theatre at the football ground. There was a dense frost prevalent in the atmosphere. I could not see anyone around me.

It was the worst result I ever faced though it was the score of only one paper-language and linguistic- rest had to come, yet I lost my comfort.

The result of second paper was horrible that I had never imagined. I was almost depressed, unable to define my state. I confined myself to the room of my own, made me isolated from rest of the world.

In these days, I came closer to Rehan and Kamal. They consoled me; encouraged me saying other paper might lift overall result. But it couldn't occur.

Flinging of sarcasm, satire and mocks over me in hostel increased more now comparatively and I bore it silently but I had made the mood firm that I would leave the hostel at any cost.

Mostly, till late night, I spent my time roaming as vagabond outside of the hostel. I studied less and minimized with the passage of days. Oft Nitesh chided me for becoming indifference toward my study. He tried to counsel. I still remember when I met him the very first time he suggested and warned me what to do what not to do. 'Flow by the surface, don't dive in-depth' 'be away from Bengali girl for they possess bewitching beauty and you will be entrapped', and he repeated ample of maxims at several occasion, now again he was reiterating same dialogues which sometime I couldn't tolerate. It panged, taste embittered. I started averting as he was to preach.

"I suggest you because you are Manish's friend, neither I don't like to opine any stranger," said he, correcting his words. "But you are no longer stranger."

And Manish used to take me for an evening walk and gave me amiable advice, "Never lose your grip on yourself. Keep believing in you. And remember the background we come from that is Hindi taught and you have chosen English. So, you have a double challenge. Keep on making your best effort. That's the only thing which will help you."

It was the on Saturday, 12 January. After tomorrow, next three days back to back it was the holiday for Makrshankranti. I liked to spend time sitting, wandering or watching boys playing at Ghats. Sometimes I went to Kamal's room unreasonably. Today we strolled to Tulsi Ghats.

Kamal always paid his ears to me, listened until I stopped. Oft he took me to roam in the campus. Rehan had no time -neither on campus nor a room. He had a very busy schedule. It was not because he remained so engaged in study whereas he trailed girls group of the class, going Lanka to bring their Xerox copy, search room for them, taking them boutique, cosmetic shop.

Sometimes he took some of them at a room to feed them chicken, fish and other non-veg recipes. And at the room, when he used to be alone, he mostly occupied with the cell phone.

One late night I saw he was sobbing hysterically sitting in a corner of his terrace behind the water tank. Later on, Kamal told me he was in love with a girl from childhood- a true one. He couldn't care of her until her father had married her to somebody else. And now he had been shedding tears vainly when she belonged to else. I was surprised when Kamal told me, still that girl talked to him and tolerating the torture of her husband's whip.

"Why doesn't he stop contacting her?"

"He doesn't understand how he is spoiling her life," said he.

I could not help without laughing at the incident from his love story that Kamal told. Kamal cited, once being angry, he had set the fire in the sack of harvested husk of grain in the farm of the girl's father.

We sat at a high stood dais followed by decreasing stairs downward leading to river's current. Occasional surges, when any engine boat passed, hit the bank. It washed the feet of people sitting there. We wanted to go there and flung our feet into the water. But Kamal refused because he didn't want to disturb a lovebird who was sitting there.

A cluster of Siberian birds followed the boat, hovered over them and dived the moment tourists threw grain toward them in water. They fluttered, flopped as they were playing the game with them. Few people called them as migrated birds, few tourist birds, few guests of Banaras; few called them Banarasi bird that flies to Siberia after winter and returns back when the suitable season for them arrived in Kashi. Whatever facts were but watching their sporty flight snatches torments from your mind.

We were watching the scenery of Ghats and Ganges. Due to frizzing cold, Ghats were not busy as it used to be in rest seasons. Still one could see fine art students rushing their pencil, brush over the canvas, local boys playing cricket, for them the direct falling ball in the water of Ganges was losing wicket rather six. Few foreigners busied with kids. And sometime Ghats reverberated with giggles of couples sitting at stairs quite at bottom splashing by hitting their legs into the water. Few elderly people were competing with youth and trying their best to cut their flying kite standing on the verge of that, seeing them my breath got stop often.

I astounded to see an old lady bathing at a distance.

"It is believed," Kamal said, "People get cure of leprosy bathing at Tulsi Ghat."

Gloominess still delayed over my face. I hid it. I averted diverting my concentration. I noticed Kamal tried to read and long to speak something.

"May I say something?" finally he uttered.

"What?" asked I, darted.

He stayed calm for next few seconds. "Nothing," said he, tried to subdue something under his soft smile. I was curious to know what that was the thing he wanted to know.

"You can ask frankly," said I.

"It's little personal," said he.

I assured him to say whatever he wanted to quote without having any spark of prejudice.

"Is there anything between Urvashi and you?" He enquired hesitating.

I shrugged and responded in 'no'. I tried to hide the fact and told him that she was a friend… just a friend. I didn't tend, she would feel embarrassing due to me.

"Just a friend!" he looked at me, through his thick spectacle's glass, suspecting . He continued after a brief pause. "It's ok if you don't want to tell. You should …because everybody has their disguise self and one must protect it from external influence."

After a little moment halt, he flung another investigating interrogation. "Do you know exactly who is she?" He glanced at me constantly until I responded to him another 'no'. This time I really was telling true.

"Really, you don't know. Didn't she tell her to you?" Now he was more emphatic. I nodded horizontally, mystified why he had all these questions about Urvashi. What had the problem?

"Why are you asking all these? What the fuck does this mean?" I agitated being asked many questions without having an answer.

"I know you both are not just a friend. But" He said drily, paused and again continued from his last word. "But I don't know what exactly you both are that I don't bother." He took a short breathing. "I don't raise any finger over her. She is not like other girls- snobby, pompous or showy- I know. But she won't matter if her score gets down in the exam. But…" He beheld me now more vigorously. "…it matter to us…to you – a bourgeois boy who received monthly expenditure counted on the finger. I don't have big dream after M.A. in English. I'm giving exam for Bank PO job, Rehan knows his future. He is staying in the class that he could escape from his father's lineal sari business. And all others had no big dream. They will pursue B.ed after post-graduation, join any school and get married. And almost everybody has some mediocre story. But it matters you like students who are talented, studious, having great possibility too and plain background. Unfortunately, if you fall, there is no parachute to rescue you."

"Say directly what you wanted to say," I said after being impatience to know his intention.

"Urvashi is the daughter of a reputed businessman. His ancestors were one of the sponsors in university and donated a great amount of money. Last year, her father donated fifty lacs rupees to university. I don't raise question over her credibility. But you mustn't forget your place. I don't say you should snap relation with people, but you must maintain a distance that your purpose can't be superseded by any unwanted things." He maneuvered his speech appreciating her. "She is simple, generous and amiable. If she wishes she needs not to put her feet on earth. She can hire any luxury hotel or her own house in Banaras, but she decided to stay at the hostel like a common student."

How simply she lived with me without any snob or pomp or pseudo etiquettes- bereft artificiality. I made her walk through crowd, stinky road. I compelled to think drastically, who was she, exactly?

"She never travelled through the train."

“Then?” I asked, waited for his answer.

There was serenity over his face answering this question. “She uses flight or luxury car. She has hundreds of servants at home. She doesn’t do any work.”

“How do you know all these,” I revealed my curiosity, gazing his face expectedly.

He smiled. “For three years we are studying here.”

My pain, only I could feel. It was brimming, overflowing, heart rendered.

“How many people know this?” asked I, dimly.

“Rehan, her room partner and…… I.”

“Her room partner…Pummy Ghosh? Asked I., he affirmed.

I understood the whole story about how he could know this. Pummy and Rehan often were caught spinning minutes together in the department, at VT, and sometimes walking on campus.

The lamppost of ghat lit up, throwing the withered pale misty light of the day. We walked back to Lanka and locked cold out of our room.

The result of poetry and prose paper published on notice board. The next morning sharp as the department opened, I found, I was the topper in poetry, but again I stayed mediocre scorer in the fourth paper. Now it was enough to the tender heart to bear. Though Urvashi was not in top three lists, she had gained comparatively better marks. I didn’t know I was jealousy to her. Whatever. But I was feeling worst, decided to return home catching the evening train.

Falling Star

Chapter 13

"It does not matter how many times you are fallen down reaching height. Sometimes rise, and fall is not in our hand. But every time it will be your own decision to stand up at your feet, start your journey again and walkthrough. And remember, stories are told in the world only of those who conquer crossing the mountains of difficulties and hardships that come in one's life. You have left the entire obstacle back till now, few are remaining. Don't give up at travelling almost your journey when you are quite far from your starting point. Mostly ordinary people stop attempting reaching near their assigned goal. Don't be dumb toward your conscience urge." Grandma mentored me. She possessed incredible wit and visionary. Oft villagers used to come for her witty counsel.

The holiday was passed. And I told Grandma my intention not to go university again and didn't want to continue my study from there. I revealed my wish to take admission in precious college. I saw she was disappointed to hear me. We were sitting by the fire at night.

"You know well how you have reached there. I cannot imagine because I hadn't ride cycle to travel eleven kilometers after working four hours already in coaching. I don't know much about education as I haven't gone to an elementary school even. Do what you think better." There was complaining in her voice that I could feel clearly.

Suddenly, the gate opened. Meera entered the house, promptly slammed the door with a thud and made biting cold air out.

"Let it remain open, Meera daughter," Grandma said, fumbled her stick to stand up. "I have to go out for the toilet." Meera helped her.

She moaned of old age joined pain. She mumbled a chain of Hindu God and Goddess name at a high pitch that meant she had drawn her warm cover over her, I just conjectured. There was little change in her nature and attitude toward me that I knew I had made her grimace.

Though it was I who had attempted every exam, attained flying colour marks, achieved rank but behind my every success it was the most furtive supporter. Though it used to be my exam, she woke up an hour before me, prepared breakfast, worked like alarm and woke me up to get ready. She had murdered her myriad untold wishes that I could choose a better life.

That only she knew. I could never imagine her strives that she had for me. She saved every single paisa that I could afford a better life. I really wounded her, discussing my intention of discontinuing my degree.

Meera sat next to me, gave a gust of puff that blew ablaze in the hearth. She was bubbling village news nonchalantly. I didn't pay any attention to her roundabout wordings. I went into my bed.

She sensed something was wrong, seeing a weird silence in the house. Mostly Grandma kept waking up till late night, sitting by the fire until the twinkling log turned into ashes. The muddy wall painted yellow with the pale light of lantern hanging by the peg on the wall.

Meera followed me to my bed. She pulled quilt and uncovered my face. She flashed the torch, focused on my face. My cheek was soaked with tears that gave bafflement to her.

"Hey…Are you okay?" asked she whispering, coming close to my face.

"Yeah. I'm ok." I said. I took a turn in the bed, making my back to her. "Go and sleep. Blow off the lantern."

" Arey wah Raja, king," said she, humorously. She picked up the cover slipped inside my bed. She held my shoulder urging to unravel the reason for strange gloominess spread in the house.

I pleaded her to stop disturbing me, although I knew she was not to leave until I disclosed her everything. She gripped me tightly hugging me by torso and made me turned to her side. Her face was next to mine. She asked, “What happen, can’t you tell me?”

There was nothing anything that I hadn’t shared with her till yet and she with me.

She wiped the moisture from my eyes and cheek dragging her fingers over my cheeks, wooing me.

I told her everything- Urvashi, my study, my result and my decision.

Since I met Urvashi, I talked less of my disguise self to her or anyone.

“But giving up isn’t any right solution. It just escapes. The much I know, you are not escapist anyway. You must continue without thinking of result. Only remember the one thing by heart why you have gone there, you won’t be diverted.” She said, brushing her finger into my hair.

The cold vanished now from my bed. She clasped me in her arms and held me gently. My head was buried in her chest. My arms wrapped her around. “It is just a gust of bad time. It will pass. And never blame anyone for your failure. A strong man always accepts his defeat and analyzes his drawback and return with being more powerful.”

Her finger’s tips gentle brushing in my head had comforted me and snatched the revolving worries from my head. The slumber glided slowly from brows into my eyes.

“Babu! Does she love you?”Asked she and reiterated it. “Babu…Babu … Babu.”

“Hmm,” I muttered in the dream. At her every calling I just muttered, and sometimes it went answerless. Slowly I was in the grip of the hibernating numbness of the night.

Fellows’ point-view was changed after the first-semester exam result. Hierarchy of image in the classroom was reframed, and I was nowhere in the elite intellectual list. What it taught me- the world does not have time to bother about you or your ways of the journey until you reach your destination and script your own story.

Also, I changed my way of life and ways of looking at the world.

I stopped purchasing the academic book, waited other to buy and got X-Rox of it. Besides, I bought my favorite books which I ever wanted to read but couldn't due to finance scarcity. My hunger for the book engulfed. The Central Library turned my soothing corner I preferred to brood or hide from the crowd.

When I reached university week after winter vacation, Urvashi was already returned from her home and elated seeing me. She walked to me promptly. But I remained indifferent, gave a cold response to her as she came to me when I was standing alone away from chirpy students of my class.

I anguished on their constant gossip on achieved grade, marks and percentage.

Urvashi asked me several queries related my health, vacation etcetera. But I didn't give any heed to her presence. I avoided her, which pinched her and me too. And she, as I inference, grieved at my rudeness.

I averted her and moved to class, she still remained standing there, waiting to have my response, but answerless. She stunned and beheld me going away every time whenever she tried to stop me holding my wrist, but I snapped with a jerk.

Throughout the lecture, she bent down her head, scribbling down something haphazardly in the notebook.

As soon as lecture got over, I snapped out of the classroom, strolled toward Matri Cafeteria. I didn't realize, she followed my tramps taciturnly. She gripped my wrist from behind when I was moving through the corridor and pulled into an adjoining room which was vacant.

"Can I know why you are..?" she burst into tears, seemed as any lump struck into her glottal, precluded her to speak furthermore. Fumbling my palm into her, she gripped, tried her best to restrain her sobbing.

I summoned all my courage, strengths and sinister ego, somewhere latent deep within me, to hold me firmly and avert her gloomy face which drenched by drizzling eyes.

It had a different picture of Urvashi. The first time, I saw her weeping. Honestly, her beauty culminated now. I blessed to see such profuse, pious, stainless love in her eyes for me. Her locks hung scattering over her face, teased her eyes that hardly, anyhow, I controlled hands to drag it behind her ears.

I unbolted her hold over my wrist. As I prolonged toward the door, her sobs escalated, but I was lamenting inside. No one could see me, however.

I wanted to cry, embrace her and bury in my chest. But sometimes, you need to fall in rude love to for the betterment of you and the people whose life is pertaining to you.

I had already snatched my hand from her grip, but my heart still haunted there with her. She tried to stop me holding my shirt from behind when I was to hold the gate to open. I unclenched her hand. Now, I was tougher, I frowned, I left her alone there.

I walked toward the canteen again, hiding sprouting tears in eyes, somehow held it at the edge of the eyes; however, I tugged backside of my palm wiped out the droplets from eyes' pit, gave a plastic smile to acquainted faces coming in the way. I pacified the melancholic man, but I can't describe the pain I was undergoing.

After a few minutes later, Pummy came to me when I was standing in the balcony of the department, beholding stagnant trees in the frizzing winter.

"Where is Urvashi?" said Pummy. I turned to her. "Have you seen her?"

I nodded in 'no'. I didn't want to give any clue of what happened a few minutes before. , It was hard to stop your emotion oozing out of your eyes, most particularly in the case if you in deep sorrow.

I denied it. I faltered uttering words. "Oh, where she could be?" she probed.

“Why do I know where is she?” Now I was rather strong in voice, agitated.

“Why are you so crying?” said she, looking at me dubiously.

“She might be in the canteen,” said I, calming down.

“Is everything okay with you?” she asked. And I nodded in affirmation. My appetite dwindled for that moment. I wanted to a complete solitary confinement. I discerned a change in me. Was there any cryptic power working mysteriously being an agent in me? I thought for a while.

In place of making a distance from her, I was running away from me- my true ambience.

“What’s the hell happening between you!” bellowed Pummy. I turned; she returned so soon unexpectedly, furiously glaring at me.

“What happen to you?” said I, ignorantly.

“Look, Sid. Don’t think me a fucking fool. Ok. I know you have made her cry.”

“May I know why you are so angry at me?” I kept on my innocent face.

“Since she returned after vacation, everything is not going well between you, which I know well. I have noticed, she doesn’t eat, nor properly sleep” she paused. “Can you tell me what’s the fuck going on?”

I didn’t reply. I stood still, gazing stagnant trees, shrouded under foggy sphere. She, after a pause, commenced speaking, “though I don’t know anything about you. But the truth, I tell you, she loves you so much. She may be garrulous, but from her untouched soul, she loves you. Don’t hurt her, whatsoever. Nor later you will regret. ’ She went downstairs.

Almost things I had changed in my routine. I understood one thing clearly; I should stop perceiving marks and knowledge with equal eyes, together. To bag good marks is just a skill, waking up a few late nights cramming before the commencement of exam schedule. It does not matter how much you have studied, throughout the session, whereas the fact is how you have performed within that three scribbling hours over plain paper bending down head in the exam hall.

Now I divided my shelves into syllabus related study notes, personal interest books.

Now, I broke off meeting with everyone. Thought better, I spent time with rickshaw wallah, gossip with cobbler than interacting with snobbish and pseudo people. I remained aloof from the scene, spent time prone in any solitary corner of the campus.

I stopped going to Sunset Adda too.

I ignored girls' lengthy 'Hiiii', which I found so irritating.

January passed, the day became a bit relax and warmer, but the night still pinched.

I reached the department by cycle, borrowed from Manish, which was unused, rotting in the tin stand.

Rehan and Kamal hailed me at the threshold.

"Scoundrel!" I called them when they were briskly walking toward classes. They paused their steps. "When will you relocate my lodging?" I joined them.

" Bhai. It will be soon. Don't worry," said Rehan. They halted at the gate of parking, waiting for me.

"I want it to change desperately," said I, pathetically. We hugged each other one by one.

"Why would you like to fuck your second semester too?" Kimal mocked. "It's still too cold. The cold will intrude in your asshole, so I'm saying, be patience until winter gets over."

"And Siddhartha," Rehan snapped in short Kamal. We were to walk toward the old building. "Why don't you shave your beard? It's quite thick and long enough, looks so weird."

"Poet," said Kamal. "It's a style. And he is a poet and lover too."

We strolled toward the same classroom, under the same roof and obviously, nowadays, we sat on the same bench.

I didn't see Urvashi in the class; she frequently bunked from the classroom in recent days.

I reverberated with sorry for all I was doing with her, but I knew, I was not to say it to her in words.

So, I walked to Sunset Adda, perhaps I could find comfort to my panic heart.

I beguiled paddling my cycle through the gate, entered into agriculture area when I was at a distance from Sunset Adda, I caught a vague image of somebody sitting there already. As I approached nearer, I found it a familiar silhouette. I anticipated, she might be Urvashi, and absolutely, it was she.

Abruptly, I turned my cycle, paddled on like the culprit, running with the feeling of burglar scared of being caught.

Was I accepted myself guilty to hurt her without telling her crime that she hadn't done? For that time, my ego didn't allow me to bend and consent to repose over what I did.

My cycle clattered as it passed over chasms of the road. It might have woken her up out of her dirge, but I hadn't turned to look her. I headed to Assi Ghat.

Let the world move on its usual pace, the things would settle down spontaneously and adjust at its righteous place. One should not stop, nor weep, - the world is enormous, where a great mass resides together- wait, and watch-right person would find you out- acclaim his authority at the right time at the right place- I tried to console myself with some soothing quote. But my heart was not ready to listen to anything except Urvashi.

It was all my self-made trouble that my silence had manufactured deep within me in a confined world. It taught me, if you become over-concerned and take cautious unnecessary, it can create a miserable state for you.

I leaned cycle by a wall, rambled through the steep road leading to buzzing Asi Ghats' solitary stairs, but I didn't stay there.

That day I walked and kept on walking, measuring stairs after stairs of Ghats, delved in soliloquies, and knitting dream with open eyes in my psyche.

At last, I checked my speedy tramp and chosen to sit at Chet Singh Ghat, in a quiet place where hardly any trespassers passed by.

At right hand, an almost nude saint was brooding, who had worn the only piece of cloth- a *langot* at genital coloured his whole body with ashes of the cremated pyre. He made his chillum ablaze from the fire. He inhaled smokes inside his lungs and then left it lingering in his surroundings. Though I had always an allergy from the smokes of cigarette, but chillum's smoke had always an alluring aroma.

A blonde European girl stood-still reaching him, gazed him and smiled at his being lost in murmurings hymns. She yearned to converse him. She sat beside him. She was uttering something which appeared ambiguous to the ascetic. The naked saint mere popped up at her, again he resumed puffing chillum.

I anticipated the hurdle of language for conveying their message between them. Thought to help, I moved to them and interpreted him her message. The conversation went for while smoothly. She stalled before to ask her question to the saint.

"Why does the saint mostly avoid wearing clothes?" said she, wryly. She glanced at ascetic, being a bit hesitated. I looked once at her, then at the saint. The saint was smiling. Even I really never drove in such questions though I have been brought up in the Banaras region, most spiritual city of India.

I was astounded how they bore such sort of chilled cold.

The saint asked the reason of perplexity. I translated her query. Gently, he spread his lips, returned a magnificent smile. He pointed toward Harishchandra Ghat's lingering funeral fire, and said pensively, "That's the truth of every human being."

We looked in the direction simultaneously. He began collecting his things scattered around to go back to his shelter. Though it was 5 o'clock in the evening, it was quite late for winter. Held his tong in his withered hand, trembling, he moved stepping ascending Ghats' arch stairs of Juna Akhara, a monastery of rumination for Naga Saints.

"Is it only the answer to the question, Baba?" I asked him as he was striving to step up, leading to his cloistered chamber.

"If you want to know more," he stopped his steps, turned his head partly toward us. "Come tomorrow."

He resumed his progress. I interpreted the same to European blonde girl.

She followed me to Asi Ghat.

"Your name?" I interrogated.

" Juliet," said she. The first time, I was hearing a live English blonde.

"You?" said she, darted at me.

"Siddhartha."

Hearing 'Siddhartha,' as if she was contemplating.

"Where are you from?" I dared.

"Britain," said she.

"You?" asked she.

"Banaras," said I. "I'm a local boy."

She looked a bit amazed. "Nope."

I chuckled and assured her. We walked a few steps without speaking any words while she was trying to restrain her smile.

"What did you think?" asked I.

"I thought you are an Irish," she giggled. We laughed.

"From where do I look like an Irish?" I questioned smiling.

"Your complexion and hair, reflect you as a European countryman," said she. She was trying to pacifying her laugh. "Sorry."

"It means," she said after a while pondering. "You know Banaras well off, right?'

I told her I was a student at the university.

"Ok," she cheered and added. "You can guide me till I'm here working on my thesis," said she, pausing. "I will pay you whatever charges you decide." Reaching Asi, she said, spreading a graceful smile, "Siddhartha, hope I will see you tomorrow at the same place." She was to detour to follow the street of her paying guest house. "Wait," she came to me. "Keep it off today's charge."

Before I could discern anything, she handed five hundred rupees. I denied her, emphasized her not to pay.

I was feeling cold enough under my only muslin shirt, so I rowed cycle using the shortcut through the zigzag streets, emerged at Lanka, BHU gate.

I glanced at my minimalist clock which told around 9 o'clock. My cell phone beeped, vibrating in my pocket. I stood under lamppost's fainted light in the mist.

Urvashi's name flashed over phone screen. I paddled cycle rolling down, slowly restraining the force of my thigh and finally stopped after at a distance. A man had set fire collecting paper, plastic. My hand turned stiff with cold as it was frizzed. I made my cycle stand over its ankle and sat over haunches. The man could be seen loitering at Lanka, people rebuked him, called him *pagalawa,* a madman. He hadn't adequate clothes over his body-put on a shaggy kurta, a torn lower and barefoot.

I fetched few edible things, a cup of tea from an adjacent tea stall and handed him. He devoured, hurling samosa and *longlata* in few swallows, finished within few minutes. Again, he kept looking me hoping for more. I bought a few fruits after searching for shops to shops.

My phone beeped once again. It was Urvashi once again. I received it; put it in the hand of that poor man. He pretended to talk in pseudo etiquette something as it was so serious talking as some trained professional. I took it back from his hand, heard a sobbing another side. After few seconds, I disconnected the call. A message displayed on the screen.

I opened.

“I don’t know the reason for your rudeness for me. I don’t what’s my fault that you believe me, culprit. I don’t know why you are indifferent. BT if you think you are better without me, I won’t disturb you anymore. But plzzzzz tell me what is my fault?”

A sadist demon inside me relished seeing her in pain, but tacitly tears rolled down escaping eyes. I thrashed my phone in front pocket of my stiff jeans. I paddled cycle, rattling through frosty night, soon disappeared over a lonely path of the university; I could see only a few furlongs and hazy faces.

Chapter 14

That day, I didn't wait for the final lecture, moved out of the classroom and hurriedly headed toward ghat. I wondered Julia was already present there next to the slack fire; there was a thin smoke billowing from the log. She had been beholding Siberian birds playing with tourists enjoying boating in the river.

She hailed me wearing a jovial smile over her lips.

You might be thinking how she was her appearing, so I tell you, she was not less than a cute full-blown blonde English girl.

As ascetic reached his decided place, I bent and touched his feet. Julia also followed me. Without taking any time, I put up my question.

"Nakedness is not exactly an issue. An ascetic rids of from all vain desires of this mundane world and its transitory pleasure." It seemed as if he was trying to recollect his conscience, closing his eyes gently. "Do you know whom human love most?" he glanced at us, questioning, and later himself answered finding us dubious. "To self."

In my mind, ample things began revolving- Grandma, Meera, my study and Urvashi's face- altogether.

I couldn't stop my curiosity, "How?"

"It's a human tendency, he travels all across the world to grasp what he gives him pleasure, that's a vain endeavor in a vain world. Whereas people are self-comprise of absolute happiness. The man always thinks about himself, whether it is about to attain or resign anything- it's all about self-pleasure. That's why; people poise themselves to attract the commend. Remember, if you are effected from outside, your happiness will be short-termed."

Simultaneously I was interpreting his sermon to Julia.

"If one success to identify his true innate self, the person will forget the world, rid of searching happiness and receives absolute pleasure constantly." The ascetic took his clay conical chillum, blowing dust out of the pipe with a gust of exhaling, clean it with clothes. He undid a bundle, removed few herbs, held that in his palm and crushed it with thumb rubbing it in another palm. It was ganja, cannabis. He continued, "Human is like musk deer, who runs entire jungle to trail the fragrance, albeit the musk is already in the neck of the deer."

He halted threshing cannabis, darted at us. "A man dreams a desirable thing what can provide pleasure to him. When he meets it, the ecstasy converts into twice volume, and when he uses it, the man reaches the culmination of pleasure. But the moment, it passes on, the pleasure also vanishes and gets over."

Now, he blew stalks out of the cannabis, grinding it between his both palms. "And *sadhak*, ascetic doesn't seek pleasure in the outer world because he knows; human soul is spring of absolute pleasure- which is Ultimate. The pleasure that a being receives in intercourse for five, ten or twenty minutes; the same aesthetic, a *sadhak* relishes for the whole day, week, and year. Remember," she stopped grinding. "Absolute pleasure is permanent, eternal and unending. It springs forever."

He stuffed his chillum with cannabis powder, stuffing with a thumb. He put chillum vertical on the floor, ablaze on the top of its chimney, he closed his eyes, murmured something as praying. "Offer everything of your to your God, whoever you believe in, things will turn into a blessing in return." He raised his face upward, set the rear of chillum at his mouth and inhaled strongly, fluctuating breathing in and releasing smoke out. After a long inhale, he retained his breathing and then puffed a thick layer of smock of his mouth, some part of flakes escaped through his nostril soaring leisurely.

Leaving smokes lingered around our noses; Julia fanned it waving her hand a couple of times, in front of her face. I found it sort of fascinating, tended to taste it but couldn't dare.

"Lord Krishna had stolen clothes of *Gopies* when they were bathing in the Yamuna." After relieving another puff, he inserted story of Lord Krishna. "He asked to come out only those Gopies, who were not even least conscious about their physical self, shunning all the vanities, shy, only having complete consciousness of their soul." He again set his fisting hand, entangled chillum between his fingers and drew inside another long breathing of flakes of smoke, restrained it next for few whiles and finally evacuated it slowly. "Do you know who those Gopies were?" He looked at us questing. He waited a while and continued. "They were *sadhak,* ascetic for several births." He paused, pensively. "One day, when God appeared before them, offered them being pleased with their pray, they could ask whatever they wished for. And those *sadhak,* ascetics revealed the utmost wills that they yearned for consummate assimilation-an intercourse of the soul with Ultimate. God smiled and promised them, He would fortune them in Dwapar Age, in the incarnation of Lord Shri Krishna."

Chillum's smoke was titillating to my nostril. I asked permission to try puff. He handed me. At first inhale, I had a series coughing. Julia held from my hand and drew in a long inhale quite professionally. When she snapped the chillum from mouth, I was looking at her face in surprise, and she had a smile at her face. It encouraged me. Afterwards, I attempted a couple of time like a successful mediocre. "And Lord had given all those ascetics, who did *tapasya*, a tough devotion for ages in the form of *Gopies*. And this way, it is famous now as Raas-Leela of Sri Krishna. Every Gopi considered at the moment of Raas, Lord Krishna was playing Raas with her, while Shri Krishna was with everyone synchronically.

Indeed, jealousy is the culmination of love. As I talk about me." He pointed himself. "I always imagine, None loves Lord Shiva, as much as I do and Lord Shiva loves me most. But the truth, He is for everyone. Equally."

"Baba," I faltered with my words. "Don't *sadhak* troubles of baser emotions of lust which is the natural impulse of a human being?"

He smiled, stirred the fire. "A true sadhak transcends oneself from the mundane world. I tell you how." he put an urn full of water by the fire to warm it, to make it drinkable. "Do you know why people need sex?"

I nodded. "Haven't experience." When I interpreted to Julia, she smiled and jerked her head vertical, signed yes.

I shared a smile.

"Sex is a sin, if it is done for just enjoyment, need of the day, but it becomes boon, a blessing if its purpose is greater. Sex is not friction or physical engagement only while it's meeting of two souls which generate an absolute pleasure- incredible. For that much amount of time, the couple doesn't concern anything of the world, not even themselves. Sex is the means of procreation- to continue the creation of God. Remember!" He stressed the word 'remember'. "Sex is the fruit of love, not the root. And a *sadhak* receives this incredible pleasure constantly, not for minutes but for hours, weeks and days after days even. For their intercourse happens with Ultimate through the soul." He looked at us. "Do you know what is the meaning of *sadhak*, ascetic?"

Again I nodded, when I explained her, she uttered, "A *sadhak* who has tamed his senses and lifted his super-conscious level beyond physical existence."

"Absolutely right," said the ascetic. I looked at her, she was smiling.

"If one has intercourse with Ultimate happens, why needs he seek that in this petty world? Why would he go for minutes, if he has enormous, eternal spring of pleasure within?"

I gazed that old man, in shabby appearance, cluster hairs twisted as thin rope. Another time, I looked around people roaming or sitting at the ghat, couple putting their hand over arms of each other. How mediocre or false life here, people lead in ignorance, believing that's ultimate. And such poor-looking ascetic, whom crowd believes wretched, how prosperous he was, I thought.

"People come here in Banaras, searching Lord Shiva. But they are the fool; they search Him in the temple, whereas He is inside everyone. One can't find God in the temple until he finds Him within." He smiled mockingly. "Those who come Banaras to worship Lord Shiva shrine, few get instant busy in abusing municipal fault for foul appearance of the city, few gaze Ghats, few draw a long tika over the forehead, and few clean their dirt in place of their sin in the Ganges. Everybody finds the reason for excuses. Remember, for any decision the man is individually responsible. If one yearns for the right path, God is always there inside of everyone to lead, forever. If you are morally strong, you will be on right track, and if you hear devil, then nobody can save you from destruction. And my dear son! This is an era of acute destruction, need to save self." It seemed as if he was reading my mind.

I astounded over his visionary dialogue and relished the flavour of cannabis occasionally. I grasped his sermon, but never yielded to his sentences. There could be many overt and covert reasons. I found an escape spending time with him. I set a good tuning with Julia and the ascetic's metaphysic and mystic talks.

I was continuing disparaging Urvashi and her lingering image from my mind, maligning myself in the smokes of cannabis. The more, I tried to make her incongruous and anachronous, the more my heart synchronized her. Now, she had occupied my mind and heart in my most of the time, even though I tried all the ways to expel her memory from my mind. I was turning hollow, dying within being away and hurting her. I realized.

I roamed with Julia, guide her about Banaras. On Sunday, I spent most of the time with her, used to go boating every evening. Recently, she shifted her guest house, at the adjacent of the ghat, so, we spent our evening in front of her hotel.

Once, such a right evening, we were sitting together under the pale light of the lamppost. A vendor passed by us, yelling 'tea…hot tea"

"Would you like to have Banarasi tea?" asked I.

She looked at me bizarre, glanced at the vendor who had muffled his head wrapping a thick woolen shawl.

The vendor poured tea into *kulhad. Kulhad*, it brought back memory spent with Urvashi at the ghat, sipping lemon tea.

She took out a cigarette packet from her pocket, ransacked lighter thrusting her hands into her pockets, front-back-side and fumbled her jacket. She stopped a while, thought something as she recalled some forgotten thing.

She put the front of the cigarette into coal fire of the grate. Her cigarette was quite unique, unlike I smoked previously. It was a long black pencil alike.

Since I tasted cannabis flavour, I stopped blocking my nose to elude odor of smoking. She looked at me once as if she was asking me 'would you like to try a puff?'

I imitated her taking sips of tea afterwards inhaling a cigarette.

There happened an abrupt and suddenness in the surrounding. Something terrible and chaotic scene happened that evening which staggered me from within, when, out of nowhere, a muscular bulky Banarasi bull arrived there swaying across the gathering at Ghats, nonchalantly strolling on. Assemblage scattered in undirected directions. Before we sensed the reason of pandemonium state in the crowd, the bull reached to us.

I pushed Julia aside but lost my balance and fell in the Ganges.

Ah! I was in the chilled water; it seemed as if thousands of spears were piercing in my body. I was frizzing. I tried hard to hold the cluttering teeth, endeavored to steady my respiratory. I choked.

The bill passed on disappeared in the mist. Julia came nearby the edge of the stairs, spread her hand for help and pulled me out. I was shivering like hell.

"O my God!" I could understand whether she was grieving or exclaiming. "You are drenched and dripping."

Stepping up the ascending stairs of the ghat, she took me to her hotel. She unlocked the door. She assisted me unbuttoning my woolen jacket, laden with water, stripped my shirt off. She brought a towel and told me to pull out my pachyderm jeans pant.

She, applying a cotton apron, attempted to drain out moisture from my head, dragging all across my body. I was helpless to imagine anything at that moment.

She flung dripping clothes into the bathroom, asked me to crawl into bed. I unbuttoned my pant, too, with trembling hands, wrapped towel by the waist. I was still tremendously shivering. I glided into her chunky luxurious bed, pulled over a quilt- a thick but light in weight. I passed sniffing after an interval.

I coiled my whole length of body, swaddled quilt around, fetched folding feet into the pit of the belly, curving back and set head near the chest. Still, my insane trembling with the cold didn't stop, though.

I felt Julia crawled down inside the bed, clutched me tightly, enclose my naked anatomy into her affable, warm arms. I didn't stir next for several minutes.

Ten, twenty, thirty minutes passed. Cold dwindled, hit generated. A biological change I sensed as her palms rowing over my limbs, made sensitized. A sort of squashy dragging from my back stopped lingering around my neck, turning my phony respiratory into never experienced homey sighing. The cold glassier inside slowly began melting, and I felt warmness under the cover.

I turned my face to her. Now, she was before the very eyes of me. The aura experienced a transformation of feeling. Gently, she pushed my shoulder, made me flat and mounted over me. She clutched my face between her both hands, smiling with her beaming eyes, caressing her both fingers dragging softly over cheeks. She held my lips between her, quite like those naked images, played on the laptop that night in the hostel.

She dragged her palms and lips as if they measured my every limb, counting every inch. Every fur of my body filled with rupture. We began sweating, she threw chunky quilt aside. Amazing. She appeared quite like any pretty blonde girl. I found her undressed physic as any mermaid or nymph in the white tube-light. I had seen European reel beauty only on screen, now it was before me, hypnotized. Being overflowed with amorous senses, tips of my fingers sojourned gliding through ebbs and flows of her smooth, geography. Eyes were closed in ecstasy.

"Let it flow on."

"Sorry," said I.

Suddenly, my eyes were opened, I struck away parting my lips from her, and still, the foggy puffs of our breathing were at a pace which could be felt stroking on our faces.

My consciousness was stricken as I closed my eyes. I envisaged if Urvashi would be cheating at my back? I shuddered.

"What happen?" said she. Still, she was over me. I could feel her acute soft, seductive curvy figure.

"I can't. It is sin," said I, apologetically. She was utterly perplexed at my sudden, changed feeling.

"What can't?" she baffled. "What do you mean?"

"I can't deceive her. Sorry."

"Who?" she probed. "Your girlfriend?"

I affirmed.

"Then, what is the problem? I also have a boyfriend in Britain."

"But I can't." I regretted.

"I respect your feeling, man." She alighted over from me, relieved me of her burden and put on her dresses.

She went out of the room and came back after half an hour. She had shopping bags full of packed food, clothes and medicines.

"Oh! Sorry, I have forgotten to take undergarment for you," said she, holding her lips under her teeth.

She commenced to say wearing a slight smile on her lips after a while of speculation, "if you haven't any problem; you can use mine, which is quite new."

"Why would I? Who is going to see your inside?" I reverted with a smile? "Bring it if you hadn't leaked."

Chapter 15

"Urvashi is not participating in Spandan," said Kamal, staring me like culprit. Don't know to whom he was accused of this- to himself or to me?

Spandan is the annual function of the university.

"Then what?" Rehan said, entered the room, holding cups of tea in both hands. He offered me one of the cups. He darted at Kamal, "*Oye*, go and take your cup from the kitchen."

"Bhai. Urvashi is three times winner in Spandan dance event, in her graduation days. But her withdrawing her name will give opportunity to new girls from the department. Art faculty is Dynamite faculty."

I heard Dynamite word often used by Art students.

"I have seen her all the time. She is marvelous in dance," said Rehan. I paused, contemplating. He continued. "One thing I don't understand why she turns so benevolent suddenly and withdrew her participation." Suddenly, seeing Kamal still etherized as patient haphazardly in the bed, he mocked. "Indeed, you are a perfect asshole of a sloth."

"*Le bhosari ke*." He leaped out of bed. "I'm going now."

I protested over their frequently used abusive slang in their talk. Kamal chuckled. "It's a sign of love and compassion in friendship." Rehan trailed his smile. "If two Banarasi friend stops using slang, understand there is something wrong in their friendship."

His cell phone danced at the table. He picked it up, put a finger at his lips to instruct us to keep quiet. "It's Abu's call."

" Aadab Abu!" "Hmm", "When?" "Where?" He put his phone down on the table and turned toward us. "It's Abbu." The expression of their faces changed into the grave and worried.

"You poise the room. I'm going to receive him, lest he misses the rout of this lodge. He hasn't come here yet." Rehan rushed out, went down through the stairs as if his feet were flying with the wind.

Kamal began winding up scattered plates, cups and fetched them into the kitchen. He set cleane-washed blanket. "His Abbu doesn't like haphazard appearance. He prefers to look the thing in organize manner. He often says to Rehan seeing his unorganized room, cleanliness is also a service toward God. it's also *imaan*."

"Then, I think I must go," I said, rising to go.

"Why? No need. Just relax. He is sort of good man," said he, assuring me. "He won't stay for a long while."

"Why?" said I.

"He often comes to see Rehan who is the only boy out of his five children." Adjusting scattered books into shelves, he said to me. "He had given her daughter a sound education." He chuckled. "He also likes reading the scripture of all religion. Whenever he visits Banaras to see Rehan,, he usually goes at *Sankat Mochan* and chanted *Ram Charit Manas* with gathering."

"Sankat Mochan temple?" I amazed.

"One of Rehan's sisters is PCS officer," said he.

We alarmed with the approaching tramp sound thumping over the adjoining stairs.

His father had worn the long curly beard, mehndi colored, worn white *kurta* and *pajama* and colored head with a white cap, he got into the room placidly. He flipped his backside of kurta before he placed down over the bed.

They behaved so tame and gentle before him, busied in his hospitality.

He asked about me.

"He is Siddhartha, my classmate," Rehan said.

He began his investigation about Rehan's study. To see a chirpy Rehan transformed into a silent tame boy was a wonderful sight. I felt laughing inside but thwarted it somehow within.

I saw a green wrapper lay dawn near me. As Kamal entered having a tray contained *namkeen,* biscuits, and teacups. Kamal put down the tray on the table.

" Kamal, how is your study?" he inquired.

"It's going good uncle," said Kamal.

"Try to counsel him too that there is no scope for him in literature. He is no impact of my words." He picked up cup, took a sip. "How long I have been trying to make him understanding, pursue MBA. He has already established the business. He is only son, and I'm getting old now." As he preceded his statement, there was pathos in his tone.

I picked up a small packet. Before I read scripted words over the wrapper and prolonged my hands toward them, inquiring about it, Kamal, who was standing by me, snatched it from my hand like lightning in heavy rain, stealthily thrashed the pouch into the pocket of his pant. And meanwhile, Rehan kept his father busy in gossip. I didn't understand why they were so horrified.

I witnessed a sign of relief over their face as he moved out of the room.

"You were to fuck me before my father," said Rehan.

"How?" I perplexed.

"You might inquire about that packet later."

"What the hell was that?" I lost my patience finally. "I thought, I must ask him whether it was a medicine, which was fallen down unknowingly."

"Don't you know what that was?" asked Rehan, gravely looking at me.

"No." I shook head into no. "I was to read the product name, he snatched from my hand," said I, complaint.

Kamal put the packet on my palm. They were seriously observing my reaction suppressing their smile.

I saw some seductive image printed over its wrapper," I read, "…, strawberry flavor." I blubbered. "What the fuck."

They burst into insane laughter and kept on for a longer time; even I couldn't control my smile.

After a week struggle, I succeed to settle my lodging at Asi Ghat, next to Ganges River. It was on the third floor of an old house owned by a Banarasi Brahmin family. From the balcony, the picturesque view of widespread Ghats and drifting boats over the stream could detain anyone's attention.

Julia urged to visit my department to meet my friends, especially to Urvashi.

One such a fine day, I invited her before she left India for her home country. Her limply acute white skin brought a change in the aura of the surrounding. Everyone became curious to see a blonde girl live. Julia gave them a gentle smile in return, shook head in reverence, saying namaskar.

She asked about Urvashi, whispering while strolling toward the classroom.

"I'm not going to tell you who is she? Where is she? You will have to recognize her in the crowd."

"I was excited to see what's unique in her, who had stopped an Indian lad to fall in the arm of a beautiful blonde." She whispered scrutinizing, moving faces across the corridor.

"Good Luck," I said.

I introduced her to Head of Department. She delineated him briefly about her three years research whiling living in India. We asked his permission for interaction with the students taking the session.

We halted in the corridor in front of the classroom, where students were gathering slowly for receiving lecture. They were my classmates, I introduced her to them. Suddenly she snapped middle of her conversation, walked toward Urvashi, who had put on her favorite attire, *Anarkali* style white suit hanging down like bell to her ankle. She looked like a mermaid in the white dress with certain quietness over face and curly locks placing over across her shoulders and back. Her eyes were lonely.

I yearned to hug her at the moment I caught her sight and whisper in her ears those three magical words. Although it was just two months, it seemed like an era had passed without her. I missed bitterly spending the hour with her at Sunset Adda.

Living away from her, I realized, I got more closure to her soul.

Julia's exotic beauty became the centre of everyone's attention. Even other department's students started coming to a pleasing glimpse of her, but mine was busy with Urvashi.

I recalled my memory of the first glimpse of her face, I had seen her in the train, that I appreciated her taciturnly. She was sitting by the window seat, gazing outside as if lost in memory looking stagnant, her hair flying back. Honestly, that time, I didn't imagine she would talk to me ever or sit with me. She seemed alien. I gazed her to relish the aesthetic through the window of my heart- both eyes.

Even I gazed her still bereft, giving her any clue as I was doing now. Within ten minutes, Julia and Urvashi both seemed like a close friend as they knew each other for a long time. They were chattering, chuckling sometimes and sharing smiles frequently. I didn't know what chemistry happened between them.

Urvashi's eyes caught me stealthily looking her; I shuddered, hesitatingly glanced to and fro to avert her when she watched me tilting her head from the side of Julia's shoulder. I was scared, Julia might tell, our guest house incident.

First time I saw a smile over her lips since I separated from her.

Tomorrow is just a fictional world until it happens. It happens in reality when it takes the shape of your idea brooding in your mind.

I don't know vigorous was the thought to be with her when I saw her on the train. She was just a dream- a reverie, but there was an invisible epiphany between us which was now the reality.

Now, I had a story with the same girl, I imagined once, to tell the world. Imagining, it made me overwhelmed, startled sometimes and by speculating this, I used to find an incredible pleasure.

But sometimes melancholic tone overcast deeply in my conscience since I stopped meeting her and checked my vagabond feet, roaming around the city and brooding at Sunset Adda.

To be worried about something is good, but too much worried might turn wrong.

Still, I could not decide why I had stopped talking to her- either to do better in the semester exam, which had taken a different course or somewhere I felt jealous to her well off background. I maintained a gap just to satiate my unconscionable heart. Oft, I felt to commute with her my most profound feeling, but my 'I'- egoism- used to come between.

Julia and Urvashi still had been chatting solemnly; jovial mien could be seen over their face.

As the clock struck ten, gradually students began moving into the class. Dr Mishra came in and introduced about Julia and requested her to mount over dais and spoke something about her research on Sanskrit, Indian Language and Culture.

As she started, culminated and the way she ended her speech, it had captivated the minds of the students, stuffed in the classroom. Their eyes broaden to realize how less they knew about their own country, culture and language.

After the dispersal of the session, I dropped Julia at the gate. I called a rickshaw wallah, who was taking nap sprawling at the back seat.

"Thank you," said she, added further, wryly. "And I will suggest you… being a friend." she put her palm over my right chest. "Mend the wall. Reconcile with her. She is a nice girl.

Once I got irritated about her when you deny me in the bed that evening, reaching the shore of pleasure. I understand how hard it was to you to yield yourself in my arms. But I was wrong. I can understand now why you had snapped me. She deserves honesty."

Though I nodded in affirmation, yet I knew it was not easy for me to mend it. My ego had made it more complex.

To knock down the wall of egoism plastered with stereotypical self-esteem is like cracking a nutshell.

And the rickshaw wallah drove her away.

I didn't know which mantras Urvashi had chanted in her ears that she began her advocacy.

I was grateful for her coming, which had enhanced popularity and impression in the eyes creatures of departments.

And most cheerful things happened. I took rid of from 'Chindi & Co.' for which I was hearty grateful to Kamal and Rehan, who helped me in searching and shifting of my lodging.

The room was on the third floor of the mansion, close to Assi Ghat. If I opened wooden window, I found flowing streams of Ganges, below the window of my room. The ray of morning sun woke me up, and white moon bid me goodnight.

Rehan and Kamal, being allured, sometimes stayed at my room. Kamal cooked cheese which used to be delicious and compelling, Rehan baked bread, and I usually knead the flour. Having dinner, we mount over the terrace of the last floor and spent time using jape in Banarasi slang, sitting at the edge of the roof dangling our feet down till late night.

I preferred to spin my hour alone, scribbling sometimes my inmost in the diary or laid down etherized in bed, sprawling books all around in the room and that day, the room stuffed with cigarette's but and smokes.

The whole room reeked with despicable stink, which could trouble if ever anyone non-smoking creature entered my room. It troubled them.

I used to cram some selected master answer which I paste in the exam. And most of the time either I imagined Urvashi, who seemed soothing as the sunlight in winter, inhaling poisonous smoke, sitting in the balcony, gazing panorama of Ghats and creeping manly creatures and flows of curvy Ganges river.

Or I read my favourite books or wrote poetry in memory of her or I gazed the widespread sandy bank across the river.

True love has no break-up. Love is totally abstract and flexible, which could be measured in the eyes and with the beating of the heart. Scrupulously, if you desire to check the honest love, you get annoyed once, pretending. The people who love you will come to you, if you matter for them.

The true love doesn't know forgetfulness; there is no delete button in its system- no break up once if it's connected. Whereas the colour of emotion for next gets profound as time passes. And then, loneliness becomes the best music which one seeks everywhere- even if he or she is surrounded by a throng of people.

Time passed. The communicational gap widened which one could discern with the way of her looking at me and mine at her.

As the news of our separation spread in campus, as sharply as the fire in the hilly jungle in summertime, a number of suitors roamed around her and continually tried to woo her but all in vain. But it troubled her.

Bhanu Singh was such sort of candidate, who loitered around her and didn't leave any chance to woo her.

I heard he followed her and trailed her throughout way going back to hostel, garrulous, which used to irritate her. Sometimes, I made me rigid like stone, ignored him, seeing him trying to persuade her. And every time her helpless glance cast at me, as if she was accusing, that made me enraged, but I controlled my insanity.

Love is the most delicate relationship on the planet. You can take your chance to persuade your counterpart but can't compel to yield your counterpart for your proposal. Form and definition might be varied person to person, but one thing remains common between two souls, that they are the sense of renunciation, compassion and silence connotation.

One after a fine morning class, he exceeded the limits, water raised above my nose, overflew when he blocked her passage, urging her to accept his rose. I was watching his melodrama standing far like others. Rehan and Kamal approached just that moment, stood beside me. His drama rose to the cathartic state for her when he held her hand, she looked at me brimming eyes.

She snatcher hand from his grip and came to me sluggishly.

"It's because of you." Hardly had she spoken these panic words, she stopped as if somebody had choked her vocal. She rushed away, wiping her tears restraining her sobs.

I felt as my head was burning like fire in anger. I couldn't control myself for that moment. I went to him and set a fierce punch over his nose abruptly and knocked him down.

For a while, he didn't understand lied down on the floor. I gave him a hard kick at him, which twisted him with a surge of pains. He screamed abusing.

Rehan and Kamal grabbed me stopping. Everyone stood still like spectator. After a few seconds, he stood up and balanced himself and was to attack me, Rehan and Kamal came between. Kamal warned him when he was spitting abuses over me. "How dare this bastard hit me?" he yelled, wiping blood oozing out of his nose.

"Look… move from here. Nor we will start," said Rehan, shuffled toward him.

"And one thing more…from today, dare not to look even from the corner of your eyes at Urvashi." Kamal threatened him.

Chapter 16

Proctorial Board suspended me for brawling in the department for one week with the warning letter. And those suspended days transformed me something more strange that I had never been.

Now, my desire to go back home dwindled. At least in those suspended days, I engaged in several things and resigned from the crowd.

I collected some of the authors' works like Nicholas Spark's The Notebook, Gayle Forman's If I Stay and its sequel, Charlotte's Jane Eyre, Emily Bronte's Wuthering Height, Murakami's Kafta on The Shore, Fitzgerald's The Great Gatsby and Hindi author, Dharmaveer Bharti's Gunaho Ka Devta, prominent. I went on leafing pages of the books puffing out whirling smokes, through rounding lips. Later on, I turned from classic love story to thriller, mystery genre books to Love Poetry of Rumi and Galib.

And I experienced, my internal philosopher still swerved.

I sprawled in the chair, setting in the balcony, gazing flows of the river and smoked cigarette, sometime chillum hectically. The butts of the cigarette were rolled all around the room- its corner, behind the door, in the balcony, everywhere.

Once upon a time, the stink of smoking I did not allow to pass by my nose, now it was imbued into the air of my room. A *kabadiwala*, scrap dealer could earn good amount, if he would collect all the butts, cans and wine bottle and sell it in the market. My lethargic fuselage did not let strike my conscience against sweeping at least once in a day, or three days or in weeks.

Everything of my life derailed from the fastidious life of hostel before I shunned Urvarshi from my life- either was it bathing, washing clothes or sweeping of the room.

I managed my meal at friends room or hostel mess. I hadn't trimmed my hairs, nor did I shave my creepy beard. I was habitual of living in filthy state; I couldn't recognize my impending hellish transformation. I most of the time remained anaesthetized in the cozy chair.

The easiest recipe for lunch or dinner what I did; I used to wash rice, then pearls and put together them mixing salt, species, chopped onion and other ingredients into the cooker and let the gas open. I never came to know what I should entitle that recipe.

Three works I had decided- either I read books off my wish list, or crammed some selected notes based on previous years question paper, or brooding Urvarshi blankly looking across the river from the height of balcony.

My perspective toward exam was changed. For me gaining marks was just a matter of skill. I discerned one thing. Clearly, you are stronger if you are counted on paper, nor are you just somebody else walking like the dummy in the crowd. The biggest fallacy of this mundane modern world, your success is the game of statics.

I met the professor whom I had seen serving an injured ox and set a good tuning with him. Afterwards, often he made me sit in the back seat of his scooter and drove to treat stray animals. Doing such benevolence deed, humility awakened inside me. I began enjoying it. Cleaning and bandaging the wounds of the mute creatures helped me to deplete the negativity I had sowed inside me. I learned and realized their pain within.

How much it is painful if somebody can't explain one's agony to the world. Thinking it, I used to feel guilty of hurting Urvashi sometimes.

Frequently I visited ascetic to inhale lucrative marijuana and puffed out my consciousness with its revolving smokes and roamed with Julia in winding Banarasi streets and Ghats. I lost my wakefulness partly after taking it - lost in sheer oblivion state; I arrived those days at the room after staggering over many obscure steps.

I hung on Julia's study about Banaras, its labyrinthine streets, culture and its chronicles, canon, which stunned me. She had enhanced horizon of my knowledge about the universe through the lance of Banaras.

Frequently, we visited Sarnath together.

Julia was a devotee of Lord Shiva, had told me many tales from scriptures about Him. She loved meditation. She played the *tabala*- an Indian hand drum, harmonium and flute so dexterously. It used to be an enlightened moment to see her sitting with saints and musing hymn.

But I moved like a waif, like a man who is without a home, like a man who has lost all hope, like a man who knows not anything about his self, like a man who is doomed.

I used to visit at Manish in his hostel room, when others were taking their class, receiving lectures. I took keys of Manish's room and use the internet on his laptop.

University had blocked all unwanted sites- erotic, Facebook, Twitter and other social media.

One day, I found a list of erotic sites on a friends' laptop. Initially, I could not understand, but the moment I typed it in Google search, it popped up 'error'. I found Google Chrome-like app, but it was not Chrome. I searched the site, some pornography web pages popped up. Next click ran the video. I became punctual to watch it, almost every day, whenever I found solitary confinement. I began wasting hours afterwards.

My total retirement from the department for a week had discredited my memory from the mind of my class fellow. I forgot to wish Urvarshi's birthday. Perhaps, my ego might not allow it. But it crossed the limit when I forgot my own birthday.

It was one beautiful February morning when somebody knocked at my door promptly, after an interval. I was drowsy.

"Come in. It's already open," said I, idly, without moving any slight. I remain still sprawling in the chair. The door glided slowly inside with the sizzle rattling.

I looked turning slightly back from the balcony into the room, without leaving my place a bit

“Who is...?” I stopped successive words in surprise.

Urvashi was standing at the threshold. Seeing her countenance, I could understand, the stink of the room was intolerable to her. She was looking around in bafflement seeing the littered room. She circumvented with the surrounding.

She had a box in her hand poised, covered with shining paper. It was the gift, I guessed.

“Hi,” said she delightedly. There was a forceful smile over her face. Her eyes were silent, travailed. She added, “Wish you a very happy birthday to you.”

“Thank you,” I said, after a pause of having self-rumination. I didn’t stir a bit from my place. I was mounted over the culmination of arrogance.

“What have you made this room?” said she, looking around. She behaved so normally as if nothing happened between us.

She put boxes on the bed, held the broom and started sweeping. She rearranged my scattered books, tackled cloth and hung them on the hanger. Within a few minutes, she had changed the filthy state into the immaculate texture of my room.

It was my first birthday occasion in Banaras, and she came to celebrate it in my room. I didn’t show warmness at her arrival. I stood up, took clothes, moved to the bathroom to change it. I was just demonstrating I was moving out and had no impact of her presence over there, completely indifferent. But in truth, it was unlike that.

“I’ve to go somewhere?” I murmured.

“It’s your birthday. I came to celebrate it with you,” said she, voicing in a low tone. She pulled the strips out from the box and began unwrapping its cover.

“Am I a beggar?” I sounded arrogant. “Do I need your sympathy?” My grimacing had rendered her bitterly. Big warm drops began rolling down her maiden cheeks. I continued my harsh tone, enjoying being sadistic in words but forbore abyss pain within parallel. “I don’t like any kind of relationship with you. What the hell is your problem?" I was louder now. "I've my dream. I don't want to spoil myself and my time behind you."

"It's ok," said she, stopping her hysteric sobs, wiping tears from cheeks. If you don't want to face me, I promise, I won't come before you, if you are thinking, I may harm your life." She picked the keys of her scooty, suddenly stopped her walking steps before snapping at the gate. "If possible, save yourself from the nemesis that you have a pet inside you."

She left the room, slamming the door behind her. The volcano of pain erupted in the arena of my heart. I remained there, still, motionless. Fainted clattering of her tramps' sound throbbed into my ears.

If you haven't experienced the ecstasy of pain in love, you haven't experienced anything marvelous while breathing is this world.

Following days, Rehan and Kamal fell into an altercation with me, taking the side of Urvashi. I decided to fuck the world off.

Be careful. Your best friend can be the most equivocating creature for you in college days; like those two scoundrels, who applauded me on wooing a metropolitan girl, as if I had won any champion trophy. Then one evening, one of them, became my good wisher and advised not to be so mingled with her because she was unlike us -a daughter of the rich father.

And now they were standing at her side.

I started attending class. Being junior, our class was going to organize a farewell party for seniors. So, the class had decided a gathering in Radhakrishnan Hall, for making a plan on how to organize farewell.

Anyway, I also followed them silently. Mostly I remained disconnected from the class, busied in writing something, sitting aloof of them.

Rehan had entitled our class - MNAREGA group of students. There were many students who had excelled in pinchpenny. If it were not mattered of reputation and some sanguine participants' effort, they would decline farewell to save their petty money-notably, a band of girls. The more, they possessed beauty and charm, equally, they were niggard.

I was sitting around three to four chairs away as I had made myself excommunicated from them. Didn't know, when they carted their discourse from farewell planning to summer vacation trip.

In fact, my class was divided into two parts- local and urban, one could detect at first glance entering into the class. The elite class was talking about foreign countries; they were to go with their family. Some of them were talking about some finest place of country- Shimala, Ladakh, Ooty and Darjeeling. And for idyllic, they knew to spend summer days sitting in their cottage with rustic folks, sharing jokes was a best entertaining package.

Pummy spoke out gladly, "Urvashi is going Switzerland with her family." Just next she realized the slip of her tongue, said apologetically. "Sorry, she had forbidden me not to tell it, anyone."

"Hey Siddhartha," out of the garrulous crowd, somebody paid attention to me. "Where are you going?"

I checked my scribbling hand, recalling, "My Home."

None ever any girl in my life had overtaken my imagination as much as she did. Literally, if I say she had hijacked my imagination, I wouldn't be exaggeration. The more I tried to be arrogant towards her, the more I was drawn hollow within the self. In those spare hours, I thought her while walking by roads, moving in the streets, travelling in trains, digging my eyes into books and communicating to people. I was drawing closer to what I tried to shun.

Interesting, sometimes we drove quite far to prove us judicial from where standing it becomes tough to turn back.

I was turned isolated. I felt lonely.

I failed to understand the secret language of terrible love.

If it happens it happens, no power can eradicate or kill it. It sojourns through eternity for it is a journey of souls, fueled by emotions. I learned what is invisible it's endurable and goes endless and visible things are transient. Even I failed to recognize the voice of her heart that used to commute to mine and mine convey to her in that separation period.

There was something there invisible between us honestly passing on, floating on. I lost so many things and several important people in my life, and I learned certain thing, once it's gone, will never return. I had made an arch wall of my self-seeking escorting and restricting me to knock it down.

Mostly, I spent my summer holiday reading my favourite collection of books and harvesting wheat crops, but this summer, vocation underwent in agonizing.

Her absence in my life sprouted a new mannerism that I started scribbling down the humdrum loneliness of my inside world vigorously. Writing in the diary, I felt as if I had been talking her, and it reclined my aching heart which carrying a pang, anonymous, unexpected and clandestine.

Chapter 17

Everyone had taken paths of their homeland after the second semester examination.

Harvesting was done; grain shacks were piled in the granary. One could see villages easily, across the translucent field, at the periphery of the outstretched open field. The folks led their cattle grazed tuft, rambling freely in the fields, they placed them under the banyan trees at a high earthen mould and had been watching their grazing pets, chattering common talks being free from stray of their cattle.

Every day early morning having breakfast, I, too, held my only cow and her heifer and joined the band of rustic folks, assembled at outskirt of the village at the pond.

The kids played games, old busied in their maxims, women discussed the domestic issues happened in their respective neighboring, few lads wandering to and fro in the field without sleeper, having a big sack, picked up left broken crops scattered in the field. Few lasses were searching dried cow dung, collecting in their bucket for fuel, held resting at their waist.

The boys engaged in playing various games - such as a boy flung a log away, another one rushed to fetch it. Other meanwhile climbed over the trees and hopped from branch to branch trying not to be touched by the boy who was beneath the tree, freed from cattle's stray whereas they were grazing grass leisurely.

I recalled the days of the adolescent when I used to take my cattle. Sometimes I had to spin my whole day grazing cows due to the scarcity of husks.

As the sun came over the head, either Meera or Grandma relieved me, giving recession that I could have bathed and lunch. Soon I returned and stayed by the evening until all the grazers returned to their homes. The cattle used to come under the trees, sit and kept ruminating.

Bhairavnath, a villager, accompanied me, sang folk songs beating a small drum.

And I took a nap and meanwhile he used to look after my cattle.

When I had to bath cow and her heifer, I tied them with stems near the pond, for they could not run away. They hopped with every sprinkle of water, whereas, quite opposite, buffaloes enjoyed rowing in the pond for hours, enraptured and ruminated as chewing something.

Oft I mounted over her back and rowed across the pond.

Grandma used to tell when she came into the village, being as a wife of Grandpa, people used to use water from the pond for drinking and cooking food.

Perhaps, I would tell my fourth generation, people used to bathe in the pond. For now, we avoid water of the pond to use for anything, except for sanitary, bathing cattle and irrigation.

Manohar Pandey gave thump down for irrigation supply to our field. Crops began getting withered. It was our sole source of earning, it was faltering now. Manohar pandey was the owner of the irrigation machine near our farms. Chhottani told me, his motive behind it was to stop our vegetable farming and began his own.

Taking out monthly expenditure, we could save some surplus cutting from our daily expenditure. It had helped us a lot.

Chhottani grieved more than me. He pleaded Manohar, ran behind him and even he offered him to pay more than other farmer but remained adamant.

I asked Chottani not to plead him time and again. It was so insulting.

Grandma had saved little money-saving one, two, three, rupees after her expenses. She was not well for weeks. I realized she was losing her health. Meera told me that her coughing turned diabolic in the night and she troubled a lot. She let not her to inform me, for she didn't want to disturb me during the exam.

When I imagined about me, I found me culprit of many - an acute selfish, an egoist and high conceited. Though people around me loved me, cared me and remained generous, in return, I always failed to equal them.

I thought not to spend my vacation in idleness. I packed up my bag, caught passenger train and backed to Varanasi next morning which was unexpected for Meera and Grandma too. Before third semester began, I arbitrated to earn some money for the coming days.

I didn't find any job. I ran a lot bereft bothering of morning, afternoon or evening, or it was burning sun or cloudy days. I visited petrol pumps, shops, coaching centre even but it was no use.

One early morning, I reached Maldahiya Chauraha, saw a throng of people-laymen, spread around waiting for a client. I went, stood among them. Suddenly I felt somebody, patted over my shoulder. The face seemed familiar; I stressed at my mind but couldn't recognize where I met him.

"Don't you remember me, brother? ... Bhulanpur station? …that evening….waiting for the train? ..hmm.?" He was curiously looking over my face waiting for my memory restored.

"Yes. Yes." I smiled, greeted him. Further, he inquired the reason for my being there. This time he was more jubilant.

"I need a job," I told him.

"Bhai," he smiled. "This place is not for you. It won't suit you. You are an educated person. Your search of your type; leave this for us like an illiterate laborer."

"I need money, and I've no job. I will be thankful if you can help me anyhow." I pleaded for him.

" *Arey Nahi bhaiya*, no ...no," said he, holding my hand. "You are making me embarrassed. It's ok. I will see something for you but..." Hesitating, he said. "How will you do it? It is not an easy task."

"Brother," said I, assuring him. "I am a farmer's lad."

He gave an approving smile, briskly walked toward assemblage along with others where a car just stopped.

It was my first day at the site. It was my first experience of earning money. It was the first experience of my physical, but titillating ache flew in every limb of my body. I was exhausted and fell etherizing on the bed. My clothes were shabby, smashed with sweat and soil.

Rehan was in Banaras. Knowing, he came to my room. I was not in the state to ask him for water even. I was completely tired. I asked him to squeeze my shoulders which brought me a heavenly bliss. Being relaxed, my eyes were closing.

"Rehan," I said.

"Hmm," said he, rubbing down my back, pressing through the fingers tips.

"Have you girlfriend?" said I

"Yes," said he. "So many."

"What do you mean by so many?" said I, moaning of relaxation.

"I love somebody since I got conscious, but she is not in the list of 'so many'," said he.

"You are equivocating the fact," I mumbled. "How can you be honest with one simultaneous busy with others too?"

"Look dear. There are two types of girl. The first one who bakes your bed and another who bake your bread. Former when you are in lust, later people believe their possession... First one quenches her and your fleshy thirst. The second one sacrifices herself for your comforts, slavishly and sheepishly. But the concept of love is different. It liberates souls."

"Don't those girls have a problem that you flirt with many more simultaneously?"

"Yeah, mostly knows it. Yesterday night I was with one such girl. She was in my lap and talking to her boyfriend on the phone." He got down, drank water and had given me too. He wiped his dripping mouth. "Yesterday, she asked how many girlfriends I have been engaged. I put a proposal before her. With every revealing, she would plant a kiss. And as I started unfolding the list of the names, she amazed and rode over me. She was gleeful." He took oil anointed my head.

"Don't you think you are cheating on them?" I said.

"No. I don't feel guilty," said I. " Brother, everyone is cheating on somebody at a time- girlfriend, parents, friends, boss, sometimes self to self." He changed his intonation. "The world is nasty and naked inside. If you dare to uncover it, you will see the ugliness of people," said he.

"What about the girl to whom you love?" asked I.

"She has married somebody else. Last month, she had come to her father house and do you know how she has introduced her kid to me?"He was looking at me chuckled and fail to hide his despair, being failed in love. "She told her child that I was her brother in front of her husband." He rubbed his eyes as if something was itching inside, but I knew he was hiding his flunk in love.

To conquer your love from the world is tougher war, than winning in Kargil. And hiding tears behind the frail smile is a common story of guys broken in love. What the hell wrong with you, if you win, you will be prized with mangalsutra, pious thread that ties in lifelong marriage and if you are the misfortune, the rakhi, a holy thread, that proclaims you her brother.

"You are lucky if you success to own and marry the girls you have loved. Mostly it has been seen that people lose the girl who has stolen their comfort of soul." He centred the point of his dialogue at me. "So I tell you if somebody loves you, don't lose her. We are always trying to prove us a gentleman guarding ourselves by making a wall of vanity around us, which consists of social taboos, self-made sugar-coated ethics- whereas the truth is different."

That day, Rehan was indifferent touch. He went on overflowing of his thoughts. "We have set a sensor when? Where? How?

What to do? Everyone has a cost to be sold, somebody sells their flesh for some rupees. Somebody gets charmed by personalities. Some falls in love at first sight." Suddenly he was almost stopped. "Don't you think you are hurting yourself by hurting Urvashi?"

I tried to escape his question, all the way I could.

"Look at yourself and ask the question to yourself whatever you are doing with her is it right. There are some few lucky people who are fortunate enough to own such love...and you are one of them," said he, mildly. "There are hundreds of handsome boys, roaming around her in campus and they are much better than you and me -bourgeois boys. But she has chosen you. Sure if you are not going to accept her, somebody else will own her. And she had to yield until or unless. But I tell you there is a cost of everyone, maybe the price is differing. It's not too late. Accept her. She is truly in love with you. I have seen in her eyes a pious intensity for you. I don't know what's the matter happened between both of you, but it can be restored only by you. No third person can do anything between you."

"How can you be so certain about her?" asked I.

"Her scribble at the back page of the notebook, I read one day. And it was only her handwriting," said he, adding further. "I had noticed sometime her bulged eyes. When I asked the reason for swelling up of her eyes, she pretended, it was an infection - that infection is you, man."

The more one tries to show oneself stronger in love, but nobody knows how feeble and fragile the person becomes covertly. The more one turns taciturn toward the world, the more they become garrulous within-a self- talking- carrying an internal struggle. Then if you get success to cross your 'I'-means ego- and speak your heartfelt to your soul mate, it brings blessing to you.

"Beauty and virtue don't go together. If it is found somewhere together, it's rarest of rare. And Urvashi is such a species."

He held my palm, pulled fingers, they sound as he gave jerk. "Destiny doesn't favour everyone to fetch a person in life-especially the person you love. Sometimes people find the soul, but loose body. And if anyhow they get success to bring a storm sensation in the body of your bed-mate, they might find themselves a failure in conquering their soul-mates soul."

Soon I realized my stomach requires food, not winding speeches. I was hungry and hadn't taken anything throughout days. I was not in the condition to cook anything, so I put on a cloth and dropped Rehan at Hyderabad gate and walked to a vendor.

After Herculean task of the day, imagining about food, it brings sweetness.

An old lady was moving shops to shops, begging money, fetching her hand to her mouth and stomach that she was hungry. Her lining wrinkled face, withered hand, curved back as like bow, which reminded me of my Grandma's face. I was tangled into nostalgic.

I couldn't help her only ten rupees. I pitied. I embarrassed to see her joining hands thankfully. I bellowed my eyes, turned back, returned to my room. I drank stomachfull water, opened all windows of the room to let the cooling wind entered in. Cloud started hovering in the sky. Caravan of the falling drops created a sonorous music in the sphere. Sometimes the wind strokes fetched some moisture in the room and sprayed over my face, which was toward the window.

I was sorry about Grandma. Her senescent image in my inward eyes flashed up, made me relentless. Her recollection lingered next for several hours until the drowsiness proclaimed over my consciousness.

Day- Twentieth

Prabha needs to visit her mother frequently as she lives lone after demise of her father. She worries to leave the Strange Man alone, concerning of his meals, medicines and routine. Twenty days has passed still the man hasn't spoken a words yet.

So she decides to carry both- the Strange Man and the Lost diary. She has started working as a visiting doctor in the Sanjivini Hospital where the Strange Man was admitted once, and parallel she begins her preparation for Civil Services.

Prabha's paternal house set almost thirty kilometers away from the city of Allahabad. Her ancestors were landlord. Her father had chosen unorthodox course unlike his father and became a reputed lawyer in Allahabad High Court who earned name and fame in very young age. He was killed in a treacherous, ghastly road accident. Some rumored it was a planed murdered, some said it was just an accident.

Prabha is the sole legatee of her parental property from village agricultural runoff, mangoes and guavas garden to city's mansions.

Her mother haunts alone in village's grand mansion. Whenever Prabha urges her to go with her and live with her in city, she often gives logic, she would never leave the place of her ancestors and husband. She believes the place a pilgrim.

Sometime, she visits Allahabad, only when Prabha persuades her for holy dips at Sangam, but she never stays there.

She is a religious, but husband's demise she has kept herself engage in chanting hymn, reading rosary beads and offering her worship in temple for hours sometimes. She spends her most of time in reading scriptures to avert the effect of inertia and lacuna of the life.

She is also a cordial patient. She has only concern that is Prabha's marriage and the concern lengthens to a profound impact over her mind after her breakup with Abhinav.

She has made urge to almost of her relatives to quest for a suitable bridegroom.

She drowns sometime in deep anxiety speculating what would happen of her daughter if some day her heartbeats get seized.

Chapter 18

I worked hard and desperately to own money in the hand at the end of the day. I managed to sell newspaper doors to doors before people peeped through their windows and got down. Stealthily I had been executing my job fairly without giving any heed to any known one.

When I fell down on the bed every evening after work, I used to be utterly drained off, sometimes moaned with aches and blubbered something vague in exhaustion lying on the bed. It helped me to obviate internal struggles.

I missed my home, Grandma, Meera, village and most often Urvarshi whose image I upheld in my mind, as pulsating my nerves. It used to be a nostalgic night after tedious and exhaustive day.

To imagine my life without Urvashi was beyond imagination. Sometimes I suspected, "Did she really exist in the world? Or was it just a fantasy? Or she is a character of some fairy tale? Sometimes I went to see her and believed, she existed in the real.

The desires to hoard money awaken in me as if I wanted to hoard a treasury of unexpected amount of wealth. My aching limbs used to get an eerily comfort when I held rupees and counted them leafing currencies before going to bed. I put them underneath the book heaves.

I sent some rupees at home, submitted my semester fees, paid my room rent and, still, I had some surplus.

Although I lost my weight, the stomach has shrunken inside, and charms of youth age was depleting down. My suffering was a purgation of my guilty soul.

Love transforms you.

One fine evening, when I was returning back to my lodging, I met Praphulla, my classmate who apprised me about the department and ask my possible date for joining the class.

“How many students already have arrived?” I enquired.

“Several,” said he.

I wanted to know whether Urvarshi returned from vacation or not. He sensed it, got my point damn well. He didn't mention her name but counted a list of girls from our class along with Urvashi. I could not help to stop without going to department very next day to see her.

When she passed by me, I saw her from the corner of my eyes and trailed her until she infiltrated into the classroom.

I relished a sense of internal comfort, quenched my eyes, which seemed, an era had gone off since last time I had seen her.

Whenever she was with me, time hurried past. But now our silence created a gap of an epoch.

I always pretended least bothered by the incident that happened between us, disguising an eerily serenity over the face. But my soul was not liberated. It seemed as if somebody had placed a huge cliff over my heart- no sense of liberation had I internally. The very thought of hurting her hackled. My psyche occupied with thoughts of people, occupation and things knitting fantasy world.

I couldn't find myself being away from the madding crowd. I turned amazingly introvert. Something or else, I chattered, laughed in lonesome hours, pondering fictitious romantic scenes characterizing her and blurting in self, meanwhile.

I discovered the cause of an accident happened that day when I was carrying gravy cement on the second floor, being lost in thoughts. My steps slipped from the ladder, rolled down through the stairs like a wrapped up carpet rolling down and my head bumped by the wall.

I got bitterly wounded. I was unable to stand on my feet and staggered; soon I realized, I got fracture my leg. Other workers rushed to me. They informed Kamal and Rehan copying their contact from my cell-phone. They headed, placing me into honing ambulance toward Sir Sunder Lal Hospital, BHU. But unfortunately, all doctors were on strike for their demands.

Jagmohan rebuked doctors abusing as he cast his eyes at my gushing down blood. Without making any delay, they took me to Heritage Hospital, which was at some distance from the university.

My face soaked with the blood clot, I was feeling giddy, and everything appeared hazy to me. I could not hold my eyelids uphold, which were slopping down every time if I tried to lift.

The doctor washed the wound, balm and bandaged me.

Landowner and his middle-aged wife stayed quite late hours next to my bed. They informed me that my right leg was fractured from the knee. As the clock struck four past thirty, Jagmohan had to go back to his home as the train's arrival time approached nearer. He was concerned, for there was no one in his house except his wife and his kids.

The landowner's wife always behaved generously, she used to call me inside the house, offered water with sweets and enquired about me and my health. Once she doubted that I didn't look like laymen, while a cute descendant of humble parentage. And every time, I tried to hide the truth.

The landowner asked me to whom he should impart the news of my accident information and summoned for assisting me in the night. I didn't want to send a message to Grandma anyhow. So I told him to call Rehan's cell number again. They phoned Rehan again.

It's a wonderful and an amazing panorama when you see a profuse love reflecting in the eyes of your beloved; especially her standing with you even when you haven't left any chance of hurting her in past months. In spite of that, she showers her affection in return.

It is sure if a girl loves somebody, she's really ready to leave her whole world, sacrifice her happiness for one person. And such a story can be seen in every house.

A woman is like a river. If she flows in the path of her dignity, carrying love, care and affection, she will turn the source of life -that's the magnitude. But if she decides to go wayward from her path, it takes the form of flooded water which can wipe out a whole city.

In last six months, she might have taken a different course, the way I treated her.

After few hours, when I opened my eyes, I found her standing next to me, having spots of parted tears over her pretty face. She appeared as if she had recently stopped drizzling and her palm wiped moisture from her cheek. Spotted wetness was telling her story still.

Her coming made me remorse. I realized she never left me. It was I wandered away from her. It was I who had created a gap between us. It was I who had set a wall of ego. She was there always, where she was ever for me from the beginning. It was she who knocked down the wall that I had set between us. She had always preserved warmness and compassion.

My world illumined with her presence. This gap had made our heartfelt more fervent and more ardent.

Nothing can be such a severe punishment than forging a guilty man's reiterates sin. It is the deed of a great, humble and pious soul. And she was a living icon of forgiveness, reconciliation and renunciation.

Finding nobody around, she strolled near me. "Non-stop hurting me," she said, lowing her tone almost at the verge of wail, whispering, that I only could listen. "I can bear miles gap distance, but I can't forbear to see you lying this way, you rascal. If you have to damage your life and then better fucked it more beautifully wasting with me. We will spoil it together."

She sat on the stool, next to my bed, clutched my hand in her and dragged her palm affectionately caressing over the bandage.

The warmness of her sacred compassion melted down the walls of high conceited self-esteemed. And my tears of repentance washed away the contaminated heart.

Tears sprouted in our eyes, irresistible and drizzled. Seeing me in an irksome state, she balanced herself and held her muslin scarf, wiped my tears and eradicated my uneasiness.

She was tense seeing me in the patient's bed.

To change her mood, I initiated talks about fellows, syllabus, class, lecture, et cetera. I realized, sometimes I succeed to draw her nearly to laugh when a slight smile floated over her visage, lightning ivory teeth blazed between her petals like the luscious lip.

As the night passed, people stick with their beds, fell asleep, attendant spread their sheet on the next of patient bed and lay down homely. Other went out to spin night in a pretty lawn in front of the building.

It was a newly founded trauma centre, well-equipped hospital for accident cases. Occasionally nurses and ward boys used to visit patients to see their progress. The ward glittered with white milky CFL limpid light.

I woke up apprehending some movements in the surrounding. I popped up my eyelids, hardly looked through. I craned to perceive around. The ward boy was checking drips of neighboring patients. He apologized, disturbing.

Seeing next tableau, it filled me with tenderness.

Urvashi, sitting on the stool, was fallen asleep, resting her head on the bed, near my right arm. Her face looks like a morning bud bloomed over delicate bough. I desired to hold her in arms, but I didn't tend to disturb her.

She woke up, labored to open her eyes; but still, she was unconscious like napping child. She twisted as I combed fingertips across her hair.

I wished I kept on beholding her pretty face forever, cherished. I moved my hands gently over her face.

She pulled my hand underneath of her head making its pillow. Beholding her I didn't know when I was fallen asleep again. Though doctor did treatment, yet she was the reason of quick recovery.

I woke up with commotion, rustled and chattering of people in the ward. Attendants of neighboring beds carried diluted tea and white-bread before they gave them morning medicines dose.

I opened my eyes and didn't see Urvashi. Suddenly she appeared coming straight toward me.

A shabby man, swarthy color, was following her. Suddenly she stopped quite at a distance from the bed, instructed him something pointing toward me.

The man pulled a rolling curtain, unfolded it and hid my bed. She turned her head away.

The man helped me to execute morning maiden task, releasing waste material of last night and set me again as usual. Urvashi came back afterwards; opened purse handed him hundreds of rupees.

She elevated the head of the bed more than 30 degrees most of the time to avert congestive heart failure, chronic pulmonary disease or respiratory.

She brought coffee and some snack.

Taking pills was a terrible thing to do every morning, but soon it turned easy as I cast my eyes at her face. An orthopaedic doctor reached to me along with his assistant, medical practitioner and few North-Indian along with several Keralites nurses.

He scrutinized my feet and checked the progress of recovery. He asked me if there was any sensation in the feet touching my toe.

I nodded slightly.

Next neurologist came. Placing fingers on the forehead, he lifted my eyelids with the thumb tenderly, blew torch into my eyes.

"Who is attendant?" ask the doctor.

Urvarshi affirmed.

"I," said Urvashi, coming in front.

He was noting down something on the paid.

Was later question relevant to ask? Was it necessary to ask who was she? Most probably, 'NO'. But this question banged me who was she to me, who was there to serve me leaving her whole work aside- spent her night half-sleep in looking after me.

This question was essential to ask me who she was she exactly to me.

If the wife should be like this, I thought, I would love to lead a life of eternity with her.

She nodded her head hesitatingly, murmured slowly, "No. We are a friend."

The doctor, in his forties, looked and smiled. "Don't mind. Take this prescription" giving her a list, he said. "He needs a slight massage at his back with Vaseline or with some moisturizer to avert skin infections"

He patted at my shoulder having a smile, wishing me 'good luck'. As they departed, she picked up her cell phone and phoned somebody.

After half an hour later Pummy arrived.

Urvashi went for brush her teeth. She suggested Pummy to stay there as the guard until she returned.

"I tell you one thing," Pummy said, as she departed. "This is not Urvashi. I know her from her graduation time. She is different and this is absolutely different"

I gave a baffled expression.

Urvashi was different than the girl, I had seen in the beginning.

"Last six month either she had talked about you or shed tears or sat silently. Even if she came to the department it was only to see me. She totally engrossed in your thoughts. She asked only question what was her fault? Really you had tortured her a lot."

"That's why I 'm here." I blurted.

“I don’t know about you, but she is crazy for you. She had to face mocking, stare and comment of fellows.” said Pummy.

“It is not fair,” said I, after a couple of days when she was giving me medicine.

She looked at me questioning

“Please. Don’t spoil your semester due to me” I said, swallowing medicine.

“I cannot leave you alone here,” said she, firmly.

“You can help me too if you attend the lecture,” I asserted.

“But I can't leave you here alone,”

“Don’t be stubborn like child,” Now I was quite firm in voice.

We stared glance, finally, I won. She yielded for attending lecture.

She explained to me whatever she studied in the classroom and sometimes she secretly recorded audio of the lecture.

Before to leave for class, she pleaded nurses, gave advance to the sweeper to help me if I needed. One afternoon she entered into the ward, delightedly distributing sweets to attendants, patient doctors and nurses and finally, her hoping feet stopped reaching to me.

“Open your mouth,” She asked me. She was in the seventh sky.

I was just gazing her bizarre.

“Open your mouth properly,” said she.

I was gazing her in bizarre.

There resembled an excitement in her voice. I opened; still looking her.

“You are the highest scorer.” She put her hand over my cheeks lovingly.

“And you?” I asked.

She leaned the fourth forgetting all, kissed over my forehead.

Kamal and Rehan arrived.

I yelled at them rebuking in typo Banarasi slang; instantly restrained my tongues glancing apologetically toward.

"You can see yourself, Urvarshi," Rehan said, mocking. "What a savage, he turns in your absence."

"Rehan if you stay here for an hour," said Urvarshi.

"Okay," Rehan affirmed.

"Kamal, you have to come with me." Urvarshi asked him.

Meeting Sky

Chapter 19

Whenever she looked around, no one noticed us, she used to apply body lotion for smoothing my back to avoid infection. She elevated the head of the bed to the comfort level, fell down softly rolling, pulled up the shirt and applied jelly at my bared back.

This is what that makes a woman an epitome of love and compassion— her playing several roles at a time.

It was second week spending in hospital bed bereft having seen natural light. I fancied about to see sunlight, sky, Lanka Gate, campus, Assi, and Banaras' streets.

One fine day, the doctor permitted me to go home. I had been waiting for this day. Urvashi didn't return. I asked the nurse numerous times since the first ray of the sun. And now she had become fed up with my queries. The needles of the clock crawled idly. Although I knew it well that it was impossible for her to arrive before 4 o'clock, as she would be in class by then.

I was leafing pages of D.H. Lawrence's 'Woman in love' which helped me to spin those tedious minutes.

She hurriedly came, began packing up- medicines, clothes, and books under my pillow.

"Rehan and Kamal are coming with the cab," said she, pulling the zip of bag which made a whizzing resound.

"Aren't we missing anything here?" she mumbled, looking around nonchalantly.

I was in acute suspension, where she was about to take me.

These fifteen days had drawn her too close to my heart and mind. She retreated back to me after a few minutes.

"Wait a while. I'm coming," Again, I kept looking at her like a child.

Hardly had she moved toward the doctor's chamber, Rehan and Kamal arrived there. They carried bags and other things and put them into the car. After ten minutes, Urvashi returned, followed by a team of nurses as courteously.

"How to shift him in the van?" Urvashi demanded.

They placed me on the stretcher and dragged me to the car. They glided the stretcher towards the gate, rolling down over the wheels. I was cruised flat on a curved plank, rolling ceiling cemented CFL lights passing past. People loitering in the corridor gave us passage as Rehan and Kamal drove navigating, halting and attaining peoples' attention.

Urvashi followed them, holding a plastic bag comprised of medicines, x-ray, and other medical reports. They shifted me into the car. Urvashi sat beside me. Kamal sat another side supporting me. Rehan sat on the front seat.

Within minutes, I was happy to see the world outside of the hospital, leaving past its medical stink, pathetic state of the patient, natural light, rambling people, yelling rickshaw wallah, honking cars, and students assembled at book vendors at Lanka Gate.

Our car, when it reached Lanka, I heard the city slang. People in Banaras event don't like to drink water bereft using '*Bhosari Ke'*. And it is the perception in Banaras; if two friends talking without using this word, they cannot find friends. They can be anything.

My reverie didn't survive long. I assumed I was going to my lodge near Hyderabad Gate, but suddenly meandering of the car threw me in the utter puzzlement. I looked through the window of the car and tried to recognize the road through the shops, banners, and landmarks. Hardly, it took ten minutes when our car reached in front of an apartment in Ravindrapuri. I had never come there before.

"Where are we now?" I asked in bafflement, peering through the window.

"Urvarshi's apartment," Kamal said. Open the gate.

"What?" I said. I looked at Urvashi questioning.

They alighted.

I was completely astonished and failed to understand what plan was running in her mind.

"Are you crazy?" said I, widening my eyes.

She nodded her head, mildly and said, "Perhaps." And she got down.

I was left alone in the cab, perplexed what to do now, what was going to happen next. I didn't want to make her a matter of gossip, mock, and mongering. I didn't get bothered from rumors but it bothered me if somebody commented on her.

Rehan and Kamal were busy in taking things out and carrying them into the apartment. Just then she opened the gate of the car and came to me. I had put my plastered leg straight.

Band-Aid wrapped around the head, seemed as if somebody tied it. It began itching oft, which was inevitable. And propelling pen or some sharp things into it, beguiled tickling.

"You will face troubles if I stay with you." I alarmed her.

"It's ok. I don't mind what people say." She blurted.

"People will mock at you taking my name, openly."

"I will love it," said she, smiling. "Why are you so bothered about what the world will say about us? It is ok." She paused for a while and asked next. "Tell me about yourself if you are uncomfortable living with me in my apartment?"

"No," I nodded.

"Then, just chill yaar," said she, jovially. "Let the world fuck off and move on." She had a titillating smile at her face. "Yes...You have to control your hormones only."

For six months, I did my best to keep away myself from her, but just an accident accommodated me into her room.

It was on the 3rd floor, 2 BHK flat, well furnished shinning color texture and poised curtains. The best place in the flat was its balcony.

She used to brush my teeth, washed my cloth, and applied body lotion as usual. Due to bandage wrap around my head, I could not have a bath for several days. Therefore she cleaned my limbs with wet cotton. She remembered my medicate schedule too. She called me meanwhile, after every lecture until she returned to the apartment.

She used to smoothen my itching of skin inside the bandage by thrusting some long and thin stuff. It relieved me of those terrible epidemic tickling.

One Sunday, she made me sit before the mirror. A thick beard had overshadowed my face, which had changed my appearance. I asked her impulsively the next step.

She succored me to sit straight on the chair, stretching legs. She brushed over my face, encrusted with white foams and soften beard.

She concentrated on moving the razor over my face. Pummy was right; she was the different girl whom I had seen for the first time on the train.

She was more bewitching in T-shirt and Capri. She compelled my mind to yell out, but I controlled and sometimes asked her to cover herself and let not give any impulsive heed, which sometimes troubled my manliness.

Sometimes she pretended of missing soaps or towel and the moment I reached the bathroom gate, she teased me in Bollywood style. That moment I could not help to stop my imagination without entering the bathroom. And my mind like any painter began drawing her curves in the blank canvas of my cognitive and created a portrait.

My eyes were casted at her cherished upper torso. She winked, “What?”

She caught my attention, paused her moving hands and slightly slammed at my check, saying, “Hello. Don’t dream.”

Her words pulled me out of the reverie.

“Sit like an ideal child and let me clean your shabby beard.” She kept on shaving.

After the final snap of razor, she showed a mirror to me. I stared at my glowing complexion. “I can flirt with you.” I cut joke.

“Don’t think of it. I will kill you,” said she humorously. She dabbed with the towel and drained off the wetness from my face.

She stood up and was about to go. I grasped her hand and stopped her. She looked at my serene face.

“What happened?” she asked.

“Thank you for everything,”

She leaned and cupped my face in her hands.

“I am happy to find you again. And this is beyond anything. It’s like the coming of monsoon after a summer draught.”

I strived to hold my overwhelmed. She sensed it. I bend, carried her face quite close my face and set her lips on mine. My eyes were closed, drops rolled down. She embraced me in her arms and held me tightly caressing to pacify me.

Chapter 20

I had developed a habit of framing plots, portraying characters, writing memories and reading classics voraciously whenever she wasn't with me.

Waiting was the toughest and torturous job for me, and that waiting was so monotonous than Vladimir and Estragon of 'Waiting for Godot'.

The moment she left for class, I was searching for reasons to spin my tedious hour. In front of my bed, the window was the only thing which introduced me to the world outside of my room. The sounds of hooting vehicles, people chattering and, often, duelling for giving passage on the jam-packed road, used to come through the window.

I flipped open her laptop, started ransacking movie folder for the sake of entertainment. I found such one but contained her exotic pictures, which I never imagined the way of her vogue. There were several other people in the photo, I thought, they were her family. The background was a pretentious mason which seems like her home having a big lawn. Some of them appeared as they were snapped abroad.

I detect it, and I found such one which had only my pictures. Mine! It was really a matter of surprise to me as I had never allowed anyone to click any pictures. Indeed I didn't know when and how she had clicked those pictures, most of them were of last six months when we were not together.

When she came during the lunch-time, I asked all the questions which were hovering in my mind. She smiled and tried to skip all my questions. When I asked her reiterating the same questions, she gave me answer with her smile.

"I had left my spy behind you."

"And Rehan, Kamal and Pummy were prominent." I gave her a throwback smile.

I recall in those days, Rehan came quite closer to me and sometimes talked about her a lot. I debug him threatening him to britches friendship if he spoke about her.

She brought a meal in one thali and sat next to me.

“Rehan was saying that Meera’s call was coming continuously.” She asked while feeding me bites. “What was she saying?” Suddenly my face color was operated, I asked her concernedly.

“I don't know. She was just asking about you. I think you should call home.”

“I haven’t called them since I got injured.” I apologized.

She made me drink water, cleaned my mouth and wiped dripping wetness. She dialed my home number.

She was looking blankly at the roof, cradling mobile by her ears, and after a few seconds, she shifted the cell phone from her to me. The ring was going. I waited inquisitively as the call rang drilling in my ear. At least call was received from the next side. It went silent for the next few minutes.

“Hello,” I said.

I was responded by another hello from the other side of the call.

Suddenly the voice changed. Meera gave the cell phone to Grandma. Her faint voice tranquillized all the tumult hovering in my mind, soothed my ears. Grandma could not understand my voice. She repeatedly said the words ‘hallo… hallo’. Meera took the cell phone again in her own hand.

“Meera?” I anticipated.

“Siddhartha!” said she. I realized a sort of delight in her voice. I heard Grandma’s exhilarating tone echoing in the background. For a while, Meera’s voice halted, I heard, Grandma’s impatience questioning remotely.

“She is not fine. She is suffering from severe chronic coughing.” I could hear, Grandma was stopping her, informing me of her state of health, but she didn’t bother.

“Have you consulted any doctor?” I asked. I was undergoing through acute agony fusion with an eerily pang of guilty.

“Not yet,” said she. “All the *paisa* I spent. And you know her well she is not ready to go to the hospital when I had arranged the money and was about to take her to the doctor. She said she didn't want to waste money anymore. She was forcing me to send that money to you.” Tears gusted down deliberately. Meera continued. “But I didn’t accept her idea. I know the situation can be worst the way she is careless about herself. You must come.” Suddenly Grandma’s coughing voice alarmed me. She was saying to Meera “Ask him where is he? And how he is? There is no call from his end for a long time? Is everything okay there?” My tongue was quiet, holding disquiet within. Meera lowered her voice and asked. “Are you okay?”

“Hmm,” I murmured, and held myself strongly. It seemed like a lump stuck in my throat “I'm ok.” I tried to handle the situation. “Listen, for some days, I cannot come. I am outside of Banaras.”

“Outside of Banaras!” She startled a bit. I sensed her. The reason was I used to share everything with her.

“Yes. For attending the seminar.”

“Seminar?”

“Yes. You will not understand.” but I knew she had understood every word of mine.

She turned silent for that moment.

“Listen Meera. I will send one of my friends. He will give you some money. Take her to the town and show him to a good doctor... Ok.”

“Hmmm,” she muttered. I knew well, her mind was speculating peevishly.

I was thrown into a no-man-land of pathos. I wished to blame but to whom? My fate? Myself? Or my selfishness? Or Ultimate?

Urvashi caressed my shoulder and pacified me.

“Can you call Kamal or Rehan?”I asked Urvashi.

She picked her phone called Kamal. Within twenty minutes, he was at our doorstep.

“You have to go to my home the next morning,” I said giving him my ATM. “Withdraw all amount and take my Grandma to hospital. And if they ask about me, pretend them anyhow.” I said, suggesting.

It was a numb afternoon of mid-August, occasional rain had made atmosphere pleasant and intoxicating. We were napping.

The doorbell rang. It went twice, then thrice and then intermittent. I woke up but could not walk to open the gate. Urvashi came out of the bedroom, unlocked the door and pulled it wide opened.

“Kamal!” She startled.

The next sight made me a statue, and I burst out, “Meera.” Chhottani also following them. Urvashi sometime looked at me sometimes at Meera. I could not understand anything. The sudden arrival of Meera made me baffled.

“Grandma forces them to come with me. I know the genuine reason. But I don't know how she knows everything. I tried my best to pretend in front of her and hide the truth though,” said Kamal, who was standing back to them.

“My heart was not ready to accept at all that you’re outside of Banaras. I guessed tentatively that something was wrong.” She was woeful seeing my bandaged body, speaking in whimpering voice and came to me.

“Now, I am ok. The doctor has said, within a week all my wound would get healed. Don’t fret. After couple of days, plaster will be cut down. And I can walk on my feet again. It’s nothing just a slight injury.”

“STOP.” She chided me, controlling her voice turning into mourn, still, she could not stop her mewling.

“How is Grandma?” I asked to avert her. “What doctor told about her health?”

"Doctor said she would get relief from the cough very soon." Again she fetched a surge of nostalgia as she began talking about Grandma. "She has repeatedly been asking about you. One morning, she was so sorry, for she had seen some ominous dream. She forced me to come to Banaras with *Chhottani.* But I didn't come leaving her alone."

"Babu," *Chhottani* shuffled toward me and said. "You suffered a lot. Why didn't you inform anybody? At least you must have called me."

"*Chhottani Bhaiya*, I didn't want to give my trouble to everyone at home. I thought, once I got well, I would come myself."

Meera was sobbing. "You were better at home. Leave this *padhayi-likhai,* study, and come with us."She said out of pathos, likely she didn't realize the meaning what she was saying in overwhelm.

Urvashi assisted her, making her stand up clutching her arms and made her sit on a chair.

"Don't worry, he is okay now. After a few days, he will be able to walk on his feet and then I will send him home."

Meera out of her teary eyes looked at Urvashi as if he was trying to recognize her. Some of the time, I had mentioned her name in the story of campus life whenever I was going back home. To help her, introduce Urvashi to Meera. "Meera, she is Urvashi."Meera shook her head, information as she acquainted her already.

"Who is with Grandma? Is she alone at home?" I was concerned as I recalled out of my contemplation, if Meera was with me, then who would be at home?

"Manju, kids and Gulabo aunty are with her to help her," said *Chhottani.* "How can we think to leave her alone?"

Laying in bed more than weeks, finally, the day came, the doctor had cut down the white thick heavy plaster which seemed as if somebody had hung mountains around my legs and the senior doctor advised Urvashi to make me walk a little every day and to gradually increase the pace and wash the fractured leg with warm salty water and massaged a prescribed oil.

Urvashi brought proteins that she used to give me before sleeping after mixing it with milk holding my hand and arms. She assisted me in walking in the spacious dining room, my steps wind wiggly. I measured every corner of the room sometimes trying to walk by the wall. Unspectacularly I got my confidence, wished her to rumble outdoor. Still, she walked behind me closely and caught me if ever I stumbled or when I was about to fall. Later she took me to ghat early morning and assisted with my walking.

An abyss fright overcast in the depth of my heart. One side, my upbringing was pure pastoral from the chore and, on other side; she was a Metropolitan elite class girl, brought up in luxuries and leisure. I did my elementary education from neighboring village school, for metric I had to paddle ten kilometers cruising cycle across zigzag pathways crossing around ten villages, fields, guava's, mangoes' garden. Sometimes we had to go on under the brooding sun through the way where there were no shelters of tree or shade. Along with it, I also used to travel to the town when I joined college for graduation.

We were coming from two different globes of the world. She was an elite class girl, and I was an idyllic boy.

I led a life in an acute crisis, she span in abundant. Would I be able to give her that kind of life?

Chapter 21

With every good morning, the campus life was slipping from the calendar with our ageing days, which was a panic point, but, on the contrary, I was looking forward to a beautiful life with Urvashi ahead. Now, we had started to increase the number of bunks from the classroom and span hours in fun and merriment.

Such a moment occurred one fine day.

I was upright at the doorway, the spectator of rambling students. Rehan entered through the main gate, perspired of cycling. He tried to control the respiratory. His steps came at pause as he reached me.

“Is there anything between you and Pummy?” I gambled words over Rehan.

“Did you drink *bhang* today?” he wiped his sweating forehead.

“This is not the answer of my question.” I pretended.

“I flirt with every girl that doesn't mean I love them. And with Pummy, it's just friendship.” He paused for a while. “But yes. She has charmed Kamal a lot.” He unraveled.

“Does he love her?” I probed.

“Of course! The way, he talks about her it seems like that. He is completely engrossed with her thoughts.”

“And what about her?” I enquired about Pummy.

“I don't know. You know what kinda…Character he is. He is such a perfect combo of Gandhiji's three monkeys in case of girls. Yup. But she likes *Kamalawa's* simplicity. Some of the time I have noticed, he gets irritated seeing her mingling with boys. And he rebuked me once when I was talking something flirtatious sort of things to her.”

He had given me adequate clues.

“So would like to participate in the game which I'm going to play with Kamal and Pummy?” I took him in confidence for a prank I was about to play with Kamal. He laughed. He phoned Pummy in the department library.

As I entered, the library attendant greeted jovially. I reached to the book issuing countered and librarian. I had set good terms with librarian and the attendants.

In those isolated days, the library was the most brooding place, I used to come to sooth my mind and avert lonesome deep-rooted.

I used to give at least one hour once every week. I swept dust from the shelves, rearranged books and sometimes even helped the attendants.

The librarian was pleased seeing me after a good amount of time. He asked me about my health wearing a smile. “I heard about your accident. I felt so bad for you.”

“How did you know?” I was puzzled.

“A girl of your class...What is her name?” “Her name is on the tip of my tongue, but I’m missing the word...I have seen her frequently with you.”

I deciphered his haziness.

“Urvashi,” I suggested.

He nodded with a broad smile on his face.

I occupied a chair at the end of the corner of the library where hardly anyone would loiter around, and our voice hardly echoed. Pummy ceased her tramps, reaching the threshold of the hall, looked searchingly to find us. Rehan waved his hand singling her to follow the location.

She pulled the chair, which made a rattling sound. She sat down. “Why have you called me?”

“Do you like Kamal?” Rehan asked, giving a mystifying expression.

“What a stupid question! I will call for this nonsense thing?” she agitated. “I came running, leaving all my important work.”

She was about to stand up.

"Wait." I stopped her. She was in an effigy posture for a while. She sat down. "What? Say soon, whatever you want to say. Go straight." She was trying to look tougher but it was apparent, I penetrated into her state of mind pretending through her grimace.

"Do you like him or not just tell me? Now tell something?"

"What's that?" asked she, strongly.

"First, you answer," said I. She got entangled in the conundrum of our questions.

"Yeah. I like him…He is such a nice guy,"

"Do you love him?" asked I.

"Another nonsense questions," she yelled. She looked at me grimly and then at Rehan. "I will break your teeth ridge if I find you are majorly behind this plotting."

Rehan tilted back.

"What if somebody likes you, it cannot mean that the person loves you," said she.

"But he loves you?" said I, emphatically.

"Yup. He talks about you a lot," added Rehan, solemnly. "He never dares to call you even he has your phone number." She turned tacit speculating. We could not leave any chance to stimulate her sleeping emotion."

She became quiet, drowned into her thoughts. We read her face; we could not leave the chance to stimulate her sleeping soul.

"I heard him muttering your name in his sleeping state." He punched.

She lifted her transformed eyelids. It was not the previous one which had egoism, rudeness and arrogance.

"Stop befooling me. Come on." She said, looking at unscrupulously still.

"No. No. It's true. You know, we are room partners," said Rehan.

We had overcome her psyche, molded it into the direction where we wanted to.

"Really?" There was a glow over her face this time.

"Haaye!" Rehan teased her.

"If you wish, we can give you his cell number," said I.

"No, no. It's ok," said she.

"You can call her right now," said Kamal, unlocking his cell-phone. "Note down." He began reading ten-digit numbers. She saved his number taping over the keypad of his cell phone, though she kept on declining.

"Remember one thing, if you will wait for his call and expect that he will call you, then you have to wait throughout your life. You know him; he is the shyest man, isn't he?"

Hardly had she gone out crossing corridors. Fortunately, Kamal came in.

"What are you doing here?" said he, looking in a manner of questioning.

"Pummy was here few minutes before of your arrival," Rehan said.

"And she was searching you," I added.

"But why?" she said curiously.

"Scoundrel, it's not 1st April."

"She is saying she loves you," said I.

"Whether you believe or not, that's not our issues. And she was right."

"What?" Kamal asked. "She was saying, you are an idiot who does'nt understand emotions."

"I have given your cell number to her. You might receive a call anytime. So talk to her carefully," said Rehan.

"What!" he exclaimed, looking at us in surprise.

Chapter 22

With her support, I descended with staggering steps through marble stairs; she made me sit on her back seat of her scooty, we drove across the vistas of campus.

The sky was a bit murky, bloom painted trees in various colours. There was a novelty all around I felt. Maybe, I was outdoor after many days.

As she zoomed, the moon was floating away, hiding behind trees and faculties' building, tranquilized soothing wind were slapping over our faces. Wandering students, faculties, everything appeared as neophyte to me.

We passed VT. I had clutched her shoulder as for support.

I grabbed her waist tightly and chin anchored at her shoulder as the scooty jerked at a breaker. Later on, she clutched break many time voluntarily.

She slowed down the speed of the scooty and crossed a narrow bar gate. Again, she headed us amidst the plants, flowers and foliages.

Finding our geriatric meeting place, Sunset Adda, after such a long time, together, the enigma inside got ended. She looked at me and smiled. I beheld around and received greeting of various species of plants- of flowers, vegetables and birds.

We sat down on our perennial bench at Sunset Adda, near a small pool of water. I remained calm to hear her flamboyant words to see me with her at there.

The fear of class difference had bridal me inside while I pleased to find her again after a passage of bitter past.

"Urvashi," said I.

She engaged in thinking something, looking blankly across the pool of water, smiled trailing off the flight of birds.

"Hmm," She mumbled.

"What am I for you?" I questioned, which drew her out offer reverie, restored her consciousness.

"What?" She tried to connote my question, she said. "What are you asking for? Haven't you understood still what you are for me?" She smiled, softly.

I reiterated my question. I faltered this time a bit before asking and waited looking at her lips to get steered for saying something.

I knew, her decision would decide my life.

"You don't know what you have brought in my life - a complete transformation." She paused looking away from and darted back at my face. "I was a spoilt child of an aristocratic father in teenage. Escaping family, I used to go to pubs , took drugs, wine and smoke and spent night out with snobbish fellows." Urvashi was narrating her story and I was hearing her silently. For me it was a mere fictional tale.

The girl, I had before me, was different one.

"I used to drink wine with dandy friends, some time took drugs, spend night out and coming late with snobbish fellows. One such night became a nightmare for me."

In fact, hearing her, I worried for a moment to hail something bitter from her past.

"Some scoundrel, who called themselves my friends, made me drink wine and molested me that night in the car. And they left me…me in an abandoned house of the city… Half naked."

She was looking away from me, hiding her face.. She was shivering with grief and pain.

"And you know," she was almost about to cry. "He was also there. That bloody..." Her whimpering turned into hysterical wailing.

"Dad neever liked me. After that incident, he didn't want to see me. I tried all possible ways to improvise my image in the eyes of my family, but Dad always disdained me." She turned to me with soaking face. "That's why I never wanted to tell you. I was afraid of…I might lose you."

I held her my arms tightly, caressed her and tried to pacify her.

After some time, as she got pacified, I asked my most itching question.

"Did your father take any action against those culprits?" I asked. Still, she wrapped her arms around across my torso, holding me tightly and resting her head on my chest.

"I don't know. But once I heard the news, they got killed in a road accident, when they were on a trip."

It was an eerily silence.

.

"Look at me," I cupped her face and looked into her eyes straight. "Don't punish yourself for somebody else infidelity. I am not accustomed to see Miss Urvashi shedding tears from her eyes. I want my Urvashi back, who is mine, who chirps like birds, who only knows to smile."

She was struggling to restrain her sobbing. She lifted her head and tried to appear normal while looking at me.

"Will you be mine?" I asked. I was overwhelmed, but honestly, I meant it.

She nodded her head, slightly bending down, with her sloppy eyes.

"Forever?" my next question.

I was successful in taking her away from her painful past remnant.

Again she nodded.

"Then promised me, you will not recall your past anymore, not ever?" I leaned my head slightly so that I could see clearly in her teary eyes.

She was silent. I waited for her response. “I want your words.” She collected herself and summoned her inner strength to convey to me.

“Please say something” I whispered.

“Stop now, I'm okay,” said she, covering her face with both her hands, she paused for a while and dragged her fingers apart over her eyes.

I chuckled.

We felt some drops falling. She assisted me in making me sit on the scooty and drove us back to the lodging.

The sun was hiding behind the facade of the building, rushing down. The silhouettes of building shimmered under diminishing daylight against grey sky.

She walked out of the rooms, possessed as a stunning looking beauty. I gazed her and gazed her and gazed her.

I woke up out of a dream when she winced and grinned indulgently assuming my open mouth. I shook my head and smiled back.

“I don't want to spoil your dressing.”

She giggled, pulled my hand and said, “Don't be crazy now. It’s getting late.”

She paused for a moment before opening the gate, stood still in front of me, constant lingering her glance at my either shoulders, mending collar, buttoning shirt, setting tie and having a bland smile at her lips.

I conjectured, she desired to say something, so I looked straight into her eyes, assuring her tacitly.

“Our living together has given the people a reason to gossip. After a long time, you will be in the department before fellows, teachers and acquaintances. It may be a little weird situation for you, but you have to be patient,” she said convincingly.

"I can't imagine how embarrassing it has become for you. The comments and mocking you had to face these days. You carried it all. You tolerated it all beacuase of me." I held both her arms delicately, leaned my head onto her shoulders.

"When you are with me, I'm unabashed. And gossiping amongst people will die a natural death."

And we hugged.

After the accident, it was my first day in the department. Urvashi had submitted my medical certificate to Head of the Department though.

As my name announced for a poetry recital, the gathering hailed me with a thunderous round of applause.

I strolled and rose to the dais. I prepared myself to read my emotional expressions as a poetry out-loud before the crowd. The clapping stopped; a deep quietness pondered everywhere in the echoing auditorium hall.

After a brief greeting and introduction, I began, my verse-

Meeting with a Stranger

You

Nobody I knew

When we met very first

Sat at a bench under the verdurous tree

Of a random park

Where tramps ramble

-laymen, old age and pairs

We shared our sour blend sweet past

We talked, laughed and shared

A gender sensation when

You touched, relieved me

Being untouched.

Her metamorphosis beauty in broad bordered Bengali sari, glittering earrings, wistful bangles style, and her charismatic smile had turned her into an aesthetically attractive princes from Venus. Sharpness, child-like traits, and frankness of her utterance vanished from her demeanour. She was now a grave, humble, and peculiarly quiet girl. She began to study late night, inspired me, too, to do the same. Though she was on the stage amidst the crowd, yet her concentration was only on me. Her dance at the fresher's party projected two different personalities of Urvashi. The moment her eyes met mine, she smiled; I was standing quite away watching her like a spectator.

She escaped friends and reached to me. It got while summing up the whole program.

"Sorry," said she, reaching to me.

"Mention not. Loved your dance," I said, smiling.

"Let's go. I feel hungry."

"Where?" I followed her. She was rushing down through the stairs.

"VT," she answered. She questioned, stepping down the stairs, "Don't you feel hungry?"

"Yes, I do," I said.

"Why didn't you tell me? "

She rode us to VT. Her hair brushed my face with the wind brisk hurriedly passing back.

The best thing I liked about her was her incredible intuition the way she knew my unquote inmost.

The sunlight, cloudy sky, numbness of the weather and munching samosa with tea allured spectators to wander at VT.

A couple was next to our table, sipping juice, smiling and whispering.

" I should write a child story for them," said I, draining the juice through the straw.

She caught sight of a couple sitting beside us, sipping juice through different two straws in one glass.

" Hello!" I spoke aloud pulling her out of her trance-like dreaming.

I leaned forth and whispered, "I don't think, two faithful people in true love need to show it to the world."

"Hmm…What?" She mumbled.

"You can't." She provoked.

Instantly, I stopped my sipping of tea, looked into her eyes. "Wait," I said. I rushed out of the restaurant, ran across the road, intruded into flower garden, usually young scientists found rambling there studying progress of foliage and petals. I caught attention of the mass gathered there.

I looked around, searching in the garden, but couldn't find anyone. Students returned to their hostels. I was amid hundreds of species of flower, bemused choosing for best. I snatched some boughs of loaded fragrance of gardenias, ruffled blooms of carnations, white Oriental lilies, twigs of orchids, Peruvian lilies with its attention-grabbing, elegant tulips. And at a point I wounded my finger while plucking a red rose. Anyway, I put rose and tulip amidst the bunch and tied them with *the Scorpion Grasses* vine.

Now it was a beautiful bouquet.

I heard some tramp behind me. I turned and saw the security guard trailing behind me like a devil.

I hurried to cross the fence.

"*Oye* stop." Seeing his bulky figure, round belly hanging like a bag, I laughed. I headed towards the nearest gate, which was already locked. He was reaching closer to me. I climbed over it without bothering its sharp spears like points and jumped across. Everybody present there was watching us, young boys and some enthusiast girls were encouraging me by shouting loud.

I reached her.

There was a gathering of youngsters. We became the centre of attraction. Everyone was watching keenly what I was about to do next.

Urvashi had been looking at me amusedly, covered her mouth with her palms, controlling her overwhelm.

"Are you crazy?" she giggled,

"Yup," I nodded widely.

"To see your pretty smile, I can go any extent of craziness." I kneeled down.

"Stupid, everyone is watching you." She whispered. I looked around and again resumed my previous posture, smiling. "I don't mind. I have to say something."

"What?" she looked at me eagerly.

I proffered the bunch of flowers to her. "I'm not a prince, not a son of the rich-cate father, nor the heir of great legacy." I collected all my courage. "I'm an idyllic romantic boy, busy in framing words into rhyme. But I can write poetry on you, whole life. So, would you like to be the muse of my poetry?"

Hushed, she received flowers from my hand, giggled and nodded in affirmative. People gathered around standing in a circle started clapping for next couple of minute feverously.

I desired to hold her into my arms, lift her up in the sky, but I checked my emotions.

We held one another's hand, looked into the eyes of each other, laughing, smiling and moved to our lodging and whispered amorous words entire ways.

Chapter 23

"Thank you," said I to Urvashi, looking at her face.

We had held each other's hands standing oppugnant of each other. She was sluggishly uplifting herself over her toes to nudge at my nose. I leaned my head, shifting my both hands at her waist. She giggled. A bike passed behind us from the pavement, for a second we faltered being found somebody in our territory. We moved to the bench and took place there.

"I am thinking to start taking tuition classes," I proposed, still holding her hands in mine, which seemed as I had soft cotton in my hand.

"Why?" she asked inquisitively.

"You have already spent a lot of money on me, and now I am ok with taking tuitions. I should do something at least."

She placed her hand over mine. She didn't want to bring down my self-esteem or hurt me.

"I know, one day the *jinn* of your self-respect would come out," she disassociated her hand from mine and took out a magazine out of her satchel, flipped the pages and finally handed me, asking me to go through the paragraphs.

No issue. I started reading it. I did retrospect, recalling vigorously as I knew that article. "I have read this somewhere…" I said wryly still glancing through the paragraph. Reaching the bottom of the article, I was amazed. "Oh my God!" Looking at her, I was in stark astonishment. I asked. "Is it mine?" I could not believe. "But I hadn't ever sent any article to anyone?" I contemplated, as once I had seen my diary in her hands. "So is it you?"

She nodded her head and was equally cherished seeing me delighted, clutching my right palm which assured me of her standing with me in every situation.

“Once I read your notepad having gone through the story, I thought, it must be published. So I sent it to a magazine. But sorry I...I...Didn't ask for your permission,” said she.

“Thank you “I just muttered, still gazing on the paragraphs, that remained in my dream. I was trying to believe that it was my write-up published in a magazine.

I hugged her in ecstasy.

“They have offered you space in their magazine weekly.” Her whispering echoed into my ears.

I was in the seventh sky. I lifted her into my arm and grabed her in gladness, thinking now I would be a writer by profession, my most desired job.

I got her down. There was an elation reflecting into her eyes.

“And they will pay you a good amount of levy on every article” said she.

I felt as I was losing my voice by being overwhelmed.

“Why you are so crazy about being thankful,” said she, laughing. She came quite close to me, Held my face into her both hands, courteously continued. “Why are you always tending to gratitude toward me? You are my life. So caring about one's life is not any way, dept.” She preens fingers of her both hands in my backside hairs.

I shrugged.

“Whenever I can do anything- love, care, anything- good for you, I receive a strange pleasure that I cannot explain into words.” She moved her sight away towards the sky as if her eyes were searching something and gasping. “It...It...Is absolutely exotic.”

She hung like garland by my neck. I grabbed her in my arms, uplifted her. Her hair fell, scattered over my face. My face was in both of my palms, her bud-like sanguine face craned toward mine and kissed on my forehead. And her lips steered to speak softly, which were magical words. “I love you.”

We spent together some hours sitting at the VT premise, clutching hands of each other. She took me in the temple covered her head with her head with a dupatta. I had been a regular visitor to the temple, but that day I couldn't decide what should I pray for. I joined my hands solicited to Lord Shiva so her wish could get fulfilled.

The glimmering lights from the shops, honking vehicles' headlights, we rode across. When she was driving scooty, I slowly dragged my both hands across her waist, reached her belly, titillating.

I averted ever to create a bashful situation.

She tilted her head back, "You can do it." I tightened my grip, wrapped my arms around her waist and set my chin at her right shoulder.

"I have done it," I whispered into her ears.

"Well done, my hero." She murmured.

I realized as thousands of butterflies were flying across my body. I didn't bother about the hue and cry of traffic passing via jam-packed evening road. I enjoyed every single moments spending with her.

She unlocked the door, threw her helmet somewhere, and plunged over me. She embraced me into her arms and madly started smooching passionately. She kissed me at my neck, at my cheek and my lips and her hands engaged for measuring the geography of my physique. I couldn't count the manifold of bubbles, I felt springing up throughout my anatomy. There was an eruption of amorous volcanoes, spontaneity inside me. She was canoodling so craftily, it transcended them.

I crawled towards the gate clutching her in my arms, pasted her lips, gliding. We struck at the side of the bed, stumbled and tossed together flat on the cushion bed.

We were tangled like vine with each other.

"You looked beautiful this evening," I said snogging. "Today, you appear like a typical Bengali belle."

“What about other days? Am I not...?”

“No. I don’t mean...”

“Ooow,” she amused. “It’s you who avoids complimenting me though all my make-up is for you, to win your eyebrows wide. But you remained silent like a stupid...” She chuckled.

Vasco De Gama and Columbus inside were trying to come out tending to explore her Island. Spontaneously, my both active hands started stripping her broad border Bengali sari. She covered her face with both hands, being sighed.

Her breathing stroked at my face, resounding in the room..

She kept her eyes closed.

We commuted without using words.

My eyes were amazed seeing her ravishing landscape, but still, I turned more inquisitive to know her the alluring sight behind her last remaining piece of cloth.

I pulled her over me. Now I was lying down. My finger fumbled at her back, searching the hook of her bra. She grasped my hand nodded her head horizontally and trying to hold my rebellious surge. .

“No…No! Sid not now.”

“Yes,” said I, rhyming with her words.

She turned her head aside.

“I think it is not right,” said she in a lower tone.

“I have every right over you. Look into my eyes, what do you see here lust or love?” I said.

She gazed. There was utterly stillness in the room.

“From now and forever, you are mine. And this stupid will be forever for you.” I said, twinkled.

She tightened her grip.

There is a very minor difference between love and lust.

I planted a kiss on her forehead. Soon after some time the room was full of ecstasy, echoing with breathing, muttering something and quite resemblance Hindi vowels sound.

We are at culmination of pleasure. I was about to get inside her, but she stopped me again.

"Where is the guard?" asked she.

For a moment, I was confused; 'guard?' looked her baffling. My racing brain pondered, recalling the meaning of the words.

"Stupid... condom," said she, giggled.

"I am ready to be father of a child without marriage," said I.

She laughed, I trailed her laughing.

Though it was just penetration, friction and erection in terms of sex, but for us, it was travelling through the light of absolute pleasure, finding eternity in each other's embrace. It was an unseen, unconquered world for me before this night.

Day- Thirty-Fifth

Prabha calls Nazarin, she takes The Strange Man to Raymond Shop that is situated in the Civil Lines. She shoped some fancy man's suit for him for going to the reception party of her friend.

The Strange Man appears debonair and handsome in black Raymond dress, knotted tie at the neck, soon he becomes the centre of showcasing and garners a positive response from the gentleman and receives admire from the beautiful ladies gathered at the party.

Suddenly, Prabha's cheerful complexion changes into dull, all enthusiasm and wanton are gutted at the appearance of Avinash in the party. She tries every way to avoid any encounter with him. She cannot bear his repatriation again in her life.

She moves aside from there leaving the Strange Man with Nazarin.

Meanwhile, a well-embellished girl in her fancy attire arrives and probes to him, "If you don't mind, you are Siddhartha sir?" she pauses, looks at him awaiting mode. "The best-selling author of the book, 'Meeting with a Stranger'."

He looks at her blankly.

"I met you once in a bookshop at Civil Lines. You remember?" asks the girl.

"Perhaps. You might have mistaken. He is not an author," asserts Nazarin.

"But he is almost resembling him," says the girl, dubiously. "Anyway. Sorry to bother you." And she walks away from there, towards the dance floor.

Prabha interrogates the reason for the girl's arrival.

"She was saying that she had seen him. She was addressing him as an author… Siddhartha," says Nazarin.

'Siddhartha- an author Siddhartha- the protagonist of the diary and the book 'Meeting with a Stranger' are mentioned in the Lost Diary too." Prabha thinks.

Prabha approaches to the girl. Nazarin watches them, trying to understand their conversation by reading their lips and gestures. She discerns a spark of delight as the girls keep on narrating sometime darting at the Strange Man.

Prabha walks back with an uninhibited smile over her lips, looks into The Strange Man's eyes as if she had found a secret world.

"Ah, how have you been carrying volcano of pain and utter no word.!" Prabha mumbles in a way that only The Strange Man can listen.

Somebody calls Prabha. The shadow she has been trying to be away from, now he is standing before her. But now particularly at that very moment-—she doesn't have a single stain of excruciation over her face.

"I'm good," she says in a cheery mood. Still, the ecstasy has been lingering all over her face, that reflected as if she is least bothered of his presence.

"Who is he?" he asks about The Stranger.

"He is Mr Siddhartha," Nazarin speaks out in the middle rashly. They share a glance and smile.

"Yup. Siddhartha," Prabha affirms. "He is the author of the bestselling book, Meeting with a Stranger. Perhaps, you have heard.

Avinash nods in approvingly and offers his hand for the shake. "Hey, how are you?"

"And Prabha is going to marry him soon." Nazarin's words shake him.

The Strange Man has been watching all these discussing as passively he is not apprised of the matter and meaning of talks.

“What!” he bursts into surprise and turns toward Prabha. She holds her lips tightly to constraints her smile. “How can you do this Prabha?” He yells.

“Why can’t she do, if you can?” says Nazarin sarcastically before Prabha opens her diplomatic mouth.

“You please shut up.” He yells at Nazarin being agitated.

Nazarin controls her laughter at his violent reaction.

“You will be fortunate to attain one more such party quite soon.” Prabha mocks. She grabs the arms of The Strange Man and strolls away from there, leaving him to watch of her departure.

“You might be thinking who that boy at the party was. He was none other than my ex-boyfriend,” says Prabha while unbuttoning her jewellery placing them in the boxes. She moves in another room to unfasten the burdensome dresses, nevertheless she keeps continuing narrating her incomplete story. “We were in the relationship. Once he was my soul-mate. I thought it was a journey of several births, but I was only like a drunken stupor in love with him. I couldn’t get him. His emotion for me was pseudo. After the demise of my father, one day, he asked me to persuade my mother to confiscate property over his name that he can start a business.” She pauses. “He pressurized me for it. Once I ignored, I did twice. I could not bear his selfishness; therefore I decided to separate from him. I wept bitterly, for I loved him. That day I realized, the pain in love has no remedy, and it’s something you can’t explain or show anyone. Now, I can’t feel your pain but understand how abyss it would be when I measure on my own experiences of pain.” She pauses to settle the lumps like something as stuck in her neck. “There was no compassion only lust – lust for my body and legacy that I had received by the inheritance from my father.”

The Strange Man has been listening to her by being stagnant in the chair, lowing his sight down on the ground and ears paid to her.

She continues. “Hardly, more than a couple of weeks had passed since he was detached from me, he found a match with another — a rich girl." She shuffles out of the room wearing a casual dress, a short kurty with a light-loose pyjama. "Sorry, I pulled you in my personal matter. I think I might not take your name as my lover, it may embarrass you." She apologizes.

He looks at her from the corner of his eyes.

"Actually, I wanted to give him the same pain that I underwent sometime back because of him." She says.

Undoubtedly, there is a great transformation that has come in Prabha's personality since the Strange Man has come in her life. She denounces the negativity, despair and all shackles that hurdle her to move on. His facade helps her in her Civil Exam's preparation. Her pain wreathen past is heart-rendered, somewhat it is volatile of his shush cosy presence in her life that reverberates her life with a soft feeling of beautiful serenade.

Next morning, she reaches books shop at Katara as earliest; hardly the shopkeeper has opened his shops and shown incessant sticks to the shelves stuffed with books.

"Do you have 'Meeting with a Stranger'?" Prabha inquires as she is in a hurry to go somewhere.

The shopkeeper doesn't wish to unchain his morning prayer, nor does he intend to disappoint the first customer of the morning. So, he indicates her with his waving hand to wait for a moment.

But she is no way in the state to wait for another minute.

She walks out of the shop. The shopkeeper rushes to the counter, hurries up and calls her back.

She retreats her steps back.

"Can you wait for a moment, please?" pleads the shopkeeper.

"How much time?" Prabha probes.

"A moment- for just a moment?" He reverts by making a sorry face. "It's *bohani* time, the first sale of the day."

He summons a lad with sticky hair who has applied mustard oil and who is flapping dusting cloths across the shelves.

“Go in haste to the Prayag Shop and bring a copy of Meeting with a Stranger.” He commands the lad.

“Better if you write it down and give him the slip,” suggests Prabha.

“No, it’s ok. It’s known to everyone. It’s a bestselling book, ma’am.” The shopkeeper asserts having a soft smile over his lips. “Readers are waiting for the next book of this author.”

The boy trots escaping morning hustle on the road- creeping cars of Professors, students headed toward the university.

The lad returns in time, even before they have finished the dialogue.

“How much?” asks Prabha.

He turns the front, then back cover of the book searching the prize, “Rupees 210 only.”

Prabha gives the money into his left hand and almost snatches the book in curiosity from his hand.

As she rotates the book in her hand and her glance falls over the picture of the author at the back page of the book, it bolts her with unexceptional wonderment.

‘It means the girl at the party was right’ Prabha soliloquies. “He is not a natural dumb. He might have lost the ability to speak. I must consult to a good doctor.”

When she reaches the house, he has been struggling to go to the washroom.

She enters in his living room, ransacks some paper or diary or something else if he has scribbled down on it, like a thief.

Minute after minute passes on, miraculously, she still has been engaged in searching, the sweat starts trickling down, but she doesn’t find any such thing. Finally, she flips the bed sheet, she has found a thin notebook in which he has written down something.

Taking it, she retires to her room. She matches the handwriting of The Strange Man and the handwriting of the lost diary. She finds an absolute match between them.

“O…My God. He is Sid.” Prabha startles.

Chapter 24

In the morning of the abounding night, her bud-like head rested over my chest.

We were still in Adam and Eve contour. I kissed on her forehead which was just bellow of my chin. I called her in low tone, tried to wake her up who was still in the grip of dawn's numbness. I called her name a bit in high pitch near her ear; she mumbled, 'hmm' and clutched resting her head as usual at my chest.

Our room was the favourite place of the city where the first light of the dawn fell travelling across the river. Our day begân with the symphony of *Subah-e-Banaras*, beaming sun from eastward and the red netting line over streams, musing birds, ragas and mantras recitation coming from ghat and after the passage of the daylight setting in the west behind the city. The moon hovered over the balcony.

"Wake up and get ready," said I, shaking her lightly.

"Why?" she mumbled, still kept closed her eyes.

"We shall go to the court," said I.

"Why?" said she.

"For marriage," said I.

She tilted her head, facing me out of her dazed eyes.

"What about the family?" she questioned, trying to come out of her sleepy mode, fluctuating her eyes.

"I will convince my Grandma. What about you?"

She steered idly, squatted on the bed beside me. My finger was caressing over her right arms.

"To Mom and Di, I can. But to Dad," she stopped in the middle. She looked at me. "Dad is a hard nut to crack. I have told you about him already. He will not be convinced easily. I need some time to make ground in the family for our marriage."

I could see the terror of her father in her tamed eyes and scared voice. I had put my right hand over her cheek, she smiled and drew closer to me, wrapped around holding me, again rested her head on my chest nonchalantly.

She alighted from the bed, picked up dresses sprawled around on the floor, thrown in the night. I watched her complete womanly fabric in morning lights coming through the partially opened pane.

"I haven't mentioned one more thing ," said she. He pulled both her hands at her back and tried to clasp her bra. She came near to me, turned her back at me. "What was that?" I tangled the hooks, planted a kiss at her back. She shuddered a bit with thrill, sensitized. "Stop" she giggled

"I have sent some sample of your novel last week to a literary agent," said she, adjusting her bra, cupping her breast to fit and pulled the panty up to guise her female organs and at last wore back her Capri and t-shirt.

"What?" She gave another jolt. "I haven't edited it. I had written leisurely."

Nerves of my forehead were taut for a moment until she made things easy.

"Relax…Relax," she said cutting off my sentence.

"I had edited it already. It was a good piece of letters. And I'm sure, they will respond positively soon," said she and sauntered to the bathroom.

"Leave the bed now," said she.

After more than three months, I was back at home. Grandma and Meera's barricade was tougher than army rules. I was strictly told not to move a bit. Meera ordered me like the general of an army. Most of the time, I spent sitting or lying on cot, stuffing something in. I was tired of eating.

Grandma's health started deteriorating. Her coughing sometimes became terrible, particularly when she used to go to bed. Meera used to massage my fractured legs with swine's oil and desi wine covering their face with the cloth, Chhottani used to arrange wine, riding cycle village to village and market to market in search of it.

She was delighted at my new expedition. She told me about her possible husband that Kaka was searching for a suitable boy to marry her. I was rather happy.

"Kaka was saying, one day he would take you to show the boy. Kaki was saying, the marriage would not be confirmed until you pass the boy," said she.

I took Grandma to the hospital with the help of Meera and Chhottani. Her health was deteriorating. The skin of her face was wilting. It turned pale, withering, and drawing countless wrinkles, overcasting her age.

I gave one thousand rupees to Meera secretly. She declined to receive it. I insisted and told about my new job – writing, "I earned a good amount of money writing for a magazine and periodicals along with the name." I bragged.

"Siddhartha," she delayed. "Won't you mind if I say something."

I nodded approving.

"Will, you both, marry each other in future or just be like couples of the city?" she checked her tongue in the middle.

I guessed her dilemma.

"We are in a live-in relationship. We shall marry after completing our degree."

"But she seemed an elite class girl."

"She is."

"Do you think she will get settled with you?"

“She has already settled with me. She is a good girl unlike snobbish, sophisticated. She is different she doesn’t care about me as I’m a son of the farmer.”

“But I was happy to see the way she cares about you” she paused. “How will you tell it all to Grandma?”

That was the daily issue, now I had to end it.

“Don't know. Once I get a suitable time I let her know.” I said with confidence.

I asked her about her marriage.

“Kaka asked for a suitable date from Pundit Ji. He said April or May is the suitable month.”

“In April,” I faltered listening to it.“There may be my exam in April.”

She grieved.

“It’s ok. I will manage,” I assured her calculating in mind.

“What is Meera’s place in your life?” asked Urvashi.

I halted while smoothing her locks. I baffled at her question. “The most important person in my life after Grandma.”

“Do you love her?” she asked.

“Obviously,” I said. Still, I didn't get what she was talking about? What was in her mind? I found a changing tint over her face promptly.

My naughty fingers’ touch had turned her silence into the sudden deep sigh.

“If you love her, then what it is with me?” she inquired. There was a feeling of insecurity in her voice. It stopped me for the moment.

“Are you crazy? What nonsense are you talking about?” I yelled. I pushed her aside. “Dam’ it.” all the excitement evaporated in the anger.

“I love her more than you. I am frank with her than any close friend. But there are many facets of love. There exists beyond petty imagination.” I thought my voice was shivering with anguish and wrath, turned louder. “Since we got consciousness, she follows me like a shadow. She cares for me like a mother, loves me like a sister, and we share everything like friends, that cannot be measured on sexual intentions.”

I stopped. I tried to control my temper.

“I never thought to give any name to our relationship and I won’t. It’s very pious and sacred. I am sure; no relationship endures without feeling and faith.”

She begged pardon and was feeling guilty. I didn’t speak to her.

“Sadhu,” called the Grandma.

I was sitting at the leg side of cot, squeezing her feet. Meera was anointing her head. Grandma always called ‘Sadhu’ which was easier to speak than Siddhartha. And I become Sadhu for Grandma, Siddhartha for class attendance register and Sid for friends.

I never understood when I had been changed my insight into the changing of my name.

“Gulab Deyiya was telling the story, about a boy from her village, who was studying in the city,” instantly she coughed terribly in a very little time. As it calmed down, she drank some swallows of water and continued. “He has married a girl against her parents will.”

Meera looked at me restraining her smile. “Kaki, your son, is also studying in the city,” she japed.

“Who?... Sadhu?... No.” Grandma said. “My son will not do such anything against my wish. He is my pride, my ego, my heart. I know him.”

I was still, motionless like a stone laying on the dais, deep drowned in speculation about my coming future with Urvashi how I would conquer social taboos and Grandma’s trust.

One morning I wore an Italian suit, and Urvashi wore a Banarsi saree. We booked a cab and reached the Court without informing anyone. Kamal, Rehan and Pummy were already there. They signed as the witness on our marriage registration form. We exchanged thick garland putting it around into one another's neck .

We got married but concealed it from the public.

Then after that we went to Lord Baba's Vishwanath's Temple. Then, we moved to a restaurant and watched a movie together. Throughout the film where everyone was engaged, Urvashi closed her fingers into mine, held tightly, rested her head on my shoulder.

For us, the world seemed absolutely different.

We roamed, rejoiced at the end of the day; we came to Dasaswamedh Ghat and reserved the boat.

I got into the boat, later I helped Urvashi holding her hand and assisted her in getting into the boat. They checked their steps at Dasaswamedh Ghat. They smiled and waved their hands. "We will meet you at Asi Ghat."

"This journey was a sort of gifts from us to you my loving wedding birds," Kamal said.

"They waved their hands and moved toward Gaudiya Chowk to catch an auto.

I looked into her eyes, which was smiling delightedly, glittering incredibly. I held her by my arms, whispering three magical words, that the boatman could not hear us and gazed ghats rolling back one after the other in series.

Many time, I did boating, but it was heavenly blissful.

We alighted at Asi Ghat, where all three of us were standing at the bank of Ganges waiting for our arrival.

Rehan and Kamal hugged me after congratulating us.

Pummy wished me, and then hugged Urvashi. I don't know what she whispered to Urvashi, which made her giggle.

Urvashi hid her mangalsutra, a sacred thread from the roaming crowd under her sari. A tiny vermilion lined between her hairs in the middle point.

I was blessed with happiness. Our relationship validated into her eyes, I could see apparently.

They parted at Lanka after wishing us. Kamal and Rehan gifted me something in the packed box, which they strictly suggested to open in the night.

Chapter 25

In the night when I opened the packed box, gifted by Kamal and Rehan, it was comprised of some strips of the *Manforce Condom*. We laughed together for the longest. For now, we were a lawfully wedded couple who were living under the same roof with no romance, sleeping in a single bed without sensual touch but had compassion in our heart.

It may be weird in listening, but it was.

The semester exam was too close, so she instructed me to govern my rising impulses.

One such fine day, she was changing her dresses after returning from the University in her room without locking the door when promptly I got there straight, my glance caught her bare shoulder. My eyes widen, finding alluring sight in front. I was tempted. For a moment, I began stepping toward her compelling in the hand of heart.

Finding me, she abruptly asked me to check my prolonging feet. I can't tell how tough it was to retreat my steps.

Nothing can't be so tormenting than lodging so close to your sweetheart but miles away from touching her.

She came to me after recasting into the domestic dress up, gave me trouser and a T-shirt and said. "Until exam gets over, you'll have to CONTROL your emotions. Remember my dear charming prince." She pulled my cheek.

I was displeased with this agreement.

"You are an unfair lady," I whined.

She grinned at my guileless whining, half-heartedly plodded into the hall. She giggled. After a pause, she said when she was about to slam the door. "You may have a kiss before going to bed every night." I turned and held the door, peeped through curiously. "But" she continued. I never found such a terrible word as 'but' which creates hurdle in the way of your success.

It's like breakers on the road which jolt your smooth journey. "If I will find your study satisfactory at the end of the day"

I never studied as I did to makc her understand the assigned topics. I used to scroll Wikipedia, browsed books at Central Library, looked into self-made notebooks, and explained her satisfactory at the end of the day and bagged a kiss before going to bed.

She always found a chance to tease me. One day, she denied saying, she had detected the method of my study that was unsystematic. She made me aspire to study about greater critics on the topics. I borrowed Kamal, Rehan and her library card and issued books of the authentic author from the library and started rummaging the pages.

My situation was like the man who was thirsty living at the bank of the river. I troubled to reside near the lake of love.

I didn't know when professors began noticing my witty replies on the theory; it made me favorite of all.

After the exam, we took the same bus, which led to Allahabad via Gopiganj- my stoppage. She was going to her Nana's house.

Every time her solicitous memories precluded me rowing in the present world and surf me into the past. I normally found me lost since I arrived at the home, that Meera and Grandma discerned it well.

Seeing my sobriety, Meera enquired about Urvashi. She suggested me, better I should visit her, which would comfort me.

I vacillated how to persuade Grandma of my leaving for Allahabad.

"You need not be always the Utopian man. Put off your wardrobe of Satya Harishchand. Tell her, you have to go for some academic works and, of course, she would not deny. And you aren't going there to do anything wrong. And when you find the right moment, you can tell about her to Grandma."

I pretended to Grandma and won her permission.

In those days, Shashank was staying in Allahabad, preparing for UPSC exam, an iconoclast, against his father's political legacy.

He received me at the station. It was an afternoon there was no sunlight due to dense foggy weather. Finding me after a long time, I could see the reflection of his ecstasy beaming from his eyes like.

I decided to spend that remaining later half of the day with Shashank. A great number of students had been brooding, said Shashank, for years in the congested cell. He told, "Every year, fifty thousand students arrived in the city for competitive exam preparation and next year, thirty thousand return to their home."

Where Shashank was living, it was divided into several quarters, having around seventy rooms. In each room, there were a minimum of two students, disbursed their hours- day and night, leafing pages, bespectacled mostly digging their eyes into books, leafing pages and scribbling important notes day and night.

The whole city was stuffed with the advertisement hoarding, banners and posters of the coaching institute.

I phoned Urvashi in the early morning. I attempted a couple more times. I guessed she would be sleeping.

"Whom you gonna trouble on such an early morning?" Shashank said from inside of his cosy bed.

"Your sister in law," I said cradling cell phone at the ear.

"*Bhabhi*" he leapt out of his cozy bed in astonishment. "Where *Bhaya?* ...When? How? Is she from Allahabad?"

Watching his caricaturing, it was unstoppable to stop my laugh. I heard 'Hello,' a soft dozing voice from the next side. Putting fingers on my lips, I signed him to remain silent .

"Hey," said I.

I thought, my 'hey' was enough to introduce myself to her. I comprehended, she was still slumbering.

"I'm Prince William. Wake up, Princess Catherine." I said humouredly.

"Sid," she twittered. "How are you?" she paused brooding. "So, early morning?"

"I'm in Allahabad," said I.

"Allahabad! … You? … So early in the morning." She amazed. Resuming her consciousness, she continued. "Where are you?"

I didn't know the name of the place. I asked him the name of the place. He told 'Katara'.

"Katara," I passed on.

"Ok. I'll receive you within half an hour." She disconnected.

I did the routine of the day, took a bath and dressed promptly.

Shashank was still prone to the lousy bed.

"Shashank, if you wish to see her, get ready soon. She is coming." I said buttoning the sleeves of my shirt.

His elation was watchable the way he hopped out, leaving the snug quilt.

We walked through the foggy serene lane, where husbands could be seen roaming, carrying milk pot. Few middle-aged office men were marching in a tracksuit to decrease their round belly. They eat carelessly, and then they sweat carefully.

We reached where she asked me to arrive. She was waiting in a silver Audi. She was in black jeans, black leather jacket, wrapped stall around her neck, and had covered her head with a woollen cap. Her long silky hair were hanging around her shoulder.

"*Bhai*, is it *Bhabhi's* car?" Shashank whispered.

"Shut your gaping mouth. Avoid behaving like newbie before her." I instructed him.

Literarily, her dressing sense remained ever unpredictable. She opened the gate, got out and couldn't stop herself without hugging me. And in that frosty morning, nobody appeared loitering around us who could see, except Shashank and a few stray bulls, coiled in the cold.

"*Namaste bhabhi ji,*" Shashank said, abruptly. Realizing his words, he pressed his tongue between his teeth.

She darted once at him and then turned to me.

"My friend," said I.

She smiled and thanked him for his compliment.

She drove the car out of the frizzed serene market, shuttered down the shops either side of the thoroughfare, sporadically people came before the car jogging out of fogs as an apparitions, the dogs squatted in the ashes near the furnace of the confessionary shop, coiling their whole flexible body and setting their head in their belly. We entered into the south campus' premises of Allahabad University crossing a fainted coloured gate, pasted some chocolaty, some bearded, some moustache boys' poster. Finally she stopped by a yellow arch wall.

Her eyes lingered on my face, smiled, and suddenly she leapt from her seat over me. She showered kisses madly- at my forehead, eyes, neck, ears and lips- everywhere, for next over ten minutes. She was utilizing advantage of foggy wintry December. She tilted her head back, stagnant and gazed at me beaming right into my eyes, and held my hand in her both delicate grab, she protracted gradually toward my face, had mine between her both smooth and tender cherries like lips and elongated slurping. She initiated me that slowly, I followed her. I lagged behind to watch the sparks whether it was flaming inside me or she was fired as she was too burning into the fire of compassion, after living away.

Her sauntered changed into a racing horse as if she would eat up my lips. Deliberately, my hand slipped down, dragged under her jacket, grabbed sort of warmest and softest things on the earth. My hands were rushing as fumbling something. Suddenly, she stopped and held my moving hands. Controlling her giggling, she said, "No".

I winced.

"Not here." she eyed me, looked through the window across the foggy sphere to scrutinize whether anyone was roaming there or spying our lovemaking secretly.

An elderly man was coming toward us, jogging. She retreated into her seat, mended the decorum of her attires and set her scattered hairs.

"Today I will show you Allahabad." Resuming her soothing voice, said she, buttoned her jacket.

"Do you know where you are now?" said she, styling her hair looking into the mirror.

"No," said I.

"This is Allahabad University Campus," she geared the car and reversed it.

She stopped the car at a tea stall at the university road. She spread her palm in front of the blazing fire.

"This is a popular tea stall of Allahabad like 'Pappu ki Ari in Varanasi," said Urvashi to me.

"Bhaiya," the leader addressed me, being elated listening words in his appreciation, rubbing his hand into a shabby *gamachha,* hanging by his shoulder. "There are hundreds of students who have become IAS, IPS sipping my tea."

The transparent puffing glass was at my lips, but I looked at him rolling my eyes. And I stared at him in amazement. "In the evening hours, the crowd swamps around the shops, sometimes I don't reach to serve them." He was sick now in self-praise and had become a pure nerd.

"It means, you are the secret of the miracle happening behind the success of Allahabad's civil services students. *Wah Bhai.*" I mocked. "Then poured down one more cup for myself."

He baffled at my witty humour.

Urvashi broke into lunatic laughter as if she had gone crazy.

Paying money, she drove us through the serene road of overcast mist. She crawled the car, drove safely through the lighting indicator of the parallel vehicles, introducing the name of roads, monument, market, lanes and thoroughfares. The hearing entitles appealed as if we were rowing through some English cities like as Smith Road, Zero Road, Stanley Road, Edin Road, Auckland Road, Thornhill Road, Clive Road, Colvin Road, Drummond Road, Cooper Road, Daltonganj and et cetera.

Reaching at the end of Civil Line, a posh area of Allahabad, our car was rolling on the periphery circling road of Patthar Girja, All Saints Cathedral Church of Allahabad.

Watching its grandeur and incredible architecture, one can guess how significant Allahabad was for the Britishers in those colonial times. It reveals the great story of its bygone era.

"I have lots of solicitous memory of my childhood days with my sister and cousins. I was the usual visitor with my family," said she, as the car stranded on the halo way. The church is located in the middle of a circular road which is named M.G. Road, a prominent road of the city.

I, too, had one of the unforgettable memories of my life, spent one fine solitary night sleeping on the bench, lying in the lawn of its yard, I recalled.

"I used to play here." She indicated fainted grassy land of the premise. She made the cross, moving her touching midst of forehead then both chest, staring to the cross at the acme of the church. I imitated her.

The memory of that night animated vividly, when I landed on the earth of Allahabad first time in my life, anyhow travelling in a cramped general carriage of the train. Next morning, I had an exam at St. Bishop School. Asking address from the crowd, I measured around five kilometres from Rambagh Station. And when I reached to the school, I was exhausted extremely. I intruded into church premise, ate the meal which Meera had kept into my bag. I lay down on an ironed bench of church campus carefree and slept soundly. It was the terrible night spent encountering with buzzing mosquitoes. After a good sleep, when I opened my eyes, I found none around me — no honking car, no two-wheelers, no auto, and no *rickshawallah*. And the next sight had shivered me from inside when a ripe mango fell over me from the tree of roadside which boughs were surpassing the boundaries of church. I got conscious of churchyard seeing Anglo-Indians tombs and gothic architecture of building at my back. I looked at the cemetery silhouettes, partly shining under the lights falling from the lamppost, partially concealed in darkness.

I clenched my bag and ran as if some ghost was chasing me. I halted at another end of the fence where already some boys were sleeping, making their bags pillow beneath their head. Likely they had also come there for the exam, thinking, I too slept down on the ground, praying Jesus Christ to guard my soul the ghosts.

Urvashi drove the car through a bar-made-gate. . Inside, the premise was not appropriately maintained- littered leaves, scattered things, covered with unwanted grasses; untrimmed plants were making it more solitary and presenting negligent of the place.

Once, I entered the church, I found immense peace and internal calmness.

Its wall was made of Chunar sandstone. It had the stained glass of the window, sculpturing was stunning and beautiful. Aesthetic of its mosaic filled with rupture. The hall echoed with the flattering of pigeon's wings and their cooing. There was no one there except us both. The benches were vacant. Some scriptures were put on the small table wrapped in the clothes, in the front crucified statue of Jesus Christ.

We set on an empty bench out of many.

"You know" she whispered. We still were gazing the idol of the Lord Jesus. "There are 42 churches in New York State." She darted at me. "In Delhi alone, it is 125." She put static data. "Sometimes I feel, religion is the main problem of all. It becomes more about population than spirituality."

"Look." I stopped her. "You should know the difference between community and religion. To be religious it is not bad, but to be communal is heinous. When religion becomes just medium of accumulation of mass, then it turns destructive. Spreading ideology is one thing. Alluring masses to join the group is another thing." She was looking at me. "You know what? Prophets, gurus, ascetic have discovered their own truth, their own way of realizing the existence of God. And people are just following their words in spite of searching their own truth." I remained calm for a while and continued. "To set temple, mosque, or churches is good if it is for spreading humanity and love for God rather than gathering community and spreading propaganda of narcissism."

Chapter 26

She drove the car detouring across Civil lines and showed me a car showroom of her *Mama*, maternal uncle. Meandering by a school, she said, showing the mason, she had studied there some classes. "Allahabad is my second home after Kolkata. My grandfather was once mayor of this city. My grandparents love me." She stopped at boisterous traffic. "Allahabad's traffic is not like Banaras's hectic traffic," said she, assuming my tense silence, whereas I was thinking about her background.

She stopped the car before a long stretched boundary of a garden.

"It's the Company's Garden. It's the same place where Chandra Shekhar Azad had got martyrdom" said Urvashi.

She bowed before his statue in his typical style- twisting moustache with the right hand and resting left on the waist.

It was a huge, long extended impressive garden that contained various species of flowers, trees, and trimmed grass. A colonial designed public library gave it an exotic look.

It was frizzing stillness, hardly middle or old aged people appeared roaming there. Couples were in good number caught rambling there wantonly.

We sat on an icy bench.

"What's the purpose of coming to Allahabad?" She inquired me.

"You," I said, instantly.

"O...Really?"

I nodded.

She grabbed my arms, leaned her head resting by my shoulder. "Honestly, I missed you terribly since I left you at Gopiganj."

"I missed you too," said I.

“But you must spend time with Grandma when you have holidays,” said she. For instance, she was right.

“Sometimes, I felt, as lust overcoming me,” I said, pitying, inhaling a heavy breathes and exhaled frosty air out of my mouth as if I had smoked cigarettes.

“Please, don’t say that’s lust,” she said. “You don’t know, it is the best part of my life. I feel I’m in heaven whenever I find you near me. And when you are not with me, it goes most panic and haunting days to spin single second.” She looked at me, smiling, and grabbed me, and regretted. “Sorry.”

I had booked tickets for the movie. It had time, so we did lunch in Haldiram Restaurant. I spotted a bookshop on the second floor; I beseeched her to go there. I pushed the pellucid glassy door, escorting Urvashi.

I picked up books, flipped its pages and read the author’s bio and the blurb of the book printed on the back page. I always loved touching books, reading them and smelling its odour.

“Excuse me, sir.” A girl of twenty patted at my shoulder.

I turned. Urvashi, who was busy in selecting the book, also looked at us.

“If I’m not wrong, you are the author of the book, Meeting with the Stranger,” said she. I saw she had my book already in her hand at the moment.

I smiled cordially, “Yes.”

“I love your writing. It has moved me a lot,” said she, ecstatic. “Autograph, please.” She handed her book to have my signature.

It caught the attention of people assembled there, who were passing by shelves to shelves in search of books.

Gradually, they strolled to get a signed copy. Urvashi was smiling at me, standing at the book counter.

I reached to her, asked her to go for the movie.

“Excuse me, sir!” A man standing across the counter said. “I’m the owner of the shop. If you can give your precious hour for putting signature over the books, I'll be grateful," said he, apologetically. "It will also be good for the book's popularity."

"Sorry, sir," I apologized. "But now I have to go somewhere."

Urvashi looked at me, pensively.

Up to now, he updated the news of my arrival at his online site, Facebook and Whatsapp group. The news of 'Meeting with the Stranger's author spread in the city. The bookworms began marching toward shops. Within few minutes, the shop was stuffed with the people.

Obviously, I was missing the chance to spent time with the prettiest girl in my life, the female protagonist of the novel. I was trying to escape them, giving casual replies to their questions.

Urvashi came near to me, and gave me a note and winced. I unfolded it. "Hello Mr Author, I'm here always for you, but these people will not come always. This is the time to cash your fortune and pleasure that you always wished to earn."

Then, I scribbled autographs on the books and shopkeepers began printing bill ledger. Reader shook hands with me, chatted about the book.

The feeling of being an author receiving respect from reader is beyond any loyalty.

Signing lots many books, I asked Urvashi to move. The shop owner stopped me, "Accept this small piece of the gift from our side."

It was a packed bundled in the paper bag. We were late for the movie already, so we hurried to the cinema and occupied our seat.

The movie couldn't hold us in the seat, except a few touchy scenes. Everyone was busy in watching the shedding tears scenes which pained her and I didn't like and finally decided together to move out. We shared kisses, caressed, and hugged when everyone was busy in watching fluctuating animation.

The whole day, I lent my ears to her voice, kept hearing her childlike intuitively zooming in her car over the smooth road till the evening- full of her giggles, sharing memoirs and lectures playing slow music in the background.

She stopped the car in the middle of an arch bridge which was beautiful, gave an exotic experience. I had heard about Naini Bridge', and its occident look. To confirm it, I asked Urvashi.

It was cold enough that day, and slowly the fog was overcasting whole sphere, so we geared back to the city.

"Don't you think, we are like two rivers?" said she, gazing at meeting points of the river at Sangam. "Do you want to visit there? It's a good time for visiting the Sangam."

I declined the option, saying. "No. Not now. Some other time."

There were thousands of cabins at the bank, and numerous people appeared creeping like ants from the bridge. It was a pious month of taking the holy dip into the meeting point of Yamuna and Ganges at Triveni. Devotees stayed there for a month. I remembered, once Grandma, too, had come here and stayed for a whole month leaving me in Gulabo auntie's custody.

The room was warm with our heat. Our eyes opened quite early. I enfolded her in my arms from back, remained still closed our eyes. The morning numbness tempted us.

She stirred, turning around, and now my lips were close to her forehead. I became flat, she placed her head in my arms, caressing her finger over my chest lightly scratching with the tips of her fingers over there.

"Sid," said she. "May I come with you to your home?"

I was awakening partially. "Why? What happen?" I mumbled, still squeezed in the cozy bed.

"I wish to meet Grandma."

It made me wake up completely out of my morning drowsiness.

"Why?" I inquired.

"Just wanna meet and touch her feet to have her blessing."

"I haven't told her yet. Only Meera knows."

"Ok. I will leave you outside of your village." She was determined.

"Ok," said I, squeezing her into my arms.

I asked her to return to Allahabad, reaching my native town-Gopiganj, but she yielded her wish to see Grandma and my native land.

I was averting to take her at my bucolic house and idyllic life existing there. My mind was busy in comparing of my mediocre life with her sophisticated profile.

I perceived a speculating reflection over her face. I decided to face reality presenting her before Grandma. I thought better, the sooner curtain of realism should be uplifted, she would be able to see my absolute life, where I breathed in.

When the car meandered from the village canal, rolling down via brick pathway manoeuvred to my home as I instructed her, there appeared none in front of the house.

Meera came out of the house hearing the horn of the car, who was sitting by the fire. Seeing us, she rushed immediately inside.

We got down. Urvashi, hardly, had prolonged steps, Meera blocked her way, holding brimful lota, an urn-like pot, urged her to halt her stepping. She poured down water before her.

"A sort of ritual," she said to Urvashi, whispering. "At the first arrival of the daughter-in-law of the house."

Urvashi hugged her, said almost in whispering. "Thank you."

"Where is *maayi?*" I asked. I used to call her '*maayi'* which means mother.

"She is inside, sitting by the fire. A few minutes before, she had gone to bed for having a nap."

Meera was leading us. I was with Urvashi, who coming close to me to speak, said, "Does Meera know about us?"

"Hmm," I hushed.

"Everything?"

"No. But many things. Not things like last night." I punned equivocating.

Meera shook Grandma softly to wake her up. She made her sit, clutching her arms gently. Grandma had covered her whole torso.

She asked my well being. Her beaming eyes fell over Urvashi, finding her a stranger, she asked us about her. Meera introduced as my classmate who had helped me in the accident. She played an emotional card.

Grandma made her sit beside her, cupped her face and showered blessing over her. The person if ever did anything good for me was the matter of importance to her.

Gulab Devi aunty also arrived there knowing somebody's arrival at my home.

"Sadhu," Gulabdeyi aunty called me nearer, said slowly that her words could not reach to any other in that chamber. "Don't leave the chance. She is very beautiful. Marry this girl. She is too white as milk…So beautiful." She was jesting.

I smiled suppressive.

Meera boiled tea in the smoking grate and served us.

The conference went on more than an hour. Meera took her to show surrounding, husbandry, mango-garden and trees which I had planted during my younger age.

"*Dadi,* grandmother," said she. She finally came to meet Grandma before she went. "I'm leaving."

Grandma put her hand over her head, blessed her. "Come again *bitiya*, daughter," said she. She gave her twenty rupees as her blessing, and she kept it in her pocket happily. She hugged Meera. I didn't know what they shared, murmuring themselves. I just watched their moving lips. Finally, she came to me, said, "Thank you."

She geared the car and drove off.

Chapter 27

Once again, I repeated history scored highest in the third-semester exam. Urvashi was on the second position.

Now, I had a name, a bit of fame. People easily recognized me.

Spandan, an annual function of the university, was at hand, and inter-faculty competition had been going on. One fine day, Dean of the Faculty called me. I went into his chamber; I stood straight still in a poised way.

"Siddhartha, son," said he, homely. He still engaged in jotting down something on the pad. While writing, he popped up his head seldom, looked at me, saying, "Last year, you had bagged the entire trophy in writing, oratory and reciting competition. What I'm thinking, others also should need a change from the department. Right?" said he. "So, if I ask you to withdraw your participation in writing, will you mind?" Asked he.

"No, sir. There is no issue of bother if you ask me to do so." I returned.

"That's nice, my boy," said he, commending.

"We have selected you as a leading volunteer from art faculty to lead participants to enhance their morale. You will be given some group of volunteer under you. And Spandan committee also has selected you as anchor and Urvashi will accompany you," said he, added. "I read your book. It's nice. And I listen to its noise in newspapers and magazines." I was about to move after the conversation, he stopped. "And keep some copies with you; we have decided to launch your book in Spandan in the presence of a famous Bollywood actor."

I told Urvashi about anchoring. She was glad to share stag with me, quite excited.

At my request, Urvashi consented to participate in the dance category.

One day, when I was passing by the Social Science faculty, I encountered Manish and Thakur. A long time had passed since the last time we had met to each other.

"Ka ho Maharaj*!* Why are you in a rush?" said Manish, coming straight to me, wrapped *gamachcha* around his neck. They glanced at me from head to toe in astonishment. "You are changed Mr Siddhartha." He added, jovially. "What happens? Is everything normal or has gone beyond?"

"How are you, Mr. Siddhartha?' asked Manish, patting on my shoulder.

"I'm fine," said I. They left the city for Delhi after completion of their degree.

"How are you both?" asked I. "And where were you?"

"Doing preparation for lectureship," said Manish.

Suddenly, his phone beeped. He snapped to receive it and walked a few steps away, bubbling something vaguely.

"Since he had secured admission in research, he became popular amongst the girls." Thakur winced me, indicating toward Manish. "He is dating a girl now."

"PhD?... O… Really? " I exclaimed.

He returned. I complained to him.

"Was busy running behind professors', that's why I couldn't get time to contact you?" said he.

I baffled 'running behind professors.'

"Means buttering in straightforward." Thakur delineated.

"Why?" asked I, dubiously. "Is it needed for research? I think you must work hard for the exam."

"Which world are you living in, *Guru?*" said Thakur.

"Look at him." He pointed to Manish, who was softly smiling. "He was the topper of the class. We have given dozen of interviews in more than seven universities, but he somehow got admission in a university, but I'm still struggling. Our rank in entrance were mostly in top five though. You know why?- because we are general!" he added further emphatically. "To be successful, you need to be skilled how to project yourself."

Just then, a boy greeted them and passed.

"Look that boy. He is receiving 30 thousand rupees as RJNF scholarship; he is nothing in subject knowledge or in the study. He had got admission at 50 marks whereas mine was 170 marks. This is the irony of this nation. He is a son of PCS officer, still deserves reservation, my father is a vendor. I had to give tuitions for the survival of my study."

I deduced anguish against class description.

"They do parties, and a genuine scholar who wants to study is deprived. The reservation must be based on financial state, not in mental efficiency. Or else the country will be the handicap in the hand of mal-skilled people," Thakur rebuked.

I heard them passively.

"But you are a man exceptionally beyond any system — an original talent," praised Manish. "I heard about your book and saw it in the bookshelf of the shops and read reviews in newspaper and magazine. Literally, I'm happy to see you growing as an author. Finally, you have become what you always desired to be."

I thanked them for paying gratitude and shaking hands.

Their further unchained statement, I received mutely, joining in their yes and no, a complete diplomatic state. Though I didn't know Nitish Thakur before coming to Banaras, almost akin, I knew Manish since graduation, his condition, in what state he had spent his three years of graduations in that isolated mediocre antique tattered room at the end of the market near buzzing stinking drainage. Still, I remembered how he wandered the whole market and at the end, he used to halt at the cheapest vegetable shop. He took tuition that he could survive at least cheaply. To save money, he used to travel forty kilometres of distance paddling cycle.

It was quite a busy schedule for Urvashi. She had to take classes, then practice, for she was participating in three different competitions- solo dance, group dance and instrument.

I tried to restrain her doing anything of the household that she could focus on her practice and give time to her study too.

Although I didn't know cooking exactly, so I packed the meal from the restaurant in Lanka. But mostly, we did breakfast at Matri Cafetaria and dinner at the room. After dispersal of class in the evening, when everyone returned at their lodging, she used to stay back in Radhakrishnan Auditorium Hall with others for rehearsal. I used to carry a bag stuffed with fruit, juice, towel and other essential things.

I abode stagnant resting in the chair, watching her. And this way, it went for a week. I had a right beard over my face.

One fine evening, when they were at their last stage of practice, solo dance and instrument were done; it had struck 8 o'clock in the evening.

I kept waiting for her sitting there for hours as a routine daily every day.

I held back, strolled in the corridor of the hall, sat at the solitary stairs showered in lamppost light, which in the day used to be buzzing with tramps of students.

As usual, I took out the book, began leafing its pages.

Urvashi came out almost drench in perspiration, completely exhausted. I put the book aside, watched her coming fainted and tiresome. She pulled her hairs, collecting and tied them into a bun. I spread my hand and assisted her in sitting beside me, letting her head resting down on my shoulder.

I rummaged the towel in the bag and pulled it out. I gave her the water bottle. She washed her face. I wiped her dripping face. She swallowed water as if she had been thirsty for many days. I fanned at her face waving book's flapping pages.

"How long will you have to stay now?" I asked her.

“Group dance’s last rehearsal is imminent,” said she, in the low tone. I dragged towel over her hands, neck to give a sponge down the wetness of sweating.

She looked a bit relaxed.

I gave her juice bottle. Taking some sips in, she urged she needed something to eat. I gave slices of fruits and some healthy stuff.

“*Arey wah,*” Pummy said emerging from the dark corridor. “What a caring buddy you have got Urvashi...*haaye!* I feel jealous.” She halted at the verge of the stairs, reminded Urvashi for practice and she retreated.

It was quite engaging schedule to me, too, as the days of celebration approached closer. At the day of the inauguration, a procession of students’ band from each faculty, swaying at the beat of DJ marched and accumulated finally in MP Theatre ground.

The chief guest was a celebrity.

Urvashi was one of the members of the group who were to welcome the guests. She was in a sari who appeared bewitching, and was an absolutely beautiful lady.

“Hello, sir,” A junior girl called me. “Urvashi Di is calling you.”

I followed the girl.

“What?” said I. I was in a hurry, as stage’s responsibility was given to me.

“Sorry,” said she, apologizing.

The smile which was blooming at her face coming there of me just vanished seeing my perturbed expression.

I held her hand, took the back side of the stage away from the gathering, and cupped her face. “I’m sorry. You are always beautiful, you need not my assurance. You are the most beautiful girl of the world for me even when you are without make-up.”

"Actually... I...Thought." She said placing her hands lightly on my chest and spoke softly. "I didn't want to go in front of anyone until your glance falls over me first. I don't want to allow anyone's eyes to look at me before you."

"Do you want, I should kiss you?" I whispered softly in her ears.

She convulsed her head.

"Maybe lipstick of your lips gets spoiled."

"Go ahead. I'll manage," said she, smiling.

In just another hour, her complexion changed, faded.

"Hey, Urvashi...Oh!" Pummy staggered seeing us as she realized she intruded in our privacy and was to retread. "You both are crazy." She smiled. "Chief Guest is to come. They have left Guest House."

I kissed at her forehead and hugged her tenderly.

"Sorry," said I. She was still silent.

"I can't go without your smile," said I.

She lifted her head, tugged her nose with mine and smiled. Eventually, I kissed at her right cheek, leaning and brisked out from there.

I, along with other volunteers, escorted distinguish to the stage. I bowed slightly to Dean of Art Faculty, as reverence. She returned a loving smile. She introduced me to Chief Guest, VC and other officials.

After the ritual of welcoming, lamp lighting before the statue of mother Saraswati, garland offering on the statue of founder of the university by chief guest and other distinguished on the stage, the band of the girls, in which Urvashi was one of them, recited kulgeet of university.

As the chief guest came over the mike, students' gathering hailed him in the chorus as in typical Banaras'style.

The leader- "…. *Bhaiya ki.*"

Of corse, I can't write his name. They trailed the slogan to its end adding Banrasi slang with name of chief guest.

That followed with the perennial slogan, "Harrrr... Harrrrr... Mahadev."

Anchor announced my name and read a few famous lines from my book that was hailed by the thunder of claps from gathering. The guests on stage launched my book.

Urvashi was clapping from the corner of the stage, peeping from the curtain. I darted at her escaping from them. She flung a flying kiss which chief guest, a famous Bollywood actor, had caught us.

"Who is she?" he whispered.

"The reason for this book."

"Keep it up. She will make you a promising author," said he, smiling.The best part of his speech which I liked, "An already drench man in the rain is not afraid of falling drops."

Setting Dawn

Chapter 28

A single spark of doubt can burn all the faith and trust you have and turn it all into ashes.

One fine February evening, we were sitting at Assi Ghat. She appeared.tacit that day. I tried to know the reason behind.

Ultimately, she opened her mouth and spoke whatever was revolving roundabout inside. She said that her sister was coming to Banaras. But I didn't find any problem in her sister's visit ofBanaras.

"Then, what's bothering in it?" said I.

"Di is not the problem," said she, lost in the trance-like state. "Actually, a boy of her hubby relative will come to see me."

"Why?" asked I, randomly.

"To see me," said she, glaring me."Dad has chosen him as groom for me," said she, lowering her head.

"DAMMIT." I yelled in pain. "How? And …" In middle, she stopped me.

"For me, their coming is not an issue, but you…if you control for a week only." She grabbed my arms, pleading. "Please. Just for me. I don't want to hurt Dad." Tears were to roll down crossing the periphery of her eyes.

"And what about me?"

"I tried my best to stop this, but couldn't."

I could sense, she was rather in more painful state than me. I moved my head away from her in despair. She urged me trying her best. I looked at her.

"Do you think I'm happy with this news?" said she, in murmuring tone as if something was choking her throat.

The pitch of her tone was diminishing; I sensed moistness in her voice. And if I stayed little longer, her eyes might begin raining. So, without delay, I turned her and asked, "Will he also stay with you?"

"No," said she. "Only Di. He has stayed in the hotel."

If you haven't experienced jealousy in love, you have experienced nothing.

Next three days, she was absent from class. I called her; her phone was either switched off orwas out of coverage area.

One day, she came as the professor was about to start his lecture. She pushed the door and plunged it open. She didn't ask permission and walked through the rows, checked her stepping reaching near my bench. She kept glaring the studentwho was sitting beside meuntil he stood up and moved to another bench. She sat down abruptly.

The whole class had set their eyes on us, but she didn't bother.

She perched, unzipped her handbag. Yes. Mostly, she carried college bag when she had to come to class, but that day, it was different.

She turned her notebook, wrote on the last page, 'Sorry' and scribbling gossip beganwhereas everyone else was rowing through the lecture on Samuel Bucket's 'Waiting for Godot', the theme of nothingness.

I ignored her and didn't see her writing on the page. She elbowed me to draw my attention. Once again, she wrote many 'sorry' that filled half of the page and still when I didn't dart, she eyed me in rage to write my response.

She got fed up. Standing from her place she, almost yelled, "I'm saying sorry to you, not to these walls. Why are you ignoring me?"

The whole class echoed with her shrieking. Everyone was stunned and they stopped their study. The professor constrained her lecture and looked at us. "Siddhartha and Urvashi do you have any problem?" she waited for our reply. "Urvashi, don't you know the difference between school and home?" said she to Urvashi, chiding.

"Mam, I need to talk to him," said she, meekly.

Everyone present in the classsomehow suppressed their laughter. I stopped my giggling with my palm, however.

She was happy now taking me out of the class. And honestly, I was happytoo, but I disguised it behind my pseudo anger. I walked in divergent to her stepping. She pulled me into another free classroom and shut the door behind.

She hung holding me around my neck, kissed at my cheek. I, as I told, tried to skip her, dramatizing my internal annoyed Romeo. She was aware of my every nerve and fragile ego. Ultimately, I smiled at her childlike behave. She cheered to see my cheery face.

Somebody knocked at the door. She opened partly and peeped outside.

"Is it room number 43?" I heard a boy's voice.

"Yes, but it is busy now." She reverted and slammed the door.

She made me sit on a bench and opened lunch box. After three days, she was in front of me which compelled me to set my eyes on her. I discovered an abundance of love; perhaps she was compensating for the absence of several days.

With every morsel, she cleaned remaining particle of food around my mouth licking. I didn't stir; neither had I wished to disrupt her overwhelming presence. I felt as if I was showered under a loaded cloud.

She fed me. She moved backed to the chair, I was sitting in. She garlanded her both arms around my neck and set her head, resting her chin on my shoulder leaning over me. Her silky hairs plummeted at my face and covered it. She ruffled my hairs courtly.

I made also her sit on the chair.

"What did you do in these three days?" asked I.

"Didi made us talk face to face. He asked about me several things," she mentioned.

"And he?" asked I. I couldn't understand why I was so prompt and possessive about her. Was it out of my love toward Urvashi or jealousy towards that NRI boy?

"Nothing. I didn't need to answer." She said, in rather strong voice. "He narrated about himself spontaneously without my asking. I kept listening her. Then he took me to a club."

"Did he touch you?" asked I.

"NO." She said emphatically. "But he thought to."

"What?"

"To touch me." she cried.

"Then?"

"Then what? I told him to mind his hand," said she. She kissed my hand gently. "You are the prince who has stolen my heart. Now nobody can own me, neither can afford me. I'm your …baby!"

I put my right hand on her cheek lovingly.

"Yesterday, I be-fooled him, sayingI had a headache. I managed to cancel his plan, however. And today, I persuaded Di that I have some important work in the department" said she, chuckling.

"How many days will it go?"

"Three to four days maximum," said she, calculating. "Yes, I saw, Di was also reading your novel 'Meeting with a Stranger'. She loves book reading. I told her, I know the author of that book. So, she wants to meet you. I haven't told her that you study in my class whom I love more than anything else."

Our faces brightened with smiles.

Next four days, I had no news of her, no calls, no clue where she was brooding? What was she doing? Being away from her, first time I caught, it was tough to breathe. My excessively imaginative mind cast unnecessarily plots between her and that NRI boy.

I got agitated every time when my phone disconnected; I kept my eyes opened whole night. I spent my time reading notebook. Regularly I went to the department, hoping she might come that day.

One evening, when the sun rushed down, I couldn't stop my wistful steps and reached her apartment. I waited outside, rambling. Ultimately, I walked upstairs, pressed the bell of her door. Coincidently she opened the door. Seeing me unexpectedly, she opened her mouth astonishingly.

"What happened?" said she, whispering.

I was looking at her silently. She shuffled me out of the room. "Tomorrow, I will come to you, I swear."

I was perplexed, why I was standing there, what I should speak. I was just gazing her blankly.

"Di is inside," said she, in rather a low tone. "Please understand."

She watched me motionless next for few seconds. She came out of the room, slammed the door noiselessly, she, stealthily, led me into a corner of the roof.

"What have you made yourself?" She moved her fingers across my unshaved beard that made me appear a gloomy lover. "Don't you take the meal on time? Just look at yourself once in the mirror." She was chiding quite like Grandma and Meera. Her chide blended with affection.

I felt as if I would start crying holding her like any whining child. But I set my eyes on my toes, however holding oozing tears. I dared not to lift it up, for I knew, it would roll down.

Seeing her I used to turn a child.

I was accumulating my courage subduing the overwhelm.

"You should go now. If Di catches us here, it would be a blunder," said she, whispering, fondling my hairs.

"Urvashi," a penetrating voice shook her. She snapped and stood apart away from me. It frightened us. I guessed it was her sister who was glaring us through her fierce eyes, in wrath.

'Speak of the devil.'

She burst over Urvashi rebuking. I was standing at a distance, listening to everything. Urvashi had been urging her not to be furious.

"Didi. STOP." She shouted at her sister when she was to turn at me with her savage words. "Not to him. You can say me whatever you want to." She looked at Urvashi. "He is my husband, MY life." Urvashi cried, pulling out her *mangalsutra*, pious thread, hanging in her neck.

Her sister went downstairs and let herself fall into the sofa with a deep sigh of exclaimation. "O my God!"

I thought better to keep silent in their family conflict, although I was the point of their duel. Urvashi prolonged with light steps toward the sofa where her sister was holding her forehead in her right hand. She knelt down at her feet, held her right hand, and persuaded her to calm down.

I watched them as a spectator to any drama scene.

"Haven't you thought about family reputation once? What dad would think when he would listen to your story?" she sneered. She added further, "You took such a big decision without concerning the creed, caste, class of the boy."

"It was not pre-planned. I thought nothing; don't know when I fell in love with him." I felt moistness in the voice of Urvashi.

"One can't spin one's life with love only," said she. "Bull shit!"

"The boy who comes here to see you, who we have chosen, is a millionaire," said her sister, calmly, holding her anger down. "He can afford your every wish and desire."

"Di, ask yourself, are you really happy marrying with a millionaire? Have you forgotten your love easily?" Urvashi threw her into her past. "He is not millionaire of course." She looked at me. “But I will have million times happiness with him. Di, I can’t imagine my life without him.”

She caught the sight of the book, ‘Meeting with a Stranger’, picked it up and commenced to speak. “You wished to meet the author of this book. He is none other than Siddhartha.” she turned the back cover of the book, shown my picture.

I discerned a melting ice on the face of her sister.

“Is he the author of this book?” said she, being ambiguously. “Seriously!”

Her mood changed immediately, finding her favorite author nearer to her. She shuffled to me.

“Do you love her?” asked she.

“She is the best part of me?” I replied.

“It’s tough to survive just with writing after falling in love,” said she.

“She is my inspiration. If she is with me, to be a millionaire will not be any dream to me, but a reality,” said I, confidently.

“Ok. You must take dinner with us,” said she, smiling.

Chapter 29

We entered a shop to have flower, milk and *prasad* for offering in the temple. We unleashed our shoes, took out phone, watch and deposited to shopkeeper. He gave us a key.

He sprinkled water in our hand to clean it before holding flowers and milk. Unexpectedly, when we, I and Kamal, marchedtowards the temple premise, Rehan followed. I looked at him questioningly, seeing him trailing us.

"What?" said he, sounding unknown to what was too imminent.

"This is temple?" said I, reminding him.

"Why are you looking at me so dubiously, you rascals," he whispered. I halted few steps before the gate where cops were checking people before theyentered the temple. "If you believe, Mahadev is master of the whole universe. Then, I'm not outside of this universe. Move ahead. You want, they issue fatwa over me? And who knows, I'm Muslim lad, except you both *Chutiyanandan*. So please don't do any stupidity here. Otherwise people will beat me." He patted me and walked.

The most amazing thing was his aptness of dialogue. It could make anyone laugh.

He murmured an Urdu sayari, poetry copied from some renowned poet.

"Insan apane sath khuda ko nahi rakh saka

Maszid bana diya taki khuda rah sake.

*(*Man couldn't keep God with self, so, people made mosque (temple) where God can live!!!")

"Let me imagine as I'm going in the premises of Mecca," saying it, he pushed me aside.

We stopped at the checking point. The policemen were searching by dragging their hands from upper torso to legs, which tickled us inside.

There were few people, wearing white *kurta -pyjama,*going inside for reading *namaz* in Gyanwapi Mosque which was close to the temple.

"I can't go inside without covering head," saying he pulled out his handkerchief and covered his head.

To avoid any sort of mishap, Kamal and I accompanied Rehan and wrapped our hanky over our head. He put his talisman inside of his pocket concealing from the public – the talisman had Mecca and Medina pics and was now hidden inside his pocket.

"Actually, covering the head is also a ritual in Hindu and Sikh," said Kamal, knotting the edges of the handkerchief stretching hands.

We walked parallel. We were protecting *prasad* from monkeys, who were hopping over the tin shed, made clattering

I thought to move with him instinctively, fearing his naughtiness. So, we put our eyes on him. We knew, if anyone suspected his identity, it might turn blunder. But he strolled confidently, glancing over the walls, golden vault of the temple, as if he was the first time watching them. And it was the fact.

"Why are you so tense about me? Relax. Just chill." He said, as preaching like any typical television Baba.

I had already come there several times before, but every time my faith in lord Mahadev renewed and rejuvenated.

We creeped in queue joining hand in praying demeanor. Some South-Indian pilgrims were murmuring some chants.

I tried my best to bestow garland and milk over the *Shivaling*.

I came out of the main temple, stood at adistance and closed my eyes, praying. The moment when I opened my eyes, Rehan was not around us.

We ran across buzzing crowd, searching him around in premises but couldn't see him anywhere. I found him finally, kneeling on the ground by the wall of temple headed westward, muttering something vaguely. Kamal reached there. He also stood there, hiding him from the crowd.

"When I was young, a maulvi used to come to teach me," as we walked out of the temple, he started narrating the story of his childhood. "My mother used to sit there till he taught. It was the everyday job for Ammi Jaan. Sometime Abbu Jaan too sat there. Ami Jaan had instructed Maulavi Saab strictly to impart only what has written in the Quran Sharif. Nothing beyond that."

Today, he appeared more different transcending his jolly nature. We halted in front of the shop to collect our things.

He pointed his finger at my chest, said, "Listen to your heart. Ammi Jaan used to say, Allah convey us of right and wrong."

Chapter 30

As the farewell approaching nearer, the fellows became amiable forgetting their past grudges, if they had ever among them. Everyone was busy accumulating sweet memories of campus days.

The pain of parting was virtually reflecting in their eyes. Few, who became close friends, could not believe how hurriedly almost two years passed away, buried under the heaves of the days which would be forever alive in their memory.

But they also had a latent ecstasy for the future, wondering what was next? At the eve of farewell day, we, one by one, confessed our sweet-sour moments of campus days, shared experiences, and bestowed our views to our fellows.

Of course. There was no certainty, whether we would meet again, once we passed out, or not.

But particularly in our case- I and Urvashi,we were thinking differently. We had decided to have an eternal compassionate journey, together. Farewell- we were not taking it as an ending, but as a real beginning of our everlasting sojourn.

I was glad for myself, remembering my first day in Banaras, like a novice boy in a world of edifying. But now I had a name, fame, a popular book, a promising future in writing and above all Urvashi- a true fellow-traveler- my love, life and strength.

That day, since morning I noticed Urvashi was a bit fatigued and a couple of times shevomited too. Unlike other days, she was not cheerful. Standing in a corner of the hall, I looked at her as sheturned towards the washroom and came out covering her mouth.

"What happened?" asked I, approaching her. "Let me take you to the hospital if there is any problem?"

She nodded in NO. "Don't fret. I'm Okay. It's some digestion problem."

"Are you sure?" I beseeched.

"Yeah." She asked for leave and walked to girls' thronging. She was talking to Pummysmilingly.

I was puzzled. What I didn't understand was whether she was okay or unwell. Anyway. I took a seat and quietly watched the performance.

After half an hour, I came out of trance-like situation lost in performances; I ran my eyes throughout the auditorium hall, searching Urvashi. I asked fellows but I didn't find her.

Gradually, as second changed into a minute, minute proceeded towardshour, the index of my anxiety rose. I asked acquainted people desperately. They simply nodded their head and moved on.

I reached at the threshold of building.

I strolledon - leaping over stairs, halted at the road and looked at either sides of it. I checked her scooty in parking-stand. I inquired the man. He told, she had taken her scooty just twenty minutes before and drove toward the main gate, Lanka.

I returned to auditorium hall. Pummy was absent from the event.

Without informing me, where would she go? I calculated.

I waited for her there with my vociferous mind and relentless heart.

I could not sit there. I stood up to move out when one of our juniors stopped reminding me for recitation at the stage.

Although I had to read on that occasion; but I didn't find any worth of it without her.

Her mysterious absence from the hall couldn't allow me to repose. So, sitting hardly few minutes, I hurriedly moved out from there. I asked a rickshaw man, who was waiting for a customer at the corner of faculty road, to peddle towards Lanka.

I was laden with speculation and anguish of her sudden mysterious absence.

I leapt out of rickshaw before it stopped. Giving fare, I ran to her apartment.

The next moment made me more mystified when I found the door already locked as it was. I hastened my flying steps downstairs leading to the basement. But I didn't find her scooty there. Millions of thoughts clashed together in the mind, creating an impending tense and messing up. My mind was enduring.

I asked the security guard at the gate. He said she hadn't returned since she left in morning with me. I was completely fatigued. So, I thought to stay there, waiting for her return and sat there on the stairs.

The clock kept revolving, the evening fell. I rushed toward the Department.

By then the function was over. People were scattered outside, conversing gladly in their gaudy dress.

"Where were you?" said Rehan, excitedly.

"Have you seen Urvashi?" asked I, concernedly.

"No." His face turned pensive. "Why?"

I swerved without saying anything further. Now, there were hundreds of questions echoed together in my mind, but I had no right answer.

I went to all possible places. I was drained off. I sat in a restaurant at VT.

A thought struck my mind and I proceeded through IIT and reached the Sunset Adda.

She was brooding on the bench alone without me, facing up the western sky, gazing covertly."You damn it." I yelled up, as I was just a few steps away from.

Haphazardly, she tilted her head, drawn her fingers to her eyes.

I stumbled over some pebbles. She turned her head at the rattling. I saw vaguely her gloomy countenance face. Just next moment, she turned her head aside and drew her fingers to her eyes abruptly as if hiding something from the corner of her eyes.

I paced to the bench where she was pondering in the faded evening. Itraced her lately wiped moisture over her face. “Hey, tears in your eyes?” I knelt down before her and peeped at her wet eyes.

Her sitting alone without having me at Sunset Adda was incongruous.

Shelabored to hold a smile over her lips. “I’m good.”

It was a phenomenally beautiful, balmy evening of late March, most suitable month to roam in BHU campus. Nursery farms were painted in a kaleidoscopic natural colour. There flowers blossomed, it scattered its fragrances that drifted in surrounding with wind blows.

Clear bluish tint resembled the musical beauty of earth. Birds chirped in, hopping and hiding in the bushes. On another side, my beloved one looked uneasy which had snatched all ease of my mind.

“Darling,” I said, squeezing her shoulders after holding tenderly, her spreading the right arms across her back. “It’s not farewell for us anyway. Here begins our bon-voyage. Got it?”

She shook her head, smiled.

Looking into her eyes, I always realized a mystic shadow which I found myself into incompatible to interpret.

“Do you know ONE THING?” I asked her gravely.

“What?” said she, softly.

“That I love you.” I deadpanned.

Her lips spread horizontally, muscles of cheeks uplifted below her beautiful eyes. Lips and eyes can explain one’s inner world, what’s going on. If I didn't fail, there was something inappropriate which she tried to hide every way.

I smiled back. I thought the best thing you can do in the tense of your friend.

“The best thing of this evening has witnessed, that’s smile at your lips,” said I.

She nodded as a little child innocently.

"Do you know what?" said she,

"What?" said I.

"You are crazy," She giggled.

Don't feel regret, shame or shy of doing what gives you pleasure.

We yielded our face toward each other. We kissed slowly.

If you want to pace down the speed of the world, kiss slowly to your soul-mate, no watch can bother you, no work can haunt you, no past can pang you, it's what can take you're a hypnotic world.

Kissing is the best remedy to delude the loneliness and pain of the heart. It's a miracle and lips are magical wand. Kissing is a sort of conveying, that you write on the lips of your soul mate. That word cannot delineate always.

Words are just a medium to reflect your insight, what you are feeling within. But that's not the whole truth. The feeling is something abstract entity which springs out from the fountain of heart. What we can't explain in words, phrase or sentences, we do silently in action.

Everything faded in the twilight, the silhouette of trees, but their images were telling they still existed.

The city's honing was turning louder. The twilight was shifting into starry night slowly. The campus glittered with lightpost.

The frail light from Gymkhana ground was coming to us as fluctuating rays of stars.

We left the bench, led to our lodging through the facade lights either side of the road. While moving through the vista, whenever I got shadow under the tree, a sort of privacy, I kissed her, clashed her in my arms. I tried to snatch her strange aloofness through using light words, jokes and laughter.

Chapter 31

Eventually, Meera's horoscope matched with a suitable boy. The date of her wedding was set quite near to my exam. At every weakened, I visited home for making the arrangement, shopping and preparation.

At every Saturday evening, I had to rush for the train and reached late evening at home and worked throughout Sunday, I used to catch evening train and return to Banaras next day.

But attending marriage was a dilemma for me.

Meera threatened me, "If you won't be present, I will not sit in wedding-mandap, temple porch."

Dangling between Banaras and village, my preparation used to get hindered.

Meanwhile, Urvashi introduced one of her longtime friends since graduation; she was visually impaired but had a profuse grasping and analytic mind and blessed with soothing and lucid voice. She loved to muse enchanting ghazal. Her ideas over any topic used to be amazing blend with witty illustration.

And she was perfect in every manner. I had given several titles to her- Miss Nightingale, Miss Fantasy and Miss Brilliant.

We all three- Urvashi, her friend and I- discussed together on conference call till late night. For I was still lodging with Kamal and Rehan, being concerned her elder sister might visit her at any hour as those days she was in Allahabad. Often, she came at her room withoutany alarm.

It was so tough to tolerate the pain living at the distance of five hundred meters away from your soul-mate living in the same city.

We could bear space for a moment, but not the length of time.

After valediction ceremony, we were engaged in exam preparation.

Meanwhile, I had to halt at home for couple of days. I took Chhottani, carried wheat sacks at the mill for grinding. I hired laymen for chopping wood apart and throwing them in open space under scorch sunlight to get it dried.

Having Gulabo aunty, Kaka and Meera, I took them to purchase jewellery andsari from our local market. There were several merchants who sold things on credit to their old costumers.

Meera accepted silently, most of time she spoke in demure without intervening in likes and dislikes of ours, and when she came before me; she did not tease or chide me like previously. Neither had she yelled nor complained against me to Grandma at my repeated misspelling of her name. I missed my childhood friend in her incompatible changed girl.

I realized, I had lost my Meera.

I terribly missed even though she stood before me.

Another concern which was eating me inside, relentlessly, was Grandma whose health was deteriorating. The clarity of her voice changed into whizzing, faded in terrible coughing.

She was unable to walk on her own. She took the support of wall if ever she had to go to relieve herself in the night. I was worried about Grandma, what would be of her after Meera's departure to her in-laws house? I was carefree of Grandma, was doing my study without any spark of tense in mind, for I knew well, she would take care of her. But now?

Whenever I got spare hours, I loved to spend with her; I sang songs, told her stories and tried caricaturing, mimicries to make her laugh.

She was not well.

Once, when I was talking to her, Meera was overhearing my jolly words, standing behind the door without making me notice.

She burst into anger at me. "Now you have studied lots, why don't you get married?" she was completely in wrath. "She needs not your bogus, boring hogwash. She needs somebody who can take care of her, look after her diets and medicines."

I did not understand exactly the reason of her wrath over me. Soon, her voice turned into sobbing, sentences came in waffling undefined words. She picked up booms, began sweeping. "I'm not your maid nor am I available always here, why don't you understand?"

"Why are you so angry at me?" I thought to ask but couldn't dare. "What happened?" I asked mildly.

"What happened? ...It's you who is asking? …You?" she was glaring me. I was dumbfounded. I didn't know whether Grandma was getting her or not, but for me, it was just like a bouncer for the batsman who comes for batting first and the pitch is wet.

She continued, "If you had taken any initiative, I wouldn't need to leave my house nor my family. You are selfish always." Before her sobbing turned vociferous, she left the place. I kept looking her haste steps.

"Dear son," Grandma patted my back. "Don't mind her words. She was saying in that manner, for she is concerned about us. But don't worry about me. I'm well. I'm not going to die until I will find a suitable girl and get you married. So, you get your degrees and become *kalattar*, magistrate… Hmm."

She was thinking, I would be magistrate after getting my study done, how could I reveal I wished to be a writer.

Hardly could I put Meera's harsh but unscrupulous words aside and now Grandma's concern made me disquiet for the whole night.

That night I sat my cot in the cowshed. I tried to close my eyes and sleep, but drowsiness eschewed away to some forbidden land. The lantern was lighting dimly, the silence of the night was occasionally broken up with the fluttering of cow's tail.

I had turned right side, closing eyes. Just then I felt as somebody got into my bed. For a while, I was astounded, but next hour I got it. It was not the first time that somebody intruded into my bed at night silently.

She was making a convulsive gasp.

I caressed her head lovingly. "You okay?"

She wrapped with me, buried face in my arms so that her sobbing could not turn louder. I could understand her situation. She had to take such a long journey after few days and would have to join an unknown family, completely new place and new faces.

I never succeeded to define our relationship into words. I can't now even.

Sobbing in my arms, she fell asleep and I didn't know when I also detained in the grip of the cozy dream, fell asleep combing fingers untangling her locks, making them smooth.

Kamal told, he had seen Urvashi twice erratically visiting the hospital.

"Why do you need to go hospital?" I asked Urvashi, taking sips of coffee sitting in Nestle Coffee shad of Madhuvan Park.

The motive of Madhuvan Park's opening was to provide a place for sitting and interacting and spending good time. But nobody knew when it turned a favourite spot for open hugging and smooches of lovebirds flowing behind its bushes. Sometimes outsiders are also seen cozying up here.

"I was not well," said she.

"What happened?" I asked worrying.

"Nothing. Had just slight fever" said she, sipping.

"How is it?" I inquired putting back on my right-hand fingers.

"Don't worry. Now, it is ok" said she, smiling.

Even though March month, the whole campus appeared beautiful because it wore verdurous foliage, multiple colored flowers of over a dozen species of trees. The facade of beautiful vistas of lofty trees at Madhuvan road can catch anyone to gaze it astonishingly, especially standing at T- point corner and looking at slightly ascending road toward Visual Art Faculty. The road which goes under-woods demonstrates as the staunching picture in as wallpaper of your android phone.

The university is a walled campus, spread over 1360 acres. Within the campusyou can witness a large number of trees, herbs, climbers, among them there are many arch fruit and wild trees primarily. These trees, like arjun, mahua, tamarind, mango, jamun, banyan, mostly stand either side of the road as high stood vistas, bless you protecting from sunlight and cast an unforgettable memory. Long trunk and canopy of several grand trees adorn campus decorum, serene and fascinating. And equally, numerous birds' species visit these trees make their shelter.

She smiled suppressing, sipped coffee.

"My detective and spies are spread in every corner of this walled campus, spread over 1360 acres," I bragged.

"Hmm. Okay." She said. "So, you have left you spies behind me!"

"You can think so," said I, promptly.

"You don't have trust in me, right?" I saw my jokes were turning into a bit into the grimace. So, I decided to end it sooner.

"No, how can I dare? I was just joking," said I, defending. I changed the topic.

1st April, a message flashed over my black &white cell phone's screen from Urvashi's number. "Congratulation. Your number has been credited with 50 Rs."

"Darling," I typed back. "I'm ready to be fooled forever in hand of you."

My phone beeped ringing my favourite tone. "Love you. That's why I'm ever ready to die at you."

"I don't want to let you die; I want to live with you for my every possible second."

"Okay…okay... Sorry." She paused, added further. "Suppose if I die, unfortunately, then what?"

At that moment I felt as if I was thrown into a dark room, and asked to find out the path to exit, having no spark, no sign of light. I didn't understand what to say on such point. To imagine about her death, for a moment, literally, I felt helpless, a patchy life.

"What a stupid question is it?" I cried and next second muted in wrath. I was not in the mood to say anything.

"Babu" She called me. I didn't reply. She reoccurred the word 'Babu' many times. "Please, say something. I'm so sorry," said she, apologetically.

"You were asking, how would one live on the planet without breathing," I said emphatically. "If you gonna talk such trivial things, I would turn myself into abyss of silence."

If I reminisced my life cannon, those two years were special-most particularly the fourth semester.

I had been lodging with Rehan and Kamal. Sometimes I spent most of the night sitting on the roof encountering bloodthirsty mosquitoes. I wrapped a blanket, covered whole body leaving face only.

Rehan and Kamal used to fall asleep soon after their dinner, snorting nose. They couldn't escape any opportunity of sleeping whether they would have to lapse their marks in their scorecard.

I used to be with her on phone in the night and in the day, we spent our hours rambling in the campus-sitting under trees, in the antic but solitary room of faculty as the session was over, and often strolled at Ghats and perched at our perpetual evening spot, Sunset Adda. She used to bring lunch for us with changed recipes, taste and flavour every day.

The whole day, we drove on scooty from one place to another. Sometimes, I followed her idiosyncrasies and paddled cycle, making her sit at the front rod.

One thing, I noticed in her- a change in her physical appearance and in demeanor. She was fatty a bit in look. Now, she was rather calm and harmonious in nature. She didn't get angry soon, nor behaved crazy as she used to do in beginning. She fatigued after having walked hardly few meters. She didn't want to leave me for a single while.

Occasionally, I spent night at her apartment in the custody of her embrace.

I knew the nerves and throbbing of her heart. But there was a mystic side which I failed ever to transcript.

Her company instilled a vicarious pleasure, her every smile was capable to thrill me with rupture. One afternoon, we spent sitting behind amphi-theatre ground resting our back by the wall of its shed, laying under the lush mango tree over a grassy floor, and shadowy, breezy place. It was less walked place.

Chapter 32

The examination days arrived.

The first day of the exam commenced on 18th of April. Gradually, all complain and guilty between fellows vanished and iceberg of grudge and ego melted down. If I recalled my whole academic journey, I found, it was the first time when I appeared in the exam without being horrified of score. I believed if I had Urvashi, I could conquer any obstacle of the world. And one day I would have my desired world.

But the Utopian world, you imagined does not occur true sometimes. Sometimes it swerved into dystopia.

At the day of the third paper, as we got into our allotted room after a brief meeting, I couldn't ignore her fainted face. I glanced at her through my lingering eyes. Before I asked her the reason of her gloominess, she moved towards her class.

I submitted my answer sheet. I readily walked toward her classroom through quietness of the corridor twenty-five minutes before the submission time.

I stopped in front of the gate, waited her patiently until the final bell rang. The assemblage rushed out of the classroom as the final bell rung as flooded water. I perused every face carefully but couldn't see her. Watching a few moments more, I went inside intruding oozing crowd.

I approached her place; she had put her head down on the desk, fainted.

I called her fondling her shoulder, placing a palm over her head, tried to checkthe temperature. Her body was burning like rock in Indian summer.

I tried to boost her, assisted her to stand up but she couldn't.

She fainted, unconscious.

I uplifted her in my arms, hanging her in my lap as in a cradle. She held me by my neck, her head rested on my right chest, eyes were closed.

Students looked us concernedly and the knownones trailed my steps making ways clear through corridor and stairs leading to ground floor. They split apart.

We became the center of attention.

Few of them found a matter of gossip, few walked near me asking the help, sympathizing, few gazed us as any classic Bollywood motion picture's shooting was going on, live.

Oft Urvashi opened her eyes, sluggishly, looked at my face and let it fell next moment as they were laden with the burden.

Pummy, Rehan and Kamal came running to me and inquired,controlling their gasping.

"She is not well," I spoke. They helped me to take her downstairs. I was drenched in perspiration, gasping. I looked asunder oscillating back and forth for vehicle.

"Wait. I'm going to call rickshaw." Kamal ran towards the gate and returned blankly."There is no rickshawallah appeared at the gate."

"Does there anyone know driving?" asked Kamal, looking away towards parking cars.

Dr. Parthana, one of the most beloved teachers, was stirring her car and was to drive out of parking. Rehan approached and said something to her pointing towards us. Urvashi was swaying in my arms unconscious. Tears rolled down spontaneous.

She made her car turned towards us. She turned down the glass, flung open the gate and asked me to take Urvashi inside.

Rehan opened the door. Pummy gripped the feet of Urvashi, helped me placing her on the back seat. She had switched on the AC of the car.

Rehan was standing outside still. He could not dare to sit in the front seat, parallel to her.

"Rehan beta, son. You come here." She opened the door herself. Rehan took the seat. She asked to tie seatbelt and drove towards the hospital.

While driving the car, she gave her cell-phone to Rehan and asked him to dial a number. Rehan handed her after dialing the number. She set phone at her ear, talked some doctor, I denoted with the tone and dictions she used. She asked the person to reach the hospital.

I was caressing her hair. Tears rolled down, dropped over her cheek seeing her miserable state. Prof. was watching me in the front mirror of the car. She consoled me.

Urvashi opened her eyes, crescent.

When we reached, a young, handsome man of thirty, was standing there with some nurses and doctor, having a stretcher, in casual attire holding stethoscope in right hand.

She slowed the car in front of the emergency department. Two nurses and a boy approached the car. Kamal was behind them.

She had been laid down on the stretcher, deployed. The nurses pulled the stretcher rolling its wheel. The young man, seemed doctor, asked me the symptoms how it had happened. I ran with the stretcher, narrating things.

"Dev," called the Prof.

The doctor turned and reached to her. She said in instructing postureand he was gravely. Then she came to me, handed her plastic card and told pin code. "Put it. You will need it. And I have told the doctor. Don't worry, my dear child! Don't be fret." said she.

The hospital is the best place to know the truth, transient nature of this muscular body. If somebody has an ego, must visit the hospital, scrutinize patients etherized over the beds once. For living in our egoist dreamland, we never imagine, this fair face will perish one day.

Staying at the reception of the emergency ward, I witnessed the pathetic state of patients.

The doctor, a young man, suggested me to admit for that moment. The word 'admit her' had filled me with a strange worrisome.

"Is there anything so serious?" I asked gravely. "She has to appear in the exam."

"When?" I quarried.

"Day after tomorrow."

"No. Not serious. She will be fine by then," said he. Patting at my shoulder he parted.

I prepared breakfast, served her tea and assisted her in bed to sit by self. She spoke less, tried to explain minimally. Sometimes, she went silent.

Next fine morning, before going to the department, she urged to visit the temple. I hired a rickshaw and took her at VT.

It was the first time, I witnessed, she covered her head with her attenuated dupatta prior entering into the temple, joined both her hands, closed her eyes, slopping her upper eyelid which met with lower as if it was intercourse of sky with land at the horizon.

Faculty masons had prevailed with an utter serenity. As we rambled, our tramps echoed in between those vacant spaces. She recalled all those days she had spent with me. Throughout she had held my arms. We walked across amphitheater ground. She giggled remembering jolly acts of our fellows, especially Rehan, a self-made clown to make laugh people in his surroundings.

Finally, we reached our alma-mater, perched on the bench at Sunset Adda.

She rested her head on my shoulder.

"It would be tremendous if time got stop now. How beautiful it will be, if we remain like this- sitting on this bench, gazing bluish boundless sky at this Sunset Adda."

She dragged her arms, clutched across my chest and upper waist.

“I’m here forever for you” I looked at her. She gave me a cryptic smile.

“I know,” said she, muzzling at my chin.

“I will adore you even when your hairs will turn grey like silver, myriad vague wrinkles emerge over face, and your eyes will be weakened in sight. Still, I will be passionate as I’m now.”

She giggled jolting her head back, constraining her laughter, said, “Really, will you love me when my hairs will turn grey as silver?”

“Yup. Perhaps that time my love will be rather profound.” I assured her, smiling into her eyes.

She used to be more fascinating, appeared exotic beautiful when she turned child-like naughty in demeanour. My glance sojourned across her facial sphere glittered blue super moon alike at such hour. I didn’t leave any chance to behold her.

“How?” She asked curiously.

“I have only two years of memory with you; I’m totally entrapped with you and your thoughts psychologically and emotionally both. Imagine, what would be at the age of eighty when I will have several amazing years with heartfelt memories span with you?”

“My dearest darling,” she mused. “I think you don’t know, you are incarnated in the world merely for me.”

Gladly, she leaned her face, planted a kiss on my cheek.

We did our dinner at Annapurna restaurant- a pure desi hotel. Next day, we had Literary Theory and Criticism’s exam.

She was apathetic towards the study that evening, seeking ways to engage in gossip. Sometimes she swung hanging by my neck, wrapping her arms around my torso, sometimes she clasped me tightly.

I asked her to focus on the study, tried to make her sit down and look into the page but in vain. When she was to leap again from her place, I clutched her wrist, pulled at her to make her sit. I sensed her fluctuating mood.

She had put on short.

I explained topics. And she signed titillating. She unfolded her bun, making her locks free to swaying over her naked shoulder which hung to waist length. She held one of the locks dangling near her ear, wrapped it circling around her finger. And when I lifted my head to address her, she smiled flashing her ivory simmering teeth.

She complained of humidity and began unbuttoning her sleeve. And next moment, she flung it away. She pretended to be too eager to study, leaning forward she asked me to explain the topic.

And, I felt, my manhood began stirring within me, which my jockey underwear tried to hold it. "Don't deviate from the topic?" said I, gravely.

"Of course. I'm focused," said she, innocently winking her eyes as seriously as nursery child.

I, too, detected a compassionate sensation in the entire fuselage, several craving surges oscillated, rising and falling amorous thoughts made me trouble.

She took the book out of my hand, put away. She minimized the space between us, crept nearer.

I controlled my inevitable sighs. Heartbeat rose, throbbing faster. I inhaled a deep breathing escaping her eyes to harmonize the vibrant romantic persona inside which busied in imagining.

She glided her palm, brushing her finger through my silky hairs and backs of my neck with her both hands and the mystique journey began with her touch which changed soon into slush sound.

She dragged her hand downward, unbuttoned my shirt at every halt of her slipping down hand. She pushed me down on the bed and mounted over me. She was crazy like anything.

I silently let her do what she liked, controlling my uncontrolled impulses. But I found it was irresistible. She turned notoriously naughty. She filled me with a thrilling sensation within ten minutes through her passionate touches.

I pulled her close to me, cupped her face, and propelled our fleshy tong deeper inside out, swirling, exploding into our mouth. I felt unyieldingness in my manhood member, stricken against the trouser which touched her belly when she sloped over me for an amorous expedition.

My hands and its fingertips were on the pleasant voyage, exploring her every sensory limb. She had closed her eyes in absolute pleasure.

My hand glided caressing her abdomen, crawled backwards of her slippery waist, then forth, and henceforth downward, unzipped her shorts to make it lose and pulled it out and threw it aside heedlessly.

She assisted me in removing her tight outfits, tucked out of her soft plumped thighs.

She had only two pieces of clothes concealing her feminine. Every time she appeared differently quite tropical to my eyes.

I kissed her, cuddled at her waist, an ardent moan came out of her mouth deliberately, and replenished the whole room with her sighs.

I slid the hand down her thigh teasingly, glided searching like any explorer in quest of some unknown world, found the strips of the silky panty. She slightly lifted her legs as likea crane, I drew out her pants.

Our every limb was busy wherever they were needed.

I unhooked her bra's hooks at above her curvy waist, kissed there, my hands sailed and found her ever soft, cozy swelled region, now, tightening. Her undressed back still sticks with my t-shirt covered chest. She twisted as my fingertips rushed at her chocolaty dark mammilla.

I fondled as ransacking some concealed archaeological land, finally found her secret love when my fingertips lightly placed at her clitoris, she burst out with sighs which soon altered into wild breathing, which I felt at my neck, a chronic warm puff.

My wandering hands still were overhauling over her marble alike glassy skin.

Sometime, a mountain size thing can't do anything to you turning a woman on in bed, what your finger's touch at her button-sized clitoris can do for you.

She turned the button of my trouser open, unzipped and freed my full swing glorious Adam and began the race of moaning, sighing and fluid motion.

After several minutes of our constant togetherness came to a halt.

We had been panting, trying to hold our labored breathing, throbbing of our heart. And again, our voyage began this time more haste. The slamming sound of bed resembled our heart beating and jolts of our breathing and ended after drenched in the shower.

We were still in bed, she cupped my face into her palm, gazed me and smiled. She craned her head and kissed my forehead.

We remained lying in bed throughout the night in the embrace of each other.

Chapter 33

After the exam got over, I left for home the same evening. Like all, this time again I reached home quite late asking lifts from strange vehicles.

I was at a distance from the house; I heard Grandma's terrible coughing and gasping which made me scary.

She was now a rather crippled old lady with a frail skinny fabric. Her sinews were loose and sense was fragile, too fragmented to remember anything for a long hour.

Meera had set her cot beside her bed.

As for custom of the village, a newly wedded girl would return to father's house spending first four days at the in-law's house.

In pale lantern light, she appeared a changed one- wearing seriousness over her face like any lady, drawn a profound vermilion line in the middle of her forged hairs, wrapped in a yellow sari and less expressive in words.

Next morning, I hospitalized Grandma, seeing her health, to a near by hospital. She had a breathing problem.

"Give medicine on time, keep her happy," said the doctor, scribbling prescription in ambiguous English fonts on the notepad. "In old age, people lose immunity power, sustainability. The more you keep her happy, would be better." Waging pen between his fingers, he said further. "Old age doesn't expect luxurious commodity. She needs respect, happiness and two pieces of bread on schedule time."

Next few days went quite crucial for her. Her voice changed into whizzing sound. She could not sit on her own. So, for sanitation, I used to lift her in lap and made her sit back side of the house, in a vast pit.

She sighed, asked me to move away. But I could not, for I could not leave her alone.

One week had gone; still, her health was deteriorating. She laboured while uttering "What would happen about Siddhartha after me?" Oft she used to talk to visitors coming to see her health.

Not always, but sometimes in solitude, when I bestowed my thoughts, speculating, I found myself blank, 'what after her?'

Since childhood, she remained like a shadow of my life, roof in rain, and warmthin chilly winter.

In the middle of the night, I woke up out of sleep at her chronic coughing; whizzing breathing, sometimes she called me for washroom. One night, nothing transpired like the routine. After several days, I remembered, first time, I slept soundly.

Next day was an unusual morning as I woke up. I found a strange silence in that smoky muddy walled house, there was no resounding sound of chronic coughing or whizzing and breathing. Neither was her early morning call for the routine wash.

As I got consciousness, I reached her cot rubbing half opened drowsy eyes. Her lightweight skeleton was still, motionless. Her eyes were closed, the mouth was open, withered lips were stretched behind her teeth ridge. Her body was cold.

I wanted to cry, but, realized, I did not know but lost the ways. I sat down holding aleg of the cot, my pain of losing most precious part of my life converted into my sobbing.

Meera came in, seeing me sobbing, she halted at the door. She apprehended the tragedy; her steps were too quick that stopped at the cot. And she could not resist herself and began crying.

Meera, then Gulabo aunty, and then neighboring folk, and then gradually whole village gathered in front of my house.

People took Grandma, laid down over a mat outdoor making her feet southward. Some orderly suggested calling priest, evoking youngster for arranging things for making pyre, last ritual.

Chhottani took the axe. He fetched two long bamboo poles.

Dindayal Pandey, who was expert in making corpse carrier, tied poles with ropes.

The woman, whom I revered and loved most in my life was tied into sack over a flat bed, made of poles and thatched, ah!

My tears had been gushing down incessantly, but no words came out of my mouth.

I have a phantom image of childhood when I had to hold urn after completing funeral rites of my Grandpa. Then I was too tender.

Villager led funeral procession reading perennial slogan which I heard in Marnikarnika gully often. Though I was greatly willing to set her cremation at most acclaimed and sacred place in Hindu mythology, Marnikarnika Ghat, but my Grandma, once, had yearned meurging to cremate her at Rampur, where Grandpa's and our other ancestors had been cremated.

How could I violate her final wish?

Reaching the border of the village, the priest asked to halt the procession. People alighted Grandma's corpse from the shoulder.

The priest made me wear a ring of pious weed, *kush*, instructed me to poured water having some rice in the palm.

The villagers marched in processionto surpass the boundary of the village as a custom.

Now, the watch struck 9 o'clock in the morning. The early May sunlight was enough to scorch people under its brooding sky.

I hired two Bolero cars. All the people who were going till cremation ghat at the Ganges sat inside and Grandma was set on the roof, tied with the railing.

Village folk, mostly, wrapped *gamachha* over their head escorting from the brooding sun. Their clothes were soaked in perspiration.

People were covered with dust layers coming through the window. We reached Rampur ghat, cremation place, where sands were hot like sand's beads frying in the grain parcher's pan.

That cremation ghat was unlike Manikarnika ghat- isolated; cattle appeared grazing turf at a distance.

The pyre was set. Completing all the rituals I was asked to set a fire in the sack of wood, where Grandma was laid down. All villagers went back and sat under a banyan tree except Chhottani who remained stood with me there until Grandma's materialistic existence dissolved and returned at their origins.

I sat down under bare sky. Chhottani beat at pyre with a long bamboo pole to make it ablaze it well.

As the fire turned her flesh into ashes, the man who was leading the ceremony flew the remnants in the currents of Ganges. As for the costume, I ordered sweets and plate of the dum-aloo recipe.I wondered I was serving sweets at the demise of my Grandma?

That day, the door of the house was missing something, and I was too.

Meera, Gulabo aunty, Chhottani's wife and children were sitting in front of the house waiting for us. I had lost the most important person of my life though, they were deprived of something.

As usual, I could not stop my step moving directly inside the house to the cot where Grandma used to rest. They all were watching me; their silence changed into sobbing.

My feet halted at the cot, knelt down, her permanent absence from there made uninhibited cry. Since morning, the ominous silence sprawled over my face; it had been swirling like any storm inside me, now it erupted as the volcano.

Meera was behind me. She sat beside me, held my shoulder; place her hand on my back, chorused with my lamentation. The more beloved she was to me; the similarly she was to Meera.

"Betawaa, dear son! Keep patience. Hold yourself." said Gulabo aunty, between her sobs. "What one can do at God's decision?" Gulabo aunty caressed my head motherly.

I was completely ignorant in the case of costumes, the ritual of *shraddha.*

Village elderly people came forth, most particularly Kashi Kaka, a veteranand a socialist of the village, who occasionally used to visit my home, conversed on the various issue related husbandry, health, and climate.

Grandma had mentioned once; Kashi Kaka and my Grandpa were childhood friend which remained long-lasting. Though Grandpa left the world years ago, he never left of his routine visiting his friend's house.

Kashi Kaka, never unabridged his routine, he told me several tales of his childhood adventure spend with my Grandma, sometimes when he had been turned nostalgic. Oft tears rolled down from his eyes recalling his sweet memory span with Grandpa.

Like all time, he arrived at my house and placed under neem's verdurous shadowand instructed me.

Every day, I was to go village pond where every neighbour followed me.

Sometimes, villagers were seen cleaning their cattle in the same pond. Buffalos used to ruminate in cool water for hours, circulating their mouth as chewing something inside.

After a bath in the pond, I offered water over a weed made stump, and afterwards everyone followed my steps as per costumes, on the priest instruction.

Whatever we see apparently is not the only truth. And truth sometimes is the mirage, which exists beyond the eyesight and mind of human being.

As for the costume, the person who had cremated the dead body would not sleep or sit on the woven cot, so I was given wooden plank.

Nobody was allowed to touch me or come near to me.

The priest told me that Grandma would receive whatever I would take in those thirteen days of *terahvi* ritual.

Meera had set her cot near my bed so that I could not be frightened of some ominous dreams in the night. She had put an iron knife under the pillow and put a blazing log.

I realized although Meera was most closed one to me, most particularly in those funeral contumely hours, I was quite away from her. She hardly wasted words with me.

One afternoon, I sent a message to Rehan, Kamal and Urvashi about the tragic incident. Both arrived till evening to see me and stayed back.

At every second-half of the day with the dropping sun in the western sky, the light turned soothing, the priest perched on a high stool and used to narrate some mythical tales from Hindu scriptures. And villages grasped his metaphysical preaching craning their head, paying their ears to him. Mostly stories were about the life death.

On tenth days, the barber arrived with a throng of his fellows, having their instrument to clean our well-flourished hairs.

I sat down, gave my head into barber's hands. With every scratching sound, a fistful hair fell down. He left a piece of hairs, churamani, in the middle of the head as if some foliage has been left from the mouth of grazing goat.

As the final day of terahvi costume approached nearer, it went more engaging to me.

On the eleventh day, at the valediction of Mahapatra ceremony, the farewell of Brahmin, quite an early morning Meera, Gulabo aunty along with neighbors set the fire in the hearth to cook recipe to serve them in the feast.

There were numbers of people assembled at the pond under the tree, including young, lad and elderly people. They sat in the queue. We began serving them recipe in leaf plate. Of course, they didn't eat but swallowed.

As they finally did their swallowing, I went through one by one, bowed partially, handed them money and touched their feet.

There was an elderly lady too, had come with them, as my disguised Grandma, whom I gifted everything that generally a person needs in day-to-day life- a new well-carpentered cot, a lantern, a set of pillows, quilt, cover, a stick, an umbrella, a sleeper, a sari. And the list was quite long.

The *gowdan*, ritual of offering cow in a donation, was next.

Chhottani had to gulp down the dust of around ten villages just to arrange a heifer.

A drain was dug out, a symbolic Baitarani river, which every human has to crossto get redemption according to Hindu belief.

The lad pulled the rope of cow across the drain hauling the boat. It is mythical belief, the holy cow by this costume help us to move across this Bhavsagar and takes us in God's kingdom.

On terahvi, I woke quite early before the dawn.

The chef was still working, busy in making the recipe with his lady gang. He was the only man.

Since morning, I rushed hailing guests at the door and looking after for their hospitality.

Kashi Kaka led me at every point with his experience visionary. He advised me to invite country folk going door to door requesting them to be present at my house. And I did.

Meanwhile, Meera took care of my meal. She gave me juices at every half an hour interval.

The swamps assembled in front of the door, sat in queues. A number of village youngsters rushed in queues holding buckets stuffed with recipe- vegetable, puri, sweets and many more.

No despair could dance over my complexion in that hastiness.Kashi Kaka scrutinized the plat of folks sitting in the rows, eating.

He yelled at young boys if supply could not reach adequately. And he yelled too at the feast eater if they spared food in the plate.

The feast went on till late night.

Next day, Kamal and Rehan carried away utensils and things that I had brought on rent for occasion and they left for their respective home.

The storm settled now.

Remaining food, Gulabo aunty had distributed among laborers, who were a partner in my strife to execute the feasting ceremony fairly.

Chhottani too along with his family went back to his home staying with me after Grandma's demise.

At late afternoon, Meera told me to have a bath then. When I returned after having the bath, she had already set plate adorned with food.

Seeing heave of meal in the plate, I suggested her deduct half of the meal from the plat. Without going against my will, she did as I instructed.

She retreated silently to her home after serving me lunch.

It was scorching afternoon. No wind blew, none appeared rambling outside. Occasionally, birds' chirruping could be heard from the throng of trees next to adjoining well.

I thought to sleep inside the house but couldn't venture to surpass the memory of Grandma. The serenity of home connoted me covertly the absolute absence of her form the planet.

I took a cot, strolled towards the cowshed uplifting it. I put the cot flat, slept over it. It seemed as if pains were also waiting for my being isolated, freed from rest burden.

With numb eyes, I hid my face in my arms, constraining my inevitable sobbing; I fell asleep with an un-tempered deepsorrow.

And when I opened my eyes, Meera was in front of my face. She was fanning at me with a homemade blower, holding tears at the verge of her eyes' periphery.

It was dusk hours. The atmosphere was salty. It was absolute silence prone all over. The darkness was prevailing over glob. The crickets were screaming piercingly.

Meera bought water gave me to wash my faint and drowsy face.

"They are coming tomorrow to take me back," said she, quietly. She gave me a glass of fresh water in left hand and a lump of the juggler in right one.

The priest had finalized her valediction quite earlier after checking the suitable date in his astrology book, around twelve days back. But due to the tragic mishap, the assigned date was postponed for further.

"But I don't want to leave you here alone?" she said, burbling.

Such a strange silence we had never witnessed before.

The sobriety prostrated in my eyes amidst the unbound tears, which constantly gushing down with warm liquids.

"I can handle myself. I'm not a child now," said I, wiping tears dragging back of my palm over the eyes.

My glib puerile voice could not abscond the truth of my pampered ambience. The phrases I was uttering were incongruous to the circumstances I was living in.

I looked at the door, which seemed as if Grandma was to come out with her frail step.

"Why don't you choose going back Banaras?" said Meera, sitting next to me, halted and continued with a heavy voice. "Nobody is here to look after you.

Chapter 34

After hours of circuitous travelling, I landed in the city of my joy which received me as if she was awaiting me spreading her arms to hold me in her embrace and let me shed down all my pains.

Pain kills pains.

Another pain was waiting for me to hail and grab me.

Importance of anything has its relevant time and space- either it is sorrow or happiness, with the passage of time it loses its validity, as every present state of emotion deludes the previous one.

Your present is the truth, rest is abstract- fictional art of your mind- either you have already span into hours and left behind into past or you will have to go for in future. To an extent, your existence is because of the power of your imagination. This is the magic of your mind that transcend you above all creature of the planet. Anyway.

I progressed straight to Urvashi's dwelling place, having my laden heart with grievances, brimful and bulging eyes.

I tapped the switch of doorbell once and waited for few while heading down patiently in front of the door. Again, I went for the second time, tapped the bell twice, and stared at the door hoping at every next second it would open swinging the plywood door wide.

After waiting quite some time, I decided to use Indian style of calling people from inside, pummeled at the door with abang sound.

A Bhabhi-style young lady flung open the door wide. I could see a scorn and frown at her face, being teased by several doorbells and bumping at her wooden gate.

"What?" said she.

She finished in one syllable, but I lost in speculation that was she- what she was doing in Urvashi's apartment.

“Who are you?” I asked in puzzlement, trying to peep her backside inside of the house suspiciously, escaping from the side of her shoulder.

“Why?” said she, indifferently.

“Where is Urvashi?” asked I, in rather strong voice.

“No Urvashi like girl stays here. We have recently owned this house on rent” she said. Finding my blank response, she slammed the door at my face with a modest thud sound.

Moving downstairs with perplexed mind and mournful heart, I dialed her cell number cuddled between the left ear and uplifting shoulder, curiously waited while drilling dialing tone.

It told it was out of coverage area. Afterwards, I attempted several times and it reverted same dialogue, ‘the number you have dialing is out of coverage area. Please dial after some time.’

I led towards Rehan’s lodging, strolling across campus by Chhittupur road.

I didn’t conscious whether I was feeling appetite I was so engrossed.

Yes. I was feeling a weakness in feet with every step. The campus was adequately serene in late May comparatively to rest months of the academic year.

Showered under perspiration, I reached to their room, Kamal was already left for his home after giving B.Ed. entrance exam where Rehan was packing up his things to move out, too.

He stopped finding me there, beheld me in slightly surprising for my sudden arrival.

Leaving everything aside, he rushed towards the kitchen. He returned back with nothing in his hand. He fondled his purse in the pocket of his pant and hurriedly moved out, telling me to have rest until he returned.

I fell in his crumbled bed lifeless, being fatigue.

He came with a packet of some edible stuff and a packet of milk. Before he said me, I unwrapped the packet. He looked me pitying. He was to move the kitchen to boil the milk, I stopped him waving the hand, for I was helpless to utter any word due to stuff my mouth with food.

After devouring all, I torn one of the edges of milk packet and set my mouth there and drew in till the last drain of the milk. And he was watching all silently, standing at a hand of bed.

"Take this key," Rehan said handing me the key to the room. "Today I will have to leave for some important work. I will return after a couple of weeks. Till then stay here. Kamal might come."

"Where is Urvashi?" asked I, without lifting my head to him, still busy with the remaining part of food in the packet.

"Should I bring something more?"

"No. Where is Urvashi?" said I, stick with my previous question.

"No" I muttered. "I don't know."

"But she is not in her flat?"

"Maybe she has also gone back to her home like all."

"Then, why did she need to vacant the flat carrying away all her things."

"Be patient. She might have some issues. Wait for some time." He held his bag to go. "Okay. Today I have to take Ruksana back to home." Ruksana was his sister, studying in MMV, girl's college of BHU. "I might have to spend time with Abu to help him in his business."

He left the room hurriedly like any ghost.

I was fancying an unusual amount of isolation even in my loved city where I hadn't felt any spark of loneliness, or any pang where the pain was itself a celebration till yet to me.

But those hours were critical to enduring.

As the time passed, being lonely I found my interest waving readily. My all thoughts gradually centered around the sudden disappearance of Urvashi from the sight.

The chime had gone far away, dimed.

Grandma's funeral smoke still lingered in the arena of my mind that Urvashi's mysterious absence had added oiled to already innate inflammation due to grief, and its flames soared higher in the cognitive firmament.

To avert that I roamed lonely in the crowd, passed from the settings where sometimes we had spent time together.

Not a single day had gone when I hadn't tried to call her phone and every time went continuous engaging or awkward beeping. Either it was out of reach or not switch to something automatic reverts.

"How can it be? How could she do with me? What's my fault?" I pondered.

'She had given preference perhaps to her father's choice- an NRI-than choosing an idyllic boy' my mind pushed another thought which shook me.

Compassion in the relationship should be the business of heart, not the infusion of logic and reason of mind. The moment of decision taking task shifts from heart to mind denounce begins. If one has given analytical approach in the matter of the heart, the mind would devour any chronic relationship. That the problem, usually, happens with the intense lover, for such creature can't tolerate distance quite longer, neither can they make themselves advocate about their partner to their soul.

Some of the days, my lunch, breakfast and dinner occurred at the tea stall at Chhittupur gate having just tea and some snacks, sometimes at little *chokha* stall.

My beards had grown up haphazardly, hairs were quite jangly, tribal-like.

My clothes used to be shabby, unwashed for unmeasured days. I used to go without having the bath for several days.

I used to go bed quite early at 9 O'clock but my eyes were on strike to not to close until she would vanish from the mind. Finally, eyes used to get tired, flipped down its thin curtain, eyelids at the end of the night when other creatures were ready to wake up.

I had stopped all my beloved hobbies- reading books, listening to music and started listening gazal on the theme of dejection in love.

"Hum Tere Shahar me Aaye Hain Musafir ki Tarah

Sirf Ek bar mulakat ka Wada Kar le"

(I have come in your city like a traveller, just give a chance to meet once.)

It used to be favorite dirge.

I realized though consciousness was the rare commodity that time, I had begun scribbling some intense stanzas some soulful paragraph, some heartbroken stories in my diaries.

I didn't know when Altaf Raja, Gulam Ali, Mohammad Rafi and Arjit Singh enrolled their names in my favorite music list.

The psyche was dogged up with haunting thoughts of Urvashi which spearheaded me towards spoiling the sterling image of her breakout from the crystalline brittle castle of faith.

Othello inside me was becoming rebellious and I, myself, feed him the meal of suspiciousness.

Rowing through the public, I had disguised my complexion with a pseudo smile.

One day, I sat in a café and typed a mail to send her.

"Dear darling,

I'm scared about you- about us. Between I left and returned to Banaras; I have gone through several changes in this short period of time. I lost Grandma. She passed away and left behind mere her memory. My pains soar higher when I didn't find you- my soul. I'm here like a breathing coffin without you. You might conjecture well how pathetic state would be I'm residing in. Your love is like the last hope for the lost vessel in Silence Sea who seek single spark of light from the lighthouse.

Hope, I'll receive your answer soon and accord the source of my existence. .

Yours craziest

Sid

After sending mail, I checked it at every quarter of the day whether I had any reply from her irrationally and it couldn't take much time changing my irrationality into a desperate state.

I logged in my mail ID and read the script of my same mail time and again. I went through the message stored on the cell phone, Facebook messenger and went through constantly.

Every morning as I wokeup and rushed to cyber-café. It used to be too early for the opening of the shop. So, I sat there. I strolled fourth and back, bending head, drowned in her thoughts pensively, sometimes I sat down at a corner on the dais near tea shop, flickered the noisy pages of the newspaper.

As the time passed being without her, I imported the distorted thoughts, hallucination and feeling of fright along with paranoia in deep abyss chore of my mind.

Love is something which can convert moor place into the lush green land, it makes life smooth on this planet but the obsession can throw you in endanger zone. And I was suffering from its brain fever. It had distorted the way I used to think, perceive the world, express myself and get connected.

So, breathing with your soul- mate is nothing like a fete. And on the contrary, breathing without him or her is nothing like deadly hell.

Then there emerges an unexplainable ache- a slow, sweet and beautiful one like the Bollywood songs of the 70s.

You can't walk away easily with the memory of the person you are living in.

UGC NET exam had passed back without my appearing.

Gradually, one by one, days converted into weeks, weeks into months, still, I had no information about her, no sign I received where she was actually residing.

I spent most time at unusual places, but football ground's isolated stairs turned my favourite one where I could sit late evening, sometimes it went on till 10 O'clock of the night, when there were throngs of insects found swamping there fluttering around the pale light of the lamp-post.

I span my days in reverie sitting on the lonely Sunset Adda, even in those early heat of evening that baked my butt.

One midnight at 12 o'clock, I set fire tore and put all the things she had gifted me as her memory.

I paused before I setfire in the diary composed by her for me- I made my heart stiff like a stone- I tore down the pages with rattling sounds and threw it into its blazing flames to turn it into ashes.

Alas! The fire failed to turn those stinking memory into ashes.

I had stuffed her FB messenger, e-mail, and message inbox with messages.

Iturned harsh in tone, used bad language in agitation which, perhaps, I should not use whatever circumstance might be, I imagine now.

But the question, why she had left me without letting me know the reason, what was my fault still haunted me even if I was in shrouded in sound sleep. I constantly tried to figure out what might be occurred, what might be gone wrong with her about me, mulling about our compassionate past.

One evening I wandered aimlessly at Lanka. Soon my fragile body got tired and placed under the tree of which either side there were buzzing stationary shops, the vendor selling government forms lied on the floor.

Suddenly, I saw that a girl, passing from therehad put a ten-rupees note in my hand.

I looked at her from behind moving away from me bemusedly. The second one, next to her halted her marching steps; she turned, hurriedly reached to me.

Being perplexed, she closed her mouth in amazement with her both hands "O my God!" She uttered in surprise. "Is it you Sid?"

I uplifted my head slightly, looked at her and the most urgent query I asked her, "Where is Urvashi?'

She looked stagnantly for a second and replied in 'No'. She extended her hand to hold my arms and pull me from there.

I didn't know why I started crying like any child finding someone known so near. Hearing my whining voice, an assemblage started gathering there which created a bewildering state for her.

She called a rickshaw and made me sit, holding me by the side of other arms. Meanwhile, she dialed some phone number over the touchscreen with her another one which was free.

"Where are you rascals?" she yelled…silent. "What sorts of friend you people are?" Silent. "You have left him alone in such miserable situation." Listened murmuring in his small phone. "Come soon in a couple of days hardly," said she, pacifying her tone, she disconnected

I understood it was one of them- Rehan or Kamal.

Chapter 35

She lived in a one BHK room along with another girl as her room partner at Durgakund, quite close to Sunbeam School, where she was teaching as guest faculty.

In Banaras or any other small city, girls don't call boy to their room - whether he is her own brother or close sibling - not due to fear of their father but because of people, landlord's slant glance from the corner of their eyes who looked at such girls as dubiousas if she has lost her virginity. .

But she was an iconoclastic girl, never bothered over what people thought.

She didn't think asking me food or any better, she rushed towards kitchen, until she returned, her room was replete with my cigarette's smoke.

I was still in reverie mode.

When she came back, she had a plate that contained some *desi-ghee* lubricant bread, two vegetable recipes along with pickles.

She was stunned, stood before me staring me, whereas I was lost in puffing out sloth ring of smoke whirling coming out of my mouth soaring upward where I had closed my eyes in rupture.

"What are you doing with yourself?" asked she, in rather yelling tone.

"*O frailty thy name is woman"* I recited Shakespearean lines in complex Hamlet mood, still lied flat on bed gazing revolving fan by ceiling.

"Do you think whatever you are doing is fair?" asked she, solemnly putting down the plate on a table.

"She is liar…she is cheater" I mumbled in trance.

"May I ask you why all these infamous blames are imposed over her?" I was to commence answering her, she cut me off before I spoke anything sarcastically, "Bcoz she couldn't receive your call? … Or she didn't response you? Or bcoz she left Banaras without telling you?" She burst over me with several *'because'* . "You are condemning her without knowing exactly the reason."

My bitter tongue was ceased, merely harked her silently. Her every single word was adequately absolute to shake me. "Actually, you all boys are having same DNA- impatient, incredulous, dubious, and lacking trust in relation, full of what, why, how types words." I sighed a heavy breath out. "I heard the tragedy happen with you. In such case, you need not to yield yourself in the hand of reason, logic. You must keep patience." She discerned my state of mind. She continued, "Might be, she had missed her phone, or else. Anything might be happened."

My feeling changed frequently, the guilty feeling Romeo woke up next morning and reached cyber-café.

Dear Darling

I feel guilty for whatever I scribbled and send you via email, messenger or phone. Really sorry. Without knowing the reason of your being silent, you might be striving in some mishap that hinders you to contact me. Neither have I known well, you can't leave me alone. Not finding you coming back Banaras after Grandma's demise,it had shattered me in pieces and I underwent through acute pain. My thoughts had gone in deeper psychological anguish with sheer hampering. So, before I decline to denouement, please leave some sign of your entity and save me being falling apart.

I am turned into a breathing coffin without you.

Looking for you eagerly

Sid

She held my arm made me sit straight and put a mirror in my hand that I could behold my reflection after several weeks, untidy, shabby.

I glanced at my own image portrait at the truthful mirror. I questioned to self, *"Is it I? Really?"*

My hairs were haphazard grown, scattered and twisted like thin rope, absolutely messy, and hung downward wayward. And above that, shabby unshaved beard over withered skin, made appearance more pity.

Below my both eyes, shining fair skin was turning blackish; lines were drawn over lips as perched in draught of several months.

And my clothes, ah! Seemingly they appeared as poorly as a wretched man spinning life under extreme economical scarcity.

Then after watchingmyportrait in the mirror, I sensed why that girl had put coins in my hand as donation when I was sitting under the tree, for I looked like nothing more than a beggar.

Next early morning, Kamal arrived in Banaras, caught me from Pummy's room and took me to saloon first, at our usual acquainted place.

The barber, who became used to of being garrulous, seeing us was baffled at my changed get up.

I settled down in the wooden chair.

"*Arey bhaiya*, after a long you have given *darshan,* appearance?" He spoke in complete astonishing manner.

Kamal winked at him, hinted him to remain quiet.

He, like all time, covered me wrapping a cloth around, for escorting my attires from falling hairs after every snaps of scissor running over it.

Returning back from there, Kamal took me for shower. Although he did not enter into bathroom but he didn't move from the door.

I was feeling fresh now though.

"Don't be childish Mr. Siddhartha. You need to learn copping up with your pain, at least. Nobody can stay for you listening your stories" said Kamal.

Turning sadist torturing to self, I found an unsaid pleasure, a self-punishment.

I measured five kilometres distance from Lanka to Madhuadih, rambling on foot over the melting charcoal road, under scorched bronze sky.

I was drenched in perspiration, soaked my clothes sticky with skin.

I reached at the foothill of high stood building, held my head uplifting towards sky, craned. Through the elevator lift, I arrived in front of flat number #301.

I tapped the bell bottom once, twice, and thrice.

With a musing voice, a young girl partially opened and peeped from the back of the door.

“Yes?” she stared me as if she was recalling all the data of her memory. “Ok you are that boy who came that evening with Rehan and Kamal, right? Who dare to denounce the beauty of Mohini?”

“May I come in or not?” I said straight before she bored me with anymore her unwanted quoting.I was without having any taint of emotion reflecting over my gloomy face and wide serene eyes.

She opened the door letting me enter into the room.

“How can I help you?” asked she, seductively.

How can a prostitute help a heart broken man in his most despair hour?

I said, “How can you help?”

She looked at me silently for a while, smiled. Hearing so straight, she was not startle anyway, but she stared mystifying.

“That’s the business every costumer seeks coming here in this room. But what you are searching here, that you can’t find at least not here. You need something else” said she.

“What?”

“Perhaps you seek a shoulder where you can rest your head and cry harder and release the liquid that you have held within the boundaries of your eyes.”

Was she a weather scientist who guessed the anticipated rain of warm liquid from my eyes? I thought.

“You need not use your mind” I said her sternly. “I know my place.”

She began stripping off her clothes. And hardly had it taken few seconds she was standing before me like any nude nymph sculptures of Khajuraho.

She fell on the bed yielding herself asunder her both legs apart in two opposite direction of each other. Her tiny whole, which asserted her feminine being and was the reason to draw her freaky customers nearer, was in front of me.

Honestly, her nudity couldn’t stir my manliness, not a slight.

“Now it’s your turn. I have surrendered before you,” said she, sprawled in front of me prone on the bed flat staring me. “Do I help you?” saying she sat on her hip and began unbuttoning my shirt and then unhooked my jeans.

Before she pulled my jeans out,

my eyes departed warm liquid, throat flagged hiccup jolting.

She was still unchanged. My sudden outburst into tears and childlike crying couldn’t impact her.

“Let it flow on. Don’t stop it,” said she. I tried to hold my wailing.

It took few seconds, I recollected my whole disturbed consciousness and I collected my scattered clothes lying here and there on the floor.

I put on as usual.

Before I walked out of there, I opened my wallet took out few strips of Indian currency and offered her.

"I accept, I'm slut. But I'm a woman also. And I don't doubt of having a heart in my bosom" said she.

According to rules of evolution, she had every right to fall in love.

I looked at her staring into her deep silent eyes, but I hadn't time to listen her story for my next book and plodded towards the gate. Scarcely had I reached near to lift, her voice stopped me.

"If you are not feeling good, stay here until you feel better."

"Thanks" I mumbled.

Amidst horning vehicles, I walked through the narrow lane and headed towards Maruadih station.

The road, around few hundred meters away from the station, struck in traffic. I navigated through the spare apace between vehicles- slanting, rotating, and sometime swerving whole body- as I was dancing.

I had no presage or any prepared plan why I was leading towards Maruadiah station.

The platform was busy with passengers waiting acutely arrival of the train.

Lots of people in throng swamped at the window for ticket, seemingly although there was no train visible there yet.

I walked too silently across the platform with stealthily steps. I saw after walking hundreds of steps a vacant bench and placed there.

Was I actually waiting for the train of my destiny? I did not reason.

The announcement harangued at the loud speaker. People, who were stagnant at the benches, suddenly stirred from there and began gazing on the track for promising arrival.

It railed from the eastern side of the station. It would go via Allahabad, I guessed.

Along with the crowd, I, too, embarked in the train without bothering the destination of the train.

I took a seat by window.

Hardly I occupied the place for ten minutes when a man came and claimed being owner of the seat.

I stood up without any insurgent attitude or revolttowards him and moved for some other place.

I walked across the compartment and halted at the gate. The strokes of the wind flew away my hair back flipping with the gust.

I was staring away blankly watching things rushing past.

The train was proceeding on the route of Allahabad.

Ticket collector seemed to cometowards me checking ticket of people, noting down something in his notepad and moved for next.

Checking every single passenger, he proceeded to me.

He asked my ticket.

I glanced at him giving a grimace look, aloofly. I nodded in negative.

He asked my destination, where I was coming from and where I was to go.

I didn't answer, remained indifferent to his responses.

He waited for a while and moved ahead.

The train was flying in jolts and jerks, clattering over the track through the dark night for more than hour.

It began to slow down the pace and finally stopped over a long-stretched bridge.

It was over Ganges River at Sangam Allahabad.

It was around ten o'clock of the night. The tickling lights simmered at the bank. Sometime in flash of the torch, some fishermen were rowing boat to trap fish.

The flows of river painted a silhouette against the twinkling sky.

Slowly the train preceded creeping, stopping.

Unexpectedly, as if I was awoken out of hypnotic state as the passengers began disembarking from the train.

I peeped through the window, I found, the train was now at a station. There was acute clamouring of tramps on the platform unlike smaller one.

I was not in any state to recall my displacement.

I stopped a passing man.

"Can you tell which station it is?" asked I.

"Allahabad Junction." He headed ahead.

I, too, flew with the swamps in the course of exit door. Coming out, I called an e-rickshaw and asked him to drive to Civil Line.

I got down at a *chauraha* from that miniature and looked at a bungalow across the road. It was same mansion where I spent one complete night with Urvashi.

I faltered a while before I stepped on.

The most essential things for the person in tough situation are to drink lots of water, take several long breathings and increase level of stoicism when one after another layer of uncoiled pain surges in the core of heart.

Henceforth, I collected my all courage and boosted inside and put all thoughts aside except Urvashi, I prolonged towards the house.

Whole night I waited sitting encountering the tiny creatures' inhabitant of the park which was just in front of the house. At the close of the dawn, I fell asleep for a while and the titillating morning rays woke me up.

I urged security guard to see Urvashi. Initially, he denied. But seeing me stubbornness, he surrendered at last, and went into the mansion asking me to wait until he returned.

An old man from the gate of main house scrutinized me, waved his hand indicating me to move inside.

"Yes. What do you want?" asked the old man, in wavy voice.

He was her grandfather most probably, I guessed. He appeared quite familiaras she had told me during my halt that night in Allahabad.

"Where is Urvashi?" my question was straight.

He scrutinized me from toe to head dragging his glance leisurely and asked after measuring me, "Who are you?"

"Siddhartha, her friend" said I, abruptly.

"But we don't know any person of such name in her friends. She never told us" said he, glancing at an orderly lady sitting at a distance on sofa.

There was an apparent glibness in his saying.

But my heart was rendered into several parts. A strange silence spread in that big spacious dining room.

"Where is she?" I asked firmly.

He was constantly looking me as if he was saying, it was over now, I might move out having my shattered last hope.

I began moving towards the door, my glance caught a snapshot resting above television in which Urvashi was smiling sitting between orderly couple.

There was sign of mortifying over his face being as if he was caught of his falsehood. It made me a bit troublesome, I found me dubious.

"Listen. We have married her with a suitable boy, up to our status" said he.

Finally, she had accepted her family choice... NRI boy, I thought.

I was shattered into pieces, hollowed inside. I had no peace left in me; no ability to apply reason, now I was able to decide what was next was to do.

Whole night I sprawled on a bench at Company Garden. Throughout night was passed gazing at twinkling sky andfighting mosquitoes. Every minute seemed as an era unfolding idly.

At early morning, I reached to her grandpa's bungalow again having my brooding mind to have queries and clarification over vacillating facts provided by the old man, her grandpa.

I was not ready to accept easily whatever he told.

I visited there at regular intervalsto meet him but I was declined every time. Even I visited him at his showroom, and there, I was humiliated by his men working there and pushed me out of there.

With every second of the needle of the clock, leisurely the day drifted to the least period of its journey.

I wandered here and there lingering on the road of the city aimlessly like a waif. And this way, I found, I headed towards the arch bridge of Naini, a salvation point for the man deserted in love.

An acute silence in one's life can doom.

You wish to talk somebody your loved one, and receive silence in return, although you have gone incessant cherished discussion sometime ago. The longer silence goes for, the louder internal struggle takes place making noise in the corner of committed person. And at a point, it turns fatal for life and pernicious to survive in the world with that silence, once which used to be muse for the ears.

Last two years campus life had overtaken the canon of my life.

I had been paid all by fortune whatever I desired and dreamed once, but I never anticipated such a catastrophic and cathartic end of this nocturnal sojourn. I never imagined a late comer in the life of twenty-four years of a young guy would desert to such fathom that I wouldn't find any spark of hopefulness, wrapped with acute darkness, treading through wilderness.

I find this life so futile and vain to breathe in now.

Next step, obviously, will take off my life, lead to end of my journey. I don't know what people, or my creator will think about my deed I'm going to commit but now I can't imagine this life any worth compatible without her.

Day- Fifty

In the evening, somewhat half an hour after shopping of clothes and other necessary things for The Strange Man to participate in a wedding reception, Prabha entered her house barely visible due to power cut. She called him, but no answer she got in return.

She turned on the torch-light of her phone to explore the path and find the switch board. She desperately searched for him throughout the house and its backyard.

He hasn't uttered a single word. He is still in mute mode which raises surges of concern and death like silence inside her where he might go.

She calls Nazarin and asks her if she has seen her or known about him where he might be. She takes her scooty and droves over the roads to search him. She has no clues what direction she should go to search the Strange Man in such a big city.

But the pages she has rowed through, there is an affinity she has realized between the man portrait in diary and The Strange Man. But it has no guarantee; he would be quite the same man.

Initially, she drove at the periphery of the university campus, checked all solitary building. Finally, she heads towards Company garden, makes stand her scooty in parking zone and perusal the jogging track, benches and lawns, she doesn't find him there anywhere.

The scale of her concern is getting higher. She moves towards Pattar Girja, where once again she fails to find him.

The droplets of sweating are trickling down from the forehead from the side of her ears. She is tired of questing him, but he hasn't appeared anywhere. He disappears like ghost. She is driving now here and there following the roads, she even doesn't aware what road she is following actually. The suddenly, when she has been driving slowly over a lonely road, she catches a sight of man's silhouette lonely sitting on a lonely bench by the pathway.

She reaches nearer scrutinizing the man. Being confirmed, she gears her drive and approaches near to him.

She takes out her helmet, just stand beside him, only gazing. He lifts his head, look at him and again bend down.

She can't decide she should be angry at him or loving after finding him having a toilsome search. If she gets angry, then with what authority? And if she turns loving, why for a stranger?

She also sits down next to him. She moves a bit to provide her a space. She breathes in, gets relax.

"I don't know how shall I react at you. If you want to go, I won't stop you. But I can't leave you until I find somebody known to you."

The Strange Man remains calm, unmoved.

"I don't know whether you are hearing me or not but one thing I know well, one can sense the essence what's spoken innately." She continues her quoting. "I don't say I help you anyway. Whereas actually you are the reason of deluding of my pains I had been suffering before you came in my life. Stay with me until I get healed of my wounds I've received from known ones and life which can't be visible but be felt. Perhaps you might too."

The Strange Man darts at her and sharply turns his head away.

"Stand up and come with me." Prabha holds his hand and pulls. He follows her swaying his head silently. She halts reaching to the scooter, tilts to find the hole for setting key.

She accelerates her scooty, leans forth urging him to sit on the back seat. She takes him to her home.

Day- After Three Years of Passing

It's a fine morning, a ramification of last night. The patting strokes of the typewriter from the perennial brooding room of Siddhartha on the roof can be heard constantly sinceearly morning when there was no sign of the sun in the eastern sky and the moon was not sunk yet, still floating. The cool fresh breeze drifted inside through the widely opened windows.

On the name of furniture, there is an only table and a chair, which Siddhartha uses for writing. At his back, there is a shelf by the wall crammed with books. The door is designed in such manner that no outsidesounds can intrude into.

Prabha pushes gently the door and she has walked a few tramps hardly. "Wait." Siddhartha's alarming voice detains her prolonging steps. "I'm coming soon."

"I'm getting late today." says she.

Prabha has left her locks open, dripping pearls like drops from her darkest-night-black hairs, drenching her clothes, which shows she is coming directly from the bathroom. To prevent the drops, she has enfolded a towel making a bun of her hairs.

"Yes," says Siddhartha, slamming the door of the room.

Prabha is engrossed in arranging breakfast on the dining table.

"You have several invitations from colleges and universities," says Prabha. She pulls the drawer and takes out some poised card indiscriminately.

"It's not possible to go anywhere. I'm rather busy with my new manuscript," says he, maneuvering to couch on the sofa.

"You should see this at least once," says she, taking one of them and hands him over. She looks at him curiously waiting for his reaction after holding the envelope.

His eyes get stagnant at the front page, reading, "Alumnae Meet."

"I'm getting late for office. Take your breakfast on time before it needs to warm again," says she, noticing his lost like state.

All the memories of past are unfolded flashing in his inward mind. For several minutes, he remains tangle with the envelope crouching on the sofa. By then, Prabha has prepared herself in her usual formal decorum- a well-poised sari. The driver has already fetched her bags.

Last year, Prabha qualified Civil Services last year and has got posting at Allahabad itself. Still, she does not take help of maid in her household work. She prefers to do all the chores- loves to wash his cloth, cook food for him with his own hand and bear his all whimsical.

"Are you free on 12th Feb?" asks he.

"I've already applied leave for that day," says she. He glances at her. She has been smiling.

Siddhartha is hailed at the arch door of the Radhakrishnan auditorium hall by some girl volunteers wearing yellowish sari.

Now, he is bestselling author of five books among them The Scorpion Grasses remains most successful and popular.

Paddling the steps of ascending stairs of the hall, his mind races against the time and fluctuates the evening hours spent together with Urvashi.

He finds himself amidst there once again as he is backed three years in the past. He realizes a slight of uneasiness. His eyes turn active spotting the same stage, arch texted wall, well- arranged chairs. It all appears as it is, as it was three years back when he also with his fellows were doing the rehearsal of Shakespearean drama, Tempest and he acted the role of Prospero and recitation performance. He garnished applause from the audiences, present faculties, and his fellows in the final performance.

Still, he can't obviate the mesmerizing dance performance of Urvashi on an occasion.

His name is announced from the stage with other honorary distinguished guests who glorify the stage with their presence.

Mounting on the stage, he throws his glance across the hall. He startles with exuberant seeing some known faces in the crowd- Rehan, Kamal and Pummy. They simper to him. He lifts his hand slightly equivocatingly without notifying anyone else except them. Prabha trails the direction of his eyes' jaunt which leads her to them. She conjures up with their appearance, who is who, as they were described in the diary.

After the welcome speech of Dean of Faculty and other distinguishes' deliveries, Question with the Author session begins.

"Sir, cathartic end of the protagonist is seen in most of your novels, most particularly The Scorpion Grasses, do you think you have anyhow justified the story?" one of the students from the audience asks.

He ponders a while, commences to speak wearing a soft smile, "A true love story has no happy ending. The summit stage of it is doom."

"There are many love stories which has a happy ending?" asks another one.

"Those love story might halt their journey in a midway and don't proceed."

"Do you think you have been prejudice while portraying the character of Urvashi, especially at the end? Aren't you trying to show her a frail lady?" asks a girl.

"If a rich girl at the climax of their decisive relationship snaps her counterpart, who is a simple boy, is a matter of question at the end," he speaks firmly.

He doesn't startle at the question asked from the crowd, for they are mostly his fellows whose question he has sensed well what they long to listen from his mouth. But not just the question, but the next person has made astonished. She is a young lady- none other than Urvashi's elder sister. She proceeds to ask, “This assumption, that she has the protagonist left for her father’s property, might be a fallacious assumption. Maybe she had some sheer problem that she resigned the protagonist suddenly.”

For a moment, he remains dumbfound, finds no suitable answer to return.

"Maybe," says he, lightly.

After some couple of discourse, the session gets ended, and people begin to move out in the lawn for refreshment. He is also accompanying with Prabha, trotting out of the hall. Meanwhile, the young student approaches him for an autograph, some shake hand. Just before reaching the threshold, he finds Urvashi's sister standing in front of her. Her eyes seem as if they have laughed last time several years ago.

She snaps out the hall, starts plodding through the serene corridor when everyone busies in taking galloping juices, eating recipes and doing gossips.

Siddhartha traces her tramps. Prabha follows him amazedly. She checks her progressive steps. Siddhartha reaches to her. Prabha thinks better to have a distance from them.

"She was not frail, nor she cheated you. She loved you truly," says she.

"What do you mean by 'was' 'cheated'?" he demands quickly. Awfulness could be seen over his countenance. Writing books, he never frightens of past tense, but today it horrifies him.

"She is no more," she pauses, put her palm over her mouth to muster her all courage. “She was suffering from cancer. She came to know at the farewell day." She tries to resist her sobs anyhow. "At the ending hours of life, I asked her if I called you. She said," she bursts into tears with choking her breathing lest her crying echoes in the corridor. "She didn't want to see the setting sun of her life in your eyes."

The lamp of the day, as on its routine journey is at its pace, rushing down the western sky - evening is ahead. Prabha notices sitting on the side seat, he drives the car in a strange direction, although she finds the roads, setting, they are familiar and reflect similarity as it is portrayed in the diary, later titled *The Scorpion Grasses*. The uninhibited showering from his eyes signifies the awakening consciousness of Urvashi in him.

Finally, he stops the car; the road ends up reaching the fence where a small gate leads outside. He comes out of the car, strolls lightly and sits down on the bench at Sunset Adda.

Prabha stands away from there, resting on the bonnet of the car and watches him remaining seated on the bench gazing the western sky. He remains there in inert posture for a while.

Gradually the sun bright crimson hues turn into a cold circle and slowly disappear splashing behind the building -far across the university fence. The scattered cloud is drifting as leisurely as if in an alcoholic tipsy. The birds are returning to their nest. The city's honking sound is getting vociferous.

Now, Prabha could see his silhouette under the greying sky from where she was standing. She approaches him, holds him in her arms affectionately and tries to console his soul.

She drives him away from there, but not far from his memory wreathen with Urvashi at Sunset Adda.

About the Author

Shivram K is a novelist, a short-story writer and a poet. He is born and brought up in a remote village of Banaras province, and now he lives in Delhi. Apart from writing, he is a passionate educator, avid traveller and voracious reader of classics. Shivram K is alumnae of KNPG College, DAV PG College, BHU Varanasi. After completing his M.A. in English Literature, he decided to follow his dream- writing and travelling, and so he moved to Delhi in 2016.

The beauty of his plotting is that it is flavoured with a poetic touch which allures readers' mind and creates a difference.

Website: www.shivramk.com

Mail ID: shivramk500@gmail.com

Facebook: @shivramkauthor

Instragram: #shivramk_